ECHOES OF ILIUM

A TALE OF THE OILFIELD

BOB CARNES

CHAPTER I

Meeting a Legend

Days, like elevators and alley cats, have personalities. The day that Mike met Buck Burnet woke up sullen and turned even nastier. The fog he had driven through to get to the Morgan City heliport kept him on the ground until it was blown away by the first norther of the year. The winds came bitter and aggressive. Mike had been offshore enough to know to be prepared for any weather, but his coat was in his bag, which was already stowed on the PHI JetRanger. The wind tugged at his hardhat before the wash from the main rotor pushed it down tighter.

In the cold helicopter cabin, the pilot handed Mike a blanket and asked him to sit in the middle seat. A pilot had never called him sir before, and it pleased him in a small way. He took the hat off and rolled it in his hands and let himself feel pride. The logo on the front was only a symbol, and he had worn symbols before, but this one, Exxon, meant something. It meant that everyone above him in the oilfield was with Exxon, too. Some would take issue with that assertion, but they would invariably be with other oil companies. He was at the top of the food

1

chain, and he let himself feel and wallow in it for the first and last time in his career.

The hat was one of the old-fashioned steel ones with the brim all the way around. The guy in Houston who issued him his safety and cold-weather gear was passing out the new plastic kind with the brim in front, but Mike talked him out of an old one he had way in the back. It still had a Humble sticker on it that you could see around the edges of the Exxon one. On the back, two more labels had been affixed, one above the other: "Drilling Engineer" and "Mike Brown." He put the hat back on, and the moment was over. In minutes they were up and over the marshes, headed south, the wide Atchafalaya River visible to the east. The Gulf of Mexico shoreline in 1972 was a sorry sight, covered as it was with debris, black oil, and the ugly yellow froth that went with it. The gulf itself was relatively calm, but the north wind was whitecapping what waves there were. The glow was gone, and he found himself wishing for someone to talk with to allay his nervousness.

Mike was starting a new job and meeting a legend on the same day. The job was drilling engineer on the Hector, a jackup rig operating around the mouth of the Mississippi. The legend was the man he would be paired with, a long-time toolpusher (rig manager) named Buck Burnet.

Mike had completed the mechanical engineering course at UT Austin working every other semester for an oil field service company on and offshore in south Louisiana. Offshore in particular there had been time for sharing stories. The tales were of the sort one would expect to hear upon entering any closed society, but the name of a single protagonist kept cropping up at different locations and in different company. Mike heard the name of Buck Burnet enough times to note it and start remembering the plots and specifics of certain stories. There were a lot of stories and all of them had a mystical quality that made them hard to believe. Still, there were at least four or five that, heard over a four year period, had enough common elements to make him think their origins might have some basis in reality.

The earliest story had Buck stepping off a through truck in Jal, New Mexico, on the western edge of the Permian Basin sometime in the early to mid-forties. He was only fourteen years old, but he was over six feet tall and lanky. The earlier stories almost universally had him resembling either Burt Lancaster or Gary Cooper. The legend held that he was born on the truck because nothing was ever learned about his previous existence. He said his name was Buck Burnet, and he had the clothes on his back and a winning smile, but no money and no way of making a living. A lady that owned a café lodged him in a back room and paid him to wash dishes. That went on for a while, and Buck was reportedly a favorite with the collection of professional and working ladies that made up the distaff side of the little boomtown. His association with professional women would be a theme that followed him through life.

It was said that the lady he worked for would never have let it happen had she known about it, but somehow Buck left the café with a rig crew going out to work on morning tour. Most drilling rigs have three shifts a day. Once drilling has started, work cannot stop until the well is finished. (The shifts are called *tours*, pronounced "towers." You ask why about things like that at first but quickly learn to adopt them and move on.) On land, the daylight tour works from seven a.m. to three p.m., evening tour from three to eleven, and morning tour, called *graveyard* in most other industries, is from eleven p.m. to seven a.m.

The lady wouldn't have objected to his being taken out on a rig—fourteen was a pretty standard starting age in those days. It was this particular crew that she would have had a problem with. They were known for being in trouble with the law, a common theme for boomtown workers, but there was something else about them. The word *pedophilia* was probably unknown in that day and at that place, but these were the kind of guys that made people's skin crawl. You just wouldn't leave anyone you cared about with them. Buck was with them, and there were people who cared about him. The café lady cast around for help and finally prevailed on a toolpusher from another company to go out to the rig in question and check on Buck.

3

By the time he got to the rig, it was breaking day. He could tell from a distance that the rig was shut down, and as he got closer, he could see no sign of life. There were lights on, so the generator was running, but there was no smoke coming from the main engines. There were no cars anywhere. A huge chunk of the side of the toolpusher's trailer was torn out and lying on the ground and light from the trailer was spilling out over the parking area. He first noticed blood on the part of the trailer on the ground, a lot of blood. He hadn't been particularly worried until then, and he quickly ran over the whole rig, afraid of what he might find. Nothing. The main engines were running at idle. The drill pipe was stood back in the derrick, and the blow-out preventer was closed.

He went back to the trailer and noticed car tracks coming from under the bloody trailer side. The car must have been there when the trailer came apart. The car left on the same road he had come in on, in the same direction, and out the other side of the location. As the light got better, he noticed grooves in the dirt near what would have been the back of the car. The grooves were from boot heels, and there was what could have been blood or oil in the dirt around them. There were two other sets of boot prints in a muddle around the area.

Oilfield people of that era were generally shy of the law, but the toolpusher couldn't avoid notifying them. He gave as little information as he could to the company dispatcher and then lit a cigarette to wait for the sheriff. The rig was in Texas. As he walked back to the trailer, the full light allowed him to see a set of footprints going in the same direction the car had gone. At one point the footprints and the car tracks coincided, and the footprints were on top. Each print was deep at front and back as if the maker had been running—after the car? Intrigued, he started his truck and followed the footprints.

After a couple of miles, he could see a figure in the road walking away from him. Carefully he eased up behind the man to what he considered a safe distance and honked his horn. The man kept walking, purposefully, but in no hurry. The figure wore no shoes, but he was big, and the toolpusher was not the kind of person who took chances. He made an end run through the mesquite bushes and drove up on the road ahead of the walking figure, coming at him from the front. A hundred feet away, he stopped his truck and got out, holding a sawed-off shotgun across his chest. He could see now that he was dealing with the boy, Buck Burnet. As he got closer, Buck asked if he had any water.

The toolpusher could hardly credit what he was seeing. There had been four people at the rig, three of them hardcases of the worst stripe. One of them had apparently left the rig in the trunk of a car, dead or badly hurt, and the two who put him there were in such a hurry that they couldn't even see to his wounds; and the one who walked away was a fourteen-year-old kid?

As Buck got close, the toolpusher could see his shirt was ripped, and he was covered in blood.

The toolpusher motioned Buck to the side of his truck, where a water cooler was mounted. Buck bypassed the furnished cups and bent down, put his mouth under the spout, and drank deeply. The toolpusher asked if he was hurt, and Buck said he was just tired — really tired. The toolpusher asked him what had happened, and Buck said, distantly, distractedly, that he didn't know. He'd been asked by the driller to go into the trailer and fill out some forms. While he was filling them out, the driller had put his hand on Buck's neck. The next thing Buck knew he was looking at the toolpusher's truck coming at him. The toolpusher told Buck to lie down in the bed of his pickup. Buck found a tarp and, pulling it over himself, fell immediately into a deep sleep.

When the toolpusher got back to the rig, there were a couple of sheriff's deputies walking around the location. The toolpusher meant to tell the men about the boy in the back of his truck, but he just couldn't do it. As soon as he got back to town, he made sure that nobody who saw Buck leave with the crew was in the way of telling anyone else about it. He and Alma Garza, the owner of the café, got Buck into his room, cleaned him up, and disposed of his bloody clothes. From that day on, the lives of Buck and the toolpusher, a man named Roman Butcher, were linked.

The next story took place some ten or so years later. By the time of the story, he was a toolpusher himself, in Calcasieu Parish, Louisiana, at a town hall somewhere southwest of Alexandria and north of Lake Charles. This is the first story where the theme of Buck's being a protector arises.

The people in the oilfield of those days were considered gypsies and interlopers by the local denizens. It must be said that there was reason for them to feel that way. The discovery of oil in an area could create a boom that drew people who were not of substance in the same way as the people who already lived there. The people who were drawn had ready money, and bars and dancehalls would spring up, sometimes many bars and dancehalls, to relieve the pressure of all that ready money. The discovery of oil could make a peaceful, beautiful town into a Wild West run of shacks and trailers overnight. The local economy would benefit—almost exclusively the landowners and banks—but the average citizens would only see a deterioration of their way of life. Naturally there was resentment. Sometimes that resentment turned into wrongs and reprisals, and sometimes the natural and constant friction turned into outright war between the original residents of the area and the people of the oilfield. The term oilfield trash became redundant, and all of the oilfield people were tarred with the same brush. Unfortunately, while some of the oilfield people were trash and didn't really care what other people thought of them, there was always an undeserving percentage of them, mainly children and wives, that suffered.

Apparently, Buck was overseeing three or four small rigs around a town named Hickory Flat when the Hickory Flat Independent School District called a meeting to discuss barring the children of oilfield trash from their schools. There was so much interest in the meeting that the school board decided to hold it at an American Legion hall near Lake Charles, so they would have enough room for everybody in case it rained. The Legion happily rented the space out, but they were somewhat sloppy about getting the word to their regular customers that they would be closed for the evening. Consequently, when the regular customers showed up and started ordering drinks, the dancehall proprietors, reluctant to forego another stream of revenue, served them and whomever of the outraged Hickory Flat residents felt parched. By meeting time the whole crowd was pretty well oiled and extremely vocal. The school board gave up trying to do any business and decamped, but the fuse had been lit and indignation about "our children" being drawn into the hedonistic lifestyle of the oilfield trash spread rampantly.

Enter our hero, Buck Burnet, the only representative of the oilfield in attendance. The dancehall had an entry area, a space about twenty feet by twenty feet with double doors on one side leading into the hall, and double doors leading out onto the gravel parking lot on the other side. Buck was backed into that room by the people in the hall and trapped there by the men who had been drinking in the parking lot and those piling out the windows to get out front. Buck had found some sort of club, and he was using it to good effect, first one way then the other. A couple of bodies in one doorway would serve to obstruct the people behind them, and then he would tend to those breaking in the other set of doors. He went on that way until a bunch of lawmen arrived, and he laid down his club and turned himself in. He was quoted as crediting those deputies with saving his life because he had been running out of steam and not running out of assailants. He wasn't sure what the club had been or how he got hold of it, but was pretty sure it was not, as quoted by one of the other participants in the local paper during his trial, "the jawbone of a ass." He had done considerable damage to local bones and egos, but he was not found to be at fault. Buck was credited with keeping oilfield children in public schools, but he was quoted as saying the real reason they stayed was the courts determined it was illegal to keep them out.

The next story took place later, but not too much later, in his early days offshore. A certain Louisiana highway patrolman resented Buck's notoriety, or maybe he just didn't like the cut of Buck's jib. There seems to have been a lot of sail envy in those days. If the officer is still alive, even he probably doesn't remember what caused him to hate Buck with such intensity.

This highway patrolman didn't like oilfield people in general and ticketed everything moving along the highways displaying an oilfield logo. His particular joy was arresting an oilfield hand for drunk driving or resisting arrest. He was a great big guy and apparently in no fear of meeting his match. Somewhere, between the point of arrest and the parish jail, the miscreant would be brutally beaten. Accounts differ on the trooper's domain — Terrebonne or Lafourche — but they all agree that the encounter with Buck took place on Grand Isle, in Jefferson Parish. These accounts also contained a lot of speculation as to what the trooper had in mind when he went down there — in his own car and wearing civilian clothes. Buck was friends with the sheriffs of all three parishes, and the trooper was universally loathed. Nearly every time Mike heard the story, the teller knew the name of the bar, but it was always a different name. Truth be told, the topography of Grand Isle is rearranged pretty regularly by hurricane, so bars come and go, literally, with the wind. The common items were that the bar was horseshoe shaped with no tables and there was no sheetrock on the walls so the studs were exposed. The tarpaper under the outside sheathing was the only interior decoration.

Buck was drinking and chatting with some of his hands. The rest of the bar turned quiet when the trooper came in, but Buck didn't seem to notice, and he continued his conversation. Accounts differ as to whether the trooper actually hit Buck or only moved to. Buck threw the trooper through the wall, taking out one of the studs and the siding. Several of the onlookers rushed outside only to see Buck throwing the trooper back through the wall in the other direction. As the confrontation wore on, even the bartender moved outside, fearing that the building was going to fall from the loss of too many structural members. Some claim that the structure had to be demolished after the event and that it only took the first nudge from the Caterpillar for it to fall. Both Buck and the trooper were taken to jail, but only the trooper went to trial. He was convicted and sent to Angola.

The next two stories are related in reverse order because the last one, the one called "the New Orleans story," is the story that defined Buck and lent most to his notoriety. The first one took place when Buck was well into middle age, and it is sort of an anomaly as it is the only story from its era.

Buck was in a grocery store in Jeanerette, a small, pretty town on Highway 90 between Morgan City and Lafayette. This in itself is anomalous since, by this time, small towns and grocery stores were not really Buck's milieu. In any case Buck was there, presumably pushing a grocery cart up and down the aisles. Once again he was attacked from behind, this time by the baddest man in Iberia Parish. This guy was so bad…Those stories go on and on. The bad man—there with his common-law wife and children, an abuser of his family and anyone else unlucky enough to cross him—had been incarcerated several times but had never been put away for good because it was so hard to get people to testify against him. Even the Iberia Parish law was loath to deal with him. Some accounts have Buck giving him a hard look when he cuffed one of his children. Others say something about the woman's demeanor triggering something from Buck's own past. In any case, the fight was on, and it was another one-sided affair. One quote that was passed on said that Buck "shook the other man like he was a rag doll." A woman who was the Jeanerette constable, the only law in town at the time, rolled up with lights flashing and came into the store in a crouch with her sidearm drawn. What she saw was Buck holding the bad man over his head, apparently preparing to bounce him off the concrete floor one more time. She said the look on Buck's face chilled her to immobility. Then, as she watched, his face relaxed and his eyes focused on her and he dropped the man in a heap. She put the bad man in an ambulance and took Buck into custody, but they never made it to any jail.

The last story, the New Orleans story, is the archetypal Buck Burnet story. It supposedly happened when Buck was still a young man but already the drilling superintendent for a New Orleans drilling company. He worked in the Shell building downtown and ran a fleet of some three or four offshore jack-up drilling rigs. Buck was in love with a prostitute who had been the mistress of the man who ran the mob in New Orleans. She was trying to sever her ties to that organization and was having a tough time of it. One thing led to another, and one night Buck found himself the objective of two assassins. They followed him into Jackson Square with the intention of cutting his throat. In a very short period of time, one of the assassins ran out of the bushes and into the Quarter. The other one staggered out, holding himself in the obvious place, screaming, "He pulled my dick off! He pulled my dick off!" Neither one of the men was ever heard from again. Normally more assassins would have followed, but the thought of losing one's manhood in such a gruesome manner was more than the local mobsters could handle. Buck had a free pass in New Orleans.

Those are the Buck Burnet stories more or less as Mike heard them. They are generally shorter and less colorful than how he heard them, but he usually heard them in bars, sometimes deep into the night. Here they have been pared to their essential elements: Buck always protecting someone (in at least one case, himself); Buck never throwing the first punch; Buck never knowing what happened; Buck exhibiting almost superhuman strength and ability; and finally, Buck never getting in trouble for his involvement.

So, how does one meet a legend? Well, as indicated earlier, one goes to work on the same rig with him.

When Mike finally graduated from school, he was hired by the world's largest oil company, mostly because of his experience in the field. He had a mechanical engineering degree but was hired as a drilling engineer; that billet usually going to a petroleum engineer, but his experience in the field tipped the scale. After a few weeks of indoctrination, it was time to be assigned to a rig. When he was being recruited his future employers seemed to be pondering where to send him, but in time he came to believe that they had hired him specifically to work on Buck's rig.

The oilfield in the Gulf of Mexico runs on a schedule of seven and seven: seven days on and seven days off. Most of the hands work twelve hour days. People like Buck and Mike Brown, supervisors, were considered to be on duty twenty-four hours a day. With the service company, Mike and the others had worked as many days as the job took, and many times he'd actually worked twenty-four-hour days. Offshore, meals, laundry, and lodging are provided, the quarters are always clean, and the food is always good. Twice a week T-bone steaks are served for supper. Like the service or a penitentiary, it is all male and you can't come and go as you please, but the companies involved do everything they can to make you as comfortable as possible. Buck's rig, the Hector, was a Bethlehem built jack-up. Strictly speaking it wasn't Buck's rig since Buck had an opposite number with his own crew that worked the rig on his days off. It's not giving too much away to say that in another, broader sense, it was indeed Buck's rig. Buck was the rig's toolpusher, the man in charge for the drilling contractor, the owners of the drilling rig. He had responsibility for the rig, the associated equipment, and all the hands employed by the contractor, including two crews of five or six hands plus assorted roustabouts, electricians, mechanics, crane operators, and so forth. The drilling engineer, sometimes called the "company man," is the representative of the operator, the oil company that is hiring the drilling contractor to drill the well. He has charge of what the rig does in the way of drilling the well and of all the service companies that come offshore to perform a task and then go back in. Who they are and what they do vary with the conditions and stages of the well. There are also cooks and people who clean the living quarters and are usually hired by the operator. The farther you go offshore, the bigger the rigs get and the more people it takes to run them; but a Bethlehem jack-up rig is restricted to a water depth of less than three hundred feet. Generally the Hector drilled in one hundred fifty to two hundred feet of water and was seldom out of sight of land.

Nominally, the toolpusher and the company man have distinct responsibilities and areas of authority, but, *Homo sapiens* being *Homo sapiens*, there are many variations on that theme. (Buck, as you might suspect, was strong and opinionated.) The representatives the company sent out tended to become subsumed by Buck to the point of ineffectiveness, or they had such huge conflicts they would show up onshore early, vowing never to go out again. Exxon was anxious to find someone who could work with Buck because the working rigs were booked years out, and they had wells that had to be drilled. Olympia was not going to be talked into replacing Buck, but if they couldn't find someone to work with him, Exxon would be forced to let the rig go. Mike was older than the usual starting engineer, having spent four years in the navy before he went to school, and he had experience offshore. His employers hoped the combination would be enough. He could see the logic of it later, but it offered him no comfort at the time. Buck was truly daunting.

When Mike stepped off the JetRanger that first day, the feeling of being special went away with the cold wind that nearly blew him off the helideck. Though the rig had been aware of his impending arrival for some time, no one greeted him. When he went into the mess decks to find someone to show him to his room, Buck was there drinking coffee with some service company people. He looked up briefly, said, "Mike Brown, is it?" and went back to his discussion. The service hands would probably have liked an introduction, but Buck wasn't offering it, and they weren't going to ask. One of the cooks came and took his bag and showed him to his room. The reception may have been more hospitable had the day itself been warmer, but the two combined to make him question the decision to take the job. At that time a power plant in Dallas seemed an inviting prospect.

Mike had a friend who had been drafted during the Vietnam mess. The friend had had a few years toward an accounting degree, so he ended up in Officer Candidate School. At the first place he was dumped in-country, he was sitting around a campfire with some other soldiers and saw what he took to be two Vietcong running up the hill across the creek. He reacted by shooting the two of them with rifle of another man. The next thing he knew he was helicoptered somewhere deep into the jungle, told, "This is your squad. You're in charge, lieutenant," and dropped off. Some of the men wore human ear necklaces and some leopard skins, and they all looked at him with eyes that gave up nothing. Mike hadn't heard the story before he met Buck, but his friend elected the same tactic Mike did, observe and keep your mouth shut. After about three days of this, the sergeant (nobody wore insignia, but it had become evident who was in charge) came up to Mike's friend and said, "We heard what you did at [name of where the first shooting incident took place]. You may be all right. If you keep your mouth shut and do what you're told, you'll live."

Mike didn't really have the option of just doing what he was told, but it was evident that he didn't have a lot of currency for doing otherwise. Buck was in charge of that rig in the same way and for the same reasons the sergeant was in charge of his men—it had worked well so far.

The first few days offshore, Mike busied himself getting settled. They were drilling but were in the upper stages of the hole, so there were no pressing decisions to be made about the well. He wandered about the rig, looking at its condition and meeting the hands as he ran into them. They were friendly enough but circumspect and quick to return to work. He had seen Buck in the mess hall from time to time but was largely ignored. About the middle of the week, he had run out of ways to keep himself occupied, so he bucked up and walked into Buck's office. Like Mike's room, Buck's had a window that looked out over the pipe rack and up at the rig floor. His desk was positioned so he could look up and out the window, which he was doing when Mike came in. Mike sat down at a chair to the side of him, and Buck didn't act as if he knew he was there.

It was Mike's first real look at the "legend." He was dark, and he had black hair showing the first tinges of gray. He was quite a handsome man in a rough-hewn, Indian sort of way. He was big. Mike had seen NFL linemen up close, and most of them looked like tall, normal-sized men carrying extra bulk. Once, he had gotten on an elevator with Bob Lilly, a Dallas player so big he seemed to fill up the small space. Bob Lilly had a head that fit his body. He was a big man that didn't require any extra bulk. Buck was that kind of big. His wrists were thick, and his hands were large. His bones must have been heavy, but he moved them as easily as Mike moved his own, relatively birdlike, ones. The impression Mike got sitting there was one of almost active stillness. Buck's body was like a machine that sat immobile until it was needed. Only then did it start up and move. It wasn't immediately apparent from a distance how he achieved legend status, but this close one could almost make stories up by looking at him.

"You know anything about drilling wells?" he said.

"No, not really," Mike said.

"Well, then, what the hell are you doing out here?"

Mike knew they both knew the answer to that one; he didn't want to risk a quaver in his voice, so he just let the question lie. The engine started up, and Buck turned his chair to look at Mike. His eyes were so dark they looked black. Mike looked back, concentrating on not betraying nervousness.

Buck said, "I talked to Snake Landry."

Once again Mike elected not to speak.

"Snake said you were the only college boy he ever had working for him that knew how to work. He said you worked your way through school with a wife and two kids. Is that true?"

Mike nodded.

"Are you still married? Did she stay with you through all that?"

Mike pulled out his wallet and opened it up to the latest picture of Sandra and the kids. She and Angela were sitting on a driftwood log at Padre Island, and Sam was jumping over it from the back. Buck took the wallet and looked at it for a long time. Mike couldn't read what Buck was thinking. He would never be able to read what Buck was thinking. If he didn't say it, Mike didn't have any idea what it was.

The engine started up, and slowly the wallet went back.

He said, "There's a load of casing that should be here today. You'll need to tally…measure it all, and log it in. Ask Nub when he can spare a couple of hands to help you with the tally. The formation we want to set it in is about seventy-five hundred feet. We should be there in a day or a day and a half."

And that's how Buck and Mike started out. Mike did everything Buck told him to, even if he thought he knew better. He acquainted himself with the rig by meeting and getting to know the hands. He got them to teach him their jobs, and until Buck got comfortable with turning things over to him, he filled his time substituting here and there around the rig. Gradually Buck realized he didn't need to tell him as much, and finally that he didn't need to tell him anything. Eventually Buck and Mike were true partners and, Mike liked to think, friends. They consulted with each other on all major decisions. They never messed up a well, they never had a blowout, and they never lost a man. Mike's employers thought enough of the relationship to pay him as if he were moving up the ranks, even though he stayed in the same job for more than two decades.

CHAPTER II

Recording a Legend

One day, after they were partners and before they were friends, Mike approached Buck about the stories. As usual, there was no sign that he had heard the question or was even aware of Mike's presence. After a long period during which Mike had many chances to regret the asking, he said, "Are you a fighter, Mike?"

Mike had expected him to shrug the question off with something like, "That was all bullshit, Mike." He hadn't expected him to be vested in the stories. Mike had been practicing a version of Buck's stillness himself, and, while he couldn't be Buck's sphinx, he put what he had into play here. The more he thought about the question, the more it seemed to be a mine-field. There had been times in Mike's life when he would have dissembled or avoided answering; but this seemed a time for honesty.

He said, "No."

The machine started up. He leaned back in his chair and looked at Mike through slitted eyes.

"That's not what I hear," he said.

Mike left that one alone then realized he hadn't expected a response when Buck said, "I'm told that you whipped Darrel Resnick a couple of times. I know Darrel Resnick, and it seems to me it would take a fighter to do it."

Mike had worked with Darrel Resnick from time to time when he was with the service company. Resnick had been doing the job for ten years, and Mike was part time, but they were doing equivalent work and receiving equal pay. There was a feeling among some of that company's workers that Mike was going to get his degree and come back and eventually become president of the company. Some of them believed being on his good side was the best course of action. Others felt like Mike had an unfair advantage and now would be the time to work out their resentment. Resnick was a member of the second group but stood out from it because he was crazy. Mike didn't know the clinical terms for his condition, but he thought it was the main reason that Resnick hadn't progressed beyond the helper position. He was smart, and he knew as much about the job as any operator Mike had worked for. He was two inches taller than Mike and outweighed him by forty solid, muscled pounds. And he hated Mike with a loathing that almost kept him from being able to form the words. Mike was going to be what he should have been, and it was Mike's fault. Mike was afraid of him, and when he was on the same location or platform, he was constantly on guard. Mike was certain that if he and Resnick ever got into a situation together with no others around, he would gladly kill Mike and dispose of the body. And he knew that he could have accomplished it with no problem.

Mike said, "I don't think that what I did to Darrel could be properly termed a *whipping*."

"Yeah?" Buck said. "I understand you and he got into it in a derrick with no ropes or safety lines, and he came out of the derrick first and ran away. That sounds like a whipping to me."

The derrick on a drilling rig is the tower that people see from a distance and think is the rig. It is centered over the well being drilled. Derricks come in different sizes; the one in question was about one hundred seventy feet tall from the crown to the surface of the water (about the height of a sixteen story building). The rig floor, where most of the work is done, is about fifty feet above the water, and the platform that the derrickman works on is ninety feet or so up from that. *Platform* is a misleading term, because what the derrickman stands on while he is handling pipe is called a *monkey board* and is about eighteen inches wide and extends some nine or ten feet to the interior of the derrick. The open space to either side of him is taken up with *fingers*, something like steel two-by-sixes attached to the inside of the derrick and pointing at the monkey board. The fingers are spaced about six inches apart and are for separating the ninety-foot stands of drill pipe while making a trip out of and into the hole. If you stood on the back of the monkey board in the derrick Buck was referring to, you were looking at about a twenty-five-by-twenty-five-foot open space, part of which was filled up by a small diving board, another part of which was intermittently filled with fingers (each of which would hold a man but give noticeably with his weight), and the rest of which was open air with a ninety-foot drop to an oak and steel floor.

Mike was working on a freeze-and-tap job, and Darrel was working on the same structure with a different operator on a production job. The rig was in a bad way. The traveling gear and the kelly were all in the derrick, and there was formation pressure on the inside of the drill pipe. Later, Mike didn't remember what he was doing up there, but the first thing he knew, Darrel was there to "help" him. Mike, on the end of the monkey board stretched out into the derrick, hadn't felt like he needed a safety line until then. Apparently Resnick thought it would be as easy as walking over and giving Mike a push. When he started down the monkey board, Mike stepped out onto one of the fingers. Mike's blood pressure was spiking and ringing bells. He didn't know if they could be seen, but he was dead certain that no one else would be able to make it there in time to do any good. When Resnick looked down before stepping out onto the fingers, Mike knew he was afraid of the height. He had chosen the wrong place for the confrontation. After that it was just a matter of waiting for him to make a move and then pushing him in the direction of the move. He swung at Mike, and Mike ducked enough to make him miss then pushed his elbow as the arm went by. Resnick fell across the fingers, and Mike went back to the monkey board. When he reached for the monkey board, Mike moved as if to step on his hand. Resnick was concentrating on the ninety-foot fall now. Mike couldn't afford to let him get hold of him, but as long as Mike stayed out of his reach, he wasn't going to get hurt. When he started making for the ladder, Mike didn't move to stop him. Mike didn't want to kill him; he just didn't want to be killed. When he was gone, Mike felt relieved but not victorious. He had just poured salt in the wound, and he was pretty sure he hadn't seen the last of Darrel Resnick.

"I didn't whip Darrel," he said. "He just chose the wrong battleground. He was afraid of heights and I wasn't. Another bad place to go up against me would be in the water."

Buck said, "The water? Were you on a swim team?"

"No. But me and my brother grew up diving off cliffs into a muddy river and swimming with the water moccasins."

Buck said, "I heard that wasn't the only confrontation. I heard you broke his arm."

Mike couldn't help but laugh at that. It always helps to have a reputation. If people think you've beaten up a known crazy like Darrel Resnick, it can only smooth your way. Actually, Buck's comment explained some of the automatic respect Mike had been afforded since coming back to the field. As a college student/part-timer, he had operated under a respect deficit. He was told by one hand back then that anything he could make up with a twenty-four the other guy could break with an eighteen. The worker was talking about pipe wrenches, but he was basically saying that Mike was weaker and less tough than he was. By working hard for the service company, Mike gained a little bit of regard from his workmates. But anybody coming into the field with a degree, especially an engineering degree, is automatically considered to have "book knowledge," which is obviously of lesser value than the knowledge most of them have gained on the job. Mike had some field experience, but that hadn't really explained the degree of deference he had been afforded. He was secretly pleased to hear that he had a reputation.

Darrel had caught Mike on a land job. Mike didn't know he was there. It was dark, and Mike was in the bushes taking a shit when he heard someone coming through the brush. He finished what he was doing and headed back to the well. When Resnick called out, Mike turned and once again got lucky. The lights from the location were in Resnick's face. Mike could see him well, but he must have been just an outline to Resnick. He had to get really close to see who Mike was. Then he made another mistake. He started telling Mike what he was going to do to him while poking him in the chest with his forefinger.

"I dislocated his finger," Mike told Buck. "It sounded like something had broken, but it hadn't. I was just reacting. Even a cornered rat will fight."

Buck looked into Mike's eyes. "I've been watching you," he said. "You're not particularly fast, but you're quick and you're plenty strong. I don't know anybody else who can climb that rope. Look at your arms."

Down at the water level was a little wharf where the supply boats tied up. Above the wharf hung ropes from the platform that were used when loading personnel. The hands would time the swells and use the ropes to swing from the boats to the wharf or vice-versa. The ropes were just the right size for climbing, and it had been Mike's habit to use them for exercise every other day or so. Mike had big arms, but it was only because he went to the trouble of making them big. They were a protective device, in the way some animals and birds puff up to make themselves look less vulnerable. Big arms will put a lot of people off you, but they don't fool the ones who really count, those who are tough and bone mean. In fact, being built up can almost be an advertisement to them that you lack what it really takes. If Buck didn't know that, it was only because he wasn't a predator or prey. He didn't routinely go around sizing people up as to whether or not he could whip them.

"The arms aren't the strength that counts. It's in the chest and shoulders and back. Anyway, my problem isn't physical. It's mental. Well, maybe not mental, but something on the inside that keeps me from acting. Some built in timidity. When I was in the navy, a couple of my shipmates decided I should be a fighter like they were. Their weekend diversion involved finding marines in bars and demonstrating to them that they couldn't whip any three sailors — thereby proving their drill instructors wrong. Anyway, these two guys took me over and counseled me in the tricks of the trade. They told me what to do, and then they showed me how to do it. After three bars of my embarrassing attempts, they gave up on me. Anybody would hate to think he was a coward, but I'm afraid that's what I am."

"I have a hard time believing that," Buck said, and then he held up his hand to forestall Mike. "I have no doubt that you believe it, but I don't. At any rate, you see how these things get blown out of proportion as they get passed around. These stories that you've heard about me — why do you care about them? Why do you think I would care about them?"

Mike said, "I haven't thought about that. The stories are exceptional. They are not just the ones passed around about people you don't know. These are about a specific person whom I do know, and they are basically the same stories whenever I hear them. It is not hard for me to believe that such stories are rooted in fact. I believe that there was probably once a warrior named Achilles who fought and killed many brave men at a city named Troy. If I had the opportunity, I would ask Achilles what he thought about the stories that followed him. Hell, even my little stories have some basis."

He said, "How is it you chose Achilles as an example? What do you know of the story?"

When he said *Achilles,* he pronounced the *ch* like the "ch" in *chip.* Mike didn't pick up on the clue at the time but would come to understand. Mike had noticed before that Buck occasionally used a word that wouldn't normally come from a formally uneducated man, but slightly mispronounced it. Another word, he'd remember, was *gesture*. He said it with a hard *g*, like the "g" in *guess*. Mike came to realize that Buck was a reader, and not just a casual reader. True enough, he liked Louis L'Amour and John D. MacDonald, but he didn't stick with the easy stuff. Naturally there were holes in his knowledge, but you could still call Buck educated. Over the years his interest and curiosity had led him to become somewhat of a minor authority on writers as diverse as Dostoevsky and Tolstoy and John Steinbeck and James Joyce. His two favorite books were the *Iliad* and *The Idiot*, both of which he had read many times and could quote from freely. Mike didn't know this at the time, and Buck didn't deign to enlighten him, hence, the following answer.

"It comes from a book, a long poem really, that was written by a blind man named Homer over twenty-five hundred years ago. It tells of the siege of a city-state named Troy by a coalition of Greek city-states. Achilles was the Greek hero, and he defeated the Trojan hero, Hector, in single combat, as well as bunches of others."

This may have not been exactly what he said, but it captures the proper tones of condescension and fatuousness. It hadn't struck Mike as odd, or even coincidental, that the name of the Trojan hero was also the name of the rig. In fact, it was way more than coincidental. Buck just sat there looking at Mike. He didn't jump, as one might have expected, on the obvious point of Homer's having been blind and therefore incapable of actually "writing" something. It turned out that the *Iliad* and *The Idiot* were sort of Buck's Old and New Testaments. He would tell Mike later that both of them spoke to him in ways that nothing else did. Mike's little speech might have helped Buck decide what he would do regarding the stories and Mike's request.

He said, "If I told you what I know and what I think, what would you do with it?"

Mike said, "I would write it up the way you told it to me. I don't know that I would do anything *with* it."

Buck looked into Mike's eyes for what seemed like a long time. Finally he said, "Let me think about it. There are some things I have to consider. I have been asked about this before, and I have always refused to comment. If I tell somebody about them then I have to expose myself to examination and possibly ridicule and I'm not sure I want that."

Mike went away thinking that there was indeed something to the stories and something else behind them and that Buck would have to trust without question whomever he told them to. Mike's question was answered however: no answer.

Mike had given up on the project when, a couple of years later after the regular meeting over breakfast, Buck asked if he would follow him to his office for a chat. That had never happened before, and it caused a little frisson of alarm. Mike thought maybe something had gone wrong with the well overnight.

When they got to Buck's office, Buck said, "I have decided that it would only be fair to myself and everyone else if we made a record of the things that have happened to me in this life. The reason I want to do it here is because I want you to take notes. I want to be sure you get it down just like I tell it to you." Then, when they were settled, he said, "Now tell me what stories you have heard." Then he corrected himself. "No, just tell me one, and we will deal with them one at a time."

Mike told him what he knew of the genesis story in Jal, New Mexico. Buck settled in and closed his eyes as Mike spoke, and listened to the whole story without comment. After the narration he said, "The names are right, though Alma got married and divorced so often that it's hard to know what her last name was at any given time. I followed Roman Butcher to Odessa and then to south Texas over a few years. He was kind of like a father to me. Alma was one of those Zorba-like, forces-of-nature people. She was lusty and loud, fiery and warmhearted, and you couldn't help but love her. She wasn't a mother, though. She didn't have a cuddling bone in her body. Physical contact with Alma was in no way nurturing; it was winner take all. Roman was kind of her between-husbands guy because he had a wife in south Texas that he was going to end up with at some point. He loved his wife, but she lived six hundred miles away, and he didn't get to see her very often. Alma had several runs at me, but I didn't really have an idea of what was being offered, and, anyway, loud and brash never really attracted me. One time, when she was trying to get me in the back room with her, she said, 'What is it? You think I'm fat?' She jerked her skirt up and put my hand on her thigh, saying, 'Feel that. Hard like a rock, no?' All I really saw was a patch of hair, but it was my first glimpse of pussy. That and the sight of a really fine pair of legs made me feel like I'd been hit with a cattle prod. I've since wished many times that I had gone in the back room with her. I would have learned something, and it would have been a kindness to her. She had seen that I was fed and housed, and I suppose you could say that she had saved my life."

"It was 1942, and I was said to be fourteen years old. I don't know how they came to agree on that number. I've since tried to figure out my real age, but maturation varies in each person so much I don't know how you'd do it. That moment with Alma is the first sexual impulse I remember, but my life before Jal is a blank, and puberty could have been earlier. They say I was born at fourteen in Jal, and in every way that matters, I guess they're right. Nobody ever located the trucker that let me out there. I'm not sure where the name Buck Burnet came from, to tell you the truth. My best guess is it was made up by Alma and some of the others when I couldn't come up with a name. There's a town up by Wichita Falls called Burkburnett, which sounds like Buck Burnet if you say it fast. There's another town not far from Austin called Burnet with only one *t* like my name, but they put the emphasis on the first syllable. They say, "Burnet, durn it, can'cha learn it?" The law in Lee County didn't have a lot of interest in another rootless kid, and I don't know that they made any effort to find out where I came from or what I might have done. For a long time, I didn't wonder about it myself, but lately I've taken to thinking about it, and there's nothing there. It's like there's a cliff and then open space with no bottom.

"The rig crew they talk about was real. After the fact I heard a lot of stories, mostly from the chippies around town, about how bad they really were. The company they worked for was sorry, and their equipment was shit. I went out to the rig thinking

I was going to learn to be a roughneck, and the other three men obviously had something else in mind. You know, lately you hear about pedophilia and child abuse like it's a new thing, but I don't think it's a new thing. I think it's been going on a long time; maybe as long as there've been men and children. I think what's new is civilization and humaneness, and I don't think we necessarily have it right, yet. The other men were drinking and saying things I didn't get and looking sideways at me and grinning, but I wasn't worried, which tells you something about the workings of my brain. I've never told anybody this, and maybe it doesn't mean anything, but my mind didn't function in words and sentences then. I communicated with other people in words, but it was almost like I had to translate in and out of the scenes I thought in. If I wasn't being asked a direct question, the words being said didn't mean anything to me. All the information I was processing came by way of feelings generated by input from all my senses. You know how they say animals can sense fear or anger? That's sort of how it was for me. They were probably telling me what they were going to do to me, but I didn't get it.

"When we got to the rig, the driller took me into the toolpusher's shack and gave me a pair of steel-toe boots and a hard hat and told me to fill out some papers. I really liked those almost-new boots, and I made to put them on. He told me to fill out the papers first. I remember looking at the papers and trying to get my mind on what I was supposed to do with them. The room started turning blue, and the blue took over and stared swirling around like a tornado, and then, all of a sudden, I was walking down a dirt road, barefoot, and Roman was standing there with a shotgun. I was so tired I almost couldn't stand up. He put me in the back of his pickup and took me back to Alma's. I don't think we went back by the rig, but we might have. Saying that the rig crew was never heard from again is not quite true. They pitched up at a hospital in Seminole, or at least two of them did. The driller is the one who was never heard from again. The two had broken ribs and other injuries that were typical results of a bar fight, which they ascribed them to. They said the driller had just taken off, and they didn't know where he was or when he might be back. When they got away from the law in Gaines County, they disappeared, too. It sounded like the driller had been killed, but there was never any evidence found."

Mike said, "So the part of the story where you didn't have any memory of what happened at the rig was true?" Buck nodded. Mike said, "That blue thing—has that ever happened since then?"

He said, "It's typical of most of the stories you're talking about. It comes and goes without thought or effort. It's nothing like sleep: when the blueness goes away, I'm fully awake, usually standing up. It feels like there has been no passage of time: like if I was lifting a fork to my mouth before, I'm waiting for the taste of the food after. But time has passed, and some kind of havoc has been wrought. The first few times, it scared me pretty bad because when I was convinced it was me that caused the damage, I was afraid of getting thrown in jail. I was jailed several times, but the blueness brought with it some kind of immunity. I was only charged once or twice and never convicted. Maybe it was just the fact that they could tell I had no real knowledge of the incident. There was also always an element of the others involved getting what they deserved and witnesses that had me being the one attacked. The blueness hasn't come on me for a while, though. It's only happened once since my fortieth birthday."

Mike said, "You talked about chippies in Jal. Is that what they called them there?"

He chuckled and said, "No, that's a south Louisiana term. I've always been reluctant to call the ladies *whores*, but I guess that's what they called them. *Chippies* seems to me a little bit kinder than most of the things they get called."

"A lot of the stories have you consorting with prostitutes. Is that characterization accurate?"

Something flickered across Buck's face that could have been either surprise or anger.

"Consorting? I guess I'm not really sure what consorting means. I like women. Truth to tell, I like women way more than whatever comes in second. I like being among them. I like the way they smell and the way they sound, the way they think and the way they feel. Prostitutes were the only ones who would ever have anything to do with me. How would a guy like me ever meet any other kind of woman? I've had so-called respectable women leave a store when I came in—because I came in. Consorting? Yes, I guess I'm guilty of consorting with prostitutes. But it's not something I apologize for. They're good and bad in just about the same proportion as the rest of us. Most of the goodness and kindness I've experienced was from prostitutes."

They left off the narrative at that point for a couple of days. Mike's notes were written as if Buck had related it all in one long session, even though they were compiled over a period of weeks or months.

When they got back together, Mike told Buck that there was a long stretch between the Jal story and the next one he wanted to talk about and asked if Buck would fill in the space a little bit. Mike had thought he might be reluctant, that there might be something in that period Buck wouldn't want to disclose. But no, he sailed right into it. "Roman put me to work as an extra hand on a daylight crew with a good driller until I could pull my weight. Then I moved as a floor hand to a morning tour crew on the same rig. The company we were working for was a good one, A. W. Thompson in Odessa. They were well run and had good equipment and hands. Eventually, as the oilfield went into a down period and Thompson had fewer rigs running, we moved to ones working closer to the office in Odessa. The need was for oil, and these deep rigs were mainly for natural gas. Finally, they only had one or two rigs running, and they didn't have jobs but for the hands that had been with them the longest. Roman went home to south Texas, and I followed him. He and his wife, Nancy, put me up for a period of time at their home in Alice. It was catch as catch can for a while. There was production, but there wasn't much drilling going on. Nancy had me in night school for a period of time, but it turned out I was a disruptive influence and could already read and add. I worked sometimes as a roustabout on existing wells, and I also worked on workover rigs when I got a chance. That was filthy work and dangerous, but the pay was good. Slowly I started catching temporary jobs on the rigs that were running. I finally stuck with a driller named Choppy Jones out of Premont, just south of Alice. He had three or four companies that liked to use him when they had a rig running, so the work was fairly steady.

"I'm not sure how Choppy got his nickname. I'm sure I heard, but all I have left is the impression that he had boxed when he was young and the name came from the way he moved in the ring. I've heard guys built short and thick like him called *chapos* by the Mexicans, and it could have come from that, too. Choppy was like Roman in some ways, mainly in that he *knew*. I don't hear that any more, but it used to say a lot in a single word. It had to do with competence in all areas of the oilfield. But where Roman was a little bit of a ladies' man, Choppy was one lady's man. Choppy's wife was known as the prettiest woman in south Texas, and I never saw anything that would make me think it wasn't true. She had the unlikely name of Halloween, and Choppy was devoted to her. Class wasn't exactly rife in south Texas, but Halloween had a lot of what there was. Her combination of beauty and charm was sure to draw a lot of interest, and she had many suitors, all of whom were turned away as gently as possible. There was one, however—a bit salesman for Hughes, I think—who was not prepared to take no for an answer. His attentions were troubling Halloween, and she was finding it hard to move around town for fear of running into this fellow. The bit salesman had been a football player for Texas A&M. A fine-looking specimen, he found it hard to believe there was a woman who could fail to give all of his qualities their due. Halloween tried to solve the problem without telling Choppy about it because she thought there might be trouble, but Choppy heard about it anyway. I don't know how he knew that the bit salesman was going to show up at his house that afternoon, but, instead of being on the rig where he was supposed to be, he was there to open the door for him. When the salesman, who stood head and shoulders over Choppy, saw him, he was surprised but not concerned. It was his intention to have Halloween, no matter how many gnomes stood in front of him. He started to say as much to Choppy, and Choppy let him have it through the screen door: one punch that ripped the screen out of its frame and knocked the bit salesman off the porch, down the steps, and flat on his back on the sidewalk, unconscious. Choppy took a lawn chair and a bucket of water down to the man, poured water on his head, and sat in the chair waiting for him to wake up. I won't speculate on what Choppy said but the guy never bothered Halloween again and, as far as anyone could tell, never even drove through Premont again. Needless to say, we never bought Hughes bits after that.

"Choppy took an interest in me and taught me as much about the work as I was prepared to accept. We were together three or four years, and he managed to get me to the point of running a rig (operating as driller) despite the fact that thinking was still pretty much an unnatural function for me. I'd guess I was sixteen or seventeen when I got there and coming into full size. I'm six feet five inches tall and was probably two hundred fifty pounds at the time, though the stories had me bigger than that. I was in the 'fullness of my youth' as they say, and I liked the work for the exercise; but what I really liked to do was hang out with loose women. That's pretty much where my time and money were spent."

Mike asked him if he did any fighting during that time. Had the world turned blue again?

He said, "I fought a lot simply because the oilfield was the kind of place where you fought a lot. I never took enjoyment in it and was mostly just careful not to let somebody crack my head open from behind. People liked to talk about the fights after they happened, but I never felt that good about beating up people who were usually drunk and wouldn't have been a match sober."

Mike asked him if he'd ever been beaten in a fight.

He said, "No, but I've been in some where neither of us wanted any more. There was one little guy in Kenedy that kept trying to bite my ear off, and it was all I could do to keep him from it. Come to think of it, I guess you could say I lost that fight. I finally had to throw him over my car, so I could get my keys out, get in the car, and drive off before he got back to the driver's side. As it was, he attacked the car, and I almost had to drive over him to get away.

"The blueness came on me a couple of times that I remember. Once was in a whorehouse in Nuevo Laredo. I don't know what brought it on, but it had something to do with the owners and some competitors. All I know is that whenever I went into that place after that, all the girls would gather around me like chicks around a mother hen. I could never pay another peso, for anything. I liked that feeling a lot, and that probably explains some of my habits even today."

CHAPTER III

Bobby Lynd

B uck said, "You said that the next story you had took place in Louisiana. Would you be interested in one from south Texas that probably means more than most of the stories you have?"

Mike said, "Of course."

"I guess what I mean is that it involves a man who means a lot to me. His name is Bobby Lynd."

Buck didn't hesitate; he started in like it was the story he had wanted to tell all along. "Bobby was an oilman—a real, true, dyed-in-the-wool entrepreneur. They call them *promoters* in the oilfield, and most of them are just what the name implies: promoters of their own welfare. The major oil companies make up most of the oil business and have done so since the twenties and thirties, but they're so big and inefficient that plenty of scraps fall off the table. The scraps make pretty good eating—so good that some of the promoters who live on them end up creating really big companies themselves. But while the scraps are still on the floor, the fighting gets pretty intense. There's plenty of double-dealing, lying, and outright thievery. Only the toughest come away with enough to eat, and only the most intelligent of those create something that lasts. Some of the most successful were the most crooked, and they are the ones people think about when they think about oilmen. Bobby is the rarest kind of oilman, though: square dealing, honest, competent, and still tough enough to come away with more than his share. A good measure of the honesty and integrity of an oilman would be how far from his base he has to go to get his ventures financed. Bobby doesn't have to go anywhere. His investors are standing at his front door, waiting to hand over their money as soon as he gets a new project put together.

"Bobby got his start in the early days of the south Texas oil and gas play, working as a bit salesman. He lived over the Hughes Tool shop in Freer and got to know everyone who was drilling any wells whatsoever. When he delivered bits, he talked to the drillers, and he eventually developed a real good idea of where production could be found, how deep it was, and what it would take to tap into it. He started by locking up the drilling rights to certain pieces of land by getting to know the owners and gaining their trust. After a while he could just buy some of the land outright.

"By the time I ran into Bobby, he had his own rig that sat idle until he had a well to drill. Choppy was his daylight driller, and if Choppy was working on another well, Bobby would wait until Choppy came free. The first time I met Bobby was at his office in Alice when Choppy and I went to see about moving the rig to a new location. Bobby lived in Alice, but most of his production was around Freer, about forty miles west. When Bobby first saw me, he was taken with the fact I was so big. He couldn't stop talking about it with Choppy, and they both talked like I couldn't hear or understand. I remember it hurting my feelings a little bit. I guess even a big, dumb roughneck doesn't like being thought of as a big, dumb roughneck. The comments were good-natured though, and I shrugged them off or occasionally played along. When Bobby came out to the rig, he and Choppy acted like a couple of kids in a schoolyard. They got a lot of amusement from my unfamiliarity with oilfield terms and my ignorance in general. One time they told me that one of the joints of drill pipe on the pipe racks needed to be turned around, that the bit they'd received connected to the other end. I think I knew they were teasing me. I don't know what they expected me to do, but when I went down and picked up the six-hundred-pound length of drill pipe from the waist-high pipe rack and turned around with it in my arms and put it back down, they almost fell off the floor. Another time they told me that the water table had sprung a leak and I needed to carry some barite up there to soak up the water. I put a one-hundred-pound sack of barite on each shoulder and carried them to the top of the derrick. When I got up there, I took each sack and threw it as far as I could toward their vehicles. I didn't hit them, but they were covered in barite, dirt, and dust—a little joke of my own. By the time I threw the second sack, they were running toward their cars, yelling, 'No! No!' The teasing stopped after that.

"We probably drilled ten or twelve wells for Bobby over a three- or four-year period. Choppy taught me most of what I know about drilling, and Bobby taught me all of what I know about production and finance, but I would almost bet that neither one of them thought I was learning very much. I was full-grown by that time, but you have to remember that in a lot of ways I was a newborn. I learned from them in the way that kids learn from their parents, mostly by observation. I didn't learn that being an honorable man was the way to be because Bobby told me so. I learned it because I could see that was what he was, and I wanted to be like him. If you did something wrong, Choppy would let you know about it, but if things were going right, he saw no reason to speak. When it came to drilling though, Choppy always made himself clear, and he never left anything to chance. When you set the rig up, you didn't set it near the marker that the geologist had left; you set it so the marker was in the exact center of the rotary table. When you set conductor pipe, it didn't lean; it was straight up and down and centered on the rotary table. You didn't guess how many joints of pipe were in the hole or how long they were;

you knew. Before you drilled into a gas bearing formation, you had the mud weight and properties right. One time some kind of government inspector came out to the rig, and he was try-ing to make a case for how dangerous drilling was and how incompetent the people were. He asked Choppy, 'Mr. Jones, what would you do if that well started coming in right now?' Choppy looked at him and said, 'Why, I would be real sur-prised.' Choppy's contention was that if you knew what you were doing and did what you knew, things didn't go wrong, even in drilling a well. Choppy never had a well come in on him and neither have I. Lost circulation can get hairy, and I've had some tense moments worrying about whether that would cause a blowout before I could get it stopped, but that was early days out here in the gulf before I learned what we were drilling in.

"What I learned from Bobby was mostly by accident: him telling stories while waiting for something to happen with the well. One time I heard him say to Choppy, 'If it ain't net, it ain't cash. And if it ain't cash, it ain't shit.' I thought that was amusing at the time, and I didn't even fully understand it. I also heard him say one time that he had seven accountants in different places, and none of them knew what the others knew. He said he didn't want any one man knowing everything about his business. He said he had been talking to a new one, one in Corpus Christi, who told him, 'Mr. Lynd, you need some tax shelters. You don't have any tax shelters.' Bobby said, 'I told him, "Son, I'm in the tax shelter bi'ness. I pay my fifty percent and fuck it."' Bobby is hard as nails, but he's a compassionate man as well.

"Anyway, I was happy doing what I was doing and noth-ing would have changed had it been up to me. We were drill-ing a well for Bobby down by Seven Sisters. I was working for Wayne Nolen on morning tour because his derrickman turned up drunk. Wayne Nolen is the same as my daylight driller out there right now, but in those days he still had both arms, and we didn't call him 'Nub.' Way up in the night, a couple of cars came out to the rig. I was mixing mud and didn't pay them much attention. They went to the side of the rig where the floor hand was working, and directly Nolen picked the bit off bottom and locked it down and went down the stairs to the other side. I could hear raised voices, so I walked around the mud pits. There were about eight men standing around in front of Nolen and the other hand, all holding gas cans and some of them with torches and clubs. I heard the leader telling Nolen, 'We mean to burn down this here rig. You can leave now or get the shit kicked out of you, but one way or the other, this rig is going to burn.' The only one who would get hurt by burning the rig and losing the well was Bobby. Whoever was paying them to do it was undoubtedly a competitor. Nolen told him they didn't bring enough men, and he looked back at me. Some of the men were impressed, but none of them thought they would need reserves. I personally was not looking forward to taking them on. It would be me and Nolen because the other hand was already edging out of the location light. I walked up behind Nolen, intending to talk it over, just as the leader clubbed him in the head. I looked down at Nolen, and the next thing I know it's full light and I'm taking a cup of coffee from Bobby. I was dead tired, and I had a sense of dread about what I was going to see when I turned around. Sure enough there were people everywhere, and none of them were upright and mobile. Nolen's floor hand was moving among them, and Choppy had Nolen sitting up and was looking at his head. Bobby said one man had been making a getaway in a car, and Bobby stopped him at the cattle guard and got the story from him. Presumably he gave Bobby the name of the person who hired them, but he never told me. Bobby was looking at me in a new way.

"He said, 'You know, if I'd known you were capable of something like this, I never would have teased you.' He looked around the location and said, 'It's hard for me to believe that any one man could do this.' By this time I was sitting on the ground with my head in my hands. Choppy had a camper on the back of his pickup, and Bobby put me in there in the space under the bed. I was out like a light, and Bobby and Choppy dealt with the law and got all the people to a hospital. When

I woke up, the pickup was parked at Bobby's office, and Bobby and Choppy were inside talking.

"When I walked in, Bobby was saying, 'Well, if we're not going to turn him in, we're going to have to get him out of the area. I don't think they're going to be looking for him too hard, but if one of those idiot deputies runs across him around here, they're going to get you and me for aiding and abetting.'

"Nolen told the sheriff that I was a hand that he had picked up for one night off the road and that he didn't even know my name. That held them off for a day or two, but as soon as my description got around, they were going to put two and two together. None of the group that came out to the rig was disposed to bring charges, and it looked like the incident would die on its own if they didn't find the 'giant' that caused the damage. Bobby kept me under cover at his office for a couple of days, and then, the second night after the incident, he came in with a set of car keys in his hand.

"He said, 'Son, you saved me a lot of money and maybe more than that when you kept those fellas from burning my rig. What I'd like to do is keep you here working for me, but it doesn't look like that's possible. I'm giving you a car and some money and the name of a friend of mine in southwest Louisiana, and I'm recommending that you go there and hit him up for a job. Another thing I'm going to suggest is that, from now on, you take half of every paycheck and send it to me, and I'll invest it for you. Roughnecks make a lot more money than they or anybody else realizes, but they piss it all away. I reckon the best thing I can do for you is to make sure that you don't wind up old and broke like most of them.'"

Mike broke into the narrative and asked Buck if he'd done that—sent half of his paychecks to Bobby Lynd.

He said, "Yep, every one I ever got, right up to and through the present moment."

Mike asked him how that worked out for him.

He smiled and chuckled and said, "It worked out real good."

That really made Mike curious, as Buck knew it would.

He said, "This is just between you and me, and I mean it." He paused and looked at Mike as if making him swear an oath. "I'm a rich man and have been for a long time. I own this rig."

It occurred to Mike that Buck had been shitting him all along. The rig belonged to the Olympia Drilling Company, and he told Buck as much.

Buck said, "The Olympia Drilling Company runs nine offshore rigs. They own six of them, but they lease three of them from a company Bobby set up for me. We bought them for pennies on the dollar during the bust before last from banks that had repossessed them. If Olympia really wanted to know who owns the rigs, they could eventually find out, but they've never gone to the trouble."

Mike said, "If you own three offshore drilling rigs, why don't you just start your own drilling company?"

"Hell, son, I don't want to run a drilling company. I worked in Olympia's office in New Orleans for a while. Running a company is not for me. I'm very comfortable spending my time running a drilling rig. Besides, these three rigs are only eight to ten percent of what I have and only fourteen to sixteen percent of my income."

This really threw Mike at the time. The rigs were worth at least five million dollars apiece. None of what Mike understood about either people or finance would lead him to think that a person with that kind of money would choose to spend time working offshore when he could be doing much more glamorous and interesting things. His salary as a toolpusher couldn't have been much more than a thousand bucks. How in the world could a person amass that kind of money in only twenty or thirty years? Mike didn't think he had ever met a millionaire before, and here was one living with him on a drilling rig in the middle of the gulf. He wore the same kind of coveralls Mike did and ate the same food. If a millionaire looked like this, who were the dudes in the Cadillac convertibles with the big cigars? As much as Mike liked and respected Buck, he didn't really believe him. The story was just too incredible.

It turned out the story was true. Buck was a rich man. But it took Mike a long time to be convinced, and his disbelief created a rift between the two that took a while to heal. A lesser man would have just shown Mike his IRS statement, but that would have been too easy for Buck. In his mind Mike had to believe him just because he had that kind of faith in him. As it was it took several weeks for Mike to ask him to continue the story. By that time the warmth that had started to develop between them had cooled, and Buck's recitations were more mechanical.

When they had spoken before, Mike usually sat at Buck's desk taking notes, and Buck sat in a chair beside it, facing him and away from the window to the rig floor. This time Buck rather pointedly turned the chair around and faced the other way, forcing Mike to speak to the side of his head. It turned out not to be that bad an arrangement because instead of looking for Mike's reactions, he was concentrating more on what had happened; but it was his way of saying that he had responsibilities and work to do and that Mike was keeping him from them. In reality, the rig ran like a top without needing much input from either one of them.

Buck asked Mike what the next story he had was, and Mike told him about the school board meeting in the town hall. He chuckled at that and said it was only partially true, and then he told him about the "jawbone of a ass" line. That quote had really tickled him, and Mike didn't know if he just liked the turn of phrase or was somehow flattered by the comparison with Samson.

"But," he said, "I'd like to fill in some before we get to it. The fellow that Bobby sent me to was a man, name of Rebel Bernard. His real name was Howard, but when he went to school at Oklahoma, his Cajun accent was so thick people could barely understand him. A Cajun isn't properly a rebel, but I wouldn't expect Oklahomans to know the difference. Rebel was a lot like Bobby in that he had principles and scruples, but where Bobby's was a bold, entrepreneurial spirit, Rebel's was more of a hunker-down-for-the-siege mentality. He was a superintendent for Sinclair at the time and, as a degreed engineer with a great deal of experience, was eligible for promotion and was frequently offered one. He liked living in Lake Charles, though, and he had a thing about not getting above the level of superintendent. He said oil companies were subject to getting bought, and when that happened, they did away with everybody above superintendent. He said that they had to keep the superintendents on down, or everything would grind to a halt; but everyone above that was dispensable. He turned out to be a prophet in that regard because, not long after I left that part of the country, Sinclair was bought out, and Rebel kept his job. Typical of a man whose occupation requires less than he's got, though, Rebel had time for other things. One of the things he liked to do most was fight with the IRS. He told me once that he considered the first return he sent in every year was the 'opening to negotiations.' Rebel and his wife, Pat, kind of semi-adopted me. Pat was an Oklahoma native who cooked great Cajun food. They didn't have any kids at the time, and they really wanted them, so I think I got some of the attention that would have been afforded the children. While I was there, they somehow learned the recipe for making kids, and I don't think they stopped until they had seven or eight.

"Rebel got me a job with the Delta Drilling Company out of Tyler, and in about six months, I broke out as a driller on a deep rig they had running around Lafayette. I stayed with Delta for a few years. We tended to drill north of Highway 90 because of where they were based. They were a good company, but they weren't growing, and they had low turnover—zero in the toolpusher ranks. I felt like I needed to be a toolpusher. Eventually I ran into a guy who was starting his own company. He went on to make me the toolpusher for his two then, finally, four rigs. His name was Niles Green, and he called it the Green Nile Drilling Company. I didn't know the difference between a legitimate operator and a hustler then, and Niles helped me sort that out by being one of the most crooked and least able oilmen I ever met. Rebel counseled me not to go with Niles, but I thought that was just his natural aversion to risk. By the time it was said and done, the Green Nile Drilling Company owed everyone in the country, and Buck Burnet was the only representative they knew. The guys that cornered me in that dancehall didn't have anything to do with anybody's school board. They were just frustrated creditors and their minions. I don't know how the school thing got into the story, though I've heard that version before myself. There were a lot of people there. Maybe some school board members got in on it just for fun. Things turned a little bit blue, but it was atypical in that I was conscious the whole time. I was at pains not to hurt anybody too badly, but it was getting harder and harder to accomplish. Finally the law got there and took me into protective custody. When I got out of jail, I took my company pickup to the little yard that Niles rented and left it there with the keys in it. I heard later that Niles tried to sue me, but he couldn't get any traction in south Louisiana, him being from Chicago and owing a bunch of people himself. I'd hurt Delta's feelings when I'd left, and they weren't in the way of taking me back. I had some hands that were loyal to me, and I could make a living and keep them alive by freelancing for people who had rigs that didn't run all the time. I found I did best if I stayed in an area east of the Sabine and south of Highway 90. I generally didn't get past Lafayette or New Iberia to the east. That was about four or five years that went by really fast because if I wasn't drilling, I was hustling for jobs. Along about then I ran into a spot of trouble that even the blue couldn't get me out of, and I ran out of work. Pat offered to put me up at their house, but I didn't feel like I could take advantage of them in that way. The truth is I already took advantage by eating at their house too often.

"That's when I first showed up at the Lilac Bloom, and that's a blue story that apparently you haven't heard. I was looking for a cheaper place to stay, and I took the Bloom for a rooming house, it having the multiple-roomed look of one and being out in the country around Hickory Flat. I knew it for a whorehouse as soon as I walked in the front door. There was a huge black lady almost filling the front hall, and she told me it was too early for customers and, anyhow, they didn't 'low no white trash in here.' Apparently they didn't cater to oilfield people, and that's how come I hadn't heard of it. I craned around her, trying to get a look at the girls. It was too early in the day for that, but the commotion attracted the attention of a woman on the second floor. She was dressed like the businesswoman she was, in a dark suit and high heels. She was probably around forty years old, but she could have been anywhere from thirty to fifty. As she came down the stairs, she held my eyes first, and then she looked me over just like you might look at a horse you were thinking of buying.

"Flora,' she said, 'why don't you just leave this fine-looking young man alone.' Then she took me by the hand and led me through a couple of rooms to the kitchen, where there was another black lady kneading dough. 'Cora, our young visitor looks hungry. Have we got anything for him to eat?'

"The lady's name was Lilah Blue, and she and the bank owned the Lilac Bloom. She ran between seven and nine girls, and she had this house and four bungalows out back. She needed someone to do odd jobs around the place; she couldn't pay me, but she could feed me and let me stay in the farthest bungalow out. I could take other jobs when I could find them. Her only stipulation was that I could talk to the girls, but I couldn't sample the merchandise under any conditions, paid for or not. When I started to protest, she said, 'What I'm packing isn't for sale. It used to be, but isn't anymore. Whenever you feel the need and I have the time, you can have a little taste of the best there is. But if you fuck one of my girls, I will kick your ass out in a New York minute.'

"Who could resist an invitation like that? Certainly not the young Buck Burnet. What Lilah didn't tell me was that she was running afoul of the consortium that handled prostitution in the area, and they were pressuring her to join up. It wouldn't have made any difference to me, though. The next six months may have been the happiest of my life. Lilah wasn't bragging when she said she had the best there was. Not only was she up for whatever I was, she was able to temper my passion and teach and coach along the way. Once the girls understood the arrangement, they delighted in trying to get me into bed, and their little stratagems were more fun than any child's game. The food was not just good, it was the best I've ever had, and I gained enough weight to start looking a little pudgy. My room was always clean, and I slept like a baby. As far as I can remember, I never did an odd job the whole time I was there. I didn't feel like I played a role, but I think I was considered a sort of low-key bouncer by the others. Lilah strove to attract a clientele that didn't require bouncing, but occasionally one would slip in. There were two other men that worked there. One was a gay piano player who was stoned on something most of the time. The other was the guy who mixed the drinks. The Bloom didn't have a bar, but the customers could buy drinks if they needed a little help in laying more money down. The drinks guy was named Tom Coleman, and he was like someone out of Dostoevsky. He seemed interesting, but I could see he had written me off as a brute; and I had the girls to talk to, anyway. My favorite time of day was about noon when most everybody would get up and have breakfast. I was the only man present, and it was like a feast for the senses. If you had Cora's biscuits one time, you would never order biscuits anywhere else again. The girls would be dressed in bright colored things that showed off their best features and talking and laughing. They seldom addressed me directly, but they would talk about me to each other. They played a game of seeing if they could embarrass or distract or get me to react in any way. When a flash of exposed breast or thigh drew my eyes, they laughed and twittered like a beautiful flock of birds. If God lets me pick my own heaven, that's where I want to spend eternity: in Cora's kitchen round about noon.

"I'd be there still, I suppose. Certainly I wouldn't have chosen to leave, but really good things, or really bad things for that matter, don't last long in this world. Lilah didn't tell me exactly what was going on until after the fact, but apparently there was at least one faction that wanted control of her business. I say 'at least one' because it seems like I heard mention made of both New Orleans and Houston. She had been under the protection of the local sheriff for unnamed fees and considerations, but the sheriff was getting pressure from these outside people. Apparently he had decided that the best course of action would be to allow the outside people in and take a bigger cut of the action himself. Lilah could see that wasn't heading any direction she wanted to take, so she was resisting. I had seen the sheriff around from time to time but hadn't paid him the mind I should have. He was a big, mean-looking guy, and I knew that none of the girls liked spending time with him. I saw him studying me occasionally, but I just took it for the natural interest of a lawman. The plan involved taking over the Lilac Bloom physically and installing their own management team. The new team and their associates showed up early one afternoon before there were any customers. They must have considered me somewhat of a threat because there were a lot more of them than one would think necessary to do the job. I was in the kitchen with Dinah, one of the prettiest girls, when I heard raised voices coming from the vestibule. I barely had time to see three men standing in front of Lilah and more on the porch before the blue took over. When I came to, I was in the front yard, and there were ten or twelve men stacked up like cordwood in the parking lot, and three cop cars coming up the drive. Lilah was standing on the porch with what I recognized as a regular customer who turned out to be the district attorney."

Mike broke into the narrative again and asked, "Was there really someone in the kitchen named Dinah?"

Buck said, "Well, I don't rightly remember her name, but if you're in the kitchen with someone and you have to make up a name, shouldn't it be Dinah?"

The ease with which he said that made Mike wonder how much license he was taking in other areas. Buck must have sensed that because he said, "Look. You come to me with some stories that you want fleshed out. If I've got to sit here and hem and haw about little details like the names of ladies of the night, then this is going to take a long time."

Mike told him he understood that, but that he thought it would just sound better if he said something like, "I was in the kitchen with one of the prettiest girls."

He said, "Fine. I'm just saying that her name could have been Dinah, and, being Dinah, it makes for a better story."

He continued, "It worked out that Lilah and the DA had the goods on the sheriff and the basis for a new working relationship. The sheriff lost his job, and, unfairly I thought, Buck Burnet lost his position as resident whatever-I-was. Lilah told me that she appreciated what I had done; but the Lilac Bloom had worked without violence before I stepped in, and she thought it would be very awkward to have me around. She said news of what had happened hadn't leaked out, and she thought it would be best for business if it didn't. If there were any tears shed at the parting, I shed them. What has occurred to me in the years since is the possibility that Lilah had just grown tired of me.

"I had done a few jobs off and on during the six months but hadn't really kept up any contacts, so I pitched back up on the doorstep of Rebel and Pat Bernard. I could tell Rebel had reservations, but Pat was happy to have me. She was pregnant for the third time and happy about everything. Rebel was interested in my stories about the Lilac Bloom, and I could see Pat listening in from time to time. She never said anything to me about them, but she stopped trying to fix me up with the daughters of her friends. Rebel had a friend—well, *acquaintance* might be more accurate—who had come by a drilling rig. He didn't exactly win it in a poker game, but I'll bet the real story wasn't far from that. He had been in the oilfield parts business but had lost that, and he got the drilling rig as some sort of settlement. There isn't anything in the world worth more per pound than a drilling rig when the business is booming, and nothing worth less when business is bad. The guy didn't know anything about drilling or hands, and he was going to lose everything if he couldn't get a handle on it and get some income. Rebel thought he was desperate enough to go partners with somebody who could turn it around.

"I found Jim Blanchard in a bar in Morgan City deep into a bottle of Jim Beam. His clothes didn't fit the place, but the rest of his appearance did. He looked like he might have played football some years back, but he didn't look fit to be playing anything now. He was thick and pasty, and his eyes didn't focus real well. He had the patter and expansive gestures of a high-rolling salesman, but there was a sour smell to him, and his hand shook when he picked up the glass. I told him who I was and what I was after. He tried to shit me for a while, but I just sat there and listened until he was ready to start talking turkey. He said he had hired the crew that was on the rig, and it looked like things were going real well. As the conversation progressed, it became apparent that the crew hadn't been hired so much as had just taken the rig over. They were somewhere back in the bayous, supposedly drilling wells, but whatever cash was flowing was finding its way past him. He said he wasn't looking for partners so much as for employees. I told him that I wasn't looking to make a paycheck; I was looking for a business to be part of. He struggled, but he didn't really have a choice. I told him I needed money for hands and supplies and the location of a legitimate well to drill. I have always suspected that Rebel fronted him the money just to get me away from Lake Charles. I know he thought a lot of me, but I was beginning to become a bit of a chore. I know for sure that the first well we drilled was for Sinclair.

"That rig was the first barge rig I had ever seen, but it didn't take long to tell that it was just a land rig rigged up on big flat barge. There was about a fifteen-by-twenty-foot window cut out of the back end of it. The floor and the rotary table were in a substructure over that hole, and the derrick was over that. The derrick was a folding one, so it could be laid down for moving, and the stand that it rested on was part of the structure of the living quarters at the front end of the barge. The deck of the barge held the mud pits and mud pumps and other storage, and everything else was supported by the substructure. It seemed like a pretty clever rig up, but I didn't have time for a detailed study. I hadn't been able to get a local crew together, so I had seven men that Roman had sent me from south Texas, among them the Nolen that I'd worked for, then and forever after known as Nub Nolen. He had lost his left arm in an accident while working on building the Bay Bridge across the channel in Corpus Christi. It left me shorthanded, but better short one hand than two."

Buck held up his hand to keep Mike from asking if he wanted him to keep that in the narrative.

"I'd told Roman that if the guys he sent me liked to fight, that would be a plus. I figured there would be five or six men aboard, and I was hoping none of them would contest us, but I was thinking it would be best to be prepared. The others spread throughout the rig, and I headed for the living quarters. On the way to the stairs, I passed a man mixing mud. I didn't like the way he dropped the sack he was holding and looked after me, but I didn't want to start anything there. I was looking to beard the lion in his den. Jim had used words like 'difficult' and 'obstinate,' but when I walked into the living quarters, I wondered if Jim had ever actually seen the man who had his rig. To call it a lion's den didn't do the place justice. It was more feral than that. The kitchen, mess hall, and common area were one big room, and it was a shambles. There were pieces of clothing and paper everywhere, and it smelled like a combination of armpits and shit. There was a stringy-haired woman doing something at the sink. She was holding one kid, and another one was dragging at her house robe. There, sitting in a lounge chair that was splayed out and a way darker color than it had been, was the aforementioned lion. It was a new type to me at the time, but I have come to know them as *Neandertals*. Neandertals were a species of man that predated *Homo sapiens*."

Mike told Buck that he knew what they were, but they were called *Neanderthals*, and they had died out thousands of years ago.

Buck continued, "The name comes from the Neander Valley, where their remains were first discovered. You see the name spelled both ways, but the most authoritative pieces I have read don't use the *h*. The reigning opinion is that the species died out forty thousand years ago, and, even though there were *Homo sapiens* around at the time, there was no contact and no interbreeding. I'm here to tell you that the proof that destroys that argument was sitting in the filthy living quarters of a rig deep in the bayous of south Louisiana, right in front of me. He didn't have a lot of hair on his head, but there was plenty to go around everywhere else. You know who he looked like? Do you read the funny papers? He looked like Alley Oop, only not so civilized. His hands were huge, and his fingers looked like sausages. His arms were the same size from wrist to elbow, and the size was large. He looked to be shorter than me, but his body was the same width as my shoulders, all the way to the floor. He didn't start when I came through the door, and he finished the piece he was reading in the newspaper before he deigned to look up. His eyes were all pupil with no white, and the color was black as coal. He said, 'Well, bless me if they didn't send young Mr. Burnet to root me out.' He moved his lipless mouth in a way that suggested he was smiling. 'You see, Mr. Burnet, you are famous. Even we godless heathens on the fringes of society have heard of you.' That was the first person that ever called me famous and the first time I had thought of the possibility. While I was considering it, he was out of the chair much faster than I thought possible and hitting me in the sternum with his huge right fist. That blow was the hardest I've ever taken. It was so hard that much of my strategy in the ensuing scuffle was directed at avoiding another one. It knocked me out the door I had just come in and down the stairs to the dragway between the pipe racks. Another theory about the Neandertals was that they were slow, but he blew that one out of the water and was in the air over me before I could register what happened."

Mike broke in and said, "Did things turn blue?"

"No, they didn't turn blue, and not for lack of me wanting them to. There were moments when I prayed for things to turn blue, or any other color, but they wouldn't. That's the first time that I realized the blueness didn't have anything to do with me. The blueness was an outside agent that was not in my control, not even subconsciously.

"He grabbed me by the shirtfront and lifted me clear of the deck with one hand. I was beginning to look for help from outside sources, but the only potential help were similarly occupied in various corners of the rig. He brought my face close to his and said, 'Mr. Burnet, welcome to the land of grownups.' Then he raised me to his shoulder and threw me down the dragway toward the rig floor. I rolled and hit my feet and ran up the fifteen-foot stairway as fast as I could. Just as my head cleared the floor, he grabbed my ankle and dragged me back down, my head hitting each step like in a cartoon. He picked me up again and was looking to hit me with that sledgehammer fist, but I twisted and pulled enough to keep him from getting a good shot. I came out of my shirt and rolled onto the pipe rack, which had a layer of ten-inch casing on it. The pipe started moving, but I scrambled across it and down onto the deck on the other side. He was gone when I looked back, but I realized he was coming under the rack and just managed to avoid him grabbing my pant leg as I sprinted for the rig floor. This time I made it and picked up a length of pipe that had been used for a cheater. I was at the top of the stairway with the pipe when he reached the base. 'This is a disappointment,' he said. 'I was looking for a fair fight from the famous Mr. Burnet.' I thought of a lot of things I should have said after the fact, but at the time I was just too tired and too preoccupied to be clever. There were three stairways to the rig floor: one in the middle of the rig at the dragway and one at the outside of each of the pipe racks. Our impasse was taking place at one of the outside ones when I saw two of my hands coming down the middle. I motioned them to the other outside one, for fear he would catch one or both of them before they could join me on the floor. Such was my respect for the Neandertal that I wasn't sure three of us were enough. He saw the two of them and scowled. 'I see some of my people didn't measure up. Such are the rewards of inbreeding for you.' At that point he decided there was just no other way than to come on up. I hit him with the pipe twice before he made it to the rig floor: once on top of the head and once on the point of a shoulder. Both blows made satisfyingly solid sounds, but they didn't visibly affect his progress. I don't remember what I was thinking, but if I wasn't thinking that I was in deep shit, it was only due to youth and ignorance. He took hold of the pipe with both hands, and for a moment we wrestled for the pipe. I fell backward, looking to pull him over onto my feet so I could flip him, but before my back hit the floor, he stopped my momentum with brute force. Then he fell on me, and the weight of him drove the air from my lungs. He put the pipe across my throat, and every molecule of my body was straining to keep that pipe from separating my head from the rest of me. I hadn't breathed for a long time, and things had turned black when I felt his weight suddenly lift off me. I was pretty sure I was dead because I was receiving no sensory input, but gradually light returned, and a face swam into view. It was Nub, and once he determined I was going to live, he started laughing. I asked him what was funny, and he said, 'When that guy pulled you down those steps, it was just like a *Tom and Jerry* cartoon.' I looked up, and the Neandertal was suspended by one of his legs from the boom of a crane attached to a leg of the derrick about sixty feet overhead. His altitude was controlled with an air winch operated by one of the two hands I had seen earlier. He said, 'Luke managed to hook that chain around his leg while he was busy strangling you. I got to keep an eye on him because if I get him too close to the mast, he'll pull himself up and get that hook loose. If I give him too much slack, he'll swing over to the derrick and get off that way. I'll tell you what: it was all this little air tugger could do to get that big son of a bitch off the floor. I don't want him where he can get to me.' I didn't say it, but I shared his sentiments. As it was, we had to keep him up there for nearly six hours before we could get any law to pick him up. I asked Nub what he had been doing that he could see me in trouble and not help out. He said he had been occupied with the woman, who had a big ass knife and was trying to cut off his other arm. A woman on a rig wasn't a usual thing, but those guys had that one out there as a common resource and cook. Apparently before she left, she was making overtures to one of my hands because I heard another one ask him why he didn't take her up on it. He said he considered it, but that finally, 'Toe jam you can see is just too much.'"

CHAPTER IV

Jeanerette

Mike didn't know what he had expected when he first started listening to Buck and taking notes. He guessed he had some vague idea of preserving a myth, of grabbing it and rooting it in reality, so those who came after wouldn't have to wonder about what kind of man Buck really was. But Mike was beginning to realize that what he was dealing with was no myth. All of the stories were a little otherworldly, but that was understandable in stories that had been passed along. It seemed a different thing when that same quality was present in tales from the source.

Mike put aside his pencil. He got up and poured a cup of coffee. One of the nice things about being with Buck was that silence didn't bother him. If you had the floor, he would wait as long as it took for you to resume. During Buck's defensive silences, Mike wasn't sure if he had any thoughts at all. He would sit there still as a stone and only come alive when you spoke.

"When you lost that fight, how did it make you feel? I mean, did you lose confidence? The next time you walked into a bar, did you have the slightest hesitancy, knowing there might be somebody in there that could beat you up?"

Buck thought about that for a long time.

"I don't know what you think about fighting," he said. "Fighting is something I have had to do from time to time, but it is not inevitable. It is not something I anticipate or expect. In fact, I avoid it whenever possible. Fighting is not me, so winning or losing at fighting doesn't affect me."

Buck still had the floor, but he considered his next very carefully.

"I am a man and I am only a man, and that's the good and the bad. In the fight that I just described to you, my opponent was, to me, a repulsive person, but he was every bit as valid a man as I was. When I burst in on him, I gave him no choice but to retaliate, which he did without hesitation. And in our confrontation, he was the grownup. He took the offensive, and I was left reacting. My first mistake had been in thinking I could not be beaten. And trying not to be beaten, probably to bolster the fiction that I couldn't be beaten, was my second mistake. The Neandertal taught me two things: one, that I could be beaten; and two, that I had to disregard my own self-image. Ninety-nine percent of the time, the winner of a fight is the one who can keep his mind clear and stay away from emotion. Fighting takes a hell of a lot of energy, and if you can just avoid taking heavy blows in the initial stages, your opponent will burn himself out, and slow enough to give you a clear shot."

Buck went quiet then. Most people would have thought the session over, but Mike knew he was getting ready to say something that he wanted to know for sure he had figured out.

"That Neandertal...Now, if Nub and them hadn't been there, he would have killed me for sure. I ran into another Neandertal just awhile ago, but he was beaten by the blue. It seems to me the universe is run on a principal of opposites — good and bad — and there's just as much of one as of the other. I can't say that each individual life comes out even in the end because I can think of too many cases where that didn't seem to be so, but when you're talking exceptional lives...When your life is occasionally taken control of by forces outside your ken, I think the highs and the lows will cancel out. Take Hector, for example; he was the baddest man on the block for a long time, but the gods were just setting him up for Achilles. Then Achilles dies from a small wound inflicted by the most craven man in the field. I've flown pretty high in my life, but I think I'm due another Neandertal, and I think the gods are planning to pull the rug out from under me."

Mike had stopped writing halfway through the last, and he sat now, thinking about just how strong and tough and rich a person had to be to feel like he didn't have to worry. If Buck wasn't there, maybe you just couldn't get there. The comment had planted the Neandertal in Mike's mind though, and he would never be far away when Mike was with Buck.

Buck stirred. "Your question makes me wonder what you think about fighting. Where did you grow up?"

"A little bit south of San Antonio."

"What was your family like? What did your father do for a living?"

"He was the sheriff of the county where we lived. His brothers were lawmen, and his father and uncles were Texas rangers at times and federal agents at others. We had a pretty normal family, I guess. My parents are Catholic, so I have a lot of brothers and sisters."

Buck said, "With that kind of tradition behind you, how is it that you're not a lawman?"

How is it that sometimes someone can sink a shaft right to your core without meaning to? Buck had turned the tables on Mike. He was just following a line of curiosity, but Buck had managed to tap into his insecurities. At least one of the reasons he wasn't a lawman was he didn't think he was tough enough.

"So your father's family are tough guys," he said. "How about your mother's family?"

Mike said, "They are cowboys and outlaws. If anything, they are even tougher than those on my father's side."

"I see," he said. "And how did you fit into that scenario?"

"Somewhat of a disappointment to both sides, I think."

Mike didn't know what Buck was doing with the information, but he turned it over in his mind for a long time before speaking, and when he did, it was about something else.

Mike told Buck that he had some reservations about the last story. He told him he thought it had a little too much of a story quality to it.

"A story is a story," Buck said. "How can a story be too much like a story?"

Mike told him that what he was trying to do was tell the stories in such a manner as to separate fact from fiction. Most people on hearing the stories he had heard would consider them largely fiction. Since the protagonist of the stories existed, Mike felt there could be some factual basis to them, and there was an opportunity to get the facts from the horse's mouth. But if what came out of the horse's mouth sounded fictional, it cast a cloud of suspicion over the whole process.

"I'm telling you what I remember and how I remember it happening. I personally don't see how a story about how some guy kicked my ass is any more fantastic than stories about how I whipped a bunch of guys on several different occasions. The truth is I remember this one and only have circumstantial knowledge of all the others. Besides, if you think I'm lying, the one who can prove the lie is right up there on the brake." He said the last while looking at Nub Nolen, who was indeed visible operating the rig.

Mike said, "Well, maybe it wasn't the facts so much as the touches — like the bad guy speaking in calm, cultured tones."

He said, "It was a long time ago, and I was a different person. Obviously I can't remember exactly what was said, but the import and the way it was said was exactly as I remember it. I know the inbred comment was his. I didn't even know what the word meant at the time. I know another thing: that guy was not human. I wasn't afraid of him at the time, but I would be if I ran into him now. And there are others like him out there — people with thick wrists and beady eyes. They are not the ones that are loud and starting fights. They tend to be quiet and out of the limelight, but they are there, and you do not want to get them stirred up. I know in my heart of hearts that I am not destined to die of old age. When my time comes, it will be a Neandertal that puts me in the ground. Hell, we got one right here on this rig. Max is a real, sure-enough Neandertal."

Mike heard Buck speaking those words about his own demise, but he didn't make anything of it at the time. The seed was planted in his subconscious, though, and there would come a time when it would blossom into his conscious mind all too vividly. Max was the mechanical superintendent and a gentle, easygoing bear of a man. There was nothing about him, other than size, that resembled the man in Buck's story, but Mike had seen him lift a full fifty-five-gallon drum of oil from the deck to a waist-high rack.

Buck said, "I was with Max one time when he was driving to New Iberia. It was night, and the car behind us had its bright lights on. Max didn't say anything, but I could see it bothered him. He would slow down to encourage the other driver to pass us, but he wouldn't do it. He just stayed there, right on our ass, bright lights and all. Finally when we came to a little town—New Iberia, I think—Max pulled up to a red light and put the car in park. He very deliberately got out and walked to the rear of the car and opened his trunk. He rummaged around in a toolbox and came up with a small ball-peen hammer. He turned to the car behind us and carefully put a small hole in each headlight. Then he stood there with his little hammer and looked at the driver's compartment of that car. The driver put his car in reverse and slowly backed down the dimly lit street. Max got back in the car, and we resumed our trip. When I finally asked him about it, he said, "I'm just glad it wasn't a little old lady that I could have scared to death." There were a lot of things that could have happened at that intersection, but the only one he was worried about was the possibility of hurting an innocent. If the options are pissing me off or pissing Max Davis off, though, I would be the safer choice.

"Anyway," he said, "What's your next story?"

Mike told him it was one about a highway patrolman that came looking for him in a bar in Grand Isle. Buck said he didn't remember that one and asked for some particulars. Mike told him what he knew.

"Well," he said, "if it's the time I'm thinking about, it wasn't in Grand Isle; it was in Venice. And it wasn't a highway patrolman; it was a constable. Plaquemines Parish has always been sort of a vipers' nest, and if you're going to be drilling out of Venice, it's a real good idea to do whatever it takes to be in good with the local officials. I was and am, but the officer in question had been the Calcasieu Parish sheriff — the very same one that got run off over the Lilac Bloom incident. I don't think there was any question what he had against me. How he ended up in Plaquemines I don't know. There aren't any cities or even towns in that parish, but the two things they have plenty of are mosquitoes and lawmen. I didn't even know he was there. I would have thought that if he were going to try to get even with me, he would have taken me into custody and done whatever he intended to while he had control. At the time I was in tight with the family that ran the parish, and maybe he felt he couldn't get away with it. Anyway, I never saw him come in the bar, and when the blue was gone, he was gone. He did get some penitentiary time out of it, and I've always kind of semi-expected him to come back around; but as far as I know, he hasn't. We didn't tear the building down, but one or both of us did go through the front wall. The parking lot was littered with boards and bits of siding. There was a highway patrolman up around Jefferson Davis or Vermilion when we were working out of Cameron that fit the description of the one you were talking about. It sounded like he was a sadist that had a hard-on for oilfield workers, but I don't remember ever meeting up with him."

Mike told Buck that the last two stories he had were the one about the two guys in Jackson Park and another one in Jeanerette that he wasn't really sure was a story about Buck.

Buck said, "I want to do some fill-in before we get to the Jackson Park story, but we might as well get the Jeanerette one off the books right now. That was me, but it wasn't the old me. That one happened just a few years ago, well after I thought the blue was gone for good. I was driving through Jeanerette on my off days, and I was hungry for some boudin. I was looking for a little market where we used to get it and found out that the guy who made it then was now working in the grocery store. I was on my way to the butcher section in the rear of the grocery when I saw the man in question. When I saw him, I got the damnedest feeling, like my stomach suddenly got heavier. The woman and the kids with him had that furtive, something-bad-could-happen-at-any-moment look. They were all dirty and underclothed. The woman had an aged look that comes with missing teeth, and both the kids' upper lips were coated with snot. The little girl was pretty, but there was something wrong with one side of her face. I looked at him, and I'm pretty sure that whatever he read in my face is what triggered the attack.

"There are a lot of things I don't understand about the blueness. Hell, there isn't anything about it I do understand, but one thing that really gets me is how it always seems to be ahead of things. That guy turned out to be one of the baddest men in southern Louisiana. He was a Neandertal for sure. He had done time, but he would have been put away for good if people hadn't been afraid to testify against him. Two good things came out of that incident. The first one was that when that guy came back from Angola, he was a model husband and father and everybody's friend. Apparently the session between him and the blue had brought him to Jesus. The second thing is that I met Laney Olson, the constable who made the call and the only law in Iberia Parish with enough balls to show up when they heard who the call was about. When I came to, I was looking at her, and she was pointing her forty-five at the middle of my chest. Her blue eyes were as big as saucers, and she was breathing so hard she was gasping. I reckon that I was as close to being killed at that moment as I ever have been. I slowly raised my hands. She was trying to tell me to lie facedown on the floor, but she couldn't get it out. I had an idea of what the store looked like behind me, but I couldn't afford to look. I knelt down, then slowly dropped to my chest and spread my arms out. Gradually she settled down. She put her knee in the middle of my back—the way they're taught—but between the gun and the handcuffs and her shaking, she couldn't get the cuffs on me. I took them away from her and put them on myself—no small trick—behind my back. She told somebody to call an ambulance. She took me out and put me in the backseat of the car and then went back in the store. She was in there a long time. The ambulance came and went. When she finally got in the car, she said, 'Mr. Burnet, it looks like you've done the parish of Iberia a favor. That man you dismantled in there has been the scourge of the parish for a number of years. I can't let you go just yet because of the damage to the store, but there's no way I can make you stay in our little jail overnight. I've tried to book you a room, but there's no room at the inn.' I ended up spending three nights at her house while she got things 'worked out.' She was from Minnesota but had fallen in love with southern Louisiana on a trip one spring break. She had chosen Jeanerette because of the beauty of the Spanish moss–covered oaks and the antebellum homes. She said she was so struck with it that things like a high poverty rate and backwardness didn't seem to be a problem. She had some kind of degree in law enforcement, and, largely because of the man who was now in full body traction in the hospital in New Orleans, nobody else wanted the job of constable. She had had the job for three years, and she spent the three years living in dread of having to confront him. She said whenever she had come across him, the way he looked at her gave her the creeps.

"She was a great cook and, when you got her out of the uniform, a really good-looking woman. If I had been twenty years younger and not a long way down a whole different road, she's the girl I should have married. I say 'should have' because I'm not at all certain that I would have had the sense to do it. My tastes in and choices of women have always been outside anyone's understanding, especially mine. Nowadays she's a parish judge in Iberia Parish. I enjoy Laney and am fond of her, and I go by and see her once in a while, but I guess she's just not mean enough or something. The New Orleans story might shed some light on that, but I think I've got to tell you how I came to be in New Orleans before we get to it.

"That barge rig where the fight with the Neandertal took place was the genesis of the B & B Drilling Company. It took us four days to make the rig livable, but when it was done, I was running my first waterborne rig. We never did get rid of the smell in the living quarters. No smell is as repulsive as that of filthy human beings. No amount of scrubbing and paint will erase it. When I spent the night on that rig, I had to take my meals and sleep outside. Even the mosquitoes couldn't force me back indoors. We drilled in the bayous and inland lakes for a year or two, mostly on a footage and turnkey."

Mike told Buck that he could imagine what a turnkey job was, but did "footage" mean they got paid for the depth they drilled?

He told him that's exactly what it was. "Footage and turnkey put the onus on the drilling contractor for drilling the well fast and completing it. It's a far riskier job for the contractor and more dangerous for its hands. In footage and turnkey drilling, there is intense pressure from the contractor's office to do things the fastest possible way, and the fastest possible way is seldom the safest and the best. As you know, your company pays Olympia a day rate, which Olympia gets paid no matter what is going on at the rig. You can imagine how much more comfortable that is for us. Lots of contractors have run into well trouble drilling footage and turnkey and lost their asses. Some contractors prefer to drill footage because, if it works out right, you make more money. But it takes a real gambler to do it. My partner Jim Blanchard was a gambler, but even he was breathing easier when times got better and things loosened up. For me drilling on day rate is a much easier thing. This way I don't have to worry about what tricks the formations might play on us. It would probably be more accurate to say that I still worry about them, but I don't worry they might lose me my living. (You're the one has to worry about that.) I think that it's better for the oil company in the final analysis, too. I think we, the contractors, do a much better and more thorough job this way.

"I was never in the habit of thinking about the future; I was much more a day-to-day man. But if you had told me that one day we would be drilling in three hundred feet of water, I'd have thought you crazy. There were people who were thinking that way, though, and they were the Jim Blanchards and Bobby Lynds of the world — the gamblers, or, a better word, the entrepreneurs. When people like me encounter obstacles, we overcome them, and we are very good at that. But we don't purposely look for problems. The problems have to be flung in front of us by the visionaries. The further we got offshore, though, the more we needed a higher level of problem solver, and that's where the engineers came in. Not all engineers have degrees, and most of the ones we got at first didn't. But when you get to using drill ships and drilling in six hundred to a thousand feet of water, just knowing how to turn a wrench or strike an arc isn't going to get you there. I'm sure you've heard the phrase, 'Engineers and O-rings fucked up the oilfield.' A lot of engineers seem pretty useless, but we couldn't have got here without the ones that weren't. There're drill ships and semi submersibles out there right now because of engineers, and I'm proud for them; but I'll stay in here where I can be attached to the earth.

"Blanchard was saying way back then that offshore was the way to go, and we bought a cobbled-together fully submersible rig that would drill in thirty feet of water. Our thinking was that we could pick up jobs near offshore and still drill in the bays and waterways if we needed to.

"While B & B just had one rig, I was one of the two toolpushers, and I did company operations on my days off. When we got the second rig, I became the drilling superintendent and began to spend more time at our office in Houma. It wasn't much, but it was downtown, and there were people around to talk to and have coffee with. Despite having lived among them all that time, I didn't start to meet and get to know the people of south Louisiana until I moved to Houma. They had a culture that was probably worth fighting for, but they were so poor they welcomed the oil-related companies and the inevitable changes.

Like any boomtown Houma had plenty of bars and clubs, and if I was out at night, that's where I was; but the Cajun people who had lived around Houma all their lives didn't hang out there. Even some of the Cajuns called themselves 'coonasses,' but the term sort of turned into a derogatory one used by the oilfield workers being drawn in from Mississippi and Alabama, so I avoided using it. The Cajuns weren't prudes by any means, but they had their own clubs, their own music, and they would just as soon keep their women to themselves. I loved their food, and I loved their music, and I would occasionally be invited to a dance. I could dance with the women, but talking to them was not encouraged. The reaction was really not different than what I had run into in other places, but the Cajun women tended to be women you would really like to talk to—somehow freer and sexier and more fun loving than the women I had seen in Texas and other parts of Louisiana. I don't know what it is about them that's so damn sexy—the way they move or look at you maybe. But the only women available to me in south Louisiana were prostitutes, and of all the ones I knew, none was Cajun.

"One time I was in Grand Isle and needing to get back to Houma. I don't remember why I didn't have a car, but I didn't. There was a guy with one of the service companies whose wife had driven down from Houma to pick him up. He offered me a ride. The guy had a German name, but all I can remember is it started with a *K*. He had one of those little fastback type cars with two bucket seats up front and a little seat in the rear. I filled up the rear of the car and was almost right on top of them while we rode. His family had lived in Houma for three generations but still hadn't been assimilated into the local culture. She was a member of a well-to-do Cajun family, and they talked like the mix was a big deal. They hadn't been married long, and he had been gone for a couple of weeks or so. The guy was sales conscious, and he was talking to me, but the wife was not interested in me or my business. I was trying to listen to the husband, but she was wearing short shorts, and there wasn't even the wisp of a hair anywhere on her legs. It became pretty evident that she was there to seduce her husband. He kept rattling on like he didn't notice, but she did a hell of a job on me. I didn't even go home when we got to Houma, just had them let me out at the chippies' place. I don't think I've ever been more worked up in my life.

"I know you've heard of Justin Wilson and how he isn't really a Cajun. He learned to talk that way from the sheriff he worked for. I don't know if that's true or not, but he sure sounds like a Cajun. In those days there were a lot of guys around who talked 'flat, lak' dat.' My favorite was a man I did a lot of work for out in Dog Lake. His name was Daniel Aucoin, Aucoin being a common French name around there. The first time he signed a ticket for me, I read his name and said, 'Mr. Dan, your last name is not Aucoin; it's O'Quinn,' because that was the way it was spelled. Apparently his family had been there long enough to be assimilated because what was spelled *O'Quinn* was pronounced 'Aucoin,' and he made certain I understood it. He spoke just like Justin Wilson, and he loved to tell stories. Just about any story he told was amusing and interesting because of the patois and the way he looked at things. There is no way I can accurately recreate it for you, so I won't try, but he told me one that has left me with an image that never fails to make me smile, and I'll just tell you the facts of that one. He said he had been out at the barge for several days one time, waiting on something to happen and getting bored. He was standing at the rail, looking out at the water in the bayou, thinking how good it would feel to take a swim, so he went down to the keyway, peeled off his clothes, and jumped into the water. He swam around a little bit and was floating by the intake of one of the centrifugal pumps used for drill water when he felt the tug of the suction. He let himself be pulled over to the side of the barge and was holding his penis up to the hole in the side of the hull where the water was going. He was waving it back and forth, thinking how good it felt, when all of a sudden the derrickman cranked up the speed of the pump. All of his genitals went into the hole, and he was sucked to the side of the barge. He yelled, and eventually the derrickman heard him and shut down the pump. The image I'm left with is Mr. Dan 'reelin' his dick back out of that hole and being so relieved when he saw that it still had a head attached to it.

"My partner, Jim Blanchard, lived in Houma, but he spent most of his time in New Orleans making 'sales calls.' He had a nice house and a nice little family, and they would have me over to eat from time to time, but we never made a real connection outside the business. I've never been married, but I've always thought that if I were married, I wouldn't be chasing tail on the side. Don't get me wrong. I've chased it all my life, and I love it, the chasing and the getting. And that's probably one of the reasons I didn't get married. If I'm hot for a woman, I fuck her until I cool down. With one exception, that has always happened. To marry one would require more than that I be hot for her. I would have to want to be around her all the time, not just for sex. I guess I would just have to respect her, and, if I respected her, I wouldn't put her through the humiliation of knowing that I was fucking someone else. Jim Blanchard was from a segment of society that I'd had no previous contact with, but with which I would become all too familiar in the next few years. He made much of being from a good family in Alabama, but my feeling is that they were just a family that wanted to be known as 'good family.' The only real calling card he had was that he had played football at Mississippi State. I accepted that he had probably played college football, but I never went to the trouble of finding how much and how well. He had stories involving semi famous names, which he liked to recount whenever he had an audience, usually in bars. One was about being drafted by a pro team—I think it was Philadelphia. He said he had been in training camp and had said something pointed about 'niggers' at his table. Two of the 'niggers' took his point and the next day on the playing field messed up his knee so badly that he could never play again. The story played well in the bars around New Orleans at the time. When I heard it, I thought that instead of being bitter, he should be grateful he could still walk. His wife was bitter, too, but it didn't seem it had to do with his running around on her. It was more that she wasn't living in the place and driving the car that suited her.

When I was at her house, she was constantly on about the 'rednecks and coonasses' in the neighborhood. She was pretty in a brittle way, and she was always made up and well dressed, but her house wasn't clean, and her kids were whiny and unruly.

"We were running three rigs when things caught up with Jim. He lost everything, and the only reason I wasn't sucked into it was because he had never put my name on anything, and I had never signed a contract. A New Orleans company got the rigs through the banks, and they never missed a day's running. The new company, the Olympia Drilling Company, had me up to their offices and out to lunch. They told me that they had heard a lot of good things about me, and part of the reason they wanted B & B's rigs is they wanted me to be their drilling superintendent. They had run off their own two months before because he was making more off their rigs than the company was. I have to tell you I was pretty flattered by the whole thing. I had already eaten in the fanciest place I had ever been. I was somewhere around thirty years old."

CHAPTER V

New Orleans

"All things taken into account, New Orleans isn't that big a city. But size is relative, and to a young Buck Burnet, it was a *really* big city. It was a really big city with a lot of interesting stuff going on. I was kind of like a kid in a department store for the first time. There were so many interesting places and so many interesting characters. I was kind of a minor celebrity myself for a while—a big, wide-eyed white boy with money to spend. I fell for most of the scams at least once, and there were a lot of scams around. Gradually there came to be vendors who would take me out and pay for everything, hoping to get business from me. Some of them were good influences, and some were not; but each one was a sort of guide, and their presence reduced to some extent my chances of getting in real trouble. New Orleans is a place where you can end up doing something that will stick with you for life. I remember some uncomfortable moments, but I never did anything that left a permanent stain.

"The French Quarter was personified for me once by a woman outside one of the louder strip joints. She was up on a little stage with a barker who was extolling the virtues of what went on inside. He called her something that sounded like "Seat-seat" and kept directing attention to her, though she had no lines. She would pose and wave and, from time to time, shake. She did it all with high style, and I could see in her eyes that she was reliving former times. Her smile could have been an effect of the heavy makeup she wore. Her costume was missing spangles and tassels and was unequal to the task of holding up huge breasts that wanted to be somewhere around her little potbelly. Her most heartbreaking aspects, though, were the skinny little legs that no longer filled up the leg holes in her costume. "Seat-seat" put a form to the illusion of New Orleans for me, and, while I don't judge it or its inhabitants, I don't enjoy it anymore, either."

Mike said, "But I thought you lived in the Quarter now."

He seemed a little bit embarrassed when he said, "True enough. I live in the Quarter for various reasons, but I don't engage in the Bourbon Street activities."

When Mike started to open his mouth again, Buck held up his hand. "The place where I live is a perfect place for me, but I assure you that no tourist knows it's there. If you stick around long enough, I may take you down there and show you around. But believe me when I tell you that my living in the Quarter has nothing to do with my disapproval of it.

"Most of the people I worked with lived in the suburbs, and that's actually where I lived at the time, too, in a nice apartment in Metairie. The clubs and restaurants out there still have a New Orleans feel, but they don't have the touristy, frenetic hubbub of the clubs in the Quarter. Our offices were at 1501 Canal Street, a little bit northwest of Rampart. I had an office that everyone made a lot about at first but which I came to realize was the one no one else wanted. I'm sure that was to be expected. I was totally out of my element, and it showed. You can never know what life is like for other people, but while I looked and functioned like an adult, I'd only had fifteen or so years of socialization. I'm pretty sure that accounts for a lot of the opinions I held and the way I acted at the time. I thought most of the people were unfriendly and snobbish, and that may have been true, but they could just as well have been reacting to my behavior, which I'm sure was boorish and abrasive. When I first showed up, I was wearing cowboy boots and blue jeans, and everyone else was dressed up like they had somewhere to go. A lot of people smoked, but I dipped snuff, and the can I carried around to spit into was an object of general disgust. Learning that, I made sure to have it prominent at every meeting.

"The president was an accountant who had been a corporate vice president of the pipeline company that had bought Olympia first and then B & B. He was a really smart man, and he understood a lot of things about business that sounded like a foreign language to me. I'm pretty sure he would have let me go early on had he known more about the actual work of drilling, but I think he consoled himself with the knowledge that I was incapable of lying and wasn't clever enough to steal.

"Only the boss above me, the vice president of operations, a big guy name Wash Stevens, had actually done any drilling. Stevens understood me far better than I gave him credit for, and I'm sure he was a big part of the reason that I stayed in the office as long as I did. He never gave me a direct order, but he would come into my office and tell me little stories that I usually didn't get and didn't pay attention to. One time, when I was being especially recalcitrant, he gave me what I've come to think of as the 'cornfield speech.' 'You're the driver of the car,' he said. 'If the owner of the car tells you to drive the car into a cornfield, it's your responsibility to tell him that driving the car into the cornfield is bad for the car. If he tells you to drive the car into the cornfield anyway, drive the damn car into the cornfield.'

"I was so arrogant and unaware that I'm sure I shortened Stevens's life. When business got really bad and we were laying off hands, I resisted every single layoff, knowing that the hands were what made the company and that we would never get these particular ones back. Stevens was trapped between me and the rest of management. He understood my position, but he also understood the reality of the situation. In an attempt to clear my vision by showing me he knew what I was talking about, he told me that after the most recent layoff, he had felt so bad that he'd had to stop by the side of the freeway on the way home and throw up. I know he was having gum trouble from stress. I treated Wash Stevens like another adversary, and a simple-minded one at that. It turned out he was neither.

Mike asked Buck if he thought all this was necessary to telling the story.

He told Mike that, in his opinion, this was the story, and if Mike was looking for a different story, he needed to look for a different storyteller. He let that soak in for a little while and then resumed.

"I know the story you're looking for is the one about the girl and the guy whose dick I pulled off, but for me the story of Buck Burnet in New Orleans is the story of a naïf in the big city. It's also the story of a man who has always made his living with knowledge and ability thrust among people who make a lot better living based on personality and social position. See, I can't even reconcile the difference today. It still makes my jaw hurt to think of an office full of people who think going to meetings and writing inconsequential letters is somehow adding value to the company. We had seven vice presidents. Wash Stevens was the vice president of operations and I know he worked hard. We had a vice president of finance who, by the time you had somebody to look after the daily usage of pencils and carbon paper, had a staff of forty. We had a vice president of legal who oversaw a secretary and a lawyer who, in turn, oversaw another secretary and a paralegal. The young lawyer worked his butt off, but the VP spent most of his time in clubs cultivating relationships with other lawyers whom he would hire whenever there was real lawyering to be done. We had a vice president of sales and a vice president of marketing, and I still don't know the difference. We had a vice president of purchasing who, if you added up all the largesse he amassed from potential vendors, probably made more money than anybody. Finally, we had a vice president of personnel whose staff did what little personnel work there was to do and who made a virtue out of doing as little company-related stuff as possible. Oddly, out of the whole bunch, he was the only one I really liked.

Two or three times a day someone would feel constrained to come into my office and fill me in on who was trying to gut me or what someone said about someone else. It wasn't just the workers who engaged in it either; it went on at the highest levels. A lunch with coworkers could end up being a war council, and if you weren't with 'em, you were agin' 'em. Our lunches went on our expense accounts, and we didn't eat in cafeterias or diners. Our secretaries were all pretty women, and I'm sure not all of them could type and take dictation. At one of our lunches, the personnel VP told me that he only had one criterion for secretaries. He said, 'I tell them to take their ears in their hands and walk toward the nearest wall. If their elbows hit the wall before their tits do, I can't hire them.' He was kidding, of course, but there was a large element of truth in what he said. I had lunch once with the legal VP and the finance VP, ostensibly to talk about something that was crucial to running the company. The whole conversation was about pipe tobacco. The lawyer had a special mix that he got from someone in another country, and he was going to get the finance guy some of it. He said he'd had women come up to him in night clubs attracted to him because they loved the smell of his pipe. When we left the place, both of them seemed satisfied that we had completed some important business, and I was left sifting the conversation for anything of substance."

Mike told Buck that he had had a similar experience in the navy. Mike had been an enlisted man seated between a senior and a junior officer in a taxi in Kowloon. They spent the whole ride talking about marmalade. Buck said it was some kind of class-oriented butt sniffing they engaged in. He thought they learned it in fraternities partly to establish their own bona fides and partly to show how far above the rest of us they were.

"Anyway," Buck said, "I was in New Orleans for about five years, and in that time I changed from a physical, totally reactive person, to one who was able to think. I have always looked like what I am, a working man from a rural environment. There's not much you can do with the surface other than wear better clothes, but those assholes in the office forced me to think, and for that I'll be forever grateful."

Mike said, "Grateful enough so that you came to like them?"

"No," he said, "it's impossible to like them. That would be akin to liking toe jam or ear wax. You know they exist, and there doesn't seem to be any way to avoid them, but you can't like them. Since we're on the subject of hygiene, let's talk about the habits of the typical office worker. Out here most of us wear coveralls, but whatever we wear is made of cotton. During the course of the day, we get actual dirt and grease on ourselves and our clothes, and we sweat, so whatever bad stuff was in us winds up on our bodies and our clothing. This leads to a certain odor that, of course, varies from individual to individual. This doesn't cause a lot of consternation because we are generally in the open air. When our day's work is done, we enter the living quarters on the lower level, peel our soiled clothing off, throw it in a pile, and take a shower. When we come out of the shower, we pick up a set of clean, washed clothes and put them on before we go upstairs to eat. My point is that whenever we are in a closed space with other people, we are clean and fresh.

"Your typical office worker wears clothes that have to be dry-cleaned. Dry-cleaning is not the same as washing. I don't know what the actual process is, but clothes that have been dry-cleaned have their own smell, right out of the wrapper. It's more of a chemical than an organic smell, but my feeling is that the body smells that were in there haven't been eradicated; they've only been covered up. Office workers don't sweat or, at least, don't realize that they sweat, and don't get dirty, so they tend to be less religious about taking daily showers. Those lacking in the olfactory department may not be religious about weekly showers. The result is that when they get into a tense situation—a meeting, say—where somebody else might be looking for something they have actually accomplished, their bodies start pushing the built-in bad stuff into their chemically laden clothing. The ones whose noses worked tried to counter this effect with cologne, and the combination of all those odors could be downright revolting."

Mike told Buck that he didn't think the hygiene of office workers was germane to the project and could potentially offend someone who might be reading this in the future.

"Keep it in there," he said. "It needs to be in there if only for the sake of some of the office workers who aren't aware of the problem."

Mike reminded Buck that he said he wore better clothes at the end. Mike asked him how he approached the problem.

"I worked out at a gym every morning to sweat and took a shower before I dressed for work. I found a cleaner in Metairie that claimed to use a special 'all natural solvent' that left the clothes smelling better, but they still never smelled fresh. Avoiding tense situations helped a lot, and I did that by making sure that I always had my job done."

Mike asked Buck about the girl, and there was a subtle shift in his posture that Mike took to be from disappointment. If a rock can become even more still, then he did, too.

"The girl wasn't a girl; she was a full-grown woman. I've never met anyone even similar to her. She robbed me of my mind (as I've said, no great feat at the time). God help me, if she walked in this room right now, I'd probably become her slave all over again. They call something like that love, but it's not love. I was talking to a junkie in the Quarter one time, trying to get at what makes a person a junkie. He had just spent fifteen minutes telling me how rotten his life was, how he screwed over his family and every friend he had time after time, how he stole everything he could get his hands on and pimped out every woman who had ever felt anything for him. He said the junk was the only thing that mattered. I asked him, 'What about pussy?' He said, 'The pussy's in the needle.'"

Mike asked Buck what her name was.

"I don't know what her name was. Her professional name was Madeleine Dupree, but I've heard some people call her

'Patty' and others call her 'Lou Ann.' My guess is they didn't know her real name, either."

Mike asked him how he met her, but Buck was so far inside himself he couldn't hear him. Mike ended the session at that point. It was several weeks before he could even catch Buck's eye, much less talk to him. When they finally did talk, Buck started out by saying, "I guess I haven't thought about any of that since I came back offshore. Being naïve is one thing, but you don't like to think of yourself as stupid. Every time I go back over that mess, the only conclusion I can come to is that I was stupid. I met her by walking into a trap — a trap that even a schoolboy could have seen and walked around.

"There was a group of women that hung out around some of the nicer places in the Quarter. They were mostly the wives of oilfield executives, a few of them wives of the guys in Olympia. They were women with plenty of money and time on their hands. I'm sure some of them had kids, but they all acted like their husbands' extramarital dealings left them the time and motive for doing whatever they pleased. They had generally gone home by seven thirty or eight, but they were a pretty constant presence from happy hour until then. I first ran into representatives of 'the group' in the ground level bar at the Royal Sonesta. Since I came into work early, I was usually out and looking for a drink and some music before the offices emptied. These women were good-looking and funny, and I enjoyed sitting and listening to them. They made a lot out of my size and my youth, and there was some good-natured squeezing going on. There must have been thirty or so in the group, but you'd see them here and there in bunches of four or more. Over time I peeled a few of them out of the pack, one at a time, and spent a pleasant early evening. Gradually, though, I realized that whatever had gone on behind closed doors was being passed among the rest of them, liberally and with elaboration. It began to seem like some kind of lottery when one or another of them would sidle up to me and her mates would have somewhere else to be. After a while it got to feeling like some kind of seedy little club, and instead of being one of the group, I was some kind of an object of the group's amusement."

Mike asked Buck if their having been married gave him any pause. He thought about it for a little while and said, "It probably would nowadays, but I don't believe it meant anything to me then. It seemed to me they should have been the ones to worry about their husbands.

"I spent some time with the alpha female of the group and the experience was something short of spectacular. I might have been guilty later of mentioning what I took to be her physical shortcomings to another woman in the group. Either that happened and she found out about it or she was so disappointed in our coming together that she devised a sordid little plan to exact retribution. I was invited for a weekend at someone's 'country place.' The country place turned out to be one of those antebellum homes on a bayou the other side of Thibodaux. You know the kind: big live oaks with Spanish moss, broad porches, and white ship-lath siding. From the front you could have been in the nineteenth century. Around back they had all the modern stuff that the nouveau riche can't do without—the main item being a really beautiful pool. There were men and women at dinner Friday evening. All the women I knew or at least recognized, but I didn't know any of the men, and they weren't the kind of people I would want to get to know. Madeleine was there, and we were introduced, but I got drunk before I could figure out something to say to her and went to bed. When I got up the next morning, there was no one around. I found something to eat in the kitchen. Nobody showed up while I was there, so I went back upstairs and put on my bathing trunks— the pool really had looked nice. When I went back down, there was only one person in the pool: Madeleine. She was floating around on a little plastic raft. She wore dark glasses and a brief, but not obscenely brief, bikini. The sight of her created a current in me as if you had hooked one pole of a truck battery to my toes and the other to the top of my head. If I had gotten into the water at that moment, I'm pretty sure I would have been electrocuted."

Buck got caught up in memory, and to bring him around Mike asked him what she looked like.

"It's hard to say what she looked like. She was medium sized to smallish. She had short brown hair and dark eyes. Her skin wanted to be brown and there were no tan lines. Her skin was as smooth as this desk right here, with no spots or bumps. Her fingers were straight and a little longer than you would have expected, and they never jumped or flitted. Her ears were like delicate ceramic things made by a master. When she smiled, her upper lip hung just a little on one eyetooth, so the smile sort of evolved. She was very pretty, but you wouldn't have thought her a movie star. When I had seen her at the function the night before, I thought her slender, even skinny. She wasn't skinny. She wasn't fat, either. She was…abundant. She had no body hair to speak of. She told me once that she had to shave a spot on one leg from time to time. Everything she had was perfectly formed, and even her shoulders and elbows promised sensual pleasure. I had the image of biting into her and having peach juice fill my mouth. I don't think either of us spoke. I stepped into the shallow end of the pool, and her raft floated over to me. I put my hand under her ass and sat her up on it as I lifted her. I held her there, away from my body, showing off but also examining her as you would a piece of pottery. I carried her out of the pool and, with my free hand, grabbed a towel off the lounge chair it was hanging on. I walked past the rose bushes at the edge of the pool deck and set her on her feet then spread the towel on the grass. Our clothes were off, and we were on the towel without hesitation.

"We fucked from Saturday morning to Monday morning. As the sun was coming up Monday morning, I made love to her, and my body malfunctioned. As soon as I got into a rhythm my body quivered and came to a stop. She rolled over on top of me and we were able to finish like that. I went to sleep and when I woke up, she was gone. I thought we were the only ones in the house for the whole weekend. I never saw anybody else. I don't think I had eaten anything since Saturday morning. I ate probably half of what I found in the fridge. I went back to my apartment and slept for more than twenty-four hours. Only then did I begin to wonder what had happened."

Mike said, "You know, I'm a friendly listener, but someone else could read into that that you raped her."

He said, "Some people could read rape into any coupling but I promise you, there was no more hesitation on her part than there was on mine. We were both at the mercy of outside agencies."

"You think you were drugged or something?"

"No," he said, "not by human beings—by something undetected but forceful. Have you ever seen a rapid chemical reaction?"

Mike told him, when he was in the tenth grade, Darrel Gardner and he were supposed to be putting up the equipment after an experiment in chemistry class. The teacher had dropped a tiny bit of sodium into a sink of water, and there was a lot of popping and fizzing until the reaction was complete. Darrel and Mike wondered if you could stop the reaction by putting a cap over the sodium, so they gave it a shot. They dropped a piece of sodium into water in the equipment room, and then Darrel placed a liter size beaker over the sodium. The beaker shattered immediately into small pieces that sprayed the room. Darrel was still holding the base of the beaker in his right hand. They were looking at each other, knowing they were lucky to be alive and whole.

"What happened after Madeleine and I looked at each other that morning was as inevitable as that beaker breaking. I didn't have the mentality to resist it. Short of one of our dying, once that meeting had happened, it had to run its course. It's the most intense thing I've ever been involved in. It was like having the blue operating on a different plane, with the exception that I was along for the ride. There wasn't a spot on her that wasn't smooth and soft and didn't taste good. Her scent, or maybe I should say scents, carried no trace of perfume or anything that wasn't woman. I appreciate smells the way some appreciate music, and she was a symphony of wonderful aromas. Let me put my nose at the base of her throat, and I would stand still as a blindfolded horse until she took it away. Her pubic hair was soft as corn silk. Her pussy was deep, and you could feel the entire length of it, like velvet, all the way to the bottom. Just being inside her ranks among the top feelings I've had."

"So, you fell in love with her," Mike said.

"I fell in what I thought was love with her," he said. "I've come to realize that love has aspects other than sexual compatibility. We didn't have time to fall in love. Over the course of the two days, I'll bet we didn't exchange more than twenty complete sentences. At the end of that time, I didn't know her name, her age, what she did, or where she was from; forget all the little things that lovers are supposed to know. The odd thing is I hadn't noticed the lack. I wound up back in New Orleans, looking for members of the group so I could get a line on her."

"Well, what did you find out?"

"Not very much, really. It took me a while to come to the conclusion that our meeting had been arranged."

"Wrath of the woman scorned?" Mike said.

"You can believe that!" he said. He said it with feeling, the way the Cajuns do. "You kin buh-lee dat!"

"I went to some of the other women in the group and they wouldn't help me, but after a time I think they began to feel sorry for me. I must have been a pitiful sight trundling around the Quarter dirty and disheveled, asking people if they knew anything of this woman whom I couldn't even describe very well. Finally, one of the women whom I hadn't even been with and who knew what had happened laid it out for me.

"Madeleine was the mistress of Marco Carlotti, the head of the New Orleans mob. Somehow she had been made to believe that the group leader's husband could get her away from Carlotti if she would do her this favor. I guess she figured I would fall for Madeleine, an unattainable woman, and that would serve me right. Evidently there were people other than the two of us around the house that weekend, though I would have told you the place was deserted. They couldn't believe the intensity of our attraction or how concentrated we were on what we were doing. They began to have misgivings about what Carlotti would think about the whole thing and what he might do to those he thought responsible. They had bundled her up and taken her back to New Orleans that Monday morning, acting like she had spent two days at a tea party. I've always wondered how that went over. My new friend told me that she and the others who were in on what they thought was going to be a prank had feared for my safety for a while, but that apparently the mob was not going to come after me after all. I don't know how she expected me to react when she told me all this, but I don't think she had any idea how deeply affected I had been by the whole thing. Without going into just how crazy I was, I can tell you that the leader moved home to live with her mother until her husband could get a transfer, and the 'group' ceased to exist. I didn't have any regard for Marco Carlotti at that point, or anyone else for that matter. In my mind Madeleine was the damsel in the tower, waiting for me to rescue her. I raged around New Orleans, very much the bull in a china shop, disturbing places of business and making life difficult for both petty criminals and cops. I finally made enough of a fuss that something had to be done. I was told where she lived, and I went to an apartment in one of the courtyards off Royal. There was a guard at her door who didn't keep me from knocking. I should have had some misgivings at that point. She answered the door, looking taller, a little older, and much slimmer than I remembered. It took her quite a while to convince me she didn't have any feelings for me and never wanted to see me again. I wanted to believe that she was performing for an audience, that she didn't really mean what she was saying, but her eyes offered even less hope than her words. I don't remember all the things she said, but it was clear she thought me a brute: 'a beast devoid of sensibility.' She didn't deny the initial physical attraction, but she didn't allude to it, and she made it clear it would never happen again."

Mike asked Buck if he thought she had been in love with him that weekend. He looked surprised by the question and thought about it for a while.

"Love was never part of the equation. What we had wasn't love on either side. What we had that weekend was lust in its rawest form. We used each other, and the crimes cancelled out. I was the only one so emotionally immature as to try to make something else out of it. She looked at the situation and reckoned it a dead-end road. I was King Kong. If you are asking me if she enjoyed that weekend, I'll tell you I think it would have been impossible for me to lose myself to the degree I did if she hadn't. I'll tell you something else, too. Though that weekend changed the course of my life and caused me a lot of heartache, I don't regret a single second of it. It was the highlight of my life. It was pleasure on an indescribable level. I am forever grateful to her and the god that created her for the experience. Did she love me? No. Did I love her? No. Do I love her now? In a strange way.

"I was distraught. I made myself persona non grata in most of the bars in the Quarter. Eventually I cooked up this story that sort of fit the conditions and had things the way I wanted them to be. Marco Carlotti was this old man who was physically incapable of fulfilling her sexual needs and psychologically incapable of comprehending it. I decided that if I could talk to him I could make him see the error of his ways. Talking to Marco Carlotti turned out to be a very difficult thing to do, though I suspect if he wanted to talk to you, it would be disturbingly easy. To this day I don't even know that she was his mistress or if he was involved in any way. Eventually I picked up a tail—the two guys that followed me into Jackson Square. The story has them assassins hired by the mob, and they might have been. They also might have been robbers or just two guys who thought I was going to try to sleep in their place that night. What I know about what happened is that they followed me into a brushy part of the square, and the blue came over me. Suddenly, the one guy is in a bush whimpering, and the other one is gone."

Mike asked him if there had been any blood. He said there was no blood, anywhere. Mike told him that when he was a newsman in Dallas, Captain Fritz told him about a case he had where a guy had gone into the bus station rest room in Dallas and sat down to take a shit. He noticed a hole in the side panel of the booth about head high while he was sitting down. All of a sudden, a big, old, hard dick came through that hole. Apparently the person who normally occupied that booth would have done something else with it, but this particular person pulled out his penknife and cut it loose from whatever it was attached to. Captain Fritz surmised all this from the hole in the panel and the three spiral rings of blood circling the adjoining booth. Mike's point being that, with the arteries involved in that particular organ, detaching it would be certain to entail a lot of blood. Buck said he had thought about that and so had the police during their investigation.

Buck said, "I don't know if it is even possible to pull one off; I mean, tendons and such as that are awfully strong. The police theorized that the only scenario that fit the descriptions was if the assailant had had some kind of tool like cable cutters or those nippers that fence builders use. Even then they would have had to be a little dull, so they could mash everything together and seal it all shut. They looked around for a tool like that but couldn't find anything. They figured the only way to get rid of it was in the river, but that would take throwing it over Decatur Street and the levee, a distance of more than a hundred yards."

"Yeah," Mike said. "And what would 'the assailant' have been doing with a tool like that in the first place?"

Buck said, "Exactly."

Buck looked at Mike like he was waiting for another question, but Mike couldn't make himself ask it.

Finally Buck said, "Anyway, once that story got around town, I couldn't find a fight in New Orleans. Not wanting to lose one's apparatus is a terrific disincentive. Bouncers, cowboys, thugs, and drunks—all of them would act like I wasn't there.

"Feeling like something had been accomplished, I went back to Madeleine's place, but she was gone. The guy who took care of the building let me in to show me how bare of anything it was. I never found out who she was, where she came from, or where she went. I only know about the part of her that stays with me."

Mike said, "Buck, I'd like to talk about the blue, about what you think it is. Do you have any idea about that? Like, is it something in your brain?"

"Of course I have an idea of what it is; but if it were something in my brain, that would make me psychotic, and I'm not ready to accept that. Besides, it doesn't fit the facts, the way I see them. When it has hit me, I have usually been unaware of the presence of danger, and there has always been a danger there. The reasons for the blue's appearances have always been really bad people whose subsequent absence from society made it better. They have been dispatched quickly and cleanly and with what can only be termed superhuman strength and speed. I have fought outside the blue, and I can assure you that none of that fits my normal MO."

He stopped talking, and Mike waited for what seemed like a long time. Finally Mike said, "What is it?"

He said, "What I'm going to tell you is what I believe, but I've only told this to one other person, and even now it's kind of sticking in my throat. I believe it's an angel—like Michael or Gabriel, you know? I don't think I become an angel. I think he takes over my body when he needs it for his own purposes. That explains why I am not able to call him up on demand. If he does it with me, he must do it with other people, and must have down through human history. That would explain things like Samson and Hercules."

"Then," Mike said, "you must believe in God."

"Believe in God? Mike, belief implies an act of will. God is because this is. God *is* this." And with that he looked around the room and then gestured to take in the world and the cosmos. "That doesn't come from any words ever said; that comes straight out of my bones. Everybody knows God exists. Some don't believe it."

Mike said, "There are some atheists who would disagree."

"Atheists just say that shit to try to draw God out. If you honestly didn't think there was a God, why would you bother saying it?"

That gave Mike food for thought, but it didn't leave him any place to go from there, so he changed the subject.

"How did you feel when it was all over? You said you made yourself persona non grata before, did you have a similar meltdown?"

"I melted down in a way, but I didn't take it out on the people around me. It took the wind out of my sails, and for the first time in my life, I lost confidence in my ability to take things on. I began to question what I was doing at work, and that destabilized the whole operation. What had been a smooth-running machine started having hitches, and there were more and more meetings at work trying to decide what to do about it. I didn't have the strength of will to tell them what to do or to do it myself. I started drinking too much and generally just wallowing in it. That's when it was decided that I would go back out into the field as a toolpusher. Believe it or not, it was meant by the company to be a kindness, and it was; but at that point, I didn't figure to be any more successful as a toolpusher than I was as a superintendent."

CHAPTER VI

The Mouse's Ear

"One night before I had been assigned the Hector, I found myself in a little place in the Quarter. I'd been by it a hundred times and never noticed it. This night someone had opened the door just as I was walking by, and I went in. It was a different kind of place, but I didn't notice that at first. The differences just kind of came to me one at a time. For one thing it was dark, not secretive dark, just nothing shining in your eyes. The air didn't smell like smoke or liquor; it smelled more like the rooms in a five-star hotel. There were people around, but the conversations were quiet. Nobody seemed looking to be noticed. The furnishings were of good quality and plush: tables in the middle of the room, piano at the back, bar along one wall, and booths on the others. I had been seated at one of the tables for some time, and nobody had asked me what I wanted to drink, but I didn't really notice the lack. I was just soaking in the surroundings and beginning to enjoy the feeling of being totally comfortable.

"Somebody sounded a jarring note by laughing too loud. I looked toward the back end of the bar, and there was a man bent over, laughing so hard that he had to lean against the bar to stay up. There was a woman standing over him with an expression that switched from vexed to worried and back. The man finally fell down and lay on his back gasping for air. I decided he was having some kind of attack and went over to see if I could help out. The woman was bent over him, and when she looked up, she was so good-looking that I almost lost track of why I was there. The man was out of breath, and I picked him up and hung him over the bar and started slapping him on the back. The flash of face I saw looked familiar, but I didn't recognize him until the lady called him 'Tom.' 'Tom Coleman?' I said. Sure enough, it was the guy who had been the bartender at the Lilac Bloom. I sat him down in a chair at a nearby table, and he said, 'Please, let me laugh. I haven't felt this good in a long time,' and continued laughing, though not as loud as before. The lady was standing beside me, and I asked her what had happened."

"'Well,' she said, 'I'm not sure. I asked him to throw you out, and when he came around the bar and saw your face, he collapsed.'

"I looked at Tom and imagined the scene he had taken in when the blue whipped all those guys outside the Lilac Bloom and started to chuckle myself. Pretty soon I was enjoying full-throated laughter, and at some point, the lady joined in. I'll tell you, there is nothing for lifting the spirits like a good laugh. I spent the rest of that evening talking to Tom and, now and again, the lady. The place was a whorehouse that the lady was just starting out. She had been a call girl in Dallas and saved her money and put it all into this place. She called it The Mouse's Ear. Tom managed the public area, and she took care of the girls, of which there weren't very many, yet. She wanted it to be a place of ultimate discretion and taste, which meant she didn't want people like me in there. I had always liked Tom, though when I was at the Lilac Bloom, we'd had nothing to talk about. Come to think about it, I never talked much to anybody in those days. It turned out that he was a kind of monk, a bartender in a whorehouse who didn't drink or fuck the help. He wasn't a

Christian in the generally accepted sense, but he had based his spiritual life on that of Jesus's. 'Jesus hung out with publicans and sinners,' he says, 'so there must be something to it.'

"I told him, 'Yeah, but by all accounts Jesus drank wine, and I'm not so sure he didn't have something going on with that other Mary.'

"That could be,' he said, 'but he wasn't in danger of becoming addicted to either.'

"The notion of 'good family' in the South is a big deal. Tom grew up in a good family, which gave him access to the children of other good families. His parents had a home in the city and a farm, and Tom seems to have spent quite a bit of his growing up time on the farm, minus his parents. He says he was raised by the Negro caretakers and still feels like they were his real parents. He's never said his father was alcoholic, but that would fit with the rest of the story. His father was great friends with another Irishman, Walt Kelly of *Pogo* fame. He had a business but wasn't really a businessman. Tom got a degree in English at Auburn and was set to marry the girl he had gone with since high school. She was beautiful and accomplished in the way of Southern belles and was also from good family. That family was having some financial problems of their own, however, and it was decided the family would be better served if she married someone of means. Tom never did say if he was actually in love with her or just following a natural path, but her family's decision cut Tom loose from his two isms: Southern- and Catholic-. He started up a band and toured the South for a couple of years. That petered out, though, since Tom wasn't a businessman either and not really that good on the guitar. (If you meet him, don't tell him I said that.) He went to India and wandered from ashram to ashram. He spent time in Tibet, China, and Japan and, by the time he got back to the States, was well versed in several of the varieties of Hinduism and Buddhism and steeped in the *Tao Te Ching*. Somewhere on his way back from the American West, he developed his current belief system. He said he wanted to be a piano player in a whorehouse, but he couldn't play piano and a guitar player in a whorehouse didn't sound right, so he learned how to tend bar. He said he had watched me with great interest at the Lilac Bloom.

"I started hanging out at the Ear regularly. The owner, Catherine Moynihan, resisted until she noticed that, when the people she considered undesirable saw me there, they left quietly and quickly on their own. She still didn't think the way I dressed and acted were appropriate, however, so she undertook to teach me how to dress and act. She alone is responsible for these impeccable manners and state of sartorial splendor."

Mike said, "Is she why you talk like a professor of Victorian literature?"

He smiled to show that he knew he spoke like that and was pleased that he did. "No, that's all Tom. Over a short period of time, I developed an affinity for Tom. He has an encyclopedic knowledge and an easygoing serenity that just makes a person want to be around him. He says that he and I are like symbiotic bookends. He says people are drawn to us: him because he is calm and seems to offer some hope for being happy, and me because they feel protected. He says they are both illusions, but in a world of illusion, they are useful and a source of comfort to others. I asked Tom to help me out with becoming more educated. I'm not sure he thought it was possible, but he gave me an old Norton's anthology he had and answered my questions. I'd go through the anthology, and when I read something I liked, I would go to the library and get more of it. I started taking classes at various junior colleges and have racked up an embarrassing number of hours. I'm not a scholar. I don't go overboard trying to figure out things I don't understand. I read it if I get something out of it, either knowledge or enjoyment, and if I don't get it, I just pass over it. I don't really know why I do it."

Mike said, "Well, from where I stand, it looks like you are hoping that Madeleine shows up some day and realizes you are no longer an uncultured brute."

He smiled again. "Kind of pathetic, isn't it? Did I mention that *The Count of Monte Cristo* was one of my early favorites?"

Mike asked if Tom tutored him in religious matters, too.

"No, when I asked him for help, I figured it would be a kind of package deal, but he won't even speak to me about spiritual matters. He pretty much avoids the word *religion* and anyone and anything associated with it, by the way."

Mike asked him if he ever got anything going with Catherine Moynihan or if he was keeping himself pure for Madeleine.

"Miz Catherine and I think a lot of each other, and occasionally a bit of cohabitation will spontaneously occur, but generally her tastes run to younger, less bulky men. I have to confess that youth has an appeal for me too, and I like at least a hint of vulnerability in my potential mates. Mostly Catherine and I are just good friends."

This ended Buck's narration of his life and times. Mike didn't know if the result was what he had had in mind when he started. He thought he was looking for the "truth," but the truth is a slippery thing. What nagged at him most was Buck's willingness and ability to tell a story. Mike felt the versions were a little too graphic and inventive. Mike had wanted Buck to measure up to his ideas of heroism, and there were instances when that did not happen. Those instances may have made him more heroic, not less, but it took Mike a lot of years to realize it. At any rate, he'd kept faith with Buck by putting it down just as he said it. He put his notes away in 1978 and forgot about them. They lay unseen until now. The next decade was relatively uneventful, but two events from the period between then and the nineties are instructive. One took place on the rig, and the other was a visit to the Mouse's Ear.

The first incident was a result of Mike's penchant for lending a hand around the rig when the opportunity presented itself. If a person has never done hard, physical labor that had to be coordinated with that of others, then it may be difficult to imagine that labor's having beauty and joy and affording deep satisfaction. If he was a member of that segment of the population that considers manual labor beneath them, then Mike felt compassion for him, for a large part of what he could have been lay undiscovered, rendering his the unexamined life. Some of Mike's best days were spent on the floor and in the derrick. He loved the teamwork and the difficulty. Walking away one day after helping out on the floor, he was brought back to reality by the appearance of an old nemesis, a wireline operator he had worked for when he was going through school. The operator would no doubt have behaved differently had he known he was working for Mike, but he saw Mike coming off the rig floor in dirty coveralls and a hard hat and figured him for a roughneck. His name was Paul Moran, and, outside of his own mind, he was a pretty nondescript sort of person. He was a Cajun but too young to have a real accent and only a couple of years older than Mike. The last time Mike had seen him, Mike was working for him on a production platform. It had been Mike's last semester in the field before he went back to school for the graduation semester. Sandra and he were out of money, and if they didn't make it in this push, he was never going to get a degree. She had stayed with the two kids in Austin in the condemned house they rented from the university. Mike had taken a bus to Houma to try to make enough money to live on for the four months it would take to finish school. Mike was really looking to get a snubbing job, but the timing wasn't working out, so he had to take a wirelining job just to get a place to sleep and food to eat. He worked for Moran for about three weeks, and there were still no snubbing jobs available when he came back onshore. For two weeks he slept on a cot in the change room of the snubbing shop and lived on a lunch he got for $1.25 at a restaurant a two-mile walk from the shop. Once he got a snubbing job again, things eased up, and he was able to live and save the required funds. The snubbing operator he worked for most of that summer, a west Texan named Lynn Boyd, was as big and good-hearted as Paul Moran wasn't.

The three weeks with Paul probably would have gone better if Mike hadn't hurt his back the first day out. He picked up something he shouldn't have before he got conditioned, and it restricted his strength and range of motion for several days. He couldn't afford to have any days off, so instead of calling it a lost-time accident and going in, he worked through it. Moran was predisposed to consider college boys, and any educated persons for that matter, essentially worthless. Mike had run into that quite a bit before but had usually been able to work hard and well enough to change their minds about him. Moran got down on him in that first week, however, and there was no pleasing him after that. Mike had saved him from having a lost-time accident on his record, but in his mind that was no match for the extra work it had caused him. He baited Mike constantly and railed about the poor job he was doing. It made for an uncomfortable period of time for Mike, but he was able to sublimate his feelings to accomplishing the goal of getting through school. Apparently Mike's equanimity just added fuel to the fire, and on their last day out, when they were cleaned up and waiting for the boat that would take them onshore, Moran went off in a verbal explosion of all the things Mike was and wasn't, finally offering to whip his ass. When Mike just stood there looking at him, he said Mike was chickenshit on top of everything else, and it put the final seal on his opinion of Mike Brown. Even though Mike didn't react and didn't agree with his assessment, his words left a mark and would return to Mike in dark periods thereafter.

They came back to Mike now as he watched Moran recognize him and drop the toolbox he was carrying, the better to confront him. "Well, well," he said, "if it isn't the chickenshit, big-time, gonna-take-over-the-company college boy. You haven't gotten a bit better looking, have you? I knew you wasn't that fucking smart. So the big man is a lowlife roughneck on a piece-of-shit rig in the Gulf." Mike looked down and saw that the logo on the coveralls he was wearing was that of Olympia, the drilling contractor. "Still a coward, too, I'll bet. Have you found the balls to fight me yet? C'mon motherfucker," he said, "c'mon and let's get this over with right now." Mike wondered how that much hate and bile can stay stored up in a person for so long. He looked up at the window in the quarters above and saw Buck watching. Mike looked back at Moran and saw a man who felt the forces of the universe arrayed against him. Most of the faces around were friendly to Mike and he could almost feel them willing him to crush this little maggot, either physically or by informing him that he ran this piece-of-shit rig and for him to get his ass off it. Naturally, Mike did neither, opting instead to walk by Moran without acknowledging him. He would never know what would have happened had he resisted Mike's passage.

Buck's first thought when he saw the confrontation taking place was to go down to the deck and intervene, but then he decided just to watch. He knew that Mike was capable of taking care of himself and that Mike was the only one who doubted it. He felt if the wireliner pushed him far enough, Mike would react and put an end to the feelings of inadequacy he harbored about his own bravery. A fight on the rig would definitely cause problems for Buck, and Mike had done the right thing, but Buck would gladly have taken the heat to see his friend's life made happier.

Typically for Mike the incident triggered a period of introspection and self-loathing. Buck came into his room while he was mentally running over all the scenarios of what could have or should have happened. Mike thought he knew what Buck was going to say, and when he said something else, it was his first intimation that Buck had been moving into the place in his mind previously reserved for older relatives. Instead of berating Mike for not taking up the gauntlet, Buck said, "You know, there were a hundred valid reasons for doing what you just did. Whatever the outcome, if you had fought that guy, it would have meant a lot of trouble for us, and maybe even big legal trouble for you. I know you'll look at that as an attempt on my part to make you feel better, but it's not. I'm here to thank you for keeping your cool." He was right. It didn't keep Mike from thinking of himself as a coward; but it did make him grateful for his wanting to help.

"You know," he said, "you have some kind of thing about fighting. Some sense that being good at it is noble and that somehow you aren't. I honestly think it's the reason you're out here and not teaching at some university (which you are capable of and would be really good at)." He put his hand in the air. "Don't get me wrong. I'm glad to have you. I couldn't do better for a partner and a friend. If it came to that, I may not even let you go. I'm just saying that you're way overqualified, and we must be subverting some kind of cosmic plan by your being out here. Being reluctant to fight doesn't make one ignoble. In fact, the truth may be the complete reverse. When I and your father and your uncles were growing up, fighting wasn't an option. It was the way things were. But things are changing. The world is becoming more civilized. The heroes now are people like Mahatma Gandhi and Martin Luther King. Fighting is the final resort of the mindless."

Able to see what Buck was trying to do, Mike still wondered if Buck believed his own words. He said, "Buck, your name is almost synonymous with fighting. Is there any way you would be where you are if you hadn't been able to do it, and well?"

"The answer to that has two or more parts. A lot of what has come to me is a result of the angel's doing. It has nothing to do with me, and I probably shouldn't be partaking in the rewards. The fighting I've done on my own has been pretty hit-or-miss if you ask me. I've never been hurt, and I suppose that's saying something, but it's probably due more to my physical makeup than any innate ability. You're plenty strong because that's something you have control over, but look at these bones." He wrapped a paw around Mike's left wrist, and with the fingertips touching his thumb, there was still plenty of space between his hand and Mike's arm. Mike put his hand around Buck's right wrist to pull it away, and his fingertips were an inch away from touching his thumb. "You're quick, but you're not fast, and if someone like me took a shot at that big head of yours, it would probably split like a melon. God made you what you are, and doing anything but working with it is insanity."

He wasn't going to change the way Mike felt because that feeling was out of reach of conscious thought, but, in a backhanded way, he was making him feel better. Mike said, sarcastically, "Thanks, Buck. That really makes me feel better." When Buck smiled, he managed to look a lot like Burt Lancaster.

"My old man was fond of saying there were two types of kids, but every time he said it, it was a different comparison. It was always blue-eyed and brown-eyed kids. The one I remember is the one about what would happen if you threw them into a flowing river. The brown-eyed kids would ride the current and enjoy the passing view. The blue-eyed kids would swim against the current, maybe making a little way, maybe not. I knew what he was trying to tell me, but I was too busy fighting upstream to listen. He didn't know this, and I'm not sure I've ever told anyone else, either, but when I was in the eighth grade, I took a test for mechanical aptitude. I scored like twenty out of one hundred. The conclusion of the testing authority was that I should stay away from anything mechanical. It didn't sound like they were any too certain that I would be able to shift gears in a car. I've often wondered if that test was why I became a mechanical engineer."

Buck smiled and said, "How are the brown-eyed kids doing?"

"Some good, some not so good. When he told the story to them, I think the brown-eyed kids were the ones fighting the current. Come to think of it though, two of the brown-eyed kids are lawyers."

Buck said, "And what am I to make of that?"

"What, indeed?"

Lawyers weren't generally very high on their lists.

Buck said, "I sent that wireline guy in. I think we'll use Camco for a while and give Otis time to reflect on why they would send an asshole out here."

For a few days, Mike thought over what they'd talked about and gave the humiliation time to synthesize and lose some of its rough edges. Buck had been right. On a rational plane, Mike had done exactly what was the "right" thing to do. But human beings have emotions, and those emotions color everything. He didn't know if he had been afraid of Moran that day or not, and even though his reaction was right and left him and everyone else better off, there was still something in his gut calling him coward.

At breakfast one morning, Mike said, "Buck, I appreciate what you said, and I know that you meant it, but the reason that you can say it and mean it is exactly what makes you different from the rest of us. Have you ever been afraid of anything or anyone?"

Buck acted like it was a ridiculous question, but when he thought about it, he couldn't remember a time when he'd been afraid.

Mike said, "That's a large part of the reason why we are all so drawn to you. We feel protected. Most of the rest of us have fears of many different things and to many different degrees. Living without fear must be the ultimate gift from God. But, it makes you incapable of understanding those of us with this little hole in our centers. I appreciate your input. It's kind of touching, in a way. But relaxing and going with what you told me would just be like covering up the hole so I couldn't see it. Some people manage to fill that hole, and they are probably the ones most to be admired. I don't know if kicking the shit out of Paul Moran would have filled my hole, but then, that's the point, isn't it? I'll never know."

Sometime in the early eighties, Buck took Mike into the Mouse's Ear and introduced him around. Everybody there seemed to feel as if they already knew him. They knew about Sandra and the kids and what they were all up to. He met Miz Catherine, Catherine Moynihan, and found her a likeable, even alluring, woman. He knew how old she had to be, but there were no clues to it in her appearance. She was beautiful in a California-girl way, and he told her that. "That's because I am a California girl," she said. She had been born and raised in Malibu, and her parents even owned a place on the beach. She had married an oilfield guy who was on temporary assignment in LA, and he had eventually taken her to Dallas. While they were there, he ginned up a limited partnership scheme that blew up in his face when the price of oil went down. She was left stranded with a huge credit card debt and no way to make a living. Her parents hadn't approved of her choice of husband, and when she went back home to live, she could see that nobody there was ever going to be able to get past it. She went back to Dallas, where she had some contacts, and got a job working in an office. Most of her contacts were married men, and she began going out with them out of boredom. The gifts they brought were good for filling in the gaps in her income. When she realized that she was basically dating men for payment, she decided to make it a career. She did "extreeeeeemely well." She was able to limit her clientele to a narrow band of very wealthy local men and, with their help, avoid the criminal element that worked the lower end of the business and the legal authorities, some of whom were on her list. When she'd made enough money to last two lifetimes, she closed up shop, changed her name, and moved down here. She saw what she did now as giving back.

Catherine and Mike enjoyed each other's company, and, before he knew it, they had put away two bottles of Poully-Fuisse, and his eyes were floating down to what looked to be a really fine pair of breasts. Buck, who had come to think of Mike's wife as an adopted daughter, noticed his attention wandering and came over to make sure he had the right woman on his mind. As he guided Mike to the bar and Tom Coleman, he said, "Now I see why you stay away from whorehouses and titty joints." Mike protested, saying that he had no intention of screwing around on his wife. Buck said, "Well, fortunately for you, you're not Catherine's type. When it comes to Catherine, your intention isn't the one that matters."

Mike, feeling like he had been making pretty good headway, said, "What's her type?"

Buck said, "She likes them…er…younger."

He left a space for Mike to fill by saying, "Do you mean better looking?" But Mike seemed satisfied with the younger comment.

Before leaving the subject of Catherine, though, a really interesting part of their conversation involved her clientele and their requirements. She claimed that a relatively small part of her job involved fucking. It sounded like she had been a sort of nanny-psychologist to most of the men that walked through her door. Pressed for details she told him about one distinguished CEO of middle years who always showed up in a suit with a briefcase. She would be dressed in something appropriate for a boarding school teenager and had to get up on the bed on her knees, bounce around, and clap her hands. The man would very carefully get undressed, open his briefcase, and extract a spray of peacock tail feathers all attached to the back end of what looked like a cork dildo. He would get down on the floor on all fours and insert the cork in his rectum then crawl about the room. While he was crawling, she was required to bounce around, clap, and say, "Ooh, look at the pretty peacock. Isn't that a pretty peacock?" Mike told Buck later that if that was what working in an office did to you, he was glad he worked outside. Catherine's story may or may not have been true. Most likely elements of it were true and others were not. But Mike was watching her eyes and listening pretty hard, and he thought she believed it. Mike considered himself generally easy when it came to believing people's stories. We all dress the facts up and move them around in our minds. Sometimes the lies we tell are more accurate indicators of the truth than the actual facts would be.

Tom Coleman was a different kind of person altogether. In fact being different was one of the driving forces of his life. He had a professorial air, a sort of attitude that he knew more than you. He certainly knew more than most people, Mike included, but no one likes to be talked down to, and Mike felt he was talking down to him. That feeling faded as the conversation progressed, however. Mike told him what Buck said about his being a monk and asked him if he was a guru.

"No," he said, "I'm not a guru. To me there are two kinds of guru. There's the truly enlightened being who speaks from a position of certainty, and there's the charlatan. The charlatan sounds like he knows what he is talking about, but he's in it for what he can get out of it. I've been around some of both kinds, and I can pretty much tell you what they will say in answer to any question. To that extent there are certain situations in which I can help. But if I were to tell you I was a guru that would automatically put me in the charlatan column."

Mike told him what Buck had said about his life and asked him if it was accurate.

"Well, it's what Buck has picked up. There are some holes in it. I don't think it's accurate to call me a monk. It's not that I don't drink; it's just that I don't drink here and don't drink very much when I do someplace else. The same thing applies to fucking. My path doesn't proscribe sex, only that no one be harmed or used during it. Finding a suitable partner when you hook those conditions to it makes sex a rarer thing than even I would like. As far as my life story goes, Buck's version is as good as any other."

Mike said, "Buck told me that you refuse to talk to him about spiritual matters. Why?"

Tom had been mixing drinks and washing and drying glasses while they spoke. Now he became totally concentrated on imaginary spots on champagne glasses. Finally looking up he said, "Buck is a special case, but I don't consider myself a spiritual teacher in any regard. If I know something and you ask me about it, I will tell you what I know. But my spiritual path is mine alone, and I have no idea what someone else's life would be by following it. It could be that what I consider good would be bad for someone else. The only real teacher is what the Buddhists call a bodhisattva, an enlightened person who has decided to stay alive and help as many people as possible. I have known such people, and that is partly why I know I am not one of them."

Once again Tom got involved in what he was doing behind the bar. Just when Mike was about to look for another conversation, he looked up. "Having said that, I try to help people when I can. Sometimes there are some obvious things that can be said. If a person is going a hundred and eighty degrees from the direction they want to go, you might not be able to get them headed toward zero, but anything past ninety or two seventy has them on a better path than they were on. You might be surprised what people will say to a bartender. I am always amazed that they seem to listen and accept what I say.

"Buck is different from the rest of us. I mean, besides being bigger, better looking, stronger, and, maybe, smarter than you and I, he's closer to God than we are. I don't know what happened to him when he was a kid, but I'm guessing it was something significant. I imagine it being something like what happened to Paul on the way to Damascus or Jesus in the desert—something that wiped out his former life and put his left brain in control. Buck is an innocent, but instead of being innocent and helpless the way most of us were when we were born, Buck was born a physical adult. Not only that, he was a natural athlete and bigger and stronger than ninety-nine percent of the other people on earth. He had nothing to fear. Can you imagine what it would be like to go through life without any fear?"

It was obvious that both Tom and Mike were men each with a variety of fears. They agreed that living without fear would be heaven on earth.

"Lao Tzu in the *Tao Te Ching* talks about the Tao in the beginning before the ten thousand things, when all was one. Buck is like a tiger in that Tao: at one with everything, with no doubt, and totally at peace. Me, teach Buck about a spiritual path? Buck is *my* teacher. I am pleased to be near him as much as possible. I am only a seeker, stumbling around trying to find my way. When I'm near Buck, I feel close to God, and I feel like someday I might see Him myself."

Mike looked into Tom's eyes when he said that and knew that he believed it absolutely. Swiveling around on his stool and taking in the scene in the Mouse's Ear though, Mike was having a little trouble agreeing with him.

The room was as Buck had described it, only more so. There was nothing to tell you that it was the waiting room of a whorehouse. It felt like an intimate dining room in a resort hotel that rich people had been coming to for generations. It was the beginning of the week, and traffic was light. There were only three or four potential customers sprinkled around talking quietly with the women. Catherine was someplace else, and Buck was seated at a table with another man and three women.

Buck had told Mike that only a few that worked here lived here, and most of them were coeds from the local universities. That had sounded improbable at the time, but these girls looked for all the world like college girls—pretty, some even beautiful. The three seated at Buck's table were ignoring the other man and totally concentrated on Buck. They were perched on his words like birds on a telephone line, and occasionally they would laugh at whatever he said or blush or put a hand on his arm. Mike was thinking that it looked like heaven to him, but he wasn't sure God would agree.

"I know what you're thinking," Tom said, "but you're wrong. All of these girls come to love Buck, but he will only rarely take one to bed. Some of them didn't have fathers, and some had fathers that abused them. All of them know that Buck is their protection. He is nearly always the father they wished they had had. Some come here because they need the money, and some have psychological reasons for selling their bodies, but all of them know that if they were to ply the trade somewhere else, they would be dealing with pimps and pushers, cops and rough trade. They don't understand how Buck makes this a haven for them, but they know he does, and they appreciate it."

Mike said, "How does Buck do it? I hear there is organized crime in New Orleans, and I hear a lot of talk about how corrupt the police are. It seems to me that both sides would want to have something like this under their control. I mean, I could walk out in the street and see a police substation."

Tom said, "I don't really understand how it's done. Catherine has made a point of meeting and becoming friends with some of the right people in government. There's the story of Buck pulling the guy's penis off, but that one is getting a little long in the tooth. Still, there is some kind of protective mystique over the place. Even on the weeks when he's offshore, this place somehow remains unnaturally calm. Buck owns this building and some others close by."

When he saw Mike's eyes widen, he said, "Yeah, and it's a bigger building than you think. It goes all the way to Wilkinson and includes the courtyard that you can see through those doors there. He's got some of the other side rented out to a federal strike force. That might have something to do with our being left alone for the time being. There is the feeling of Camelot about it—like it can't last forever. It's a lovely place to be for now, though."

Buck came up behind Mike, grabbed his elbow, and asked if he was hungry. He was. "Well," he said, "let's go see what they have in the kitchen." Something about the way he said it made Mike realize how much pride he took in this place. It put a whole new face on a man that he thought he knew through and through. Mike looked around to see if Miz Catherine might be joining them. Buck's eyes twinkled as he said, "I think keeping you and Miz Catherine apart is the best thing for everyone concerned." Mike protested, but Buck just smiled a bigger smile and kept walking. As he walked ahead of Mike out onto the courtyard, Mike noticed how fine and comfortable Buck looked in what had to be expensive clothes. The Poully-Fuisse was still operative, and it loosened his tongue enough for him to ask, "Do those clothes cost a lot of money?"

He said, "They cost a lot of money, but they could cost even more and not look as good. Catherine taught me that what counts is the store where you shop. Catherine could make a lot of money just shopping for men. The right store has employees that have been there for years and who are helpful enough to make suggestions without insulting you. If you listen to them, you'll get the right fabrics and cuts, and their in-house tailors will take little tucks and let things out, and pretty soon you look like a million bucks."

As Mike watched Buck, it occurred to him that if your body didn't go from bigger to smaller from the top down, clothes weren't going to hang like that, tailors and fabrics aside. Mike asked him where he shopped, and he said, "You can't afford it." He said it as a point of information, not to be mean, but it still hurt Mike's feelings a little bit.

Buck motioned to the right and said, "The Ear's rooms are behind us and over there, and that's where we'll put you up tonight." Motioning to the left, he said, "That's a small, very chic hotel over there. Up there are offices currently leased to the US government." They were looking up at windows four stories high. The courtyard had a fountain in its center and was got up with all kinds of plants — a very cool and inviting place.

"And this," Buck said with a flourish, "is the kitchen." And indeed it was a kitchen or, at least, a room at one end of a kitchen that must have been seventy-five feet long. There were twenty or so people dressed in white and engaged in activities of all kinds around gleaming pots and flaring pans. The intensity and concentration was of the level you would hope to see in an operating room where a loved one was being worked on. Buck and Mike stood watching, appreciating the precision and coordination as only ones who routinely orchestrate organized chaos can do. Finally one of the chefs caught sight of Buck and raised the alarm. The cry, "Buck!" came at them almost in unison. There was a shout at the far end of the room; it didn't stop with "Buck," and it continued, the source working its way through the crowd. Eventually it resolved itself into words from a single individual, a very, very large black woman who was having to push people into benches and tables to get through. She was apparently remonstrating with Buck, though Mike was having a hard time understanding what she was saying. New Orleans is home to many accents, three of which Mike could differentiate, and of the three, the New Orleans black patois was the richest and the most fun to listen to. This lady was so fluent in it that understanding required concentration. Mike looked at Buck, and he was grinning, something he'd never seen before, and, as she reached him, still yelling at the top of her voice, Buck swept her up and swung her around, something Mike was pretty sure didn't happen to her very often. She shrieked and pummeled his chest, obviously thoroughly enjoying Buck's attention. When she settled down, Buck looked at Mike and said, "I know you've heard of Andre's Kitchen. Well, it should be called Jaybelle's Kitchen because this lady right here is the one who makes it work." Jaybelle beamed, and Buck continued, "Jaybelle, this is my good friend and coworker

Mike Brown. I've been telling him for years that he needs to quit bypassing New Orleans on his way to Texas and come in here and try some real red beans and rice."

That last part wasn't true. At the time Mike didn't know there was a dish called "red beans and rice." God knew he'd had plenty of beans in his life, and they were sort of reddish, and he'd occasionally had them with rice, but the combination wasn't something he'd have ordered in a restaurant, certainly not a starred restaurant in the French Quarter.

When Jaybelle turned her attention on a person, the effect was something like walking into a comfortable room. All small annoyances faded away, and the person was somehow looser and more at ease.

"Well, Mike Brown," she said, "sit yourself down right here, and I'll see if I can whip up something suitable for the friend of a friend and landlord."

Her English didn't have a trace of an accent. She left them at the kitchen table and headed back for the busy end of the room. In answer to Mike's widened eyes, Buck said, "Jaybelle is a Cordon Bleu chef. She grew up here but studied in Paris and worked there and in London on her way to Andre's. She talks to me in black because she knows I love it, but I guess she didn't want you thinking she was Aunt Jemimah."

The table was a large rectangle that looked like it seated sixteen to twenty people. It must have been where the staff ate. A waiter with a wine bottle appeared and showed the label to Buck. Buck nodded then took the bottle when it was uncorked and poured some for both of them. It was a really nice red.

"Is there an Andre?"

"There was. He got old and unable to do the kind of watchdogging it takes to maintain a place like this. When I bought the building, the restaurant was actually a liability and part of the reason I got it for such a good price."

Mike asked if Jaybelle came with the place.

"No. Shortly after I had made the deal, I was sitting in the front room there, wondering what in the world I had gotten myself and Bobby into, and a black lady walked in looking for work. I told her I wasn't in the way of hiring anybody just yet, and I didn't know if it would even be a restaurant. She stood there talking long enough for me to be aware she was feeling me out. She asked me if I would be interested in a Cordon Bleu chef that was running the kitchen for a big hotel in London. She said her cousin was visiting her at the time. She wasn't looking for anything because she didn't think she would ever get what she wanted in the States, but this cousin thought she could get her down here if I was interested. I wasn't really, but I didn't think it would hurt anything to meet her. The rest, as they say, is history. She hired an imperious guy named Gustav to run the front, and she is queen of the kitchen, and she loves it."

Another waiter showed up with a couple of salads and some bread, either or both of which Mike could have made a meal of. "God damn," he said, "I had no idea rabbit food could taste this good."

Buck chuckled and said, "If I didn't have time off on the rig, I'd be big as a house."

He was joking because both of them loved the cooking on the rig, as well. Mike was thinking about Buck's life, and without thinking, he blurted, "Why haven't you ever gotten married?" As soon as he said it, he had a feeling it wasn't the right thing to say. The question sucked the life out of the party, and the clinking of forks on plates sounded like it was being made in a well. Buck finished his salad before he looked up.

"I know you didn't mean that to be judgmental, but it was. I know it came from a desire to see me happy, and that's the reason I'm not slapping you about the head and shoulders. I also know that it comes out of your lack of experience and conventional ideas of what it takes to be happy. The fact is, I am happy and wouldn't have my life changed one whit. You and Sandra love each other, and you have two fine, really loveable kids. I'm pleased for you that you have a 'normal' life and are so well suited to it. But I wouldn't trade places with you."

He might not have traded places with Mike, but Mike knew that wasn't the whole story. He sat there looking at Buck — well, at a button on his shirt. He must have thought he'd hurt Mike's feelings because, uncharacteristically, he offered more.

"It's a question of time and timing. You and Sandra got married at the perfect time. You were old enough to have an idea of what you were looking for in a partner and young enough not to have too many requirements. In my experience that doesn't happen very often."

Jaybelle swayed up from the depths of the kitchen and put a plate down in front of each of them. It looked like beans with chunks of sausage spread over rice. It didn't look all that great. Once, when Mike was in the navy, they got some stores by helicopter. They'd been thirty days in the South China Sea, and tasty food was a memory. One of the bags contained a package for Mike, a pecan pie sent by his mother. All the handling had rendered it unrecognizable as foodstuff, and none of the sailors around him knew the smell. Protocol required that he offer everyone a piece, but they all turned up their noses. Mike had the pie half eaten before the first person decided to try a bite. He got nothing after that, but it was OK: the looks of the pie had held everybody off long enough for him to get his fill. For the rest of his time in the navy, people were asking him to request another pecan pie. Remembering that pie helped him get the first forkful of red beans and rice to his mouth, and the result was the same. It was impossible to reconcile the taste with the looks. The dish was sublime.

After Jaybelle put the plate in front of Buck, she put a large arm around his neck and hugged him. "After you get rid of that hunger, we'll take care of that other problem," she said, and gave a low, deep laugh. Mike thought Buck blushed. Jaybelle sat down across the table from Mike and talked to them while they were savoring the meal.

When they were finished and drinking coffee, Buck said, "There are families and there are families; and, believe it or not, I have several families of which I am very proud and from which I get as much satisfaction and pleasure as anyone gets from more conventional arrangements. I have wives and mothers and brothers and sons that I chose myself, and sisters and daughters that fate placed in my hands. It's not a conventional life in any sense, but I have to say, in my life, I haven't had to pay too much attention to convention."

Mike settled down and enjoyed the company, but in the back of his mind was a thought building about something Tom had said, something about what had happened to Buck when he was fourteen. Buck had become a real person to Mike, and it was obvious that he wasn't born at fourteen, and that something had happened to him. The fourteen-year blank space made Buck different to begin with, and Mike recalled Buck's comment about Neandertals and the inevitability of his being done in by one. Was there a Neandertal in Buck's first fourteen years?

CHAPTER VI

Val Campbell

Days, like old cars and young children, have personalities. The day that Val Campbell went aboard the Hector was sluggish and fitful and seemed on the verge of a tantrum. Venice, Louisiana, sits on the narrow strip of land that follows the Mississippi down to the Gulf of Mexico from New Orleans. It lies exposed to the elements, and its inhabitants are set on edge by uncertain weather.

The *Delacroix*, a workboat contracted to Exxon, was tied up stern to that company's pier B. It was spring, 1991. The *Delacroix* was big but moved uneasily on its lines. The sky was overcast, and everything that could be seen was its own depressing shade of gray. Groups of men were standing around bundles and stacks of supplies on the fantail. They smoked and talked, duffels already loaded in the cabin. The boat's engines throbbed underfoot, anxious to be doing something. In the pilot house, the captain, Cappy Leroux, and the company man for the Hector, Mike Brown, drank coffee and talked idly, but their attention was really on the little patch of road from the main gate of the Exxon compound to the dock just back of the boat. Buck

Burnet and the men that rode with him from New Orleans were late, and they would have to come down that road to Buck's reserved parking space. This was the first time anyone could remember Buck's having been late. The Exxon yard dispatcher was anxious to get the boat out of the way. The toolpusher whose crew was due to be relieved on the rig was adding to the tension with frequent calls. When the protestations turned into a constant stream, Leroux turned the volume down on his radio until the voices became a scratch. The weather was worsening, and both men were eager to get the trip over with. The Hector was located not far offshore, but the open water section of the trip involved a relatively long stretch where both wind and waves would be coming athwart ships. Brown wasn't as concerned about the ship's motion as he was about the transfer of men at the rig. The transfer was not a risk-free operation on the calmest of days, but rough water made it difficult, and ten-foot seas were being predicted for later in the day.

"Buck's car must'a broke down," Leroux said. "Dat's da problem wit havin' a fancy car like dat. Was he drivin' a model T, he could fix dat wit a piece of bailin' wire. But a Rolls Royce? Who in sout' Louisiana knows how to fix a Rolls Royce?"

"It's a Bentley," Brown said. "I think they are very much alike, but the advantage to having either one is that it's never supposed to break down. I'd be very surprised if it broke down, though. Buck has that guy in Gretna who takes care of it practically on retainer."

"Broke-down car or not, the reason Buck is late is something he didn't plan on, and it ain't gon' leave him too happy. He's gon' pitch up here in a bad mood, and then he's gon' to see Little Lord Fauntleroy down there, and all hell's gon' break loose."

Brown could just see the head of the boy Leroux was talking about, standing about midway between the stern and the boathouse on the fantail. He had the same worry. Nobody had ever seen the boy before, but it took no more than a glance to tell what he was. This was the time of year that oilfield executives liked to send their collegiate sons to work in the field to let them "learn the business from the bottom up." The boys themselves didn't think much of the idea and generally felt compelled to demonstrate their disdain by being surly and doing as little work as possible, knowing they wouldn't be fired because of their father's influence. They would do that for one or two summers and spend the rest of their lives in break rooms and boardrooms talking about what it was like when they were "roughnecks." Most rigs and production facilities got one or two every summer, and they endured them, like they would a summer cold or a morning headache, but the Hector was different. Buck had early on made it known that he was not going to nursemaid anybody's little boy, no matter who or how powerful he was. Olympia's personnel department, which, like every other department in the company, had a tentative if not adversarial relationship with Buck, had sent a few out, over Buck's objections, with disastrous results. One had been the son of an Olympia executive who left the company in the resulting furor. Another had been the son of the CEO of a large independent oil company, who refused to do business with Olympia afterward. Buck's response on both occasions: "Everybody should be grateful that he made it back to the bank alive." The boy on the fantail's mere presence was testament to how much stroke the father had. He had to be high up in Exxon itself. One could almost hear the father vowing to "make a man" of him. If the father was an Exxon exec, that would have ramifications for the rig and its crew and for Brown himself, an Exxon employee.

"Look at dat'," said Leroux, while looking at the Exxon jack on the bow of the boat. "Da wind — she wants to blow; she just don't know which way to do it."

The presence of the boy, Buck's lateness, and the weather swirled around the workboat's bridge, and the day advanced reluctantly, malevolently. It was eight o'clock, a full two hours past Buck's usual arrival time, when Brown finally saw the big car make the turn off the road onto the shell pad. Crushed oyster shell doesn't generate a lot of dust, but the Bentley managed to stir up a pretty good cloud on its way to the dock. Brown dropped his paper cup into a trashcan and dropped into the stairway to the main deck. He was hoping to play the part of spoiler in the chemical reaction that would be inevitable when Buck saw the boy. Leroux had been right: Buck was going to be in a foul mood because of whatever it was that made him late, and the boy's presence would have infuriated him had he shown up in a sunny state. Buck was the leader and protector of nearly everyone on the boat, and few of them had seen him really angry, but they all felt privileged to be on his good side and sensed—knew—that they didn't want to piss him off. Brown walked up beside the boy who, he noticed, was two to three inches taller than himself and broader, but so slim as to be almost skeletal.

Herman Trahan, one of the daylight workers, got out of the shotgun seat and moved the fifty-five-gallon barrel that reserved Buck's space, and Buck jerked the car into it. The other hands got out of the car with alacrity and stood clear of the back end, waiting for the trunk lid to come up. Buck's movements when he got out of the car confirmed that he was not happy. The hands got their bags out of the trunk, and one of them moved to get Buck's then thought better of it and backed away. Buck snatched two bags up and slammed the trunk lid so hard that the Bentley momentarily sat down. He held both bags over his right shoulder as he stepped over the transom onto the deck of the boat. Buck's reaction when he saw the boy would have been comic in another situation: his jaw dropped, and his eyes opened wide in a parody of disbelief. As he strode toward the boy, his jaw was working, but no words were coming out. He had to bend down slightly to get at eye level with the boy, and even Brown recoiled, but the boy didn't. Buck's mouth barely opened as he said, "Get your coddled ass off this boat and take your grandmother's bag with you," the latter a reference to the flowered suitcase at the boy's feet, which was undoubtedly the latest in fashionable young men's travel accessories, but which did look sort of twenties' cruise worthy. With a last hard look for punctuation, Buck headed for the substructure and disappeared into a watertight door.

"Well," said Brown to the boy, "that went a lot better than I expected."

The boy turned to Brown and said, "That isn't fair."

Looking into the boy's face at close range was a little bit of a shock for Brown. Beautiful probably wasn't appropriate, but he was certainly at the upper limit of handsome. Brown found himself wondering what his parents looked like: if they were similarly attractive or if he might have been a one-off from normal people. Being from Texas Brown was only familiar with breeding of livestock.

"No," Brown said, "it is decidedly not fair. But that confrontation you just had was with what passes for the law of the land offshore. I'm—"

"I know who you are," said the boy. "You're Mike Brown, drilling engineer for the Hector, and I know who and what he was, and I know my rights. I've been through a lot to get this job, and I'm not about to quit before I even get to the rig."

Brown heard this with some trepidation: firstly because he couldn't think of a single benign reason why a newly hired roughneck would know who he was, and, secondly, why said roughneck would know that he couldn't be fired without just cause and that by stepping off the boat he would be quitting. Despite himself Brown couldn't help liking the boy. "Look, son, I'm sure you are a nice boy and a good person. But Buck has already decided he doesn't like you, and if you come out to the rig, your life will be hell. Let me help you with your bag, and I will talk to your bosses and see if I can't get you a billet on another rig."

"With all due respect, Mr. Brown, I don't want another rig. I didn't expect the job to be easy. I'm staying on this boat."

Brown had the authority to order him off the boat, and he briefly considered doing it but didn't, and not only because he thought the boy's father might have his job for doing so. He knew the boy's presence on the rig would create upheaval and trouble between himself and Buck, but he saw in the boy a kind of better-bred, better-looking, richer version of himself. He knew the boy had little chance of making it on the rig, and that it was only a matter of time before he left voluntarily, but he didn't want to be the source of his disappointment.

"If you stay," Brown said, "know that you are letting yourself in for a world of hurt. Buck Burnet is a fair man in almost every way, but he's got a blind spot when it comes to privilege. You would be in for a hard time if every man on the rig was behind you, but you're not going to have any friends out here."

"Well," the boy said, "I've got you," and smiled a smile that any orthodontist would have been proud of. He stuck out his hand and said, "I'm Val Campbell." Brown shook it, surprised by the firmness in a hand softer than his own.

"Yeah," Brown said ruefully, "and that's doing neither one of us any good."

Buck stomped into the pilot house where Leroux was waiting and said, "We're all here. Have you got everything you're waiting for?"

"And a good morning to you, too, M'sieu Burnet." The captain pronounced it "Bur-nay," as if it were French. He knew it wasn't. They'd had this discussion before.

Buck said, "I got a damned speeding ticket in Plaquemines Parish, and those dumb sons of bitches in personnel sent out somebody's son for me to put to work."

Leroux said, "Wa'al I can sure see why you might be out of sorts, but if you're gonna act like dat, you can ride in the crew's quarters like the rest of the oilfield trash. Cappy Leroux doesn't have to put up with dat kind of shit. I'll kick your ass, I will. I ain't a' scared of you, no." There was no doubt in either man's mind that Leroux would try to do just that if he were feeling disrespected, but the prospect of its actually happening was patently absurd. Leroux was a little stick of a man with a smoker's cough.

By way of apology, Buck said, "What have we got for weather? I didn't like the way the sky was looking this morning. Are we going to have some weather?"

The captain said, "Yeah. We lookin' at maybe six or eight feet. Waves out da southeast. Somethin' goin' on the other side of the islands. Shouldn't be no problem."

"One of the Perez boys catch you?"

Buck said, "I don't think he was blood kin. He didn't look like the rest of them. I told him to check with his boss, but he wouldn't do it. Took me in his car all the way to the justice of the peace and pulled him out of bed. The JP was mad at him, but it didn't matter. He still fined me two hundred dollars."

Buck said, "That fucking rich kid put the icing on the cake. You should have seen the bag he had—looked like Zsa Zsa Gabor waiting for a red cap."

"He might have trouble gettin' off the boat today."

"I sent him packing. He's probably headed for Daddy's office right now."

Leroux was about to say he hadn't seen him get off the boat when Mike Brown came into the pilot house.

"Actually," Brown said, "He's not headed for Daddy's office. He knows his rights, and he wants to stay. I told him he'd be better off finding another rig, but he specifically wants to work on the Hector."

"I don't give a fuck what he wants. I'm not going to have him on my rig."

Brown said, "Buck. There's every indication that this boy's family is way high up in the oilfield food chain. Think about it. Your personnel department surely knows how you feel about these things. If they sent him out here, it was for one of two reasons. Either the order to hire him came from so high up that they couldn't say no, or they figured you would do just what you did and come under fire, maybe lose your job over it. Come to think of it, it's probably both things."

"I'm not worried about losing my job, and you know why."

"Lose your job; lose work for the rig—same thing. Exxon can hire any one of the hundred stacked-out rigs in the Gulf right now. Exxon loves you up to a certain level, but my guess is that that boy's father loves him and that he's at a level that he doesn't even know the names of the companies working for him, much less who the toolpushers are. You don't have to worry about it, but what about the crew?"

Buck signaled that he wasn't listening any more by walking over to the starboard side of the pilot house and staring out to sea. The three rode in a silence punctuated by the horns of the passing boats and ships in the channel. It seemed that they were the only vessel headed out. Everyone else was looking for safe harbor.

The motion of the boat changed immediately as they cleared the channel. An oilfield workboat is built something like an oceangoing tug, except that it's broader in the beam, and the main deck level of the stern is stretched out to provide a platform for carrying heavy equipment and supplies. The relief rig crew was sometimes taken to the rig on a personnel boat: smaller and faster than the big workboat but much more responsive to wave motion. The hands who thought about such things were probably glad to be riding the workboat today, but the ones who were prey to seasickness didn't notice the distinction. The boat rolled steeply from side to side while it rocked fore and aft with a different frequency. Those who could got in the bunks, and the rest looked for something solid to put their arms around. The new boy sat at one of the dining tables and held onto the edges. He didn't seem to be affected by the boat's motion, though there would have been general satisfaction if he'd joined the contingent in the head. The others figured he'd probably spent a lot of time on yachts. The boat's motion was accentuated in the pilot house because of its height, but nobody in the pilot house was thinking about his stomach. Their minds were on the state of the sea and the upcoming personnel transfer.

There were two ways to transfer personnel from a boat to a jack-up rig and back. When the seas were calm, the usual way was for the boat to back up to a landing platform that was attached to one of the rig's legs and that floated up and down with the tides. From the body of the rig overhead, there hung thick ropes for holding while the transition was made. From that platform, a ladder led to the lower deck, some thirty feet up. In rougher water, the crew were taken up in personnel baskets by one of the rig's cranes, which were mounted on the main deck. The transfer from deck to basket was tricky with the motion created by large waves, but today's motion would make it almost impossible for the crane operator and the boat captain to achieve the coordination necessary to safely get the basket on and off the boat's deck. All three men were wishing they had pulled the plug and spent the extra time and money it would have taken to move the men on helicopters. Cappy hadn't wanted to mention it because he didn't want to be stuck in port with a load of supplies and equipment; but there would be no question of transferring that stuff to the rig in the present conditions. Buck had been distracted and angry and hadn't taken the time to think it through. Mike Brown, who normally traveled to the rig and back on helicopters anyway, was in the habit of leaving personnel matters to Buck and was only now letting himself realize that an accident would be as much his responsibility as it was Buck's. Had the trio known what they were in for, they would still, this close to the rig, have turned back to the helicopters or left the transfer for another day.

Without looking anyone in the face, Buck told the windshield that if that kid was going to stay on the rig, Buck didn't want to have to deal with him. He would be on the roustabout crew, and he better know that his number one priority was staying out of Buck's sight. Brown was secretly pleased to hear this; he had been dreading a further confrontation. Buck was as much as telling him that he could keep the boy on the rig, but that he was doing it for his sake. It left the door open for future confrontations, but how hard could it be just to keep the boy out of Buck's way?

When Buck and Brown reached the main deck, the crew was huddled under the overhang of the superstructure. They were looking out over the stern at the rig, which looked curiously small in the face of this day's version of Nature. Pallets stacked with thousands of pounds of mud and chemicals, which normally seemed rooted to the deck, had become mobile and formed a sort of moving gauntlet between them and the stern. The deck was moving more than anybody liked here, but, seventy-five feet away, the very back of the boat was heaving and pitching as if it had a life of its own. Most of the men were seasoned offshore workers and had gotten on and off rigs and platforms under all kinds of conditions, but this was something special. This was daunting. Nobody there really wanted to be the first to leave the relative safety of the boathouse, but nobody wanted to be the one who said he wouldn't. Recognizing the situation Brown started making his way through the hands to Buck, whom he intended to tell that they should shut it down and go back to port. Just as he reached him, he saw Buck looking at the new kid, and his heart sank because he knew Buck was beyond suggestion.

"All right!" Buck shouted. "We'll go one at a time. I'll go back first, and when I get set, you start coming back. Don't leave here until the man back there is on the ladder to the rig. When you get to me, hand me your bag and hold on to the transom. When I've got your bag on the platform, grab one of the ropes and time the surges. When you feel us going up, grab the rope as high as you can and swing across. Get up the ladder as fast as you can. The platform is awash, too. Don't move unless you can move safely. We'll take as long as it takes. Don't be foolish," he said as he left, and the irony of that statement hung in the air.

Nub Nolen put the strap from his bag over his neck and grabbed up one of Buck's bags. When he could see that Buck had safely reached the back of the boat, he started out. The deck had a tread-like coating but was slippery in spite of that. Staying upright demanded total concentration on the boat's motion, and that one be in a place where he could get support at the end of each roll. It was important to stay near the boat's midline for the reduced motion and to keep from getting wet. The pallets in back had been tied down and afforded something solid as support and places to rest. It must have been harder for someone missing an arm, but Nub made it look easier than it was. Nub took his and Buck's bags up as soon as he got over, but then disobeyed orders by coming back down to the little landing platform to help out as the men swung to it. One by one the men wended their way to the rear of the boat.

Brown was certain that Buck had initiated the exercise solely to dissuade the boy from getting on the rig, and was equally as certain the tactic would work. But looking at the boy now, he saw no sign that he was put off. Seeing the set of his jaw, Brown felt the boy was going to try it, but he could see in his eyes the knowledge that he could die in the attempt. Brown decided to order him to stay on the boat, but the boy seemed to sense his intent and grabbed up his bag to be the next one out on the deck. Brown yelled but to no effect, and then he saw Max Davis start out right after the boy, and he felt better. The boy might have navigated the trip unloaded, but the weight of his luggage took him off time and pulled him one way and another. Had not Max been there, he would surely have lost at least his bag overboard and possibly himself. By the time they reached Buck, Max had the boy around the waist and the boy's bag with his own in the other hand. Brown could see a discussion ensue between Buck and Max, and finally, reluctantly it seemed, Max swung over to the rig by himself.

What happened next happened in seconds but seemed to play out over a much longer time. The bags were already over, and the boy was standing close to Buck, who was yelling at him. Brown couldn't hear the words, but he could tell he wasn't shouting encouragement. The boy made a grab at one of the ropes at the wrong time, and the rope lifted him off the deck slightly before he let go. He then turned away from Buck and appeared to be timing the boat's motion. But it was his first time, and he didn't have the right feel for it. When he did grab a rope, it wasn't high enough to clear the platform, and he didn't have the forward motion to get there in any case. The boat fell away, and the boy was left hanging between the landing platform and the stern of the boat. Cappy gunned the engines to move the boat away from the platform, but the boat had been sliding down the previous swell, and when it came up, it was moving to pinch the boy between the stern and the platform. The boy disappeared behind the transom, and the boat crashed into the platform's supporting posts, and Brown actually thought he could feel an extra tremor in the boat as the boy was crushed. When the boat fell away, though, the boy could be seen floating, unharmed, but free from the rope he had been hanging on. The boat's screws finally gained some traction and moved the boat away from the rig, but the boy was on the verge of being swept away. Buck was on the transom and had leaped to one of the ropes so quickly that it takes a lot longer to say it. His actions were so smooth they seemed almost rehearsed. Buck hung from the rope by one arm and waited for the next swell to bring the boy back up to him; then he used the boy's upward momentum to help propel him over his head to the platform's little deck. He then waited for the boat to come back to the platform and lightly dropped onto the deck, ready for the next man to come down.

A couple of years later, Brown would watch Michael Jordan in action and regain some of the wonder of witnessing the boy's rescue. What he had seen was almost superhuman, yet Buck had accomplished it seemingly without effort. He looked up to the after-control station to see if Leroux had seen it too, but the little Cajun was too intent on keeping the boat on station to be looking at anything else. Brown's heart was still in his throat, and his whole body was a jangled nerve. The men around him must have felt the same. None of them had yet moved toward the stern despite Buck's glowering and motioning them on. He looked back at the landing platform and saw Nub Nolen helping the boy into a sitting position. Then Nub picked up the absurd bag and waited for the boy to crawl over to the ladder and start up it. Somebody moved toward Buck, and the spell was broken. Brown was the last one down, and by the time he reached the transom, Buck had leaped across and was already out of sight on the rig. Brown took that to mean that Buck was blaming him for what had happened. Brown wasn't so much mad at Buck as he was disappointed. He had only watched, but he was so spent by the experience that it was all he could do to heave his bag over to the landing platform. His timing was off, and he stood at the stern, letting the rope slide through his hands while the boat lurched up and down and sideways. He heard Cappy yelling at him from the after controls. Finally, a swell came that was high enough, and he swung across. Cat engines don't roar, so much as throb more deeply, but Brown could feel the big engines pushing the workboat away from the rig. Cappy turned the boat in a long arc on a path to port. There would be no equipment and supply transfer today. When Brown got to his room, he found the boy seated at his desk, true to his class, unconcernedly dripping saltwater onto Brown's leather chair, floral bag at his feet.

"Get the fuck out of that chair. And what the hell are you doing in here anyway?" Brown said.

The boy jumped up and stood at the bulkhead between the window and the door. "The one armed man brought me here and told me to stay here until he could get me situated," he said.

"More likely to keep you out of Buck's way," Brown thought.

Brown looked at the papers on his desk, drilling reports and ledgers from the previous week that Curt Petersen, his opposite number, had left for him. Petersen had had something personal to attend to on land, and that was why Brown was out a day early and why he had been on the boat in the first place. He didn't see anything alarming or needing his immediate attention.

"This is probably a big lark for you," Brown said, turning from the desk, "but do you have any idea how close to death you came today?"

The boy was soaked and shivering. Through clenched teeth he said something that sounded like, "I wasn't going to die within reach of Buck Burnet." Brown knew that wasn't it, because there was no way the boy knew anything about Buck, but his attention wasn't on what he said but on how he said it.

Brown said a heartfelt, "Shit!" and got up and opened the door to his small bathroom. "Get in here and stand in the hot shower until you warm up."

After the boy had walked stiffly into the bathroom, Brown picked up his bag with the idea of getting something dry out of it for him to wear, but the bag and everything in it was damp with salt water. Resentful for being burdened with it but seeing no way out, Brown carried the bag down to the laundry room and asked the attendant to wash everything in the bag. He considered the possibility that he might have something in there he wouldn't want washed, but such was Brown's pique that he let it go anyway, thinking it served him right. He fumbled around in the lost and found for a pair of coveralls that would fit, some underwear and socks, and a pair of left-behind slippers. On the way back to his room, he ran into Nub Nolen.

Nub said, "Don't let Buck see you with those. He's been on a tear looking for that boy. I've just about got him convinced that he left on the chopper with the other crew. I'm afraid if he sees him before he gets settled down, he'll throw him in the gulf."

"Buck isn't going to throw anybody in the gulf, no matter how mad he gets, but I agree we need to keep them apart for a while. If he still wants to stay, and it looks to me like he does, we'll put him on the roustabout crew. If you see Max, ask him to come up to my room." Such was the political situation aboard the rig that anything Brown wanted done by a crew member was made in the form of a request. What Brown meant and what Nolen took him to mean was "Find Max for me and send him up to my room."

As it was Max nearly beat him there. They walked into the room together, and Brown walked to the bathroom door and put the clothes on the sink. Max had to bend down to get into the space and stayed hunched a little bit to keep his head clear of the overhead. There was a little dance as Brown went between Max and the bed to get back to the desk. Max almost took up the whole room by himself.

As much as he looked like a yeti, Barnes knew Max to be an intelligent and insightful person, so he didn't bother explaining the situation. "I made a deal with Buck to put this kid on the roustabout crew. That would make him your responsibility, but I'll think of something else if you don't think you can take the heat."

Max noticed the little hook about his being able to take the heat and smiled, but he didn't bite. "The way I see it, this is a situation where we have to protect Buck from himself. I'm happy to have an extra hand, even though it looks like we'll have to teach the boy how to put paint on a brush. Is that who I hear just finishing up a shower?"

"Yeah, Nub put him up here to keep him out of the way. He was freezing to death. You never know about these guys. You may have to teach him everything, but if he wants to learn, he won't have any trouble doing it. Most of them aren't worth a shit, but every once in a while you'll run across one that's worth the trouble."

"Present company not excluded," Max said, and Brown colored a little at the implied compliment. Praise from those under you generally came pretty cheap, but praise from Max was a rare and valuable thing.

Val Campbell stepped out of the bathroom in the provided coveralls and was taken aback at the sight and nearness of the big man.

"Val Campbell, meet Max Davis, your new boss," said Brown.

Campbell's hand came out and was enveloped by that of the superintendent. Brown watched Max closely for any sign of judgment but could detect nothing. The personal Max had emerged briefly but was now back in place, totally hidden from the outside world. Brown decided that Campbell could do a lot worse than be Max's responsibility.

CHAPTER VIII

Life Offshore

By the next day, the weather had improved and so had the mood aboard the Hector. During the rest of the week, nothing was seen of the new crew member. When asked about him by Brown, Max said he had had him scraping and painting the deck of the engine room. He wasn't very strong, but he didn't seem to mind work. He seemed to know that the best thing he could do was work hard and keep his mouth shut. Max had him eating early and late, and as far as he knew, Buck had forgotten about him. Brown said he wouldn't count on that and asked Max to watch over things on the boat trip back to the bank tomorrow. Max did that, physically shielding Campbell from Buck's vision and keeping him aboard the boat until Buck's car had left the lot.

"I feel like some kind of fish that's in danger of being eaten by one of its parents," Campbell said.

Max looked at him steadily, and when his voice came, it was deep and peaceful. "Son, on this rig you aren't even a little fish. You're more like a little gnat. Buck is the one I and everybody else cares about. We all love our jobs and working for Buck. If you disappeared, it wouldn't matter one whit to anyone else on this rig; but if we lost Buck, it would hurt all of us. Buck doesn't hate many things, but he can't abide people who come by things without having to work for them, and you and your father are definitely of that group. It's up to you whether you show up for work next week. I would advise against it. But, if you do, know that you are paddling upstream in a swift current, and you don't have any help. Mr. Brown is more like you than the rest of us, but he and Buck are way tighter than you think. If it comes to the nut cutting, Mike is with Buck."

Campbell watched Max as he spoke, and tears welled up in his eyes; but his chin came up slightly, and his gaze didn't waver. As he turned away, he said, "See you next week." When he said that, Max knew he had lied when he said nobody cared about the boy. At least one crew member was pulling for him.

There was no hiding him from Buck the next time out, but Buck chose to ignore him. The crew, however, had picked up on Buck's feelings about the boy, and they snubbed him in the myriad ways that people have. Campbell took the comments and jabs with equanimity, and there was no sign of his feelings being hurt. The transfer from the boat to the rig went without incident. He had gotten a reasonable-looking duffel to replace the flowered bag (which, in fact, was his grandmother's), and the clothes he wore were more suitable for one faced with manual labor. He showed up for work on time, and though he had very little natural ability and almost no knowledge of how to accomplish the simplest tasks, he set to each one with concentration and alacrity. Max had to show him how to hold a paint brush and how to mix paint, what the scraper was for, and how to use it. No matter how dirty and menial the job, Campbell seemed pleased to do it.

Most of the roustabouts, and the rig hands for that matter, were from farms or small towns and had grown up working on heavy equipment and cars. Knowing how to accomplish tasks from plowing and planting to dressing a deer or butchering a hog were points of pride. Such things were what allowed them to feel superior to city folk and how they were able to look down on "book learnin'." They figured book learners would be the first to die when catastrophe struck. They had an almost innate knowledge of how things like pumps and motors worked. Campbell was the ultimate book learner with many facts and theories at his disposal, yet he was a babe in this milieu, and he had only Max to help him survive. Max found himself teaching Campbell everything, no matter how basic. He mocked up a single-sleeve pump to demonstrate how the inlet and outlet valves worked. He tore down hydraulic pumps and motors and went over in detail how they worked, then had Campbell put them back together. Originally astounded at the depth of Campbell's ignorance (Campbell hadn't known the difference between Philips head and slotted screwdrivers or even, for that matter, exactly what a screwdriver was) he became amazed at how quickly Campbell picked things up and to what depth. Eventually he began asking questions that pushed Max, finally going beyond Max's ken. When that happened, Campbell began coming back from his days off with the requested information. Max knew he himself had an intellect far beyond that of the normal rig hand, but he had never really had it challenged—not even by Mike Brown, until now the smartest man he knew. Max didn't know how much smarter than he himself Val Campbell was, but he knew it was a lot.

As green as he was and with Buck's feelings about him common knowledge, Campbell fell prey to a little more than the standard worm's harassment. He spent some time looking for "relative bearing grease" and wrenches with odd names. Steak nights were traditionally Mondays and Fridays, and, offshore, steak meant T-bones. As every steak eater knows, on one side of the T is a big piece of meat, and the other side is small. They also know that the small side is the tender, or filet, side. For the first three or four outings, the steak that Campbell received was minus a piece of meat on the small side. Campbell apparently didn't notice the snickering that went on around him as he took his portion and visibly enjoyed every bite. Finally after one of the meals, Campbell approached the cook and thanked him for removing the tasteless, pasty side of his steak just like his mother did. He said they fed that side to the dogs and asked if the ones he cut off were already earmarked for someone else's pets. The cook didn't have an answer, but Campbell got steaks like everyone else after that.

The hazing culminated in a variation of the "three-man pickup," a stunt that opens with a discussion of who is strong and who not. The discussion eventually centers around one of the participants who is capable of picking up three men at one time. In this case it was Leon Mavis, one of the stronger and, it must be said, smarter of the roustabout crew. In order to perform the lift, it is necessary for the initiate, Campbell, to lie on his back on the deck. Two other participants lie down either side of him and lock their legs around his and their arms around his arms and shoulders. Thus incapacitated, the initiate suffers the — hilarious to the others — indignity of having his pants opened and pulled down and some noxious substance, pipe dope or the like, applied to his private parts. Campbell had a hard time grasping the concept and had the others explaining to the point that they became edgy and over anxious. In order to hurry the proceedings, Mavis demonstrated the technique by assuming the middle position and locking together with the other two whereupon Campbell, loath to waste an opportunity, administered the pipe dope application to Mavis, Mavis protesting loudly and strenuously the while. Why the other two hadn't released him when they saw the prank was going wrong was the subject of heated debate for years to come.

While Campbell didn't know much about practical matters, he seemed to know an awful lot about things that didn't seem knowable, and, at some primitive level, it began to generate respect among the other hands. Max once heard him explaining why the fish that were swimming around the legs of the rig weren't where they looked to be. The hands knew that you had to shoot your arrow under the fish to hit him, but when he told them about the refraction of light, they didn't believe him. They also didn't believe that the sun had already been down for ten minutes by the time they witnessed the sunset. They knew that when salt water was flowing in a pipe, the pipe warmed up, and a gas flow would cool the pipe, even causing it to freeze up, but Campbell told them about phase changes and friction. They didn't really understand it but were incapable of refuting it. Eventually they started going to Mike Brown, but what Brown said seemed to agree with Campbell's explanation. What most intrigued Max however was that he knew things that he shouldn't have known—things that he didn't have any logical reason for knowing.

Once Max was reading a book in the living quarters within earshot of the television, and he was half listening to the show that was on, a documentary about the shooting that had taken place in the University of Texas tower some years before. It was just wrapping up, and two of the hands got into an argument about how many people had been killed. About that time Mike Brown came through a door to the outside, and one of the hands said, "Mike, you went to the University of Texas, didn't you?"

Brown said he had.

"How many people did Charles Whitman kill that day?"

Brown said, "Sixteen."

The asker turned around with an "I told you so" look on his face, and his detractor said, "Aw hell, Mike, how would you know?"

Brown said, "I was there. I shot ten rolls of sixteen millimeter film of it."

"Bullshit," the other man said, and Brown just looked at him and walked on through.

Max knew that Brown had been a TV newsman in Dallas before he went back to school, and if he said it, it was probably true. He was surprised by the fact that he hadn't heard it before, though, that being the sort of thing that would come up over time. Maybe the time for telling had just never been right. Brown's input added fuel to the argument however, which quickly took on additional voices and volume. Suddenly there was a loud "What!" and the room grew silent.

Max distinctly heard Campbell's quiet voice when he said, "Not only is it true, he got an Associated Press award for the story."

"Bullshit," cried the dissenter, and the argument resumed, but Max had heard what he had heard, and he tucked the incident away in the mental file labeled "oddities."

Summer came and went, and the time for college interns to go back to their respective schools passed with no sign from Campbell that he was leaving. That troubled Max without his really knowing why, and he sought out Nub Nolen for counsel. There was a console with remote controls inside the driller's shack for handling normal drilling operations, but Nub frequently drilled from the driller's console on the drawworks. He got some kind of additional information by having his hands on the iron. That's where Max found him. The situation suited Max fine because, though they were in full view of anyone on the rig who cared to look up there, Buck for instance, he knew it would look like they were talking about some rig problem. There were the added advantages that nobody could slip up on them without their knowing, and the squeaking of the brake would assure no one could hear them.

When Nub saw Max, he started and his eyes widened, but then he smiled warmly. Max was conscious of being big, but he had long since stopped being pleased by the reactions it caused. He didn't regret his size; in fact he considered it a blessing, but he wished he could have human interactions without size being a factor. The people that knew him well should know they had nothing to fear from him, but somehow there was always a little hesitancy. The only ones who didn't react that way were Buck and, incredibly, Campbell.

Nub said, "I can't remember the last time I saw you up here on the floor, Max. Is something wrong?"

"Probably, but I don't know what it is yet."

Nub chuckled to show he knew it was a joke.

"I came up here because I've got a little bit of a personnel problem, and I need somebody to talk it over with. You know that boy that came out a few months ago, Val Campbell?"

"Yeah, I remember him real good. What I know is that, if you want to get Buck in a bad mood real fast, just mention his name."

"Yeah," Max said. "That's part of the problem."

Nub said, "You know, Max, you haven't done yourself any favors by taking him under your wing. Buck figures you know how much Buck is against him, and you must be mentoring him out of spite."

"I'm pretty sure Buck doesn't like me being nice to him, but I know he knows I'm not doing it to spite him. I may be doing it in spite of knowing how Buck feels about him, but I'm not doing it just *to* spite Buck."

"Well, it doesn't matter now. He'll go back to school, and everything will get back to normal."

"That's the problem. He's not going back to school. The semester is starting up right now, and he acts like that doesn't mean anything to him."

"Well," said Nub, "that ain't your problem. The time for interns is up. He's got to leave."

"I checked with the office last time I was in. He wasn't hired on as an intern. He was hired permanent."

"And his probationary period…"

"Was up two weeks ago."

"Shit. That means we can't fire him without just cause."

"Now you're beginning to see my problem."

"Well, what about cause?"

"He's the best hand I've got. He's already learned everything I can teach him. He works hard twelve hours a day, he never bitches, and the other hands have taken to following his lead. I've been trying to get them to paint out the substructure and the moon pool area for years. Nobody wanted to do it because it's so wet and shitty under there, and they're hanging over water most of the time. To tell you the truth, I didn't blame them. I mentioned — mentioned — it to Campbell six weeks ago. He got his bosun's chair and his shit and crawled up under there and started it by himself. Washing and scraping and painting. He'd come out looking like a tar baby, but there'd be another good-sized patch all sparkly and clean. The others would go under there and razz him, but after a while they could see that he was going to do the whole son of a bitch by himself. I swear it was like Tom Sawyer. He had them up on stages and bosun's chairs, cleaning and painting like they liked it. They finished it off in a couple of days and all proud of themselves as they could be. Buck noticed it right away and started praising me, and I couldn't tell him what had really happened for fear he'd make us fuck it all up again."

Nub said, "I haven't been under there in a while. Let's go look at it."

After calling Joe Tom up to watch the brake, the two of them walked down to the main deck and looked in at the moon pool. The underside of the floor was a gleaming white, the beams and pillars of the substructure were light gray, and the blowout preventer stack was as red as the day it had first come aboard.

"I'll be," said Nub. "Did they put some more lights in? It looks a lot brighter than I remember it."

"They replaced a few that were out, but there ain't any more lights than there were before."

"Well, it looks brand new," Nub said. "I just can't feature that boy being that kind of worker. Have you heard who his father is?"

"Nope. I don't know ary about him. He's friendly, and he talks a lot when you're around him, but I've never heard him give out any personal information. There's no end of rumors about who he might be, but I've never heard anything I would consider a fact. The other hands are always poking around trying to get information about him, but I don't think they've come up with the first thing. He laughs and kids and tells obvious lies based on their suggestions, but he's a mystery to them, too. This boy is not what he seems: and that could be bad or it could be good. My natural caution tells me to get rid of him, but for the life of me, I can't come up with a single reason to do that. Besides that I have a feeling firing him would cause a shit storm the likes of which we've never seen."

"Well, Buck wouldn't have any trouble firing him."

"It doesn't matter who fired him; we'd still be swimming in shit."

"OK, Max," Nub said, "let's get around to why you're telling me all this."

Max smiled. He knew Nub for an ace drilling hand, but he didn't figure him for quick on the draw in other matters. He would have to count Nub more subtle in the future.

"Well, partly I wanted to talk to you about it because what happens will affect all of us, and I wanted your opinion. And partly, he's outgrown the roustabout crew." Nub turned around and headed for the ladder. "Now hold on; just hear me out." Nub stopped at the first step, head down. "For whatever reason he wants to be a drilling hand. If we can't fire him, then I think we should put him to work on the floor."

Nub said, "You keep saying we, Max, and all I see is you. I can't think of anything that would make me want to make an enemy out of Buck Burnet." Nub made it halfway up the ladder and turned his head around. "If I was you, I'd talk to Mike. I don't know what in the world he could do, but he would come closer to helping than anyone else. As it is, you and him are the only reasons that boy hasn't been packed up in a crate and sent to shore long ago."

Max sat on it for a couple of days and was on the verge of telling Campbell he was fired several times. But it just didn't feel right to him. Take away the threat of the boy's all-powerful father turning their world upside down; take away Buck's hatred of his kind; even take away the boy's charm and general likeability—there was something about him that didn't fit with the general preconception; something good and worthwhile. In the end he did as Nub advised; he went to see Brown.

Mike Brown sat quietly in his office, watching Max as he spoke. Brown marveled, not for the first time, at the gentle soul that resided in this warrior's body. He looked for all the world like the big Ajax: dark facial hair crowded his eyes and nose, and the hair over his eyes came to a widow's peak. It was easy to imagine the combination as a helmet, plumes from the crest reaching high overhead. Everything about him was huge and hirsute, and here he sat speaking with great compassion about a person who could only bring him harm. Brown had been surreptitiously watching the boy with interest since he had first come aboard and was amazed himself that he was still aboard and working. He had thought him way too slender and soft to weather the vagaries of rig life, but not only had he weathered them, he had thrived on them. Brown estimated that he was carrying thirty more pounds than the day he first climbed the steps to the rig. His carriage was straighter, his skin was tanned, and his face glowed with health. He had gained the confidence that comes from being able to do hard, physical labor. Brown pondered the paradox. Had Buck not had this blind spot about people of his class, Val Campbell would have been just the kind of boy he would want to mentor himself. Max had the right of it. This was a problem that kept turning in circles with no apparent outlet. He heard him out, agreeing with everything he said, but when Max finished up, he still had no clear idea of the direction to proceed.

Brown said, "Do you know what school he goes to? What his major is?"

"I honestly don't know anything about him. He talks but he doesn't say much. You get the feeling that he doesn't give anything up on purpose. He seems to have knowledge in a lot of areas. I would say engineering, but he seems too up on things like archeology and history. No offense intended, but engineers don't generally know anything but engineering."

"True," said the engineer. "I checked at the office, and there are some Campbells higher up in Exxon, but there's no way of knowing if he's kin to any of them. I even went over to Olympia, but they wouldn't tell me anything but he was just some guy who came in and made application." The idea of Campbell's just being some guy looking for a job was a patent absurdity in both of their minds. "They said he was from the southwest part of Louisiana, but wouldn't tell me where."

Brown looked out his window and mused. "Let's think this thing over. What's the worst possible case? Let's say he's the son or nephew or something of somebody high up in Exxon or some other company able to apply a lot of pressure. Why this rig? Why did he, or whoever hired him, choose this rig? The only thing I can come up with is the Olympia personnel department sent him here just to get at Buck." Max nodded. "That makes Campbell an unwitting pawn who just happened to wind up in the shit and is somehow making meat patties out of it. If he was going to run whining to Papa, he would surely have done it by now, and we would have felt the repercussions. In fact he doesn't show any sign of running to Papa. One of the cooks told me a story about Campbell and that ex-marine with Shotco we used to perforate the last well. The marine had spotted Campbell as easy meat and slipped up on him with a glass of cold water when he was showering. After he and his helper had finished perforating, he went into the showers to clean up, and there sat Campbell on a chair he had drug in with one of those industrial-sized peach cans on his lap full of ice water. The ex-marine cajoled and threatened, ranted and raved, and Campbell just sat there, seemingly unconcerned. In the end the ex-marine couldn't get in the shower for thinking about taking that cold bath, and he headed for the bank in clean clothes with a dirty body. He threatened to meet Campbell on the bank, but I reckon nothing came of that. That doesn't seem like the actions of a man about to run to anybody. I guess the point is that Campbell seems blameless, and our taking anything out on him would be pretty cruel."

Max let out a sigh and settled back in his chair. Max had another reason for wanting Campbell off the roustabout crew, one that he hadn't even told himself. Having Campbell working for him was a source of pressure, and Max didn't like pressure. That's why he was in this line of work. Campbell seemed to be a bottomless pit that you threw knowledge into, and Max felt like he had to keep learning things himself, just to stay ahead of him. Campbell was always showing up ahead of the expected time, asking what he could do, too. Max would have to take time away from whatever he was doing to find something for Campbell. Max's real passion was building boats, and that's what he did on his days off. All he asked from his offshore job was that it enable him to live the way he wanted to and sleep easy at night. Worrying about whatever Campbell was going to come up with had been interfering with the latter.

Brown went on, "That still doesn't say anything about what he's doing out here and why he's not going back to school. Maybe his dad wants to start a drilling company and wants to have him know something about it." Brown was musing now, looking into space and not making conversation. "Maybe he just wanted to know how the other half lives. Maybe just about anything. It doesn't appear that that's any of our business, but I can't see any legitimate reason not to let him try his hand on the drill floor, if that's what he wants to do."

"Yeah, but...," Max said.

"Yeah, but...I'll have to have a talk with Buck. If it doesn't go well, would you see that my remains get back to my wife in Austin?"

Max knew he was only partially kidding.

Mike Brown had been with Buck for a good long time and enjoyed equal footing with him in almost every area of operations. The one area in which that was not true was that of rig personnel. The crew was Buck's alone to administer, and while he might listen to suggestions from Brown out of courtesy, there was absolutely no pressure that could be brought to bear to make him change his mind about a made decision. Just letting Campbell aboard was a huge concession on Buck's part, and Buck had set out the terms pretty clearly at the time. Brown went looking for a meeting with Buck knowing full well he held no cards. He knew his trepidations were well founded when he stuck his head inside Buck's office door and Buck said, "I wondered who they were going to send."

CHAPTER IX

The Rig Standoff

Brown closed the door and walked over to Buck's spare chair. He sat trying to marshal all the arguments he had been going over, but Buck's knowing why he was there had taken the wind out of his sails.

Buck sat looking out the window, and Brown's attention was drawn that way. A couple of hands were moving casing on the pipe racks, and Nub was circulating the hole with the bit on the bottom, conditioning it. The sky was clear, and the wind was still, and there were shore birds flitting about. The silence dragged on as Buck thought, and Brown knew it wouldn't do for him to say anything. Brown gradually came to feel that Buck was searching for a bottom to push off of. By the time Buck finally turned to Brown, the floor that had been sunlit was mostly in shade. Buck's voice broke slightly from disuse.

"When I was a young man, maybe twenty-five to thirty, I was running a couple of broken-down rigs in and around Cameron Parish. We were drilling for a consortium of independents, but the operator was an old man named Mr. Gene. He had started out in the oilfield working for his dad on a cable tool rig. He was at Spindletop when it started, and if there was anything to be known about drilling in east Texas or Louisiana, Mr. Gene knew it. He reminded me some of Bobby Lynd, but he wasn't the businessman Bobby was. Of course, Bobby likely wasn't the drilling hand that Mr. Gene was. Mr. Gene taught me most of what I know about drilling. If I'd been able to buckle down and take on learning as an assignment, he could have taught me a lot more. He liked me and wanted to help me, but my carousing frustrated him.

"Anyhow, one of the partners in the consortium was a company out of Houston. The company name was the same as that of the family that owned it, and anybody of any consequence in the company was a member of the family. You'd know the name if I told it to you. They're even bigger now than they were then. Every so often one or another family member would show up at the well site and expect to be shown around. Mr. Gene usually did the honors, and if I happened to be at that rig, he would take me out to eat lunch with them. Most of them carried that money attitude — that expectation that people would defer to them. Most of them were so steeped in it they didn't even see it as a pose. Mr. Gene didn't kowtow to them, but even he was more polite than usual. Only one of them I met didn't act like he was better than you, and I expect they've managed to bring him into the fold by now. His name was George, and he was the one that was out there most frequently. "

"This guy George was a wild kid and had aspirations of being a maverick. He went out with me a few times, and he was fun for a while, but he didn't have a lot of staying power. He drove a pickup that he thought looked suitably rugged and official, and I would see it parked at his motel well past noon the next day. He told stories on his family that I'm pretty sure they wouldn't want passed around. He was one of four grandchildren of the old man who had started the whole thing. The old man was still in charge, but his son, George's father, was the titular head. He had the dumbest name I've ever heard for someone raised in the lap of luxury: 'Pard'. I can see some prep school swells hanging that one on you, but why would you keep it?"

Mike's eyebrow arched and he said "swells?" before he could stop himself.

Buck said, "Look it up."

Mike said, "I've read it, I just never heard it before."

"The old man had a nickname for a first name, too. There was another grandson out there from time to time, but, unlike George, he didn't feel any need to be one of the guys. I don't remember his name, but he was a calculating piece of work. Both of them had "been" to school at places that sounded toney and were in fraternities that they mentioned often, but neither had seen a reason to put forth the effort required to actually get a degree. George's mother was either Pard's current wife or one of the former ones, but this other boy's lineage was a little murkier. A lot of George's devil-may-care attitude came from knowing he had ultimate backup, but the other seemed to feel he needed to make a showing to be cut in on the take, and there was a sweatiness to him that George lacked. They considered "big rich" the only success and saw themselves as heirs apparent. Both of them were taken with me, though, and apparently talked me up when they got home, because one day I received a summons to their ranch west of Houston.

"They had a name for the place that I don't remember, but it could as well have been Elsinore. Only Shakespeare could really do it justice. A mansion out in the middle of a great big mesquite patch. Dead animals on the walls and in the corners. Dark wood and leather and fireplaces everywhere. A young Mexican guy took my bag and motioned me to the room where everyone else had already congregated. They all had cigars and drinks in their hands. The old man and Pard sat in leather chairs, and George and the other one stood between the chairs and the fireplace. The fireplace was big enough for me to walk into upright, and the fire in it could have warmed three or four normal-sized houses. Pard got up to shake my hand, but the old man stayed seated. That was less an insult than a matter of practicality as his frame seemed to be packing more suet than muscle. Pard was a six-foot-ish kind of guy in shirtsleeves and suspenders. He was thick wasted too, and with the suspenders holding his pants at half-mast, he looked like he just couldn't wait to look like his father. Both older men wore glasses and held their cigars with their forefingers like there would be holes there if not plugged up with cigar. Everybody seemed very happy to see me. There was another man outside the circle of family that I didn't notice at first, and they introduced him as the ranch manager. I don't remember his name, but they called him the Marlboro Man, and he did look very much like that guy on the billboards. With the exception of the Marlboro Man, who stayed quiet and in the background, it was a merry group, and I basked in the warmth of a lot of attention. Much scotch was drunk, bourbon for me, and I felt loved and expansive. Supper was served in another room by more young Mexican men. I had what was by far the tastiest and most tender rib-eye I've ever eaten.

"I was clearly there to receive some kind of offer, but there was never an overt offer made. It was more like everybody, including myself, knew what was on the table, and we were celebrating my having accepted it. Mention was made of some property they had acquired (land was never bought: the mineral rights were acquired and the land sometimes came with them) in Alaska, and they were forming their own drilling company to explore and develop it. I got the idea that I was expected to run that operation. No titles were mentioned or money or any-thing else typically associated with job discussions. It was kind of like I would just become part of the family and naturally be recompensed beyond my wildest expectations. There was a ranch house on the place with a trout stream out the back door. Elk grazed the land like cattle. They all wished they could live in the wild like that, but—sigh—businesses took a lot of hard work and attention. I wish I could tell you I was observing all this with a discerning ear and a wary eye, but that would not be true. I was wallowing in it like the yokel they took me for. I was having visions of living large and well. I've never had an inclination to live in the country, but that night it sounded like the finest thing possible. Never having to worry about money sounded like a good thing, too.

"We were back in the big room after supper, and waiting for us there was a young woman. I'm going to tell you she was breathtakingly beautiful because I actually had trouble breathing when I first saw her. She had dark eyes and hair, and her skin was as smooth and fine-grained as patent leather. She was tall and dressed elegantly and simply. She moved around the room making sure that our glasses were full and making small talk here and there. The business discussions went on, but I didn't hear them because all my attention was on the woman named Mary. When she sat on the couch next to me, I had the breath thing again, and I think my heart stopped for a couple of beats. Her voice was soft and beautiful, and her laugh was low and throaty. She French inhaled her cigarette smoke, and I thought it was the most sophisticated thing I had ever seen. Her father was a big league baseball manager, or had been, whose name I would have known had I followed baseball. She had a child (it wasn't clear where the child was), and she was sort of a housekeeper for the ranch. If a preacher had shown up, I would have married her on the spot. To say that I was intoxicated by her would be no exaggeration because when I managed to tear myself away and look around, we were the only two people there. She graciously offered to show me to my room. Once there she turned down the bed and turned back to me as I held the door. She walked up to me and made as if to put her hand behind my head but couldn't reach it and was left grasping my collar to pull my head down. I've never been so thoroughly kissed, before or since. Now, finally, there were alarm bells ringing in my head, but they were muted by all I had drunk and the smell and feel of her.

"If I know, or hope, that I'm going to be making love, I drink very little or, preferably, nothing. Drink dulls my senses and reduces my ability to perform, but mostly, it reduces my enjoyment. She was a fine woman, and I would dearly love another chance with her with my faculties intact. As it was she praised everything about me, but I was left not enjoying any of it and regretting having even done it. When I woke up the next morning, her side of the bed wasn't unmade, and I had the worst hangover of my life. There was nothing of her left in the room, not even her scent. I stumbled around the house looking for something to eat and found George having coffee in the dining room where we had eaten the night before. The two older men and the other son were at work in the city. Either everyone else had drunk a lot less than it had seemed at the time, or the bourbon was stronger than the scotch. Mary was somewhere else, too. Apparently she didn't actually live at the ranch. George was chipper, but I felt like I was walking around in a warm, dusty fog. George had somewhere to go, and he could either take me to the airport now, or the Marlboro Man could take me when I got ready. He said they would be getting in touch with me when things were ready for me to make the move. As far as I can remember, I didn't say a single word.

"I opted for the Marlboro Man and went back to my room to sleep some more. I ended up throwing up several times before I could sleep, and when I woke up, it was dark again. I found some of the young Mexicans. They didn't seem to speak any English, but I managed to get another really good meal out of them anyway. When I woke up the next morning, I felt good again, and my mind was processing everything that had happened. The Marlboro Man was as taciturn as his nickname would indicate, and the ride to the airport was long and largely silent. I tried to draw him out, but he answered questions as close to yes or no as he could possibly get. Finally I just came out and asked him if what the others had been talking about sounded like a good deal to him. His eyes were glued to the road ahead, and for a long time, I thought he wasn't going to answer me. Finally he said, so low I could barely hear it, 'Sooner or later, we all make our deal with the devil.'

"When I got back to Louisiana, I found Mr. Gene in a café in town. I told him what had happened, and he listened like he knew what I was going to say. Mr. Gene wasn't the sort of guy to avoid things, but when I asked him what he thought, his eyes kind of slid off to the side. He told me he couldn't see as I had any choice and that a lot of guys would kill for an opportunity like that. He said he hadn't ever been to Alaska, but he had heard a lot about it and would love to go there. He said he heard the hunting was fantastic. He didn't shake my hand or slap my back or smile.

"The next time George came down to the rig, I told him that I thought Alaska sounded too cold for me, but I appreciated the offer. George got cold himself all of a sudden and asked me what offer was that. That was my first intimation of exactly how vindictive they could be. When I talked to Mr. Gene, he told me he was sorry, but he was going to have to let me go. When I protested, he told me he wasn't talking about the hands or the rigs, just me. He said my office had already sent someone out to take my place. I went without work for a couple of months before I finally realized that there wasn't any work for me in the oilfield, and that's the real story of how I pitched up at that whorehouse. It was literally my only option. I'm pretty sure that, even now, if I were to make a big show and call myself to their attention, they could still make things very uncomfortable for me. I understand that they tapped into a big gas field in Alaska and made even more money. Like they say, 'Them as has, gets.'

"I guess what I'm trying to say is that there is a certain class of people who run the state and maybe the country who are so far removed from you and me they don't even see us as being from the same species. The only way you can get into that class is to be born into it. Even people that marry in never quite belong. It's the same system that drove people over here from Europe in the first place. It's not formalized and named, but it's real and functioning nonetheless. These people have the power of life and death over us, but we don't seem to know it. We either do their bidding outright, or they manipulate us into doing what they want. All that money puts them high enough to see the big picture. The rest of us can only see the ground in front as we plod about in our daily lives trying to survive. If they want us to go in that direction, they put something we want over there, and we scuttle to it. Every once in a while, one of us looks up and realizes what's going on and gets stomped on for the effort.

"That boy, George, told me a story one time that was meant to show how competitive he was. He had lived for a period of time in the north part of San Antonio. He said that one summer he and some of the other boys on his block had a contest to see who could grow the best vegetable garden. One of the other boys was on his way to being the clear winner. George could see that garden as he told me about it: big ripe tomatoes, two different kinds of squash, several kinds of beans. Before the day of the final judging, George crept over to that garden in the middle of the night and poured gasoline all over it. By morning it was just a mass of yellowed leaves strewn over the ground. George told me that last with as much satisfaction as if he had won the contest legitimately."

Brown said, "George didn't end up shooting his ex-wife and killing her boyfriend and daughter by any chance, did he?"

"No, wrong family, but from exactly the same social group. It has been made pretty plain to me that I am unable to act against that kind of people, but I'm goddamned if I'm going to enable or help them in any way. That boy…" And here Buck stammered, looking for the name. "That boy is one of them, and I don't care how good or how able he is, I'm not taking him to my breast."

Buck seemed to have a knack for saying something right before it was your turn to talk that took your mind off the subject and what you had been planning to say. The mental image of Buck's taking anyone to his breast was so absurd that Brown was left dealing with it long after he should have been responding to Buck. When Brown finally stirred, the room, except for the area around Buck near the desk lamp, was dark. The men on the floor, tripping pipe out of the hole, looked like actors on a well-lit stage, but the rest of the rig was in shadow. Brown searched for words. He felt like he had been given a peek at the real Buck Burnet, that somehow the experience Buck described had more than a little to do with shaping present-day Buck. Brown thought he knew the family Buck had referred to because he happened to know of a private group that was active and successful in Alaska, but they weren't from Houston. He knew Buck thought a lot of Bobby Lynd, so he started there.

"Isn't Bobby Lynd just the kind of guy you are talking about?"

Brown could tell by the way Buck looked at him that Buck had asked himself that question in the past and dealt with it.

"Bobby Lynd is an entrepreneur, not a greedy, controlling asshole. The old man, Pard's father, and Bobby would probably make a valid comparison, but even that breaks down when personality and character are taken into account. I don't believe Bobby ever cheated anyone in his life whereas people like the… like them believe cheating is business."

Brown said, "You're a rich man yourself. Doesn't that sort of put you in their league?"

"You're not listening. It's not money that makes the difference between people like that and people like us. It's entitlement. It's in coming up with a generation or two of people who assume that, since they were born richer and more powerful than the rest of us, they have the right to be richer and more powerful and to get even richer and more powerful. And we, most of us, are complicit. In fact, they couldn't do it without our help. If all of us could be content with what we have, they would have no leverage. As it happens, there's no shortage of people who will sell their souls to get just a little taste of what they can deal out. Families like that intermarry and consolidate fortunes. They buy or heavily influence legislatures and judicial systems. Sometimes they come right out and get elected and rule themselves. A classic example of that is John Kennedy, president of the United States. All right, he wasn't so bad, but what if he was an ignorant, grasping playboy like George. Just think of the damage he could do."

Brown said, "I don't know people like you're talking about, but I know they exist, and I'm prepared to believe they are evil and that the world would be better off without them. I just have a problem believing Val Campbell is one of them. Right enough, we don't know much about him. He's obviously smart and well educated. He knows a lot about certain things that would take some effort to find out—"

Buck broke in. "Like what, for instance?"

"Well, like you for instance. He seems to know a lot about you—and me. He knows things about me that I don't remember having told anyone. And he knows how things work. Not like which way do they screw on and off, but how they work at a molecular level. And he knows about people: who they are and what they do. Like the prime minister of England or what political party is in control in Singapore. The hands have started asking him questions and using him for the ultimate source on bets and stuff." Brown could see this line wasn't calming any fears, but he realized they were things that had been gnawing at his own mind. Still, they weren't the sorts of things that should keep a man from being hired. In certain situations they would be reasons to hire him.

"Well, there you go," said Buck, "the son of a bitch is a spy. He's here to worm his way into my operation and destabilize it. Why else would he be out here making friends of people he normally wouldn't be in the same restaurant with?"

"Buck, you can't be that paranoid. I think he probably is up to something, but I don't think it has anything to do with destabilizing the rig. There is just no way he or anyone else has a motive to do that. I don't know what his game is, but I'm sure it is a game; and I have to tell you, I'm very interested in finding out about it. I'm pretty sure we aren't going to know what it is until he wants to tell us."

"Well, I, for one, don't give a shit what his game is. I just don't want him playing it on my rig. I want him off my rig." He added, "He knows things about me like what?"

"I don't know—just things. You don't have cause to fire him, and if you did it anyway, we'd be living in a legal shit storm for years. The fact is he's become one of your better hands, and I'm pretty sure the other crew members would testify to that."

Buck started to say something, but Brown cut him off.

"I know you don't care if they fire you, but you're not thinking about the rest of us. The crew have given you their loyalty and best effort for a lot of years, all in return for having a safe and secure place to work—and me, too. I've hung here in a dead-end job because of you. I know I wouldn't have gotten the job without you, but you have to admit that I've become more than just a guy who won't piss you off. I've turned in some pretty good work, and in a just world, I would be several steps up the ladder now. And you would throw that away for what? Nobody understands your objections to Val, and I'm beginning to think you don't understand them either. You can't fire a guy because he might belong to a class of people you don't like."

"I won't fire him until he sets a foot wrong, but I'm goddamn sure not going to promote him to the floor. Did you ever hear the old saw about the frog carrying the scorpion across the creek?"

"Probably about thirty times from you."

Brown surprised himself by saying that. Buck wasn't used to people pointing out his foibles, and a cloud crossed his face, but he decided to let the comment pass.

"Well, the saying holds here. That boy is a goddamn scorpion, and I'm not going to let him destroy this rig."

Brown knew when a discussion was over, and this one was over. He left Buck's office equally angry at the man's obstinacy and puzzled by his refusal to examine his own motives. He knew Buck for an intelligent, open-minded, and fair man, and in this case he was seeing none of those qualities. Nub and Max were hanging around down the corridor from Buck's office, but they didn't have to ask how the session went. All three men walked into the dining room and filled shot-sized Luzianne paper cups with the dark, aromatic brew. They sat at a table looking at each other, feeling no need for conversation. Directly Buck came in, spotted the three of them, and pointedly carried his coffee to the other side of the room. Somehow, despite the years of working together and the fraternal feelings that had been generated, lines had been drawn. In Buck's mind Val was the problem and his absence the solution. The others knew this. They were all thinking of times in the past when they disagreed with Buck and deferred to him. Buck was, after all, the boss, and on top of that, he was usually right. What then, they thought, was different about this situation? All they had to do was to agree that Campbell be fired, and instantly the clouds would go, and the sun would shine again. Buck would be his old self, and the rig would be a smooth-running machine. But somehow, and this was all communicated with looks and minute gestures, they decided that Buck was wrong, and they would not condone his actions. He had the upper hand, and a frontal assault would be folly, but they all resolved not to show approval in any way. Meanwhile Buck was having a lively conversation with a cook's assistant, whose name he probably didn't know. All three men picked up their cups and slowly, almost mournfully, filed past the trash can and out the door.

Over the following days and weeks, the mood aboard the Hector deteriorated to that of a normal workplace environment and lower. Buck was cheerful and almost talkative, spending time with members of the crew with whom he had spoken very little in the past. Those crew members reveled in the attention and took to talking to each other a lot and loudly about very little. The respect they had shown for the natural leaders of the crew began to dissipate, and they waxed rough and rude to Nub, and even to Brown. Only Max was spared their disapproval. They were slow and ignorant, but they weren't suicidal.

Only Brown had an idea of how much the little charade was costing Buck. Buck had worked hard making the organization of the rig what it was: intelligent, knowledgeable people at the top and people who were content to take orders in the jobs where boredom could otherwise be a problem. Buck had told him that when he first started out, he thought the perfect rig would be one on which every hand was ambitious and had the knowledge of a driller. When he first gained control of the Hector, he had put that theory into practice. He said it had been chaos. Nothing was done because of the clash of egos. He essentially had sixty or so people doing what they thought should be done. Only the truly intelligent among them could see what was happening and tried to bring the others together in a spirit of cooperation. Their efforts were rebuffed the more strongly for their conciliatory tones. After that Buck came up with the current model: intelligent and quick thinking at the top; strong, physically adept, and with a solid work ethic at the bottom.

And here he was, himself turning the rig he loved on its head. Buck hated clichés, and he was talking about cows pissing on flat rocks and Mabel's pussy like he had just thought them up. He normally refused to have discussions without content, and he was talking about the bars between Venice and Belle Chasse like he had been in one in the last twenty years. Max seemed to be handling the situation with equanimity, and Brown knew it for something that couldn't last forever, but Nub was taking it to heart. Nub was old compared to the rest of the men on the crew, but no one had actually factored his age into their opinions of him. It seemed he had been that old since everyone knew him and would be that old when they died. But lately his movements had slowed, and his eyesight had dimmed. It took him longer to climb the ladder to the floor, and working the brake cost him some effort. When he was off duty, he spent more time in the rack, and he had totally given up laughter. Brown felt like Buck might have some reservations when it came to his feelings about Max and himself, but he knew Buck loved Nub Nolen as much as he could love anyone; and he knew that if the three of them had any leverage at all, that was it.

One day Nub missed the helicopter going to the rig at the beginning of the shift. Buck was worried, and he called everyone he could think of including law enforcement offices and the Coast Guard inquiring as to his whereabouts. Nub's wife said he had left Rockport at the regular time in his old pickup. She said it usually took him about ten hours. She gave Buck the name of the motel in Harvey where he usually stayed, and the people at the motel said he had checked out at four o'clock that morning, in plenty of time to make the boat at six.

Finally, Nub showed up on a later chopper, seemingly bemused at the fuss. His pickup had been pulling to the right, and the guy at the garage had taken longer than he thought it would to locate the problem. He hadn't called because he didn't know the rig's number. He had never had occasion to call it before. It wasn't obvious from the outside, but those who knew him best knew Buck had been in a state. He didn't say anything to Nub after seeing him safely off the chopper, just locked himself in his office for a couple of hours. Sometime before lunch the same day, Brown was on the floor with Nub conferring about the state of the well. They stopped talking and stared as Buck appeared on the ladder. It had been a while since he had purposely showed up where one of them was, let alone where they both were. There was no warmth in his voice, and he looked over their heads as he spoke.

"All right. I'm not going to be responsible for the death of one of the few friends I've got, just to make a point. I want you to understand that I still don't agree with you. I still think that, ultimately, Campbell's presence on this rig will be its undoing. But if things go on the way they have been, it will be undone in a different way. Put him on the floor if you must, and know that I will be watching for the first fuck-up. Mark my words"—and here he looked Brown in the eye for the first time—"that boy will pour gasoline on your garden, and I won't hesitate to say I told you so."

Buck stomped off the floor like the teenaged girl who couldn't go to the party. Brown looked at Nub and swore there was a sparkle in his eye. It was then Brown realized that kindly old Nub Nolen, the guy that played Gabby Hayes to both Buck and him on an ongoing basis, was far smarter and more artful than he had imagined.

Brown said, "Aren't you going to ask what he meant about pouring gas on the garden?"

Nub said, "No, I heard the 'gas on the garden' story a long time ago.

"Well," said Nub, "let's see what the boy's got." And with that he used his one hand and his butt to slide down one rail of the ladder, feet not touching until he reached the pipe rack floor.

CHAPTER X

Val's Story

Val Campbell was sitting in the chair in his bunkroom reading a mystery novel when Nub found him and told him that he would be starting in the worm's corner the next day. He was gladdened by the news, but it wasn't totally unexpected. He knew there had been a bit of a tug-of-war going on, and he was hoping for this outcome. The book he was reading was about a guy living on a houseboat in Miami who recovered money for people who had no legal recourse. The premise was ridiculous, but it was imaginative and well written, and the lead character was likeable. It wasn't Dostoevsky, but he enjoyed it, and it passed the time. Once he finished this author, he was keen to find others who were equally engaging. It was yet another of the simple pleasures he had discovered since coming offshore.

He felt coming offshore to have been, in many ways, his making. His life up to this point had been lived largely for the sake of other people. Not that he was forced to live a certain way, just expected to by people he loved and wanted to please. However, he thought, twenty-four years was long enough to

149

donate to other people's aspirations. His life to this point had been spent in the "halls of academe," and he was the proud, if somewhat bemused, possessor of a doctorate of philosophy in anthropology. He had distinguished himself sufficiently to be the receptor of several tempting offers from fine schools around the country. The problem was that he could find nothing in himself that wanted to be in school, however comfortable the position might be. The degree had been his goal for almost all of his twenty-four years, and he had sublimated his life to it. Friends, girls, hobbies, sports—all were seen as potential threats to his achieving the goal, therefore dispensed with. As soon as the degree was assured, even before he received it, he began to look around and was amazed and a little horrified at his singleness of purpose. He could see clearly what the effort had cost him; familiar with the details of the lives of many other people, he could not come up with a single detail of his own that he considered worthy of note. He had been protected, but he had protected himself as well. He found himself ready, even eager, to leave the nest, but he realized that his wings would only support him in the heady air surrounding ivory towers. He could imagine conditions under which that would have been enough. He knew people who spent their time there and couldn't imagine doing anything else, but it seemed to him too easy—too much like floating on the surface and just imagining what was below.

He didn't particularly like himself, and that seemed a shame because he thought he was, at bottom, a genial and worthwhile fellow. Jack London was one of his secret heroes (secret because, like Kipling and Tennyson, he was considered a little too common by the establishment), and he sort of felt himself to be living Jack London's life in reverse. London had grown up in a physical, dangerous world and came late to letters. Val was born and bred in literature, and here he was, twenty-three years later, only peeking out from the ruins of his shell. When he compared himself to any of the characters or authors he loved, he invariably came up wanting. He felt himself too pretty for one thing. His features were crisp and delicate, and his skin was clear and smooth. He had what he considered a good frame, but his body lacked tone and definition. He had no muscle other than what was needed for sitting or standing. Though he couldn't play a note, he had the long delicate hands of a pianist. For another thing he had no social skills. He had no idea how to interact with others of any sort—male, female, professional, or worker. He did quite well in the milieu of his degree, of course, but conversations he might have in that arena elicited blank stares and sometimes open derision when carried on elsewhere. Occasionally, he had caught himself ambling down that path out here. He had cut short the discourse to find the audience looking at him like they might have at a new species of animal or an intergalactic alien. He was aware that there were people who looked down upon physical labor and the people who did it, but, perhaps because of the research he had been engaged in over the last few years, he didn't share that view. In fact, when he started thinking of things to do, physical labor became a required component of any candidate endeavor. He tried to consider everything (logging and trains were high on his list), but it was almost inevitable that he end up here, on this rig in the Gulf of Mexico, working for the man who was the subject of that research and his PhD dissertation.

Getting the job hadn't been easy. The Jones Act, another name for the Merchant Marine Act of 1920, makes an accident offshore much more costly for the operator of a vessel, or a rig, than a similar accident onshore. For that reason, hands hired for offshore positions are almost universally required to have mastered the same duties on land before they are considered eligible. He was rejected out of hand when he applied by letter, so he went to New Orleans to apply in person. He had no luck there initially, but over two days of waiting in the lobby of the Olympia Drilling Company for an interview, he made a friend of the receptionist, Ms. Helen Price. She was a very dignified lady of fifty or so and, as the company's first line of defense against people who would waste the executives' time, had the ability to change her tone from warm to frosty at the drop of a business card. She was very good at her job, and she was cool to Val for the first day or so, as she was required to be, but being a naturally good and compassionate person, she could only resist him for so long. She finally prevailed on someone in the personnel department to see Val, certain when she did so that it would be a short visit. It would have been — should have been — a short visit, had not Val lucked into Vip Short, one of the people with the least use for Buck Burnet in the company.

He started out by telling Val that there was no way he was going to be hired. He did this in a very businesslike, no-nonsense manner. When Val just sat in front of him with a look of mild interest, Short sought to fill the silence with all the reasons he could not be hired. This led to a discussion of Buck and why Val wouldn't want to be on the rig in any case. The more he talked about Buck, the more he remembered why and how much he didn't like him. The man had been a major thorn in his side for the full time he worked in the office, and the mere thought of him, hulking up and down the halls like something looking for prey, still gave Short indigestion. He, Vip Short, was the vice-president for God's sake. Never had he received the least shred of respect from him. He never listened when Vip was holding forth in a meeting, and anyone would tell you Vip Short was one of the best at meetings. If you tried to call him on it, he would just sit and look at you like you were a bug or something. At some point Vip began thinking how much Buck would hate to have Val show up at his rig. At first he just toyed with the idea of hiring Val. He would not be able to justify the action if someone ever questioned it. (And he knew someone, specifically his so-called assistant, Teresa Mendoza, would raise flags and run up and down the hallway with them if she got wind of it.) But the more he talked and played with the idea, the more irresistible it became. Finally he hired Val and created and put through all the paperwork himself (so as to avoid prying eyes). Short was very pleased with himself and remained so until around three o'clock the next morning when he woke up bathed in sweat with a sharp pain in his stomach. That pain returned frequently for a period of months and only receded when it became obvious that Val was not going to die or create a catastrophe—a catastrophe being anything that would reflect badly on Vip Short.

Physical attributes aside, Campbell possessed a mental toughness as deep and strong as it was unapparent on the surface. He had walked onto the boat that first day without a clue about what was in store, but he did it with full confidence that he could handle whatever came his way. That confidence evaporated while he was hanging from the rope and dropping into the ocean, but even then he wasn't in fear of losing his life. He was probably the only person present that day who was absolutely, one hundred percent sure that Buck Burnet would not let him, or any other man in his charge, be harmed. Everybody knew Buck Burnet the legend, but he was the only one who knew Buck Burnet, the man—and that included Buck Burnet. That event had been extremely unfortunate, however, because Buck had taken himself to be responsible for the near accident, which, in Val's opinion, he was. It left Buck angry at himself and, by association, angry at Val. He had still not given Val the time of day and even seemed to be actively trying to get Val to leave the rig. Val knew before he applied for the job that it would take Buck a long time to warm to him. He knew Buck had a thing about privilege and that Val looked like he was from money, but he figured the truth would become evident over time. Buck was a little bit like a celebrity in that he felt no need to increase his circle of friends, and he was naturally brusque and dismissive to just about anyone new. But in the ultimate analysis, he was a fair man, and Val was sure that when Buck came to know him, they would be great friends. Until that day Val would simply stay low and keep his mouth shut whenever he was around Buck, which was amazingly seldom given the relatively small size of their world.

His first weeks on the rig had been difficult, but he looked upon the work as a learning assignment. He had studied culture, of course; culture was one of his things. But he quickly realized that what he knew of cultures in the aggregate had not prepared him for being thrust into the specific one of the offshore oilfield. Specific *ones* would be the more accurate term for, while there was an ethos associated with working the offshore rigs, all of the hands were from different regions and backgrounds, and it made for a real hodgepodge. He was beginning to believe he could create a credible and valid thesis around almost any one of the men he had been working with. The majority were from Texas. He had been told that that was because of the way the oilfield grew; the big play just before coming offshore to drill had been in Texas. The Texas Gulf coast would have been the logical place to start offshore exploration, but Texas got into a fight with the federal government about how far offshore Texas' rights extended. By the time the lawsuit was settled Louisiana was well ahead in infrastructure built and wells drilled. More and more Louisiana hands were being trained, and they made up the second-largest component. Mississippians and Oklahomans formed the last contingent, with a smattering from the other Southern states and one each from the Midwest and New England. Most of them were working class people, but a surprising number came from middle- and even upper-middle-class homes. The last were especially noticeable among the crews sent out to the rig by service companies. The most entertaining were the south Louisianans — generally Cajuns. The people from north Louisiana were more like the rednecks of Arkansas or Mississippi than like their brothers to the south. In fact Val had heard one young service hand reply when asked if he was from Louisiana, "No, sir. I'm from north Louisiana." The south Louisianans had a pleasing, lilting way of speaking the patois that came out of the bayous, but only the older ones sounded like Justin Wilson. Even so, they could make the most common story funny and enjoyable. In the forties and fifties, so the story went, the government had made a concerted effort to stamp out the French language and the Cajun culture, and had succeeded to the extent that most of the young people spoke only English. Val couldn't help but believe that the government had done the people of Louisiana and the world a huge disservice. He had known and been around Cajuns all his life, of course, but he had never gotten to know them the way he had since working with them every day.

Getting off on the wrong foot with Buck had made his initial footing on the rig an iffy proposition. Nobody believed he would be there very long, and some of the stupider hands on the roustabout crew felt even freer than they normally would have to ride and haze him. He recognized what was happening and went along with most of it in the name of being a good sport. Some of the verbal taunts got to be a little much, but he let them roll off his back, as well. Near the end of the first week, he woke up and slipped his foot into a sock to find somebody had deposited a wad of semen into it. To say he had read widely would have been a huge understatement, but in all his reading, he had never come across an incident of someone's masturbating into someone else's sock. The act seemed to have sadistic overtones—not to mention the revulsion felt when one's toes encountered someone else's cold ejaculate. Turning the other cheek didn't really seem the thing to do in this instance. Practical jokes were to be expected, but this was over that line. He could have talked to somebody, but, given his status on the rig, he couldn't see his being listened to seriously. He also didn't want the story to get out of the room if he could avoid it. There were only four people in the room, and he figured the odds were good that all of the other three were complicit in the prank. He found a plastic pail in the bathroom and filled it with chilled water from a fountain in the hall. He divided the contents of the pail among the three pair of boots and slipped back into bed. The first of his bunkmates up actually put a foot into one of the boots and created a near riot with his screaming and threats. That was the first time anyone had ever promised to kick Val's ass. Apparently the strictures against fighting offshore were firm enough to keep anyone from doing it there. All the ass kicking was going to take place when they made it back to shore. There was no doubt in his mind that the least of these could kick his ass without much trouble. He wasn't quite sure how one went about doing it or how one defended himself from it. At any rate, though he worried about it quite a bit on the way in, everybody went home without bringing it up again. The hazing didn't stop, but it slowed quite a bit, and the tone got less vicious. He was to find out that there was generally a lot less ass kicking in the oilfield than was talked about.

He could tell that the jobs he got early on were the ones nobody else wanted to do. He willed himself not to mind it and gradually came even to enjoy it, if not the specific jobs then at least the fact that he could not be made to protest, or even grouse. The jobs got easier and better, and he found himself growing stronger and tougher. He began to take pride in what he did and to find a connection between working with one's body and hands and a feeling of satisfaction, even peace. He mentally filed the subject of the interaction between manual labor and contentedness as a future area of study. As a member of the roustabout crew, Val technically worked for Max Davis, a sort of mechanical superintendent and electrician who doubled as the crane operator, but he hardly ever saw him, and it was a month before he spoke to him.

It was a rainy day, and all the work that the roustabout crew had underway involved painting in the open air. Rather than put themselves in the way of someone who might give them a job to do indoors, the whole roustabout crew plus some contract laborers, welders and the like, were holed up in the mechanical storeroom, a large room with shelves and work benches and pieces of shop equipment here and there. The mood was merry for who, being paid by the hour, doesn't enjoy being paid for doing nothing. The stories and the bullshit had petered out around ten o'clock, and somebody had suggested the vise grip game. A vise grip is a hand tool that looks something like a regular pair of pliers except that the handle that fits in one's palm is a tube with a knurled screw fitted into its base. The other handle is actually two handles, one riding inside the other. Used for its intended purpose, you put whatever you want to manipulate in the toothed mouth at the business end—a frozen nut, say—and squeeze. You will feel the bottom handle go past a detent, and the vise grip will be locked onto the nut. It is a really useful device, and it comes in sizes from very small to nobody's got hands that big. If you adjust the screw in the upper tube far enough clockwise, the mouth of the device will close on itself, and if you squeeze it past the detent in that position, the vise grip will lock on itself. To open it requires that you push the inside handle on the other side out against the outside part, thereby taking it over the detent in the opposite direction. If you then turn the screw a little further to the right, it will operate the same way but require significantly more squeezing force to get it past the detent. In the game someone puts the vise grip screw at a nominal setting, squeezes it shut, opens it, and passes the tool to the next person. After everybody has had a try, the screw is tightened slightly and passed around again. Usually the vise grip will make a couple of rounds before people start dropping out, unable to muster the hand strength needed to get it closed. On this particular day, it was on its first round, and Val could not get it closed. He, and probably everyone else present, had known that he was not very strong, but not to get the vise grip closed on the easiest setting betrayed a lack of strength, in their minds, beyond weakness. "How does a person no stronger than that manage to zip up his pants?" It was so embarrassing that nobody said anything—no gibes, no comments, just a general looking away, as if by ignoring him, Val would cease to exist. He was prepared for, even expected, derision. He didn't expect it to hurt. He had never felt like this before. If he left, it would seem like he was running away, but staying meant being subjected to the rest of the game, which went another round or two before other people started dropping out.

Finally one of the service hands, a welder from Mississippi named Deats, closed the vise grips on a setting no one else could match. Campbell found him an interesting fellow. He was only about five foot six, but he weighed over two hundred pounds and wasn't fat. (The "how much do you weigh" game had happened earlier in the morning. Campbell had come in at one hundred sixty-two, coveralls, boots and all, much to the amusement of the other hands.) Deats was a balding redhead of thirty-five or so, and thick, ginger-colored hair covered his arms and spilled out the neck of his shirt, front and back. His forearms were huge, and his hands and wrists were thick. Earlier that morning he had regaled the group with the story of a wrestling match he had attended in Mobile. The bad guy had thrown Deats's favorite into the stands behind him and then jumped over the ropes after him. As the wrestler passed him, Deats hit him flush on the jaw, rendering him unconscious. Deats had escaped in the confusion. He was presently haranguing the group about what a bunch of pussies they were. Campbell had read about *vaunting* many times, but this was the first time he had ever witnessed it. He got a vivid mental picture of one of the Greek heroes, Little Ajax, maybe, holding a pair of vise grips aloft and shouting down at the Trojans running away.

Max had entered the room without anyone's having noticed, so no one knew how long he had been there when he cleared his throat. "Mrs. Deats got herself a real brute, didn't she?" he said. The odd thing was that *brute* is exactly the word Campbell had in mind. Max seemed to fill up the room, and people to his back and sides started filtering out the door. "Is that a pair of vise grips you have there, Deats?" Deats handed over the tool along with some inane words having to do with why he happened to have them in a space where no useful work was taking place. Max looked at the vise grips like he had never seen any before. He took the knurled screw daintily between right forefinger and thumb and cranked it down a full turn then handed the tool back to Deats. Strong as he was, it had been all Deats could do to get the vise grips closed at the previous setting. He and everyone else in the room knew that nobody, with one hand, could get those vise grips closed. For one thing the handles were so far apart at that setting a normal hand couldn't span the handles far enough back to get any leverage. He handed them back to Max. He didn't say anything, but the dare was implicit. Max held the tool loosely, looking into Deats's eyes. "How about you get to doing something that the company's paying you for, Deats," Max said, dropping the tool onto a nearby workbench as he did so. He held Deats's eyes with his own while the smaller man backed out of the door. Then he swung and caught Campbell's eyes, pinning him in place. By this time he and Val were the only ones in the room. "Were you part of that game?" he said.

Campbell said, "Not for very long."

Max's eyes squinted in what Campbell would come to recognize as a smile. "A lot of this has to do with what God gave you, but people like Deats think they themselves are responsible." He took Campbell's right hand in a huge paw and turned it over to look at the palm. "You're getting some calluses. Just keep working hard, and you'll come along. When you're not doing something else, opening and closing a pair of vise grips is a good way to strengthen the forearms. Body builders and such as that don't think about the forearms, but look at a successful baseball player."

Val hadn't seen him this close since his first day on the rig. Buck was big in a different way. Max was like standing close to a bear or a gorilla. He was Val's height, but he must have weighed twice as much. He didn't have a neck, and his shoulders melded into arms with no evident transition. He seemed to be pretty much the same thickness from top to bottom, and the irony was that he was calling someone else "brute." But his eyes were something different. Val saw in them some of what he had hoped to see in Buck's: intelligence, wisdom, even warmth. Max made as if to leave, and Campbell said, "Do you mind if I ask you something?" When Max turned to him, Val noticed something else: he moved like a much lighter person.

Max didn't say anything.

"Why didn't you try to close the vise grips?"

"Because I didn't have to. I could see in his eyes that he knew I could do it. I had made my point. You don't humiliate a man just to look bigger yourself."

Val continued to look at Max speculatively. Max looked back. Holding Val's gaze, he moved to the workbench and picked up the vise grips in his left hand, positioning them so as to grip the handles with his right. Even with his huge hand, he could only get the first joints of the first three fingers around the handle, and he closed the tool without apparent effort. Then he handed them to Campbell and said, "Now you open them up." Campbell ended up putting the top handle in a vise and hitting the bottom handle with a twelve pound sledge hammer. He got the tool open, but it was unusable after that.

Following the day in the mechanical room, Campbell began to see Max more and more often. Mostly he would show up where Val was working and offer criticism or a better way to do things. Val had taken a lot of science in undergraduate school and engineering courses in later years. His excuse had been so he could understand carbon dating and all the other technology that was increasingly being brought to bear in his chosen field, but the real reason he took them was he was just curious about the way things worked. Max had a lock on the way things worked, but he would be at a frequent loss when it came to finding ways to explain them. Their discussions taught both men a lot. Max was easily as intelligent as any professor Val had ever had. He had studied the world around him and had amassed a store of wisdom that would only be considered homespun because of the words and terms he used to divulge it. Val came to see Max as a mentor and a valued resource; and, for his part, Max obviously thought a lot of Campbell, and he seemed at pains to protect him from Buck. Once when Val was painting a landing on the outside of the platform, Max joined him. He said, "You see that little sheen on the water when you shake your brush over it? Buck will send you to the bank immediately if he knows you put it there. Buck's got a notion that the chemicals we use aren't good for the Gulf. I can help you in a lot of areas, but God himself couldn't protect you if you polluted the water around the Hector."

Over the weeks and months that Val was on the roustabout crew, he came to know Max better and better. In fact, he thought, Val probably knew him better than any other person alive. Max was an insightful observer of other people, but he didn't really relate to them in any visceral or even intellectual way. Campbell thought he was the most solitary person he had ever met, but it wasn't because he was shy or afraid of human contact; he just didn't see what possible value it could have.

Val once asked him if his parents were outsized people, like himself.

"I never knew my father, but my mother said he was bigger than she was. I don't think she cared too much for him though, so the picture may not be entirely accurate. Mother was my size, maybe a little larger. She looked a lot like me, too, so you can imagine how her life went. She was the kind of woman who, when people saw her headed for the lady's restroom, would try to redirect her to the men's. She had a seamstress and tailor shop in Yazoo, the little town in Mississippi where we lived. She could turn out a quilt you wouldn't believe in a day. She did this kind of art that was wall hangings made of fabric and other bits and pieces. They were truly beautiful, and they let you see what she was like on the inside. People tried to get her to turn them out in commercial quantities, but she was happy with the money she made from the shop, and anyway, she said, 'How could something that was done to make money be a true expression of anything?' I was the light of her life, and I loved her more than I can say."

Max and his mother lived on a small acreage in the country outside Yazoo and kept goats and chickens and a few dogs. Max was aware of being different. "I've looked like this since I was born and been about this size since I was thirteen." But it took him most of his growing-up years before he actually began to feel different. He said his mother would never tell him the full story or where it had happened, but apparently her father had been executed for killing a man. She said if he had been a normal-sized man, he would have been let go because it was self-defense; but, she said, the jury convicted him out of their own fear of him. She was devastated, and from his earliest days, she taught Max self-control and to never, under any circumstances, hit or otherwise injure another person.

Val asked him if that was true. "Have you never hit another person?"

"She died when I was fifteen. I'm not even sure what from. Almost the last thing she did was to get me to swear that I never would, and I never have and won't ever. I've had to *restrain* people from time to time, hold them immobile until they calmed down. It's kind of scary when you think of it, really. I could pop a normal man's head like a gourd just by squeezing it with one hand. In a different time and place, I might have been a warrior and a valuable member of society. But to tell you the truth, I like the no-hitting part. I'm a peaceful man at heart."

Val said it was strange that no one ever picked him to play football, and Max just said, "Yeah. Well, that would involve hitting another person, wouldn't it?"

Max had never been married, and he claimed to be asexual. He said he missed his mother and wouldn't mind living with someone that was like her, but then, he said, "There's not likely to be another like her, is there?" He spent his time off rebuilding boats at a little yard he owned in Gulfport, and he considered himself a happy person. "Beyond happy," he said.

When Val said that didn't seem very likely, given Max's perpetually morose mien, Max said, "You're just like everyone else. You judge by what's on the outside. Appearance is a liar. Appearance only tells you whatever that person wants you to know. I happen to have a very active, rich, and satisfying internal life. You're a nice-looking young man, and I'm sure there are any number of people who are attracted to you because of the way you look; but that's not why I started talking to you. I engaged with you because of what's going on inside you, and you like me for the same reason, whether you know it or not."

Val said, "Well, I know there are good and bad people, but it seems to me that before you can really judge which they are, you've got to observe them over a period of time and watch their actions."

"That's certainly part of it. You can tell a lot by their actions over time, but you have so much more than that to go by. Your body and your mind know so much more than you do. You only have to listen to them."

"But my body and my mind is all I've got. I am my body and my mind."

"No. You're not, and I'll prove it to you. Do you control your own breathing?"

"Yes."

"No, you don't. Your body breathes on its own. You can will it to stop breathing, and it will, for a while. As soon as you go unconscious, it goes right on breathing again. Your heart is controlled by something other than you or your mind. Short of stabbing it or shooting it, there is no way you can get it to stop."

"I've heard of yogis that can stop their heartbeats."

"Yeah? Well, I don't know any yogis, but I can tell you right now that that's a load of horseshit. The body has its own intelligence, and the mind is an amazing thing, but it's not supernatural. It's just a wonderful machine that's available for our use. Whatever 'I' is, it is not our bodies or our minds. The I is like a temporary resident that gets to make use of the premises for a limited period of time. What most people who think they are their bodies and their minds don't realize is exactly how much of a gift they are."

"Are you saying you believe in the afterlife?"

"I don't *believe* in anything. I know that my body is like its own little universe. It's like all these diverse cells decided that it would be easier to survive if they all got together and made themselves look like one of something else. 'We'll put ourselves together and call ourselves a man. We set up the lines of communication so everyone gets his share of the booty.' What they didn't plan on was somehow the organism would get the idea that he was more than a collection of cells and start making their lives miserable by not listening to them and making random choices. What I'm telling you is, if you learn to listen to the cells of your body, you can be just as happy as I am. Tell me something: do you know what it feels like to take a shit?"

"Um, yes."

"No. To really *feel* it. Next time you take a shit, stop reading the paper or your novel for a while and think about what your body is feeling as that turd slides out. You'll be amazed at how good that feeling really is. The same goes for taking a piss. Forget about that little burn at first and just listen to that part of your body rejoicing. You obviously feel sorry for me because I don't have sex, but I feel sorry for you because you think that is the only reward the body gets. Who was it said that thing about the sensation of sex being fleeting and the position ridiculous? He was right. Plus your body can't do it just anytime it feels like it. If it involves another person, then the odds against its happening go out of sight. Messy and potentially demeaning, sex has poor odds for making your life happy. Nobody I know has ever had to make monthly payments for something he dropped down a toilet bowl years before. And relieving yourself is only the grossest example of the rewards that can be had for listening to your body. Your body will tell you what to eat, when, and how much. It will tell you when to lie down and give you hours of blissful sleep. It will smell its various parts and droppings and make adjustments accordingly. It will keep you healthy and feeling good, and all you have to do is listen and enjoy."

"I'm not sure how I listen to something that can't speak."

"Now you're being purposely dense. Do you think that a dog picks up words when he sniffs another dog's butt? He probably doesn't even know what information he's just received, but it's likely to come in real handy. If you walk into a restaurant and pick up a smell you don't like, turn around and find another place to eat. If you get an odd feeling when you put something in your mouth, spit it out. The most obvious example is pain. If something hurts, stop doing it. Those are things even someone dense as you can understand, but our bodies operate on far subtler levels as well, and all the time. We started out talking about judging people. Next time you meet someone, don't think about him. Just keep your mouth shut and be around him. Watching his actions is part of it but not all, by any means. After a while you will get an idea of what that person is really like, and that impression will be far more accurate than anything your conscious mind could have come up with."

Campbell had heard of people having and reading each other's auras. One of his mother's suitors was a guy from California that had a whole ethos built out of auras and ethers, but Campbell could tell that even he didn't really believe it. What Max was talking about was different, though. He seemed to lump the mind in with the body, and he wasn't talking about spirits or other worlds. What he was talking about seemed very much rooted in this world. At another time Val asked Max if he had ever had any religious training, and Max said, "As far as I know, I've never set foot in any church or spoken about religion with anyone. I talked about some things with Mama, but what I think about things I pretty much came up with on my own hook. There might be something to religion, but I've never felt a need for whatever it is." Val knew Max was capable of putting him on if he wanted to, but he seemed sincere.

It turned out he was right about going to the bathroom.

When Val found out he was going to be a roughneck, Max was the one he went to talk to. Max told him, "Buck has a thing about you. I've told him you aren't what he thinks you are, but he's angry at himself, and he's trying to deflect it at you. He'll wake up one day and be even angrier at himself, but until then you are in his sights. While you were down here, I could shield you to a certain extent; but when you move to the floor, you're going to be in front of him a lot more. All I can tell you is Buck is not who you see now, and the real Buck is well worth having as a friend. You have worked with me for more than seven months now, and in that time I've watched you fill out and toughen up and become a man. The floor is going to require you to grow more and become even tougher. Here you worked at your own pace; up there you have to keep up with the big boys, and it's louder, faster, and a lot scarier. Hang in there. Nub will watch out for you, but you have to watch out for yourself. There's a reason so many roughnecks are missing body parts. Mr. Brown is an ally. He can be a valuable resource for information and even aid. You can trust him."

Val said, "It's not like I'm going to be in another place. I'll still see you all the time."

Max's eyes squinted slightly. "I'll become almost invisible when you're working up there, but, remember, I'll always be here if you need me."

CHAPTER XI

Working Floors

As a roustabout on the Hector, Val's workday had begun at seven o'clock in the morning and ended at six o'clock in the evening with a half hour off for lunch. Since the well the rig was drilling could never go unattended, and the roughnecks were the attendants, the roughneck's duties were split into two twelve-hour periods. Some rigs had two tours starting and ending at seven o'clock, but it was Buck's preference to divide the hours of darkness between the tours, and the Hector's schedule was twelve to twelve; daylight tour started at noon, and morning tour at midnight. Each tour had two regular meals (breakfast and lunch for days and lunch and supper for mornings) and had a meal in a sack delivered to the rig floor between times. If the situation was such that they could come to the dining hall during their tour, they could do so, but most opted not to because they didn't want to be the ones not at their station if something went wrong.

Val ate a hot lunch for the first time aboard the Hector (the roustabouts got a sack lunch at noon) and then walked up the stairs to the drill floor for the first time as a roughneck.

Everyone aboard the Hector was a member of the team, and the company went to pains to push that message. Even so, there was a natural segregation between roustabout and roughneck. The roustabouts were the people on the line, the ones doing the dirty work. The roughnecks were the skill players, the ones who handled the ball and made the scores. The roughneck's job was high pressure and dangerous, and he was paid accordingly. Val was feeling equal parts of pride and fear as his boots rang on the grating of the steps. He took in the floor as he reached it. The drive bushing was down on the rotary table and turning, and most of the kelly was showing above it, so they weren't on the verge of making a connection right now. Val relaxed slightly. He knew as much as he could learn about the operations on the floor from asking questions at a distance, but understanding what was going on and doing it were two different things. There was a man washing mud off the floor with a hose, so he surmised that a connection had just been made. The hole they were drilling wasn't very deep yet, so the drilling would be pretty fast, and another connection might need to be made within minutes. As his eyes swung past the drawworks and the brake, he saw Nub motioning to him from the doorway of the driller's shack, a small structure just outside the base of the derrick. Nub was a short, rounded man with a slight hunch. Nub smiled as he walked up, and Val immediately felt better.

"Right on time," Nub said. "Only right on time on the drill floor is fifteen minutes before the hour. We get up here a little ahead of time, so we can check in with our opposite numbers and pick up where they leave off."

Val nodded that he understood.

"OK," he said, "how does it feel to be up here in the light?"

"It feels good," said Val, noticing for the first time that it was a beautiful day.

"What do they call you?"

"Well, it sort of depends on who 'they' is. 'Val' is good for me."

"OK, 'Val' it is. It's been a long time since I've had to teach somebody from scratch, but I think I can remember all the steps. To tell you the truth, I'm sort of looking forward to it. You've already heard a lot about safety. I think we get some kind of break on insurance the more programs on safety we have. But Buck and me have other reasons for making sure everyone operates safe, and it's not just our own asses we're worried about. We will not tolerate unsafe behavior. Until you know" — and here Nub was using the oilfield *know*, meaning knowing everything there was to know about drilling a well offshore — "if something happens and you don't know what to do, don't do anything. You got that?"

Val nodded.

"Just freeze and wait till I tell you what to do," he said, and paused looking for confirmation.

"This here's Stanley Ketch," Nub said and stepped backward out of the doorway to indicate an even smaller and older man seated on a stool with a cup of coffee in his hand. "Stanley's our daylight motorman. Onshore a motorman is the one that takes care of the engines and such, but out here it just means he is the senior floor hand. He'll be looking over you, along with me, and helping you learn the ropes."

Val got the distinct impression that Stanley wasn't all that keen on helping out.

"That's Stanley's son Roon out there washing up. They're both from Victoria, Texas. The other floor hand, Herman Trahan, is normally on days with us, but he's working the worm's corner on mornings, and that's the position you'll be training for. We'll train you up at all the floor positions on days, and then, when we think you're ready, you'll swap places with Herman and go to work for Odell Sipko on the morning tour. The reason we're training you on days is because it's less dangerous than at night. The truth is you can lose a body part or your life in the blink of an eye on any tour."

Val wanted to ask the obvious question but didn't feel comfortable doing so. It didn't matter though because Nub answered it without being asked.

"No, I didn't lose it on a drilling rig, though the cathead's good for getting arms. I was working building the Corpus

Christi Bay Bridge, and the arm got between two fifty-four-inch H beams. It wasn't no contest. The reason I was working there is because my wife thought drilling was too dangerous. I came back to the oilfield after that, and she never says anything, but I think that she expects sooner or later I won't show up. You look around, and you'll see missing fingers and toes; but I'll tell you this: nobody who had his mind on what he was doing and was working with a crew that had their minds on the job ever lost anything. A quick young feller like you might even get bored with what he was doing, but the snake is laying there all the time; and the second you take your eye off him, he'll bite. Keep your mind on what you're doing as long as you're on the floor, and you'll walk off tour every evening whole. That's a promise."

Nub walked Val out of the shack and onto the floor.

"We're going to take it slow and easy," Nub said. "We're standing on the drill floor," he said, indicating an area of about forty feet by forty feet delineated by the corners of the derrick that stretched overhead. "That's the drawworks—that big, blue thing across the back of the floor. It's really just a big winch, but we got to call it something different so people won't think we're sailors." Stanley Ketch snorted his approval of the joke, but Val's face was blank. "They don't call them big winches on ships, either. They call them windlasses, or they turn them sideways and call them capstans. We have capstans too, but we call them catheads. That's the things that's turning on either end of the drawworks. Buck says everybody calls things something different, so people who aren't in the know won't know what they're talking about. If it was up to him, they'd all be winches.

"Anyway, the drawworks reels in the drilling line or lets it out thereby raising that big yellow traveling block up there or letting it down. The block is generally attached to something else that we want to raise or lower like the drill string alone or the drill string and the swivel and kelly, what it's attached to right now." Val made as if to tell him that he already knew a lot of this, but Nub held up his hand and said, "Later on you can tell me what it is you think you know, but for right now you just listen to me. Or was you going to ask a question?" Val shook his head.

As they spoke the kelly and bushing continued to turn, and the drawworks squeaked as the automatic driller released and reset the brake. The kelly and the swivel gradually approached floor level as the bit made headway at the bottom of the hole. Nub went on in the same vein explaining the basic functions of the rig while keeping an eye on the progress of the kelly. When there was about four feet of the kelly showing, he broke off and walked to the driller's position at the brake. He put his hand along the side of the control panel, and Val heard a distant horn.

"Until you get comfortable, Joe Tom is going to be helping us make connections."

Joe Tom was Joe Tom Wright, the daylight derrickman and the only black man on the rig. Some said the only black man in the oilfield. Val had seen him from time to time, but the two had never spoken. He came onto the floor and joined Val in the worm's corner. He was shorter than Val, maybe five ten or eleven, and perfectly proportioned. Val had never seen anyone who moved so economically and gracefully. It was as if he were moving to music no one else could hear.

"Do you know what it is you're going to do?" He had a voice like Grandma's molasses and spoke with a little bit of a Texas accent.

Val said, "I've been told, but I'm not sure I know."

He showed a beautiful set of teeth. "Just remember nobody is going to jump you about being too careful. Don't make no sudden moves."

Joe Tom put his hand on the set of tongs that were hanging from the derrick just in front of them. "We make and break pipe connections just like a plumber. Our pipes are bigger than his, so our wrenches are bigger, too. You put the jaws up against the pipe, latch 'em, then pull in with this hand and back with the other to make 'em bite. Try it."

Val fumbled with the latching mechanism and pushed at the tong. The tong was five feet or so in length and weighed about two hundred pounds. It resisted being moved at first and, once it began to move, resisted being stopped. His boots slipped on the wet floor, and his body slid under the tool. He only avoided landing on the floor by hanging onto the tongs. As he scrambled back up, he was acutely aware of the derisive looks of the other two floor hands. His heartbeat was already thumping in his ears, and he was out of breath.

"Settle down, now; settle down." Joe Tom used exactly the same voice he might on a skittish horse. "You're not going to get hurt, and you're not going to fuck anything up. That's why I'm here. Now, breathe."

Val felt like he had been underwater.

Joe Tom said, "It's all in knowing what you want to do ahead of time. You have to have the tongs moving in the direction you want them before you need them there."

The kelly was going up, and Stanley and Roon each had a hand on handles of the slips, a heavy steel implement about two feet tall with three attached segments. The inside of the segments had teeth that fitted the drill pipe, and the outsides were tapered and slick. When the bottom of the kelly came by, they dropped the slips into the tapered hole in the rotary table. Nub dropped the drill string slightly, and the slips bit on the top length of drill pipe about ten inches below the upset. The whole weight of the drill string shifted to the rotary table, and the derrick gave off small sounds of relief. Joe Tom had Val's hands on the set of tongs and was pushing them toward the well center. Roon already had the other set of tongs on the upset of the pipe, and Val and Joe Tom pushed his set onto the bottom of the kelly. "Make 'em bite," said Joe Tom, pushing hard with his left hand and pulling with the right. Val would have fallen if Joe Tom hadn't been there, not holding him up so much as just being an immovable object in the direction he would have fallen. The rotary table turned a few times, and the pin of the kelly was out of the pipe, and the two floor hands were swinging the bottom of the kelly out in the direction of the V-door. A joint of pipe Val hadn't noticed before was sticking out of the mousehole just in front of the rotary table, and they guided the pin of the kelly into its box. Joe Tom had Val's hands back on his tongs and was guiding them to the drill pipe sticking up in the rotary table, then pushing them down below the upset. "Latch 'em; don't make 'em bite yet," Joe Tom said, and then did it for him. Val heard a noise like a motor scooter overhead, and the kelly spun itself into the joint in the mousehole. Kelly and drill pipe went up into the air, and, as the pin of the joint cleared the mousehole, Roon grabbed the joint and rode it, feet sliding on the muddy floor, back to well center. Stanley had latched the other set of tongs on the joint in the rotary table, and both were riding loosely. Roon guided the bottom of the new joint into the one in the rotary table. Val heard the motor scooter sound again (an air motor at the bottom of the swivel), and the joint on the kelly spun into the joint in the rotary table. "Make 'em bite," Joe Tom said, and then made the bottom tongs bite. Stanley and Roon pulled the slips as Nub picked up on the string. As the kelly came back down, they set the slips again to torque up on the kelly–drill pipe connection. The slips were pulled, and the kelly continued its downward travel. The pins on the kelly drive bushing located the holes on the rotary table, the rotary table started turning to the right, and they were back to drilling.

The whole operation had taken two minutes or less, and Val felt like he had already done a day's work. He had watched connections being made from the quarters numerous times, and it had seemed a much more relaxed operation. He was bathed in sweat, his knees felt weak, his shoulders and arms ached from effort, and he had a cut on his right hand because he hadn't remembered to put that glove on. Everything was heavy and slick and moving so fast. "Lord God," he said under his breath, "are you sure this is where I'm meant to be?" Joe Tom patted him on the back, thrust a hose into his hand, and told him to wash off the floor before he walked away.

Roon took the hose away from him, and Nub grabbed his hand to look at the cut. Apparently he didn't think it worthy of attention because he dropped the hand while saying, "That's why we always wear gloves." And Val was left to contemplate the next tornado.

He was to find the experience similar with each new function learned. No matter how simple a job seemed at the outset, there was a period, sometimes as long as two or three weeks, during which he felt totally incompetent. Much later Nub would tell him, "You can work derricks, or derricks can work you." He found the same was true for all the jobs. There was a timing and a rhythm to each one that, once found, geometrically reduced the physical effort required.

Thankfully, they didn't make a trip that first week, so he was able to practice his moves on connections. The moves on a trip were very similar but they had to be made faster, and they came right on top of one another. The rig is very vulnerable during a trip, and no one is breathing easy until the bit is back on bottom and turning to the right. For that reason the pressure is on to make the trip as smooth and easy as possible.

Another thing that made the trip more difficult was that Joe Tom was in the derrick and not standing behind him. Apparently his presence had had a dampening effect on the Ketch Kids because in his absence they felt free to offer verbal input—constant, abusive, and at high volume. Very little of it was helpful, and Val eventually came to the conclusion that it wasn't meant to be. What it did do was make him even more nervous and prone to misstep. If they weren't having at him, they were complaining to Nub and whoever else could hear that he was never going to make it. Nub would shut them up from time to time, but Val sometimes wondered if even he didn't have his doubts. Stanley and Roon had decided they didn't like Val, and when they weren't making connections or trips, they completely ignored him. He listened to the conversations they had between themselves from time to time though, and he never heard any he would have wanted to join. He found himself trying to imagine their home life and not really being able to pin it down. It involved a lot of beer (and, in Roon's case, other things including Quaaludes and marijuana), shifting conjugal relationships (it was hard to keep track of who was fucking whom), and shooting guns off the front porch (apparently they lived in the country). They managed to forestall his competency to some degree, but the day did arrive when he could hold his own in the worm's corner. The constant chatter didn't stop, but the subject matter shifted, and the volume dropped. He endured similar periods of abuse when he learned to tail pipe, work the make-up tongs, and throw the chain, but once he had shown the ability to master the first position, they couldn't seem to really get their hearts into it. He came to realize their attitudes had come from a sense of being one up on him and not wanting to lose the advantage, though he would have been perfectly willing to cede them whatever feeling they wanted.

Buck was a different matter, however. He hadn't shown up on the floor at all until it became evident that Val had mastered the worm's corner; then he started showing up all too often. Val had misjudged the degree of Buck's animosity. Buck apparently hated him, or at least what he thought he represented. At first he would just stand in the doorway of the driller's shack and glare at him and Nub. When that wasn't unsettling enough, he started offering opinions about the quality of work, all of which "could have been done better by a competent team of fourth graders." Val felt he could have defused the situation by informing Buck of a few things, but he wasn't sure at this stage if Buck would even listen. Besides, he had wanted to accomplish this without any tricks or subplots. He was also starting to lose a little of his respect for Buck. He felt he understood Buck and his motivations, but he thought that a true hero — and Buck was a certified hero — should be able to overcome his baser instincts in the face of overwhelming evidence to the contrary.

For his part becoming competent in all the positions and feeling at home on the rig floor was its own reward. Never had he felt a sense of accomplishment like this! He particularly enjoyed throwing the chain. The task was equal parts of skill and art and involved perfect timing between the thrower and the driller. Once he and Nub got in sync there was a small joy with each successful throw that built, like an ion engine, to an elation that lasted hours after a trip. Never had he felt so alive, so at home in his own body, such a sense of being able to tackle anything. Food tasted better. He went to sleep as soon as his head hit the pillow and woke up refreshed just before the alarm went off. He marveled as he washed his body and felt the hard muscles. In the mirror now he saw a man, vagueness and baby fat replaced with a steady gaze and hard edges. He wondered how office workers had managed to sell the story that they were superior to those who made a living by using their bodies in the out of doors. Surely, any woman who had slept with both could put the lie to that.

When he had first come aboard the rig, most of the men treated him as if he were a virgin. It was almost as if they wanted him to be deficient in all areas of life, like it would be confirmation of all the things they thought about "his kind." Since he didn't say anything to deny it, it became a factoid, and a lot of the discourse around and about him alluded to it. In fact, making love was one area in which he came to the rig far ahead of just about anyone else; and he owed it all to his grandmother, she being the main reason for his dedicated run at an advanced degree.

His grandmother had been the main parental figure in his life, his mother being present but with other interests and concerns. His grandmother was French—not Cajun French, but French from France French. According to her, her mother had been a courtesan and that—and growing up in a relatively permissive society—left her with views on life in general and sexuality in particular more than slightly apart from the American mainstream. For her, sex for a young person was a given. She would no more have attempted to keep Val from having sex than she would have tried to still the wind. When she noticed the first signs of puberty on his bed sheets, she took him to her "boudoir" and sat him down.

"You know I love America," she said. Actually he hadn't known, but he considered it useful information. "I love American people. I love their energy and their optimism. But Americans have strange ideas about making love. There is a feeling, I think it comes from the Irish—but no, the English are repressed as well. Well, it wasn't from any warm country. They think sex is a bad thing, and people who engage in it are bad people. Sex is a very hard thing not to engage in, so naturally they do engage in it anyway, but, because they believe it to be bad, they can't do it openly and enjoy it. They have to sneak around and feel guilty about it.

"Unfortunately, people who don't believe as they do are not free to go and have sex just nilly-nilly, either, because we must live here among them and not be shunned. You have attained *puberté*. (It sounds so much nicer than puberty, don't you think?) You are becoming a young man now, and things are going to start seeming very different to you (Well, maybe not all that different — you have always been a little precocious. Remember that little girl, Marie, who lived in the rent house behind us? You were like little rabbits, you two. I think the father gave up his job, and they moved just to get her away from you. Ah, well…Good luck to him keeping that one away from boys.) At any rate, what was a pleasant thing then is going to seem like something that must be done, now, and I want to make sure you don't do something that will keep you from becoming a *professeur*, yes?"

"Yes, but, Mère, when do you have sex?" The question was not entirely innocent. He took an opening to ask something he had wondered about before. His mother saw men from time to time, and he had assumed weekend trips out of town entailed sex, but to his knowledge his grandmother had had no contact with men since he had been capable of thought.

She had obviously been prepared for the question. "I am the only one I have sex with these years since your grandfather died. It is not my preference, but I have not wanted to do anything that might put your chances under a cloud." She didn't play those cards very often, but when she did, they counted. "All I ask of you is when you feel you must have sex with someone else or die, you must come and tell me. Yes?"

That day did come, when he was fifteen or sixteen. There was a girl in his algebra class in the next row, one seat forward, who had really shapely legs. It had gotten to the point that when he walked out of class, all he could remember was those legs. That day she had dropped her pencil, and they both reached for it at the same time. He acted as if he had missed and grabbed her about halfway up the forearm. Her eyes came up, and she actually shuddered. He took that for a good sign. What he expected his grandmother to do was give him some condoms, but she surprised him.

"There is no good thing that can come from your fucking any young girl in Hickory Flat, or anywhere else for that matter. There is only one possible positive outcome, and it is extremely unlikely that any young girl is going to enjoy the experience and then forget about it. The only logical thing for you to do is spend these formative years with older women — women who are not likely to fall in love and who have in mind no more than the pleasant passage of time with a comely member of the opposite gender. I have identified just such a woman here and have discussed the possibility of her hiring you to help out around the house."

Val objected, but she said, "Shu...shu...shush. I would not select for you a pig or a dried-up old prune. This woman is in her prime, but she has married someone older and rich, and she is slowly going crazy for the lack of young male companionship. She doesn't know it however, so whatever happens, you must allow her to initiate it." So saying she marched him three blocks over to where there were two giant new houses taking up a full block. She introduced him to the lady of one of the houses, who did seem way too young for the role. The lady invited his grandmother and him into the house for tea. During the course of their discussion, which involved all the tasks around the house that needed doing and which, apparently, could not be handled by the ancient gardener working in the back yard or the handyman working on the lights in the foyer, the lady could not stop looking at Val and smiling, and Val himself totally forgot about the girl in algebra.

He helped out around that house until he left for college, and that was the last procuring his grandmother had to do for him. It turned out, if you knew what you were looking for, there were many, many houses that needed a helping hand. The ladies of those houses were invariably enthusiastic and accommodating, and not infrequently generous. He learned many things while performing his tasks and, by the time he went offshore, reckoned himself an expert in the arts of lovemaking though he had never had a date or learned how to dance.

When he got his degree, he promised to indulge in all the things he had denied himself, girlfriends being topmost on that list. Ironically, being fully equipped and able to take care of any situation in the bedroom, he found himself without the knowledge of how to get in the front door. At university he had turned away so many girls he had a reputation for being gay, and he had found that perception useful. After university he had moved into an apartment complex in Metairie that was full of good-looking women, and he thought that maybe the gay reputation had preceded him. Either that or he looked like a serial killer. The more likely explanation was that he had become so used to not being welcoming that something in the way he looked or moved warned them off. It was his intention to date eligible young women: to observe and interact, learn the proper ways of presenting himself, and eventually pick one to live with the rest of his life. He didn't think in those terms, of course. His intention had been formed unconsciously, as a result of and reaction to the way he himself was raised. No one who knew him would think of him as unconventional, neither would he think so of himself, but he was, and for that reason, he very much desired the cloak of conventionality.

He was sure his grandmother would have been able to help him out, but their communication had become somewhat strained since he had elected to come offshore and become a "tradesman." He regretted that, but he was aware that for too long he had been the focus of her life, and he had to allow her to get on with her own. She had wanted him to accept one of the university positions offered, preferably close. ("Rice seems like such a nice place, or even Vanderbilt.") In his youth he had taken her care and attention as a matter of course, but, since breaking loose, he realized it would be extremely selfish of him to do other than fend for himself. He just wasn't sure that she was, indeed, getting on with her life. His mother, on the other hand, another theoretical source of life information, had been getting on with her own life as long as Val had known her. He didn't understand his mother and didn't really know much about her. Her relationship with Val was the elephant in the room when either two or all three were together, but they all ignored it. Val had long since decided that the way to keep from being hurt by his mother was to treat her the way she did him, brusquely and with resignation.

Val had picked up little things that gave him a vague, fairy-tale idea of how things came to be thus and, though he gave it no conscious credit, couldn't help adding and taking away little bits as they came along. His grandfather had been president of the very college where his mother now taught. He had become embroiled in a scandal involving state monies and solved the problem by ending his own life. In Val's fictional version of events, his death or its manner unhinged his mother, who had adored her father, and forever blighted any possible relationship with males. When she was in college, she desperately wanted a daughter and formed some type of union with one of her professors in order to create one. Bitterly disappointed when the girl came with male parts, she gave it an untenable name then threw herself into her studies in an attempt to forget she had ever given birth. Some ten years later, the desire for a daughter drove her to try again, this time with one of her colleagues, a Chinese math professor whom Val had actually met. He had been in love with and wanted to marry his mother, and it had begun to look as if his mother would let that happen, but the daughter they produced developed meningitis as an infant. The combination of his offspring's being female and defective was too much for the man, and he disappeared from their lives. Far from turning her back on the child, as had been her wont with babies, his mother not only accepted the poor little thing but welcomed her, treating her with a love and tenderness of which Val had considered her incapable. He loved Olivia too, and she seemed to take comfort in his presence, but there was no having a relationship with her, and, in any case, his mother kept him away out of some sort of protective instinct. If anything, the addition of a sibling drove his mother and him even further apart and his grandmother and him even closer together.

The irony of the situation—his being a student of social interaction but not knowing how to engage in it—did not escape him. He tried hanging around the pool, but the gaiety of the other residents and their obvious pleasure in being part of the group made him feel even more alone. The other males present seemed to exclude him almost consciously, and their verbalizations were forced and loud. One day when he had mistimed the washing and drying of clothes and was left in the laundry room for more than a short time, a pretty young woman whom he had seen around the complex asked him if he needed help. Instead of telling her that he had been washing his own clothes for many years, he asked her about different kinds of soap. Oddly, he thought, that was all the social skill that was required. Almost before you could say it, they were in her bed making love. "Making love" is what she called it. Val thought of it as masturbating with a partner. Pretty soon there was a stream of young women showing up at his door. Initially he felt an obligation to service them, but after a while it got to be too much of an imposition. It seemed like some sort of odd ritual, something they had to get out of the way. They worked very hard at having fun. There were body parts of a very high quality that he enjoyed playing with for a while, but there was precious little social interaction of the kind he was looking for. It was like, in looking for a drink of water, he had locked the valve in the open position, and instead of being sustained, he was drowning. When not answering the door was not enough, he moved into a single room in an old house downtown. He vowed to extra caution in the future.

CHAPTER XII

Joe Tom Wright

Val knew that the original intention had been to train him in the worm's corner and then shift him to the morning tour, but that isn't the way it turned out. Once he was fully proficient in the worm's corner, Nub set him to tailing pipe, then, when he knew what he was doing there, to throwing the chain. The result was that he spent nearly six months in a training slot. Val suspected the real reason for the change in direction was the fact that Nub liked him and just wanted him to be around. He could tell from Buck's comments that it didn't sit well with him, but somehow Nub resisted the pressure to move him to the other tour. Being on days was fine with Val, but there was a lot of time while drilling when what they were doing was busy work. Busy work always leads to discussion, of course, and much of the ongoing discussion was conducted by the Ketch Kids. They had become more open to his inclusion, but the topics remained the same, and once Val had made a mental list of the topics and the general directions taken, he felt he didn't stand to learn anything more and had nothing to add. That left Nub.

Nub was a really nice man, and Val had grown quite fond of him, but Nub had only three or four topics himself. There was a limit to how much he wanted to know about the Corpus Christi Bay Bridge and gigging flounders, and when he had heard every story at least twenty times, he figured he had gleaned as much as he could from them. The first time Nub sent him down in the platform to help Joe Tom mix drilling mud, he was grateful and doubtful in about equal amounts; mud didn't sound like something he wanted to have a lot to do with. The mud wasn't great, but he loved being around Joe Tom.

As he dropped onto the pump deck, Val saw Joe Tom in the mud room, where he had a couple of chemical sacks cut open and was slowly feeding the contents into a jet mixer. Joe Tom made him think of a leaf, and he cast around in his mind for why that should be so. Finally he remembered sitting in Audubon Park the previous autumn, watching the leaves fall from a big tree; he didn't know what kind. Over time it became apparent that the shape each leaf had attained by the time of death mattered. Most had been a little bit odd to begin with, and others had warped and twisted as they withered. The more symmetrical they were, the farther the wind carried them before they touched down, but only a few of them escaped the perimeter of the tree's outer branches. Then he caught sight of one breaking loose from very near the top of the tree. He could tell from the ground that it was well-formed, and it floated on the air like a perfectly made paper airplane. Slowly it fell, making large, lazy circles in the air, all the while being carried gently by the breeze. It dropped a full twenty feet farther from the tree than its closest sibling. The leaf had had no hand in its shape or its location on the tree, but of all the hundreds of leaves on the tree, it had been the one most favored. Did the other leaves stand in envy or admiration? Did that one leaf know itself closest to the model?

If Joe Tom knew himself a perfect specimen, you couldn't tell it. The Cheshire Cat smile appeared in the dark little room, and Val heard, "Ho, college boy, how you doin'?"

The derrickman was from Oklahoma, and the reason he didn't speak in a black dialect was because he hadn't grown up around other black people. Val had mistaken his accent for Texan at first, but listening to him over time, he began to pick up the differences.

Work around the mud pits was more leisurely than that around the floor. Only once was his help really needed, and that was when the well went through a short period of lost circulation. Then it was four hours of the most intense activity Val had ever seen. He and Joe Tom were racing up and down the six-foot stair to the mud pits with hundred-pound sacks of mica and barite. By the end of the four hours, mica flakes were flickering in the air around the pits and coating their lungs just like they did the well bore. Val was left light-headed and gasping for breath, and even Joe Tom had lost his smile and was slow to speak. But most of the time, the work was light and the conversation interesting. Joe Tom seemed open and inviting, and Val considered himself a skilled interviewer, but Val found the openness to be an illusion. It took months to get enough bits out of him to put together a cohesive story. Val found it fascinating and thought Joe Tom fit the classic Western hero profile — the Virginian, say — better than did Buck himself.

Joe Tom Wright was raised on a four-section ranch southeast of Hinton, Oklahoma. When he was born, his father was looking after it for the man owner, a doctor in Oklahoma City. The doctor spent his weekends at the ranch during hunting season, but, for the most part, Joe Tom and his father were there alone. Joe Tom's mother was a Cherokee who had gone back to the reservation to live with her family. His father thought he might be part Kiowa, but he never offered details and was generally circumspect about his life before Joe Tom. He never spoke of Joe Tom's mother and didn't seem to miss her, but he didn't seek female companionship anywhere else either. For his part Joe Tom didn't know he was missing anything, and he loved his life on the ranch. His father wasn't an educated man, but he knew everything he needed to about living life in the country. He was a skilled cowboy and horseman. They ran cattle and hunted. They had a huge garden that produced something nearly year-round, and they were usually putting something up or eating something that had been put up. Joe Tom was almost a wild child, and he ran in the woods and swam in the ponds and rode the horses. He generally lived in heaven, until the first day that a school bus from Hinton pulled up and waited for him to climb aboard.

He hadn't really been aware of an existence outside the two-mile square he called home, and it was a bit of a shock to discover there were a lot of people in the world (Hinton, pop. 1,853) and that most of them didn't look remotely like him. He was the only black child in school and was a bit of a celebrity for being so. He felt that if he had looked like his mother, he would have been discriminated against, but, as it was, he was always one of the most popular kids. He did OK with the books, but recess was really his best subject. Early on, he played sports but gravitated to rodeo, and he ended up winning state in bull riding his final two years. He went pro in bull riding out of high school and spent four and a half years traipsing from venue to venue. He said there was a reason most bull riders were little, wiry guys. Once he got his full growth, he spent most of the time injured. Part of the ethos of bull riding is riding hurt, but when he started having visions of becoming a crippled old man at a young age, he rethought the pro rodeo thing. About the time he moved home, the Oklahoma City surgeon who owned the place was shot and killed by his wife, and they found out that he had left the place to Joe Tom's dad. That was a heady feeling for a while, but it dawned on them that ownership carried with it responsibilities. The place wasn't big enough to pay for itself the way they had been using it. They could make some money raising cattle and breeding horses, but both those endeavors had ups and downs, and a down cycle would have left them vulnerable. Neither one of them had a taste for clearing some of the flat land in the south and growing wheat. If Joe Tom could get a job and cover taxes, utilities, and maintenance, they could feel comfortable, and that decision is how he came to be in the oilfield. He started on the little rigs around the west side of Oklahoma City and then went to the big rigs in the western part of the state. Roughnecking was good money, but they were dependent on it; so when the action moved to south Louisiana, he moved with it. The intention was to get a job offshore, so he could spend half his time on the place, but the move to south Louisiana put a hitch in the plans. He had heard the word *nigger* before but never applied to himself. He knew it was a trigger word for some, but it inspired no emotional response in him. When someone called him that, his usual reaction was to look at the speaker with compassion, as if saying, "I'm sorry you're such a dumbass." Usually that was the one response that the speaker couldn't stomach. The companies felt like they had to hire him when he applied, but they were obviously relieved when they could fire him for fighting. He never initiated a fight, but the white guy with whom he had fought always got to keep his job. He had been close to running out of companies to work for when Buck showed up. Since he had come to work for Buck, there had been no discrimination, and for that he was thankful; but the experience in south Louisiana had helped him to understand some of his father's ways. He could see how a Negro in the Deep South could — almost surely would — be an angry young man.

He had long since saved enough money to live full time in Oklahoma but had stayed out here partly from loyalty to Buck. Since he was able to be there every other week, the horse breeding was going well, and the price of beef was headed back up. He didn't talk about her a lot, but he had gone back and married a girl he had met when he was on the pro rodeo circuit. Val hadn't picked up enough hard information to conclude she was a Las Vegas showgirl, but somehow that was the impression he was left with. He had two little girls that he loved very much. They were beautiful things in the pictures he showed Val, and, if the mother hadn't been a showgirl, she must have looked like one. Every young man feels like he was bad between high school and marriage, but Val got the sense that Joe Tom was ashamed and a little bit plagued by some of the things he had done. He had undergone some kind of transformation while working on the rigs around Hinton, and one day when Val was probing him about it, he said, "I knew this guy, Jesus."

"You knew Jesus? Like, you were born again?" Somehow it didn't fit.

"No, no. I knew this guy. His name wasn't really Jesus, but that's what we called him when he wasn't around."

"Was he a preacher?"

"No, he wasn't a preacher. I don't know as I ever heard him say a single word that sounded like a preacher. He looked a little like Jesus. His hair was kind of long, and men weren't wearing long hair then, at least not men in central Oklahoma. We didn't call him Jesus because of the way he looked; it was because of the way he was: the way he moved and acted and talked. He was just so damned…kind. He was the best hand on the rig—the best hand I've ever seen. He worked daylight floors, but he could fill in anyplace on the rig and do the job the way it was supposed to be done. He's the one that taught me to work derricks. He said, 'If you can work derricks, you will never be out of a job.' Even the driller and the toolpusher got to where they leaned on him when they weren't quite certain what to do. He finally came to the attention of our drilling superintendent, a young guy who was an engineer that the company was trying to train up for management."

Val said, "You're losing me. You're saying this guy, Jesus, could have been a toolpusher and he voluntarily worked as a floor hand?"

"As a floor hand—and preferred it. In fact, he wouldn't accept any other job. The superintendent saw what a quality guy he was and kept after him to break out as a derrickman or even a driller. He just couldn't understand why, if he had the ability, a man wouldn't take on more responsibility and more money. (I should be able to think of the guy's real name, but, somehow, *Jesus* is all I can come up with.) Anyway, Jesus finally got tired of the superintendent's pestering him and decided to hang 'em up. Everybody was upset about it. The toolpusher offered to give him part of his check if he would stay. I wanted to go with him. I swear, what he had must have been very much like what Jesus had when those fishermen followed him. My father called it *medicine*. I was in the derrick when the superintendent brought out Jesus's final check. Jesus drove a pickup with a camper on it, and he was pulling one of those little Airstream trailers. The superintendent couldn't resist giving one last pitch. He was taking it harder than anybody because he wanted to upgrade his personnel. Anyway, while they were talking, two little kids ran out from behind the trailer, and they were the prettiest kids I've ever seen. I was up there watching them and trying to figure out if they were boys or girls, and their mother stepped out. She was dressed kind of like a hippie, but you could tell from the way she walked that what she was wearing wouldn't matter. Confident—you know what I mean? Nothing wasted. Nothing for show. Just bone-in graceful and sure. She put her hands on her hips and watched the kids. Then she looked at the rig, and her eyes swung up to me. It was like stepping out from the shade of a tree into the the sun. We were an easy hundred and fifty feet apart, and it was like she was on the monkey board with me."

"She was really good-looking, huh?"

"She was beautiful, but that wasn't the main thing she had going for her. I didn't want her; I wanted to be her child. I wanted to put my head on her chest and put my arms around her and close my eyes and stay there. I'll bet they weren't even married, Jesus and her. Did you ever read the book *Hondo* by Louis L'Amour?"

"I don't think so."

"Hondo is always with this dog, and everybody calls it his dog. Hondo tells them, 'He ain't my dog. We just run together.' Or something like that. I don't think the lady with Jesus was ever owned by anybody. When she looked away, all I could think of was this girl in Nevada I had walked away from because I didn't think she would ever make an obedient wife. I went back and found her, and it took a lot of walking and talking, but I finally got her to move to Oklahoma with me. I was right, though. She never did make an obedient wife.

"The superintendent told me he made a last pitch to get him to stay. When Jesus turned him down, he finally started to get a little glimmering that Jesus really was different. When he opened the back of the camper to put his check inside, the superintendent looked in. He said the camper was chock-full of toolboxes and cases and tools hung on racks. There were carpenter's tools and electrician's tools and all a mechanic would need to fix a car or probably anything else. The superintendent said that all he could think of while Jesus was pulling away was 'master of all trades.'

"Anyway, knowing Jesus changed the way my life was headed. Just knowing what a person could be made me want to be better. I don't know if I would have had a wife and kids now if I hadn't met him. I do know we're all happier than we would have been."

CHAPTER XIII

Morning Tour

Nub had taught Val how to fish and supplied him with the requisite equipment. He had developed the very pleasant habit of going down to the boat landing platform and fishing in the hours before going to work. He was often there when the company man, Mike Brown, came down for his daily exercise and climbed up and down one of the ropes used for swinging on and off boats. Most of the time, Brown would nod or say "good morning," but one morning after he had finished with the rope, he sat on the steps and seemed ready to engage.

Val said, "That seems like really good exercise."

"It is. It is," said Brown. "This and running in place is about all we have in the way of exercise for its sake. You guys get plenty in other ways, but we sedentary types have to make things up."

Val asked if Buck worked out, too.

"Not that I know of. If he doesn't, he doesn't need to. Except for his hair being grayer, he looks very much like the man I met nineteen years ago. I guess it's in the genes or something. Hell, you saw how he can move on your first day out here."

"Actually I didn't see it, but I can imagine it was very impressive."

"What is your discipline?"

The question came as a surprise — so much so that Val wasn't sure he had heard him right. The question could mean only one thing, but Val had never said anything to anyone about his academic life for fear that it would make them react to him differently. Val said, "What do you think it is?"

"It could be engineering. You seem to have some theoretical knowledge, and some applications, too, but I'm betting if it's engineering you don't have your degree yet."

"And if it isn't engineering?"

"Then I'm betting it's history or literature or something like that, and you have at least one advanced degree."

"What would explain the engineering knowledge?"

"No accounting for taste or curiosity. I have twenty-four hours of English and the university only required six."

"I told them I needed the engineering hours to keep up with the tools of the trade."

"And the trade is?"

"Anthropology."

"And you have a…?"

"PhD."

"Damn," said Brown. "I love being right. Where did you go to school?"

"My baccalaureate is from Auburn, but I did my graduate work at the University of Chicago." Val was visibly troubled. "I'd rather not have this become common knowledge."

"Well, I'm not going to tell anybody, but I doubt that there's a person out here who thinks you're a high school dropout. What are you doing out here? Studying us? Are you going to write a book about the Hector? Do you have a specialization?"

It occurred to Val that maybe that was what he was doing. "I don't think it will ever become an actual book. Maybe a part of one. An anthropologist has a lot of latitude. If you had to put a name to it, you could call me an ethnographer since I deal with people in the present."

"So your father isn't a big oil executive?"

"No. Not even close." Val was leaving a lot out, but he was reluctant to give up any information he didn't have to. He had become comfortable with his life and his role aboard the Hector. He knew subconsciously that it couldn't last forever, but he had put out of his mind the day that he would have to become an adult and take up a real life. This felt a lot like being flushed out, and he didn't want to be in the open, yet.

Brown asked him what he thought about working offshore, and Val felt a little easier.

"I like it. I like it a lot. I expected to like it. I weaned myself on Jack London and Joseph Conrad. Being at sea and becoming strong through physical work just seemed like something one should do. But, to tell you the truth, there were elements of it that I wasn't prepared for. Not outside, but inside. I mean, I expected—wanted—to change my outside, but I didn't reckon on it's affecting my inside."

Brown's stillness told Val that he hadn't lost him yet, but he was puzzled.

"I was—am—confident in academe. But the confidence I feel now is fuller—three dimensional. I feel an easiness…a relaxation that I've never felt before, like there aren't any dark places I need to stay away from, no doors that I'm afraid to enter."

Brown understood, as Val knew he would.

Brown said, "Your life would be a whole lot easier if you told Buck what you've just told me."

The sun was bouncing off the calm surface of the gulf as Val squinted up at Brown. The drilling engineer was a dark outline, and it was impossible to read his expression. Brown was obviously an intelligent and intuitive man. He had guessed a lot already. How much more did he know? It would be impossible to explain how he felt about Buck in a few words. It might be impossible to explain Buck's role in his life with any number of words. Could you admit to another person to having been obsessed with someone? What would

Brown think if he told him that Buck had been his hero from a very early age, an artificial father that he'd ginned up to fill the hole in his life that no one else ever spoke about? He had made Buck what he wanted him to be—an outsized paragon of strength and goodness. When he had started work on his dissertation, it had been with the idea of recording the genesis of a mythical hero. As he traveled around gathering stories and data, it became evident that there had actually been a person named Buck Burnet and, finally, that he was still alive and working. It had taken a while to process that knowledge and rearrange the premises of his thesis, but it wasn't until he was getting close to the end of his work that he began to toy with the idea of actually meeting, talking to, and even working for the man. He knew it was inevitable that the real man would be at odds with the myth, but he thought that would show itself as the real Buck's being smaller or less tough or less eloquent than the myth. This rejection of himself based totally on assumptions generated by his appearance was unexpected and in his mind betrayed a serious lack in Buck's personality. He wasn't yet able to separate his feelings from the facts and look at things the way Buck must have seen them. He didn't know now if he even wanted any longer to have the heart-to-heart with Buck that he had dreamed of. At any rate, telling Buck what he was would be letting Buck off the hook. If Buck was going to come around, he wanted it to be because he recognized Val as a contemporary and someone capable of succeeding in Buck's world.

"I wouldn't mind my life's being easier, but I don't want it so much that I'd let Buck cheat. There's plenty of evidence lying around that indicates he's been wrong about me. If he's capable of it, he needs to come to that knowledge on his own."

Brown stayed in the sun, and Val thought he heard a chuckle. The final sentence had spoken volumes to Brown, a man who had been studying relationships for years. He might as well have told him all the things he'd been thinking.

Brown said, "Buck is an exceptional man in a lot of ways, but he is, after all, just a man. We are all of us capable of being wrong and of letting our egos get wrapped up in our wrong-ness. I'm sure you've heard of the Gordian knot. Well, Buck is knotted up in his own emotions, and it's going to take some-one's slicing through it to get him out. I personally don't think it will ever happen."

Brown sat down on the platform next to Val, taking him-self out of the sun and indicating a feeling of closeness, even kinship. Val looked at Brown up close for the first time since the day on the boat, and he was struck by how rough his fea-tures were. He had heard some service hands refer to Brown as "Paladin." When he asked them about it, they said there had been a Western hero on old TV that they thought he looked like. It was hard to imagine a TV hero this ill-favored. His nose was large and oddly shaped, almost like an Idaho potato. His eyes were blue and twinkled from time to time, but they were a little too closely set. Val felt ashamed for staring and had to almost consciously tear his gaze away. Brown didn't seem to have noticed, indeed, seemed blithely unaware of his condi-tion. Both of them had forgotten about the rod that Val still held in his right hand, bait and hook in his left.

"Nub says you're fully qualified on the floor. I probably shouldn't tell you, but he says you're the best hand he's got. I asked him if he was going to move you to the morning tour, but he doesn't want to let you go. He's talking about qualifying you as a derrickman. That suggestion may be enough to make Buck's heart stop. Herman's been hanging around Buck, piss-ing about wanting to get back on days."

The two were sat facing the inside of the rig. Below them in the water were numerous fish of various species. Prominent were the buck-toothed sheepshead and a smattering of pom-pano. Brown asked him what he was fishing for. Val told him he was trying for the red snappers on the bottom, but he was having trouble getting his bait past the barracuda. Only then did Brown notice the long sliver of silver hanging around the outside of the pack.

"You might as well pack it in," said Brown. "There's no way you can get past him."

Val didn't hear what happened when Nub approached Buck about training him to be a derrickman, but Val was summarily assigned to morning tour at the beginning of the next hitch. If Buck's heart had stopped, it must have been temporarily, because he was his imperious self on the boat going out. Val had known the change was coming, but he was disappointed anyway. He liked working for Nub and being outdoors in the afternoon and evening hours and had grown comfortable in his routine.

He had been around the morning tour driller on several occasions but had yet to talk to him. Odell Sipko was what a Dickens character would be if Dickens had been born and raised in central Mississippi. He was a sullen man, morose almost, and his mien and the darkness of the hour created an ominous air. The late-evening chill, so welcome after a hard day of working in the sun, was unsettling and uncomfortable at the start of a tour. Val, with a sinking heart, watched Nub walk off the floor and turned to Sipko for instructions. He was to learn that Sipko didn't give instructions. Sipko expected everyone to know what to do at any given time and to that end remained totally silent and looked only at inanimate objects. When something went wrong, which happened frequently for the first few weeks because of small differences in the ways the two tours did things, Sipko brought the operation to a halt and leaned on the brake, looking at the floor until things were ready to go again. Sometimes it was easy to tell what was wrong. At other times Val, or another miscreant, would be left frantically trying this and that until he somehow remedied the situation. Sipko obviously didn't like Val, but he was also cool with everyone else. The morning tour derrickman didn't like Val, and he took every opportunity to show it was personal. He was average size, if thicker in the chest and neck than usual, but he had an odd, feral presence. His arms seemed a little bit longer than they needed to be, and his legs a little shorter. His name was Charlie Bates, and Val had learned that his father was the toolpusher of the crew that took over the Hector from Buck's every other week. Val had seen the elder Bates briefly several times during changeover, and he was a larger version of Charlie. True to his name, Charlie baited Val constantly, mostly about his not being competent on the floor. Charlie bragged that he could handle all the jobs on the floor at one time, and proceeded to prove it by making a connection all by himself. It was an impressive showing, and when it was over, Charlie looked at Val like he was inviting him to do something about it. Val was nonplussed. He wasn't going to try to make a connection by himself; he was one hundred percent sure he couldn't do it. If he was asking for a fight, Val wasn't going to do that either, though he was beginning to think that, sooner or later, it was going to happen. Val had become strong and confident, but he had never once engaged in fisticuffs or anything like it, and he didn't have an idea of what it took. He resolved to find a karate place and join when he got back to town, but before he got the chance, something happened that convinced him no amount of instruction would be enough.

It was a Monday night, the first night back out, and when they came on tour, Charlie seemed to be still hopped up on whatever he had been imbibing on his days off. It was a cold night in the middle of winter, and Charlie was bouncing around the floor like a pinball. About ten feet off the floor and circling its perimeter was a temporary structure made of two-inch pipe from which windbreaks hung like curtains. On this night the tarps were pulled back, and the pipes shone in the air like horizontal bars in a gym. Suddenly Charlie stripped all his clothes off down to his socks. Three things struck Val about the resulting vision. One: despite being almost totally bald, Charlie was covered with thick, dark hair. Two: Charlie had outsized forearms like Popeye, and Val immediately thought of what Max had told him. Three: between his legs was the largest set of male genitalia he had ever seen. Granted, he hadn't seen that many but these things seemed to hang almost halfway to his knees, and they flopped around obscenely. Without hesitation Charlie broke for the edge of the floor over the pipe racks and seemed to be going to jump out onto them, but, just as he cleared the handrail, his hands smacked on to the two-inch windbreak pipe, and his body arced up into the air. He swung almost horizontal, then his body came back the other way, and he swung into a perfect handstand— out of the light, in the air ten feet from the floor and nearly thirty from the pipe rack deck, all the while making a joyous noise somewhere between keening and groaning. He stayed there several seconds, balls hanging the wrong direction, then swung back and went into a series of giant circles, pipe bending in the direction of pull and threatening to give at any moment. Finally, he swung back and dropped lightly to the deck, put his clothes on, and went down to the mud pump room.

Val had seen the chest beating display of a mountain gorilla in films but never in person. After witnessing Charlie's little show, he had a lot more respect for the photographers who had held their ground while the displays were taking place. The display was meant to intimidate, and Charlie's had certainly had that effect on Val. He immediately shifted his strategy from one of preparing to fight him to one of avoiding fighting with him at all costs. The mountain gorilla display was usually sufficient, but if a fight did ensue, somebody died. Val was no longer under any illusions about whom that would be if he and Charlie came to blows. Sometime later Val would tell Buck that he stayed away from Charlie and why. Buck would say, "Yeah, well that's always been my preferred method of dealing with Neandertals."

The motorman on the morning tour was a Cajun from Dulac named Dubois (no apparent first name), a dark-skinned, pleasant sort of guy who talked mostly about food. Val once timed him while he talked about how to make a roux, to him the basis for all decent cuisine: thirty-six and a half minutes. Another favorite subject was sauce piquante. The other floor hand, Willard Cox, was from DeKalb County in Alabama (not DeKalb County in Georgia). Val had to ask for the spelling of DeKalb because when Cox said it, it sounded nothing like it looks. Cox was a natural storyteller with a penchant for making the worst of any situation. He was also unconsciously funny, and one of the few people Val met who could wring laughter from tragedy.

One memorable story had the teenaged Willard being sent to fetch the family milk cow from a pasture across the road and near the river about a mile away. It was Sunday afternoon, and all the relatives were at his parents' house. Dinner was over, and everyone else was lounging around on the front porch, letting things settle and talking about nothing in particular. Willard said he had actually thought about changing out of his Sunday go-to-meeting clothes, but he thought, "No, the ground is dry," and he could "stay in the lane." The cow, a Jersey with sloe eyes and a provocative manner, was right where he knew she'd be, chewing a cud and waiting to be taken back and milked. Willard cradled her head in his arms then ran his hands down her soft side. On a whim, being it was a nice warm day and no one was around, Willard decided to knock off a quick piece. He assumed the position, dropped his pants to his knees, lifted her tail to the side, and entered her, something he had apparently been doing on a regular basis. Only this time she reciprocated, unleashing a load of runny cow shit that covered him from belly button to toenails and filled his go-to-meeting pants. His description of trying to get back to the house without being seen was hilarious. He didn't make it, of course, and the story was still a Sunday afternoon favorite at the Cox house. Val was struck by the casualness with which he told the story, the assumption that everybody routinely fucked livestock.

It made him think of what Willard had said in answer to someone who was trying to get a rise out of him by offering conjectures about what his wife might be doing while he was offshore. "Two can't get in it, and one can't hurt it." If it mattered to you, and you had any doubts about your wife or girl-friend's faithfulness, offshore was not the place for you.

The major source of entertainment above decks late was listening to the marine radio. Somehow they could route it to the loudspeaker on the floor. You could only hear half the conversation, that of the person on land. There were a lot of people calling wives and a lot of "love you" and "miss you" and "when you comin' home," but one night a guy called to find out from his mother that his wife wasn't home. That news initiated a series of calls to kin and close friends and finally bars and nightclubs. The last friend he talked to rang off by saying, "OK, call me when you get to the dock, and I'll pick you up." The whole search took about an hour and a half and was the source of great amusement to the rest of the crew. It was one of the saddest things Val had ever heard.

Another morning about two o'clock, the crew had just finished making a connection when they heard a thump, like someone had launched a big sack of sand from the derrick and hit the main deck. A big flare in the middle distance to the west drew their attention away from the Hector. Another rig, almost identical to the Hector, was on fire. The well had come in on them, and the flames were shooting high into the sky. It was a windless, damp night, and a lot of the smoke didn't go up but seemed to linger around the rig. Sporadically you could see the rig and figures jumping into the water. Boats started coming from all directions, and you could tell they were trying to pick up the men in the water, but the smoke had to be hampering them, and they seemed to be getting in each other's ways. Eventually a Coast Guard cutter showed up and then three big oceangoing tugs. The tugs sprayed huge streams of water onto the rig, and the steam mixed with the smoke and further obscured the operations. One of the boats came to the Hector and let some men off then went back for more. Just after dawn the derrick laid itself over like it was tired, and shortly after that the rest of the substructure caved in. Val and the rest of the morning tour crew had to leave periodically and tend to the Hector's well, but they watched as much of the disaster as they could. Val was the designated person to go in at breakfast and try to pick up some details. There was an old man sitting at one of the tables with Buck and some others. The rig had been a Storm rig, and he had been the lead toolpusher on it since they pulled it out of the shipyard. He had been in bed asleep when it happened. He had headed for the rig floor, but the heat was already so intense on that side of the rig you couldn't even touch the door to the outside. He got out the door on the port side of the living quarters and was driven to the back by the heat. People were yelling and running, and he had to feel his way because of the smoke. He found himself trapped on a platform with some other people. He could tell there were boats down there, but they seemed to be running into each other. There were sirens and horns. The other people climbed down a rope from the platform, but he couldn't see what happened to them at the bottom. He didn't want to go down the rope because he couldn't swim. He was deathly afraid of the water. Finally the heat was so intense there was nothing for it but to slide down that rope. His worst fears were confirmed when the rope ran out and there wasn't any place to go. He was steady praying, and now it was just him and God. He held on as long as he could, and finally his hands and arms gave out. And then…"God picked me up by the scruff of my neck and set me down on that boat that brought me over here." He said he knew that was what happened because he didn't have a drop of water on him. He left after he told the story, and the people of the Hector stayed sitting in a somber silence. After what seemed like a long time, Buck said, "He may be wishing God had let him drop into the gulf when he realizes what happened and that he's responsible. Now you see why I'm such a hardass. I guarantee you that whatever happened built up over a period of time. I'll thank God if I make it through all my years and not have something like that happen to me."

Val wasn't really affected by it, but there was a new round of training sessions for all the rig supervisors, and all the drillers and derrickmen had to go back to the blowout school at Oklahoma University.

CHAPTER XIV

The Reckoning

The only good thing about working morning tour was that Buck had fewer opportunities to snipe at Val; but that luxury came at a relatively high price in terms of personal well-being. He couldn't get used to sleeping during the day and frequently ate supper without having been to bed. The most sleep he could get then was four or five hours. His performance on the job suffered, and he felt that by being physically slow and mentally distracted he was losing much of the ground gained in the previous year. By the end of each seven days on, he was so fatigued that he slept for most of the first day or two off. His sunny disposition evaporated, and he was grouchy and generally unfriendly. He was beginning not to like himself very much, and he was beginning not to like Buck a lot.

Evidence that he was losing his judgment came one evening after supper. He was tired and irritable, and Buck was sitting at the next table over with his back to him, in on the perpetual game of bourré. The people at Val's table were on one of their favorite subjects: what Val's home life must be like. Usually there was speculation about how many homes his family must have and where they were and how many servants and so forth, but tonight they were on his schooling and what sort of subjects he might be taking. Suddenly, loud enough so Buck could hear, he said, "I don't know why you're ragging on me. I'm not even the most educated man on the rig." Buck didn't move so much as a hair, but Mike Brown, who was sitting at the table with Buck, moved over, so he could see Val around Buck. The conversation at Val's table stopped, each of the participants absorbed in trying to figure out what Val meant. They knew by now that, when Val said something, he knew it to be true and could demonstrate it. Val himself was slightly abashed, surprised that he had blurted it out. Best educated might have been an arguable point, but the most educated man on the rig was Buck Burnet, the holder of more than three hundred college credit hours, amassed over a twenty-year period at various junior colleges in south Louisiana and Mississippi. Only Buck knew why he felt the need for so much knowledge, and only Buck knew why he didn't advertise it; but Val knew clearly if he had wanted it out, he would have put it out himself. Mike Brown's face showed curiosity, but Buck's stillness spoke volumes. Val began to regret having said it, and the silence hung in the air like a real thing. Finally one of the other hands said, "That's right, Mike has a master's degree." That broke the tension, and everyone went back to what he was doing. Val started breathing again, and he realized he was going to have to get off morning tour, one way or another.

It all came to a head during a trip one morning. Sipko needed to go to the bathroom, and Buck was spelling him on the brake. The trip wasn't going well, and Val knew it was mostly because of him. He couldn't quite get the tongs in the right place in time, and occasionally it took two tries to stab the pipe. Sipko never said anything, whatever he thought, but Buck was a different kind of rig runner. Buck started by riding him the way he normally did, but the criticism gradually got harsher and more personal. Val began to suspect that Sipko hadn't really needed to take a shit—that Buck was up here by design. Val tried to let it all go by, but some of the barbs were beginning to snag him. The more Buck yelled, the harder it got to keep up; and the more he messed up, the more Buck yelled. For the first time since childhood, Val started to tear up, and the shame of crying in front of the others made him angry. Buck said, "Is the baby boy crying? Where's your big shot father now, pussy? Are you going to run crying to him?"

In total, unthinking reaction, Val leaped over the tongs and rushed over to get in Buck's face. Buck's reaction was almost comic in its surprise. Val said something, but nobody could hear what it was. They heard Buck say, "What did you say?" Everybody heard Val's reply very clearly. "I said, I don't have a father, you dumb son of a bitch. I'm a bastard, just like you."

The rig came to a standstill, and the only sound was the exhaust from the engines down in the platform. The other hands were standing with mouths open, waiting for Buck to make a grease spot of Val. Val was still in front of Buck but wishing mightily he wasn't. It was the first time in his life that he had ever challenged anyone physically, and he'd chosen Buck Burnet, of all people. He knew very well what Buck was capable of. The heat of the moment had passed quickly, and he now felt a chill. For his part Buck was still looking at Val, but his mind was on a loop. The words *bastard* and *father* kept replacing each other. He didn't think he had just been called a bastard. He thought he had just been told he was a bastard, and somehow that resonated with him and kept his brain from engaging with his body. All the tension drained from Val, and suddenly all he could think of was getting some sleep. He stepped away from Buck and walked to the edge of the floor. When he turned, Buck was still in the same position. Val thought, "Oh, what the hell," and started down the V-door stairs to take a shower.

Mike Brown stepped into Buck's office and realized that he had never seen the shades on Buck's window drawn before. There were no lights on, and Buck was lying on his back on the bed. Brown sat in Buck's chair and waited.

"I really fucked this one up, didn't I?"

"That is probably a valid assessment."

"I would say, 'Why didn't you tell me?' But you did tell me, didn't you?"

"I tried."

"Do you know him? Do you know what he is? What he's after?" Without waiting for an answer, Buck went on. "He said I was a bastard, but he wasn't just calling me a name. I get the feeling he knows more about me than I do, and that I am, in fact, a bastard."

Brown resisted saying that he had heard that from other people.

"You know what the good thing about that is? That means that I didn't kill my father. If you don't have a father, you can't be guilty of fratricide. I was always afraid that I had done something like that, and that was why I couldn't remember. What's he going to do?"

"He's sleeping now, but I think he has every intention of taking the first means of egress."

"That'd be a damn shame. It's not like I couldn't see how good he was. His being good only made me hate him more. Perverse."

"Perverse," echoed Brown.

"You know, my past has tried to come back to me a few times. It was all there, in a box like Pandora's, trying to get out, and every time it happened, I would sit on it—hold it down. It hasn't happened so much lately. I've been lying here trying to let it come back, but it's like trying to remember a dream that you've left just that little bit too long. But something tells me that whatever is in there can't be good. I have to tell you that I like my life. My conscious mind is perfectly sanguine with the whole born-at-fourteen story. So, do you know him? What do you know about him?"

"Not a lot, really. I know he feels let down by you in some way. I know he knows a lot about you. He's a PhD anthropologist, and he can't be long out of school. He got his last degree from the University of Chicago, but I think he's from somewhere in the western part of south Louisiana. He's obviously intelligent and seems to be a nice guy. He's nonconfrontational but has a way of making his point. I've heard he's complained of having trouble getting dates."

"Do you think he's gay?"

"I don't have any reason to think that. Anyway, it seemed to be girls he wasn't getting dates with."

"I just find that a little hard to believe. I know women that would literally eat him."

"I think his problem is meeting them. He spent so much time on his schooling that he never really talked to them."

"How hard can talking to a woman be?"

"Says the guy who's never approached a woman in his life."

"That's ridiculous."

"What about that girl in the church in Houma you told me about?"

"That was different. There was no way in hell that girl was going to talk to me."

"Did you ever try? Did you ever once even look her in the eye when she walked by?"

"Her parents were with her every Sunday. You could tell just by looking at them that they weren't going to stand for any oilfield trash being with their daughter."

"Yeah," said Brown, "that could very well be true. In fact, it's almost certainly true. But we're never going to know for sure, are we? By the way, how did you come to be in that church, anyway? You didn't see her walk in there one Sunday and follow her in, and then come back every Sunday after that just to look at her, did you?"

Buck said, "Why don't you take him down to the Mouse's Ear? Any of the girls there will talk to him for the price of a drink, and he doesn't even have to know it's a whorehouse."

Actually, Mike thought, that's not a bad idea. Most of the women at the Mouse's Ear were college girls, and all of them were interesting to talk to. He realized that, without saying it, Buck and he had entered into an agreement to do whatever it took to keep Val Campbell as a member of the crew. The Mouse's Ear could be just the thing. A person could easily go there and have drinks and leave not knowing that drinks weren't the main source of revenue. The girls were conversant on a variety of subjects, and quite a few of their customers paid for just that.

Mike said, "Why don't *you* take him to the Mouse's Ear?"

"I don't think he's in a mood to have a drink with me."

"That's probably true. Sandra is at her parents with the kids, and I don't have to be in Austin until Thursday. I might be able to take a night off and drop by the old Mouse's Ear."

"Just remember that what you're there for doesn't require spending time with Miz Catherine or, for that matter, any of the girls."

The next morning Val was on the first JetRanger headed for Venice, and, just as the helicopter was about to lift off, Buck got on. There were three seats in the back, but another person could not have squeezed into the one between them. Val had cooled off some from the day before, but he still didn't feel the need to converse with the man who had been trying to make his life hell. As soon as they gained altitude and the noise abated somewhat, Buck leaned over.

"I know you don't want to talk to me, and I can't say that I blame you." Buck had to speak loudly to be heard. "I couldn't let you leave without telling you that I'm sorry for the way I've been acting. I have a blind spot, and you fit into it perfectly. I want you to come back out to the rig and work. I know you're not out here for life, but I want you to come back for as long as it takes you to accomplish whatever it is you came for. Everyone I normally listen to likes you and considers you an exceptional young man. For my part I want to get to know you without having myself in the way. You don't owe me a thing, but I would consider it a personal favor if you showed up next hitch." With that Buck settled back into his seat and turned his attention to what was outside the window.

Val sat looking forward and reran Buck's words several times. Gradually he became aware of a warm spot in his neck just under the nape. The warmth grew until it had suffused his whole body. He recognized the feeling as happiness and wondered how long it had been since he last felt it. He didn't miss the irony in the situation, but it didn't surprise him either. Buck's revelation took longer and was harder to come by than he had imagined, but it just might be the sweeter for that. He knew that once you were on Buck's good list, there was almost no way to get off. He finished the ride basking in the glow. After he retrieved his bag, he stood outside the wash of the propeller, waiting for Buck, so he could tell him he would be back, but the copter lifted off without discharging Buck. He had gotten aboard for the sole reason of talking to Val.

Val took the St. Charles trolley to the edge of the Quarter and hoofed it south from there. Mike Brown had given him the address of the Mouse's Ear without telling him the name of it or what it was, but as soon as he saw the outside, he recognized it. He had been to the outside of it before. He had eaten in Andre's on the other side and even been in the courtyard between the two but hadn't been inside the Mouse's Ear. At the time he hadn't known why he was so reluctant to enter, but now he knew it was for this: so he could walk in the front door and not be spotted for the guy who had been asking so many questions about Buck Burnet. He knew all about the Mouse's Ear, of course, and about Buck's association with it. He also knew a considerable amount about the proprietress, Catherine Moynihan, and her assistant manager cum bartender, Tom Coleman. Even though he had been eager for information about Buck, he had never approached either one. Now, he could walk into the Mouse's Ear without any explanation or dissembling, which he proceeded to do with a light heart. When he got inside, he wondered if maybe another reason for not going in earlier was he had been afraid of liking it too much. A guy could spend a lot of time in here. It was nothing like the bars farther north in the Quarter. It had a much softer, more genteel feel. The women at the tables could have been the daughters or even the young wives of the men they were with, and the talk was at a low level and pleasant. Mike Brown was already there and sitting at a table with a woman who seemed too young to be "Miz Catherine" but who must have been. She was striking, and Val liked her immediately. As he approached their table, he was wondering what Brown might have been telling her about him. They took his smile for pleasure at meeting them, but it was there at least as much because of what he was thinking.

Val knew of her proclivity for young men and wasn't surprised that, whenever Mike would try to get young girls to the table, Catherine would wave them off. Brown was famously monogamous, but Val could see that he had anticipated spending more time with Miz Catherine alone. Catherine couldn't keep her eyes off Val and shamelessly plied him with wine and hors d'oeuvres. Val wouldn't have been surprised if at some point she had looked at him, fluttered her eyelashes, and said, "Why don't you come up sometime and see me." It wasn't all camp, though. She was an intelligent and entertaining woman and extremely artful with peeks and light touches. By the time he followed her up to her room, he was beyond ready.

As soon as Val and Catherine left, there was a flurry of activity at the bar. When Brown got there, he saw that two of the girls were drawing a grid of sixty squares on a sheet of letter paper. Then they started selling the squares for ten dollars apiece. It took Brown a while to figure out that the squares represented minutes in the hour. The winner was the square of the minute when Catherine and Val showed back up: Catherine presumably purring, and Val licking his wounds. Brown noticed that the only minutes that were selling were in the early part of the hour. He waited until there were no more comers then bought the final thirty minutes for fifty dollars. When thirty minutes had passed, he was looking like a genius. When the next thirty minutes passed, the hilarity was beginning to turn to wonder. Everybody agreed that this had never happened before. It was decided to shift the bets to the second hour, but at the end of that hour, the bettors all got their money back. Four and a half hours into it, at around three o'clock in the morning, the phone behind the bar rang, and Tom came away from it saying, "They want breakfast and coffee." Mike Brown went back to his hotel, and Tom Coleman locked up after the last customer.

Buck was reading the morning paper and drinking coffee in the courtyard when Catherine came down. "Good afternoon, bright eyes," he said, then added, "Catherine, are you all right?" The Catherine he knew never—never—appeared in public looking less than stunning. This Catherine had made an attempt at fixing up, but she had missed the mark. There were whole strands of hair out of place, her face was blotchy, and her eyes were red and underscored with bags. She had obviously not spent any time picking out the gown she was wearing, and her shoes were definitely bedroom slippers.

"If you mean am I going to die any time soon, the answer is no. The truth is I wish dying were an option."

"Did that kid hurt you?"

"That's so sweet." She said this in a way that indicated she didn't really think it was sweet—macho and dumb, maybe, but not sweet.

"What would you do if he had hurt me? Beat him up?"

Buck realized that his good friend, the hardened, cynical madam, had been crying and was still perilously close to tears. He felt sympathy but was at a total loss as to what to say.

"Hurt me? Hurt me?" She dabbed at her eyes with a large handkerchief she had tucked in a sleeve. "He gave me the best night's loving I've ever had. That's what he did to me."

Buck was confused on every level his mind was capable of.

"You fucking men! You fucking men!"

Buck didn't feel taking the heat for an entire gender was fair, but fortunately he held his tongue.

"I know men. I know men. I know them for the venal, posturing, craven animals that they are. I've built my life on that knowledge. I was happy with my life. I have the power. I have everything I needed. Then, all of a sudden, one person comes along—one beautiful, strong, gentle person—and the whole world is turned upside down. If there's one, there had to have been others. How could you know they existed? What would have been the clue?"

She sat, staring at something on the other side of the courtyard. Buck waited, still not sure of what to say. He went back over what he had heard. Val and Catherine had gone up to her room last evening and, apparently, spent the night together. But the "person" she was talking about didn't match up with the Val he knew. Could Val's innocence alone be what had so affected her?

"That boy, by the way, was no virgin last night, and he certainly isn't this morning. Most men—yesterday I would have said all men—don't have any idea of the concept of making love. They reach a climax as soon as they possibly can and congratulate themselves because the woman made sounds like she had been satisfied. Then they lie there in their arrogance and stupidity and expect to be thanked, or even praised. If the woman was lucky, the guy was good-looking or smart or charming enough for her to have gotten ahead of the game in her mind. If he wasn't, she's left with no illusions about what she just endured, and there's not a lot in the sex act itself that offers solace."

She went quiet again, and Buck was hoping he wasn't expected to say something. It didn't sound like the sort of thing he could agree with for the sake of being agreeable. She seemed more reflective than upset, now, and he took that to be a good thing. Looking at her face in repose, he realized she was older than he had thought—older, but somehow more appealing.

"That's why I never have a long-term relationship. I fuck them in my mind until reality starts to intrude, then I send them back to mama. I just lick the icing off, so to speak."

Buck supposed that the images conjured up by that last sentence were different for the two of them, but he realized that what she said about herself was true. He had thought that her fickleness meant she was more like a man than most women. They had their times together, he and Catherine, and they were good; but they always seemed to end before he was ready.

"That's how I maintain control. I always leave them wanting more. That's the way I stay ahead of the game. Men can hurt you in several ways, but they can't hurt you if they can't catch you."

This was a Catherine he had never seen—that he hadn't even been aware existed. There were long spaces between sentences now. She seemed to be reaching deep inside herself and far into the past.

"I've never been hurt physically, but I think that was just the luck of the draw. Well, I guess I have you to thank for that these last years. New Orleans would be a dangerous place for a woman in my position if she didn't have someone like you, close."

Her eyes focused on Buck, and she looked over his face as if she hadn't seen it before.

"Buck, you're the best. I play the tough broad, but I've always known you were behind me. You're more sensitive than anyone would imagine, but your main value lies in your being a paragon of manhood. The man every man wants to be, and the man every woman wants. I've come to love you more than I've ever loved any other man, but your very maleness has kept me from being 'in love' with you. You are my protector. You are my guardian angel. You are the father and brother I didn't have. But you were the best of a bad lot, at least until now."

Buck was beginning to feel very sad. He realized that he had failed her and, by extension, every woman, in some way, and the sad part was he couldn't figure out why or how.

"Val Campbell. I guess most women start out thinking, hoping they are going to meet a Val Campbell. I gave that up early on. I decided he didn't exist—not based on the examples I had seen. I let myself turn cynical and hard, and I became the one who dealt out the pain. I have always told myself that the women I've seen in the salons and the shops were dumb and oppressed, going about their dull, deluded lives while I was living the high life and fucking their stupid husbands. But, you know, at least some of those women are genuinely happy, knowing they are going home to a Val Campbell. What must they think of me, those women? You know, they probably don't even think of me. What reason would they have to look at another woman in a mall and admire her, or envy her, or, God in heaven, pity her. They are treasured. They are listened to. They are partners, equals, in a loving relationship. They have no reason to think others are any different. I wonder if any of them realize how lucky they are."

This wasn't the first time that Buck had begun to tire of hearing the name Val Campbell. OK, he was educated. He got that he was intelligent and self-made. He was a good-looking guy, and everybody seemed to like him. But when it came to satisfying a woman, Buck would take a backseat to no man. Well, he wouldn't have before. If anyone knew about such things, it would be Catherine. But what she was talking about went way beyond having a bigger dick or being able to fuck eight times in a night. For one scary moment, he felt like he had said that out loud, but no, she wasn't drawn back in horror. She was still looking at Buck in that motherly way.

"You're perfectly adequate, Buck."

Oh, no. Maybe he had said it out loud.

"Val's not the man you are from a physical or even sexual standpoint." When she chuckled, he realized she had just been reading his mind. "When a woman makes love to you or to any man like you, she has to be going on how exceptional you are. You know, she's telling herself, 'This is the biggest or the strongest or the hairiest (or whatever her particular fetish) man I've ever fucked.' The oddness and variety of our tastes are common to both sexes. It's easy for a woman to get a fantasy going by looking at you. But what I'm telling you is that that fantasy is a crucial thing. Remember that girl Julie from Texas with the big tits? She didn't have a clue about how to please a trick, but it was all right because most men got off on those tits. That's why after lovemaking sometimes you feel a little depressed. Because what was actually happening didn't match what was going on in your mind. Well, you're the big-time lover because most women seduce themselves with your image ahead of time."

Well, that was just totally untrue, there. Buck knew himself to be a gentle and considerate lover.

"No, you're not."

"What?"

"You're not a particularly great lover. Like I said, you're the best of a bad lot."

Damn. He was sure he hadn't said that out loud. She was right about the mind thing, though. The girl from Texas she was talking about was so passive he could have been fucking a mannequin. Her tits were more than big, though; they were truly beautiful. And, if he told himself the truth, he had seen the odd bit of disappointment in a woman's eye here and there.

"When Val Campbell followed me to the room last night, he was as horny as any man I've ever been with. Yet, before he climaxed once, I had been there twice. I hadn't even seen his penis until shortly before the second time. His brain was in control of his dick! He knew how to touch and where and when. He knew what to say and when not to talk. Every once in a while, you get a guy that works at it. He's read something in one of those pornographic men's magazines, and he wants you to think he's a sensitive and caring lover. This wasn't like that. There was no work or artifice involved. It was as natural as stepping into a warm river and letting it carry you to places you've never been. It was like a racehorse must feel when the right jockey takes the reins. After the first session, we talked. I asked him where he learned all that. He said the only learning required was how to tap into what was already there. He said his grandmother was mostly responsible for the way he is. He said she was father and mother to him. He said she put him onto frustrated married women as soon as he reached puberty as a way of keeping him out of trouble. Two climaxes is a sort of record for me, but I wasn't finished. I lost count—for both of us. I think I just passed out after a while and had the purest, most dreamless sleep I've ever had."

She went really quiet after that.

Buck rethought what he knew about Val. What Catherine was talking about wasn't just a kid with a knack. Somehow Buck understood her. Buck was what he was. It wasn't in him to be the sort of lover Val was. He could see how Val would be better for a woman, but he, Buck, couldn't get there. What she was describing was a lover who was a woman with a dick. If anyone said that about Val in Buck's hearing, Buck would squash him like a bug because the comment would undoubtedly be derogatory, but the concept wasn't derogatory on its own. Who wouldn't rather have a woman for a lover? Who wouldn't rather have someone who really cared about you? Who wouldn't rather have someone who placed your well-being above his or her own? Buck felt like he had discovered a rare species deep in a primeval forest, and his first thought was to understand it, so he could better protect it. Val Campbell was going to require some study.

"When I woke up, I felt like I was in heaven. I had no tension, no worries. Then I looked over, and there he was, sitting at the window, drinking coffee, and watching the seagulls playing in the wind. He looked like a little boy, and the difference in that picture and the one from last night was like a fist that grabbed my heart and gave it a twist. It was God's way of showing me what could have been — two what-could-have-beens. He could have been my soul mate. He could have been my child, too. Either one would have made my current life seem like a shell."

It was too sad. Buck still had no words, but he knew what she meant and knew the same to be true of himself. His life looked a lot better than it was. Then Buck committed one of the kindest and most spontaneous acts of his life. He rose and picked her up, robe and all, and sat back down with her on his lap. She put her face in his neck and cried until she was cried out.

She whispered, "I wish to God I had never heard of Val Campbell."

CHAPTER XV

Mike Brown

Mike Brown's take on New Orleans differed from Buck's in a number of ways, he thought because of the difference in their vantage points. Buck was a denizen; through the years he had become part of the lore himself. As such he was entitled to criticize the city. Mike, on the other hand, was a tourist — not a first-time, don't-know-where-to-get-a-beignet tourist, but a tourist, nonetheless. He was still allowed to be amazed and amused by the variety and ingenuity of the hustlers, the quality of music available on every corner, and the near-constant stream of odd and interesting people. Famously, there is good food to be had in New Orleans, some of it, though not very much, in the French Quarter. Andre's in Buck's building and the Bon Ton were Mike's favorites, and both were in the unlighted periphery of the Quarter. The food quality degraded and the price inflated the closer you were to the intersection of Bourbon and Orleans. The French Quarter is the symbol of the city and what gives it its wicked reputation, but another New Orleans lies outside the Quarter in the numerous little neighborhoods. New Orleans is surrounded by

Cajuns and, outside of them, rednecks, and here, in the deepest of the Deep South, the people speak…Brooklynese. Brown only ran across real New Orleanians when he wound up in some eddy of downtown, a sandwich shop or the like, but when he did, it was like being among a group of extras for *The Godfather*. Brown had never been part of a neighborhood, and he envied locals their ease and familiarity with each other and their pure enjoyment of intercourse.

He was in such a shop right now listening to the owner berate everyone who came in, as he had Mike. He was a big, Irish-looking guy with a deep, loud voice. It was midmorning, and he was still in the process of opening up. Most of the traffic was food deliverymen and secretaries buying bagels for the surrounding offices. He obviously knew everyone, and he seemed to be performing a little bit for Brown. When he delivered an especially good zinger, he would look around to see if Mike appreciated it. Brown was killing time. He was here attending a convention of the International Association of Drilling Contractors. When he had told Campbell he would be in town, Val insisted that they meet for lunch one day, and this was the designated day. He had left the hotel early, acting like he was headed for the convention center, and then hopped across Poydras and into the business district. He had stumbled across this shop hidden away in the bottom of one of the office buildings. He was about a block off St. Charles, where he planned to catch a trolley. Val had asked if he had ever been to the zoo. Mike told him he had taken his kids to the aquarium, but he didn't even know New Orleans had a zoo. "Well," Val had said, "it's no San Diego, but it's a pretty good zoo, and the weather should be fine." They had agreed to meet at the seal pond at eleven. Mike figured a fifteen-minute trolley ride and fifteen minutes to find the seal pond. With a cushion it was time to leave.

The zoo turned out not to be where Mike thought it was, just off St. Charles, and he used up his time cushion finding a cab and getting down to Magazine. Once inside the zoo, it took longer than fifteen minutes to find the seal pond. Museums and zoos seem to feel constrained to make their maps more artistic than useful. Val was there, watching the seals.

Mike was struck, as he had been on the first day, by how good-looking Val was. The face had been subtly reshaped and no longer verged on the feminine. The body was now filled out and athletic. He stood leaning against a big rock, looking for all the world like a model ready for a photo shoot. Mike felt a swell of paternal pride and momentarily pitied the sire who would never be able to feel it for himself.

"Look at this young guy right here," Val said. "He's the reason I like to come here. Look at that face and tell me that seals don't think."

The mammal of the moment was a handsome fellow, too. He was treading water and looking up with big, expressive eyes. He looked at Mike, then, sure he had his attention, swam furiously around a rock and out of sight into a cave. Seconds later he breached the surface of the water to Mike's right, having come from the opposite direction. It was very much what a human child would do. "Hey, Dad, watch this." Then, with one's attention, think up some kind of trick to justify the call.

"That's actually a pretty good trick," Mike said.

"He's got a million of 'em," Val said. "He'll do them for as long as you'll sit and watch."

"Do you secretly feed him fish or something? I'm pretty sure that's not allowed."

"No. He does it purely for love of theater."

Mike sat down on a bench across the pathway from the pond. Meeting at the zoo was not a normal way to start a lunch, but then, Val was not the normal kind of guy. Mike watched the people walking by, most of whom seemed to be New Orleanais—all colors and sizes. He breathed the perfumed air and looked around at the foliage; all in all, he thought, not a bad place to be.

Val crossed the path and sat beside him on the bench. He asked Mike how the convention was going and if he was a member of the organization holding it. Mike told him he wasn't, that some of the hands on the rig had figured out a new and better way of transferring casing from a barge to the rig. He had written it up, listed the hands as coauthors, and submitted it as a paper to the IADC. They had asked him to present it at the meeting before it was published. Mike said he wasn't really interested in whatever else was going on there, so he was happy for a break.

Val said, "I wanted a chance to talk in a quiet place, and this is one of my favorite places to be. I hope it wasn't too much trouble."

"It wasn't any trouble, and I'm enjoying being here. How is learning derricks going?"

After the scene on the rig, Buck had given the OK to teaching Val to work derricks. Mike knew that it was not going well from the comments of some of the other hands, and he immediately regretted asking about it.

Val looked at him ruefully and said, "I haven't killed myself yet, but I think I've come pretty close. It's entirely possible that I've bitten off more than I can chew."

"So, are you going to stop trying?"

"I've considered it, but something in me finds that distasteful."

"You know," Mike said, "I've been meaning to ask you about something I heard. Somebody told me that you said that I had won an Associated Press award. That happens to be true, but it made me wonder how and why you would know it."

Val was quiet for a while. He was trying to think of how much he had let out and to whom. He finally decided that he had been engaged in a child's game of hide-and-seek and that there was no point in not telling Brown the truth. "I told you that I had written a dissertation and gotten a degree, but I didn't tell you what it was about."

Mike realized that was true. He thought back to the original conversation and remembered how smoothly Val had avoided questions.

"My dissertation was about Buck Burnet. I've spent the last three years learning everything there is to know about Buck Burnet. In doing that I naturally learned something about the people close to him, you being the major one of those. I found you so interesting that I actually made side trips to Austin to fill in some blank spots."

Mike was used to being ahead in any conversation, but this thought hadn't even occurred to him. "As flattering as that is, I can't really believe that there's that much about me that could be of interest. I'm about as average and vanilla a guy as you're likely to run across."

"So it would seem," Val said. "So it would seem. Still, when I think over my research, the things that cause my mind to itch aren't about Buck. They are about you."

Mike was surprised. "Things like what?"

"I know everything I can from looking into records and interviewing people who knew you. I know you got out of the navy in 1965 and enrolled at the University of Texas at Austin in spring of 1966."

"We didn't bother saying 'at Austin' in those days. There was only one."

"Not strictly true, but I take your meaning. I know you went to work for KHFI-TV as a night receptionist, and the news department taught you how to shoot film, so you could cover the boring banquets for them. I know you met your future wife, Sandra, there at the station."

"She had won a dance contest at Barton Springs. She and another girl were got up in bikinis, and I was filming them as a promo for an AP convention. I thought she was a singer in a bar."

"And it turns out she was a coed—a majorette, actually."

"Actually, she would tell you she was a Texas Star."

"Yes. I know that when Charles Whitman climbed up into the tower, all the 'real' newsmen were out-of-pocket, and you took a camera and a bunch of film and went down to the campus and got the only action shots taken that day. That was where the AP award came in."

"There wasn't much made of it. The 'real' newsmen were up in arms because they felt like it had just 'happened' to me, that there was no real news work in what I had done."

"I know you were hired by an independent television station in Fort Worth. You married Sandra on September 10 and moved to Irving. By January 1967 you were working in the Dallas bureau for the NBC station for the metro area, WBAP. Here is what I don't understand. Everybody I talked to thought you were doing great. They said you weren't what they thought you were when they hired you, but that by the time you left, you were doing exceptional work and looking at a bright future. Then, after a couple of years, you just disappeared from Dallas. When I asked them why you left, not a one could come up with a credible answer."

"Who did you talk to?"

"Jimmy Darnell and Russ Thornton were the main ones. Alex Burton, Jack Brown...several others I can't remember right off. Jimmy Kerr. Johnny Rutledge."

"Doyle Vinson was—"

"Dead."

Mike appeared to be smiling and looking Val in the eyes, but Val knew neither was true. His mind was in the past, communing with the people mentioned. Mike started to speak then stopped, looked away.

Mike stayed inside himself for some time. Rather than break in on his thoughts, Val occupied himself with the people strolling by. Finally Mike turned back to him and said, "I've asked myself why I got out of the news business many times. I had what I thought were a lot of valid reasons then. I knew I liked doing physical work outside, and being a newsman wasn't going to entail anything like that. I didn't make much money, and the guys who had been around a lot longer didn't seem to make much more than I did. We mixed easily with the movers and shakers, but there wasn't much of a chance of becoming one of them. I didn't have an air-quality voice, so I was never going to be on the air. One thing I told those who asked me was that I thought the country was going to undergo a period of reckoning, and that newsmen—being they didn't really have anything material to add to the equation—would be the first ones to lose their jobs."

Val didn't react, and Mike said, "It should actually be funnier now than it was then."

Apparently Val missed the humor of it at either time.

"Closer to the bone was that I didn't have a degree, and everyone else did. I could have gotten an English or journalism degree on my days and nights off, but those subjects were so easy for me that they hardly seemed worth the effort. Russ Thornton, who was my boss above Doyle, told me not to get a journalism degree. He said that's what everybody else had, and just about anything else would come in a lot handier. That didn't tip the scales, but it did seem as though I should have a go at the hardest thing I could qualify for. That turned out to be engineering. An engineering degree pays so much out of school that it didn't occur to anyone that I might want to go back to the news business after getting one; therefore, it didn't occur to me. I found a company, Otis Engineering, who would give me a job offshore and allow me to go back and forth to school. I went to work for them when I graduated."

"That's the next question," Val said. "You worked for Otis as a design engineer for a year; once again, you were doing well, showing a true talent for machine design, then you quit to go offshore with Exxon." Val could tell the word *quit* didn't sit well with Brown, but then he hadn't meant it to. He could see Brown dealing with the pique and finally putting it to rest. Val wondered if he had ever thought about these things before. Mike got up and started walking, and Val followed him.

"I heard that one of my former bosses said of me that I was an odd combination of confidence and lack of confidence— that if I could have been confident all the time, I would easily have gone to the top. I didn't understand that then, and I don't understand it now, but something about it rings true all the same. I'm confident when I'm sure of my position, but I don't have the ability to appear confident about something I'm not sure of. I don't understand why I made those decisions myself. Fear of failure? Fear of success? Distrustful of early and easy success? Surely. I'm pretty sure it all goes way, way back. Unhappy childhoods are almost de rigueur nowadays. I don't know how mine compared to others, but I do remember thinking that I would rather be doing something else." Val made as if to interrupt, but Mike said, "We don't have time enough, and I have no desire to go into the specifics of that. I remember vividly lying in bed once, looking at a full moon, sometime after I had reached puberty. There were four other beds in the room with sleeping siblings. I didn't normally pray; I don't think I felt I had the right to ask for anything, but I prayed that night. I asked God for someone to love who would love me. Pretty simple stuff but I must have meant it because I obviously remembered it. Things got better in the navy, away from my parents and the allergens that I discovered had been making me feel bad physically. But things didn't start to really improve until I met Sandra. Until then I had lived in daydreams and subsisted on bullshit. She was the first real thing that ever happened to me. I started to view myself through her eyes; her view was much more favorable than mine. I have always believed she was an unmistakable answer to that long ago prayer. She was a solid eight and a half then, and she has since worked herself up to nine-ness. I was a five based on some pretty iffy stuff, and I consider myself an unequivocal six now. She provided the frame upon which I started building a real person, and I guess what you see is the final product. But those early decisions were taken when that person was in the beginning stages and based on emotion and God knows what else. The wonder of it for me was that Sandra stayed with me and not begrudgingly — happy and helpful through it all. She didn't like the decisions you mentioned, but she went along with them anyway."

Val found it interesting that Mike considered himself a six. He might average out to that. The only thing about him that wasn't an eight or nine was his looks. In that regard only the kindest person would afford him a two.

Mike had paused on a bridge overlooking a savannah, but he wasn't looking at the animals; he was still looking in. "I guess I'm attributing those decisions to immaturity. Certainly I didn't realize what I was giving up, in either case. Those people you mentioned were some of the most creative and clever people

I've known. Ben Stevens and Jimmy Darnell could both be hilarious. Jimmy's worth a book, all on his own. Being around them day after day was the most fun I've had in a work setting. If I'd been older, that would certainly have weighed in more heavily than it did. And I did have a good start at Otis, but just because I was a good designer didn't mean that I looked forward to sitting at a drawing table the rest of my life. Now that I think about it, I enjoyed the people at Otis, too. I wish I still had access to all those people now. I have been terrible about not keeping up with any of the friends I've made along the way. I put that down to self-absorption." Mike's attention almost visibly snapped back to the present, and he looked at Val and said, "So, that's about as good as I can do for you on that score. I'm hungry, and you owe me a good lunch."

Val wasn't fully satisfied with the answers Mike had given, but what Mike had said about his wife had gone some way toward answering another question he had. He decided he was hungry, too, and he led Mike to where he had his car parked on the street. Val drove north across St. Charles, and Mike spotted Loyola University to the left. Two or three blocks in, they turned to the right and then left, and Mike lost track of where they were. Val parked in a dirt lot behind a row of stores, then guided him into the backdoor of what turned out to be a combination bar and deli. It was not a place or even a part of town Mike would have picked on his own. The bar took up half the room, going from back to front, and there were a few tables along the wall on the left. Most of the people were black, but the entrance of two white people didn't create any kind of commotion. There was water standing in puddles on the floor, and Mike found himself hoping that it had been raining here even though he hadn't seen any clouds. Any other source he could think of would be unsettling. Several of the people greeted Val warmly, and the bartender, a large white man with long hair and tattoos, was effusive. Val introduced them, but Mike didn't catch the bartender's name. He just remembered it wasn't something simple like Fred or Joe. Mike asked for an amber ale, and Val said he would have one, too. Val recommended a shrimp po'boy, and Mike said that sounded good. After the beers were drawn, Val led Mike to the outside in front where a bench and a few chairs were set along the wall. They sat on the bench, and Mike sipped his beer, a local brew that was incredibly good and cold. There was a black Harley backed to the curb, and Mike figured it for the bartender's.

Mike said, "Are you going to tell Buck about your research?"

"Yeah. I've nearly told him several times already, but I haven't yet. I guess I'm still a little angry about the way he treated me. It's childish, I know — "

"I think it's remarkably mature of you to be talking to him at all. Did you find out anything about where he came from?"

Val winced. "Possibly, but in all fairness I think he should be the one to find out first."

"Fair enough," Mike said. "Fair enough."

The block across the street was a jumble of old, zero-lot line houses, two- and three-story, some with storefronts, some not. Their side of the block was a line of stores with what looked like apartments overhead. The rest of the street as far as Mike could see was a mishmash of businesses, houses, and apartment blocks. None of it looked as if it had been built after 1950. As a Texan Mike wasn't used to seeing people walking on the streets, but here the pedestrian traffic was heavy. Like the people at the zoo, these came in all shapes and sizes, ages and colors. Mike wasn't used to seeing interracial couples, either, but here they seemed to be common, and he was the only one noticing. Often people would nod or speak to Val, and occasionally one would stop and have a short conversation. As he sat, Mike became aware of the constant, subtle attention Val was receiving. Old women, young women, big ones and small — not a single one passed that wasn't conscious of Val. For his part, Val was smiling, sipping, and enjoying the parade.

Val said, "This is what a neighborhood should be. That's my apartment over there." He gestured at a two-story structure with a bookstore on the bottom floor. "I love this place."

Mike said, "How are you doing on the girl front?"

Val grinned. "I'm no longer having trouble getting dates. I've determined that quantity is not what I'm looking for, but I'm having trouble judging quality from the outside. I don't think I'm in the right place to find the girl I'm looking for, but I don't know what the right place is."

As they spoke a white Mercedes pulled up in front of Val's place. A really good-looking woman got out and walked around it, headed for the door of Val's apartment.

Mike turned to comment on it, but Val had gone inside. He didn't reappear for five or ten minutes by which time the girl had given up and left. When he came back out, he had their po'boys with him.

Mike said, "Did you go inside because our sandwiches were ready or to get out of sight of that girl in the Mercedes?"

"Kind of a combination, I guess. They come on like it's all fun and games; then they show up the next day wanting to move in."

They sat without speaking, both involved in the po'boys, which were beyond excellent. People continued to drift by, at least a quarter of them young families with children. Brown thought, not for the first time, that that was what was wrong with the subdivision where they lived in Austin. Everybody there was just like Sandra and him, middle-aged and white. There was something natural and relaxing about being here. The shade they sat in worked its way out to the curb, and they sipped on fresh beers and spoke of many things.

Mike and Val were comfortable outside the bar. Occasionally people, usually men, would sit in one of the chairs and attempt to join the conversation. One was a short, young man who claimed to be a welder/diver offshore. His mouth was wired shut, and he drank his beer with a straw through a hole where a tooth was missing. He said he had been in a fight, and his jaw was broken in seven places. He said he was looking for the guy who did it, and he intended to kill him. Val asked him how many times the guy had hit him, and he said, "Once." Val said, "I believe if a guy could do that much damage with one punch, I'd be pleased not ever to see him again." Sometime in the midafternoon, a young woman sat in the chair on the other side of Val. Though he didn't pay her a lot of attention, she was obviously taken with Val. She said she was visiting from Dallas, that she had just been through a divorce. She was dressed in a little cotton shift and sandals and carried a straw purse. Mike never heard how she came to be this far outside the tourist track. Most of her early conversation concerned her "ex." Her name was Jennifer. Over the course of the afternoon, it became apparent that she was looking to forget her "ex" in the arms of another man, and, increasingly, Val was looking like the man of choice. She was plain with a weak chin, but her skin was the color and texture of porcelain, and her breasts, unfettered by anything but the thin cotton, were beautiful.

After an especially long quiet spell, Mike moved to the unoccupied chair. Val shifted to his side of the bench. Mike said, "We lived out in the country because my father didn't want to pay higher rent. Five boys and two girls then, and I was the oldest. Daddy was an intermittent alcoholic, but we were the only ones who knew it. Everyone else thought he was the greatest. When he was drinking, most of his salary went to alcohol, but he always acted like we were poor because of his having to clothe and feed us, the kids. His binges had a pattern of four stages, and during only one of the stages was he a nice person. My mother and I took the brunt of it. I hated him and felt guilty for hating him. When he was in his early fifties, he sobered up and turned into the person he was meant to be. I wrote him a letter once to 'clear the air.' I thought I was just getting some things off my chest, but somewhere down deep I think I intended to hurt him. He took it like the man he was, but it did hurt him, badly. We became friends after that, but there had been a lot of damage done, and we have never developed the kind of relationship that I hope to enjoy with my son. When I was a kid, I didn't know we weren't the only ones who lived that way, and I reckon that's why I still have trouble talking about it. Isolated the way we were, there was no one else to talk to, no one to be friends with. I put the world together the way

I saw it, and it turns out the pieces I made didn't fit. It seems like it's been relatively recently that I've started to see relationships and social interaction outside the family as valuable and even necessary."

Val pondered the irony of it: not having a father and feeling loss on his side and having one that you wished you didn't on Mike's. He didn't know if there was such a thing as an "intermittent alcoholic," but he figured it must have meaning for Brown. The story went a long way to explaining a gifted man who seemed to be happy with less than he could have had. Val was content being here, listening to the music coming from inside the bar. He didn't have many friends either, and he found himself hoping that he and Mike were in the process of forming a friendship now. The age difference was the only thing separating them, and it seemed to be fading as they spoke.

The shadows had grown to the other side of the street. Midday had been hot, but the air was softening now. The girl, Jennifer, was still with them. She was twenty-one years old and had some sort of office job. Mike and Val had been drinking beer for a while, but slowly. Neither was drunk, but both were far mellower than usual. Mike had just said something about being in love with other women, and Val was seeking clarification.

"I don't love Sandra any less for loving other women. In fact I think it all goes into a pool that she draws from. I love them in the way an art lover loves certain works of art. I can't see them and be around them without appreciating them. I don't have to possess them. I don't even have to talk to them. Every once in a while, one is so great that I just have to fall in love with her. I don't say anything, and, if she knows it, she doesn't say anything either. The danger would be in acting on it. Sandra wouldn't put up with it, and there's nothing I would risk losing Sandra for."

"They are lovely," Val said. Mike's diction was falling off, and he didn't seem as coherent as he had been. Maybe they were mellower than Val had thought. Mike's story about other women had the ring of rationalization, and it must have shown on his face because Mike felt constrained to elucidate.

Mike said, "Yeah. I wouldn't have gone for that when I was your age, either. In any case, women are what I love most. What else? I mean, what else? If not for women, life would literally not be worth living. They are the only reward."

Val decided that he was probably the same way. A person might be defined by what he liked, what he appreciated most. Val liked a lot of things, but none of them were even in the same league as women. He knew that he wanted more from a woman than what he was finding, but aside from looks, intelligence, and a basic decency he couldn't name, the other attributes he was looking for were nebulous and unnamed. Wouldn't it be nice if it were as easy as when his grandmother picked out his first amour?

Jennifer had apparently given up on Val. Mike hadn't noticed when she left, but she had been gone for a while. Mike knew there were always two sides, but it sounded to him like she had gotten a raw deal. Mike felt bad for her and hoped she fared well. She seemed awfully vulnerable to be poking around in places like this one. Mike stirred and said, "When we were talking about WBAP earlier, it sort of shifted some things around in the attic. Another reason for leaving, and I have no idea at this point if it was the main reason or just a side note, was a defect in my personality that I suspected would keep me from going very far in the news business. It's a timidity — an inability to press people. If you're going to be a journalist, you're going to have to ask some tough questions, and I just had a hell of time doing that. I think it's also why I'm so reluctant to fight.

"No," Mike said, "I didn't say that very well. Let me tell you a story about when I was in the navy. Are you up for a story?"

Val said, "Yeah. Give me a minute to go to the bathroom. You ready for another beer?"

Mike said, "I will be by the time you get back."

Val grabbed the other chair when he got back and pulled it up across from Mike.

"There were two striptease joints on Oahu, one on Hotel Street in downtown Honolulu and the other between downtown and Waikiki. I met Billy Kidd in the Waikiki joint. She was billed as "Billy Kidd and Her Flaming Tassels," but she was just smoldering when she sat at the bar. I had just witnessed her act. She had been backstage and put on a dress before coming out. I wasn't yet familiar with the Caucasian female body close up, but hers compared favorably with the many I had seen in *Playboy*. Two seats away she was much smaller than she looked onstage. Her gaze fell on me, and, instead of looking away or spilling my drink, I returned it and started talking to her. My hands didn't shake as I lit her cigarette, and my words were reasonably calm and coherent. I was in my Hong Kong–made, Italian-silk suit. I was two years past full grown and had recently attained passable facial hair. I suspect I appeared more sophisticated than I was. I invited her out when she finished her night, and she accepted. I was able to drive her away in an Alfa Romeo Spider Veloce of relatively recent vintage. So far so good.

"The Alfa was mine if that's the right way of saying that; I made payments on it almost equaling my monthly salary. The suit I had made on a WestPac trip some months earlier. Both items were of very high quality and afforded me much pleasure while they were in my custody. It has been another of my shortcomings not to have fully appreciated the fine things that have come my way. Two troubling aspects of my nature: observing and not acting, the first; consuming and not savoring, the second. We drove down to the bay where Elvis got married in *Blue Hawaii*, and I talked to her the same way I would have talked to any girl on a date. No doubt most men would have been making moves, and no doubt she was expecting me to. She considered what she did art and refused to believe that I and the other men in the audience were looking at her as a sex object. That sounds like denial and maybe it was, but during the conversation I gradually turned away from the image of beautiful, sexy airhead that went with the territory and began to see her as an intelligent, honest, if unfortunate, being. Yes, I was naïve. But no destroyer sailor is really naïve about bar girls and hustles, and I knew that she was not hustling me. I can't remember her real last name, but her first name was Shirley.

"She lived in a single-story apartment in a high-dollar area northeast of Fort de Russy on Waikiki. When I parked my car in her unused carport, we come to the first of two events that are my reasons for relating this story. When we met in front of her apartment door, we kissed. I don't remember the quality of the kiss itself, but I remember clearly the contact between my erection and her body. I was trying to figure out what my next move was. All of my dates to this point had ended with this kiss, and all of my assignations with prostitutes hadn't started with what amounted to a date. I suppose what was required was ripping her bodice (as they say) and taking her. Certainly I felt like doing that. But I was incapable then, as I'm sure I would be even now, of taking her or anyone by force. I had heard all the male stories about how *no* really meant *yes*, how girls really wanted to but felt like they were being bad if they hadn't been forced. I had heard all that, but something, some defect deep in my core, wouldn't let me believe it. I was waiting for her to ask me in and to let me make love to her. That didn't happen. Though I dated her for a period of weeks, I never made love to her. I don't remember ever kissing her again. It wasn't nobility that kept me from taking Billy Kidd, tassels and all; it was some fear that I've never ferreted out. And it is not lack of ability, or desire, but that same fear that doomed me to a life of observation and inaction."

Maybe it was Val's imagination, but Mike seemed to be sobering up. Possibly Val was just getting drunker.

"After the abortive moment at the door, she invited me in, and we began what I have always thought of as a brother-sister relationship. It wasn't that I wanted it to be that way. There wasn't a moment that went by when I didn't want her to ask me to fuck her. The apartment was large and well furnished. Somebody obviously cleaned for her, and when she was hungry, she had food delivered by cab. She seemed to like my taking her places, and I certainly liked taking her. She garnered a lot of attention, and it was almost as if she used me as a buffer, a way of saying she was with someone, so don't bother her. When we were in, we talked. Well, mostly, she talked. She had gone for a long time with a local horn player. She said they had recently broken up. She wasn't going to be a stripper forever. She had plans to be a jazz singer. The problem with that was she had a very high-pitched voice. When she spoke quietly, it left you with the illusion that you were speaking with a child. When she raised her voice, it was irritating, even grating. I wasn't musical, but I couldn't see that voice translating into anything worth listening to for its own sake.

"One Sunday afternoon she asked me to take her to a jam session at a club about halfway to Pearl Harbor. She knew the band that was playing, and she felt like they would ask her to sing with them. We sat at the table with 'friends of the band.' The band was five or six people, but the only one I remember was the lead guitar, a nondescript black guy. His girlfriend was sat next to me, and Shirley was on my other side. 'Black men are physically superior to white men,' the girlfriend said across me, and then again in case Shirley hadn't gotten the full meaning. The insult was an invitation to argue with her, but I couldn't see any percentage in taking the bait. Besides, in my opinion, black men, generally, were physically superior. We listened to the band, and Shirley and the other people at the table chatted. She was hoping to catch the lead guy at the break and get on stage, but before that he introduced her from the stage. 'Billy Kidd and Her Flaming Tassels,' he intoned, and then he said something about her being the girl to go to.

"What he said must have been derogatory because shortly after that Shirley told me she wanted to leave. I asked her if there was anything wrong, and she shook her head; but something was clearly amiss, and it had to do with what had been said from the stage. I've played the scene over in my mind a thousand times, and the right thing always turns out to be my going up to the bandstand and doing some damage to the lead guy. But that isn't what happened. I gathered Shirley up, and we left. Shirley deserved being defended, and I hadn't defended her. The person I wanted to be wouldn't have hesitated. Maybe it was fear of physical harm that kept me from discharging my duty, but I'm inclined to believe it a more insidious thing connected to not wanting to make or be in trouble. I've spent these years telling myself that it didn't have anything to do with her profession or the things I had heard about her, but I can't be sure about that, either. She was crying on the way home, quietly; but I could see the tracks of her tears in the light of passing cars. Whatever I had felt in the club, she was now just a girl whose feelings had been badly hurt. I took her home and went back to the ship.

"It was several weeks before I went back onshore, and in the interim she had moved to the other strip club, the one on Hotel Street downtown. I took a seat in a corner and asked the waitress to tell Billy that I was there. Before the waitress got back with my drink, two men showed up and sat down at my table. One was a beefy-looking white guy, and the other was a Hawaiian who was bigger than Buck. They told me that Billy didn't want to see me, and it would be better if I just left the club and didn't come there ever again. Taking on those two would have been an act of lunacy, but when I kept looking at the white guy, he lifted up his shirt to show me the forty-five in his waistband. I don't know if Shirley really didn't want to see me. She could have been disappointed in me, but I don't really think she expected me to or would have appreciated my making a scene at the jazz club. It could have been that her handlers didn't care for our non-revenue-producing relationship and decided to end it. There was little likelihood that I could have wrested her from their grasp and put her on a path to a better life, but the thing is, I knew her phone number and where she lived and could have asked her. I didn't. Six weeks later I was out of the navy and on my way to Texas."

Mike had delivered the story in the way of someone divulging a deep, shameful secret. Val had never thought of Mike as weak, and he was sure no one else did, either, but it was apparent that Mike did. It occurred to him that this is what friends did; they confided in each other. Val didn't yet know himself well enough to offer anything in return. Of the two, Buck was far the more vivid character, but the longer he knew Mike, the more interesting he became. He seemed to have cast himself as Buck's sidekick, but an intelligent person working around them for any time would come to the conclusion that they were equally powerful. He had decided that Mike absolutely didn't know he wasn't good-looking. Maybe it was in the way of a plain girl being sexy if she believed herself sexy. Val had seen the girl's, Jennifer's, reaction when she first saw Mike—almost a comic double-take. She had obviously stayed because she was interested in Val, but, as the day wore on, she seemed more and more drawn to Mike. She was finally hanging on his every word. He didn't know if Mike knew he could have had her, but the reason she left was because he wouldn't pick up on the numerous hints she was dropping. It was full dark now, and the story seemed to have used up all the conversation Mike had. Val asked him if he wanted to go get some supper, and Mike said it was past his suppertime. Val offered to take him back to the hotel, and Mike thanked him but said he would just call a taxi since Val was already home. When the taxi got there, Mike shook his hand and told him he had enjoyed the day. He turned when he got to the taxi and said, "Hang in there on working derricks. It'll get easier, soon."

CHAPTER XVI

Campbell's Books

Days, like diesel engines and racehorses, have personalities. The day that Buck met Val Campbell's family held nothing in reserve. It was open and direct—full out before noon. It was south Louisiana in the summertime, and the damp morning cool had given way to muggy heat. Buck could feel the first few beads of sweat forming on his chest as he sat in his car on the main street of Hickory Flat. Since the incident at the Mouse's Ear, he had been occupied with how Val Campbell came to be the way he was. He had come to know him in the months since and even to admire him, but Val was still very close with the details of his life. Finally, curiosity had dictated this trip. Buck knew Val had grown up in this town, his family still lived here, and his last name was a part of the sign on the bookstore across the street: Campbell's Books. That Val and the owner of the store would be related was not too far-fetched, since the number of non-French surnames in a town this size in south Louisiana had to be minimal. He had driven the two hundred or so miles from New Orleans, eaten an excellent breakfast, and been sitting here the hour since wondering what to do. He didn't feel like watching the storefront was accomplishing much, but anything else carried with it the threat of social contact. Finally, deciding that social contact was going to be necessary if this weren't to be a wasted trip, he opened the door and got out.

Earl Guidry was known informally as the "Sheriff of Hickory Flat." He was actually a deputy sheriff of the parish of Calcasieu, though Hickory Flat was his principal responsibility. He was born here, raised here, and, in all likelihood, would die here. Earl was on his third sheriff, a testament to how well he performed his duties and to how popular he was with the citizens of Hickory Flat and the surrounding area. He had been asked to run for sheriff on several occasions, but had always demurred. He felt himself to be wholly competent in Hickory Flat, but Lake Charles, or any big city, gave him the willies. He hadn't any family since his folks had passed away, but he felt himself to be an interested and useful member of the larger family. His role of protector is what brought him to his current position, standing in the shade on the boardwalk in front of the Campbell bookstore, watching as the big man got out of the big car across the street and headed his way. Beside the car, Buck looked almost normal sized, but that illusion was shattered as soon as he began to move. He walked with a bit of a roll, almost like John Wayne, but Earl could tell the gait was due to his toes being turned in slightly and not an affectation. Earl was alert to such things ever since he had started noticing that a pigeon-toed man was nigh impossible to put on the ground. Buck obviously wasn't a young man, but there was no hint that he was near the age Guidry knew he had to be. The man was erect, his shoulders broad and still square. Earl unconsciously pulled in his own gut when he noticed Buck didn't have one. Earl didn't know much about expensive clothes, but he knew Buck's hadn't been bought at J. C. Penney's. The way they fell straight when not touched by a body part made them seem something other than cloth. He saw Buck notice him and slightly alter direction. Guidry was a Cajun, and as a small child, his family had lived hand-to-mouth; but when the oilfield swept over the area, his father took a job working on the rigs, and their fortunes took a turn for the better. Roughnecking paid a lot of money, and if you didn't spend it on booze, you could actually acquire some property and eventually be seen as someone of substance, which is what his father did. Earl still lived in the brick house his father had built. As an original resident and the son of a roughneck, Earl grew up in a position to see both sides of the oilfield controversy. He fully understood the pride the oilfield kids took in telling the stories of the giant roughneck who could right all wrongs. He retold many of the stories himself, having no idea that they weren't total fabrications. It wasn't until he became a lawman and started talking to some of the older deputies that he found out Buck Burnet was no myth. He regretted never having seen him, and now, here he was. Earl himself was no small man, but he was looking Buck in the eye when Buck was still in the street. Seeing him in the flesh was worth the price of admission.

Buck noticed the man in the shade when he was about half-way across the street and realized he should have expected "the small-town sheriff." He was aware that the man would already have checked out his license number and gotten his description; sheriffs in south Louisiana didn't have a lot to do, and giving outsiders a hard time was one of their few diversions. Buck had dealt with many such men, and he didn't for a second take the attention lightly.

"Hello. How we doin' today?"

Hearty—this guy saw himself as source for a movie. The lawman positioned himself to put Buck at the edge of the boardwalk with his back to the street.

"Hello," Buck said. He moved carefully and kept his voice even and low. "How you doin?"

"Great. Great," the man in the hat said. "Can I he'p you find something?"

Buck noticed that the badge said deputy and the deputy's being under six feet Buck took as a matter for concern. The apparent intelligence behind what the deputy meant to be piercing brown eyes he took for a hopeful sign.

For his part Guidry was trying to analyze all the parts that made up Buck's presence. Buck's physicality certainly matched the boyhood stories, but there was more to him than the stories conveyed. There was a confidence that was almost palpable. There was gentleness, too. The stories, re-examined in the light of his years of experience, had convinced him that Buck, while certainly strong and tough, was not a mean person. Here, almost in Buck's chest, he was glad for the gentleness, because he was past the point where help from another quarter would have done him any good. Guidry's bluff, good-old-boy manner, developed as a tool to disarm and sometimes intimidate, was ringing hollow in this situation, and his question seemed to be echoing around the storefront.

"No," Buck said, "I believe I've got 'er found. I'm just going in here to look for a book."

"You come all the way up here from New Orleans just to find a book?" The look said he didn't think Buck could read, but telling him he knew he was from New Orleans meant he was willing to play fair.

"No," he said, carefully, deciding to get as near the truth as possible. "I might get a book, but I mainly came looking for relatives of one of my hands."

"Who might that be?"

"His name is Val Campbell. I thought he might be kin to the owner of this store."

"Well, you'd be right there. His grandmother, Mrs. Sylvie Campbell, owns and runs it. She's most likely in there right now. You say Val is one of your hands?" This wasn't rhetorical, he was genuinely surprised.

"That's right. I'm a toolpusher on a drilling rig in the gulf. Val has been working for me about a year."

"Well, I'll be damned. I didn't think he had it in him—physically, I mean."

As the big man's eyes met his own, Guidry realized that he hadn't seen them before, and an odd feeling came over the back of his neck. This was the famous Buck Burnet, and he had heard so much about him, for so long, that he felt like he knew him. But he didn't know him, and he felt compelled to explain.

"Val Campbell is liked and respected around here, but he is known to be one more for the books than physical activity. He hasn't been hurt, has he?"

The eyes moved away, and the feeling went with them. Buck had recorded genuine concern in the eyes of the deputy. Buck said, "No, no. He's fine."

"Well, you tell Miz Sylvie that Earl Guidry said hello, now, would you? Have a nice day…and welcome to Hickory Flat."

Buck nodded that he would have a nice day. Guidry was protective of his charges, but there was nothing undue in his approach. Buck mentally paid the deputy the respect due another competent person, and decided the deputy would be someone he would like to know. He turned back to the bookstore.

A bell tinkled overhead as Buck forced the old door open. The wood floor, gray paint worn off the planks' curled edges, sloped toward the rear, at least until becoming lost in a poorly lit welter of shelves and books. He could see no one at the front, so he headed down one of what appeared to be aisles, so narrow that he had to turn sideways to make his way. The books were not the modern texts one might expect in the bookstore of a college town, but then, the old part of downtown is not the place a college bookstore would likely be located. They were mostly old and arranged in no quickly discernible order. They were clean and cared for, though, and as he reached the back of the store, he realized that the musty bookstore smell was missing as well. Part of his mind toyed with that while the rest peered about, trying to make things out of dark shapes. He focused on what seemed to be reflected light in the left rear corner of the store. Moving toward the light, a voice saying, "May I help you," coming from one of the aisles on his left, made the hair on his neck rise. Buck felt more surprised than threatened, and his body went still while he sorted things out. The voice had been female: not old, not young but so near that he couldn't believe he hadn't sensed her presence earlier. He turned slowly toward the voice. He tried to say something, but as he had nothing ready to say, nothing came out.

"May I help you?" she said again. By this time he had identified the source as a white shape three buttons up from his waist and about twice that distance away. The voice was firm and genuinely interrogatory. He thought fleetingly of the two old ladies on the farm in Ruark's *Uhuru*. "I'm looking for a copy of *Uhuru*," he said. "I was told you might be the one to have it." By now the shape had become a face. There was no fear in it, and Buck wondered at that. A little fear on her part would have been a reasonable response. She was no girl, but neither could Buck see her as the grandmother of a grown man. Her hair gave the impression of being white here in the darkness, but there was nothing old about her scent, or her presence. She was three feet away, but he felt as if she were standing right in front of him, touching him. Buck had never been this close to a woman of this quality before, and he decided that whatever it was that caused this feeling in the pit of his stomach wasn't personal; it probably radiated off her in all directions, all the time. There was light, but something close to night vision was still required. She was taller than average. Her eyes were bright and searching. She was taking him in as Buck was trying to her. Silence was a big part of his conversation, but she waited long enough to make him nervous.

"I don't think much of Ruark," she said. "If there's anything worse than forced machismo, it's second-hand forced machismo. Come over to the files, and I'll see if I have a copy."

Buck thought of Marlene Dietrich then and thought he noticed an accent. No, maybe not.

Making their way at her pace to the light he had seen earlier, he was at pains to avoid bumping into things that were as much felt as seen. The light was atop a huge roll-top desk situated along the north wall just out of sight of the rear aisle. A wooden armchair was rolled out and turned toward a little reading table, which held an open book. She had been reading when Buck came in. He wondered briefly how she had gotten to her defensive position without his hearing. The defense theory was confirmed by the shotgun, which thumped when she set it by the desk.

As she set the gun down Sylvie thought she should either load it or get rid of it. She was mentally castigating herself for not locking the door when she spotted the Bentley. She thought she should have asked Earl to run him out of town, though Earl might not have been up to it. Valiant always played up this one's intelligence, but he looked like just another big, stupid workman to her. *Uhuru* — for God's sake. He may as well like Hemingway, or Kipling.

As it happened Buck didn't care much for Hemingway, but he liked Kipling a lot.

Buck had a good feeling about her. There were four or five rolodexes on the desk, and she went to one of them and started flipping through it. By the time she told him she didn't have one, he'd been able to come up with the name of a book he really wanted. Her manner brightened when he told her he was looking for a copy of the *Iliad*.

"Now that is a book worth the reading," she said, "but the only copy I've got is in French."

He told her that he had enough copies of it to qualify as a collector but that he still couldn't see the use of owning a book he couldn't read. He said he would be interested in a Greek just out of curiosity but that most of the bad things that happened in his life had been French. Her laughter was surprising and pleasing: pleasing because it was soft and warm; surprising because she had recognized that he meant it as a joke. For whatever reason, very few people who didn't know him could tell when Buck was joking. She asked him the author of his favorite copy, and he told her that he wasn't a collector in that sense. He didn't remember the names of the translators (although the name of one of them did come to mind while he was saying he didn't). He realized she thought he was making it all up when she began talking about how all men thought of themselves as Achilles and how every man dreamed of having a woman like "her." Buck felt that no man with half a brain would ask to be

Achilles, and the brief references to Helen told one little more than that she was beautiful and had run off with an idiot.

"Yes," he said. "It's true. Probably the reason I've never been married is because I've never found her."

The grandmother, Sylvie, was somehow disappointed. She would put him about fifty-five, a few years younger than her own...however many there were now.

"Don't worry. Some day you will find your Helen."

"Helen?" he said. "I thought we were talking about Andromache."

Buck felt that to be a bit of a cheap shot, but condescension got on his nerves. He could tell by a slight widening of her eyes that she recognized the retort for what it was.

As he sat in the hard-backed chair, the upper part of his chest and his face stayed out of the pool of light formed by her reading lamp. She briefly considered adjusting the lamp shade and decided not to. It was hard to get past the sheer size of him. How large was he? Bigger than what? He was the largest human being she had ever been close to. No animal comparison occurred to her. He was more like a large piece of construction machinery. He was so still. There was a driver in there somewhere. In this light, his eyes were as black and motionless as the rest of him. His face was cruel, and she thought what a good model he would make for a pirate. She imagined he was the origin of many a kidnap or rape fantasy. He was the rapist one would choose. He wore the air of command the way he wore his hair, almost as if he were unaware of it. What was she going to say now? Something about his choice between Helen and Andromache had intrigued her. What, in the *Iliad*, made him think Andromache a better choice? How many of the implications did he understand? How much of a mind was inside there? His pride in the knowledge of the difference between the two women was a little school boyish, but somehow endearing for that. She had to force herself to remember that this was the man who had made all their lives miserable for a considerable period of time.

She said, "What are you really looking for, Mr. Burnet?"

That was the second time in ten minutes she had surprised him. She had either communicated with the deputy or knew him from a picture, which, as he thought about it, was not that coincidental.

"I'm sorry," she said. "I called Deputy Guidry when I saw your car over there earlier this morning, and he called me back with who you are."

Buck slowly put his hand out, and after a moment's hesitation, she put hers into it. The shock was almost electric when he realized it was Val's hand. He reacted somehow, and her eyes smiled slightly.

"I've noticed that he has my hands, too," she said. "They are capable and useful hands, but I would imagine his are no longer as soft."

Oddly, Buck thought, they are. But soft wasn't what one thought of on gripping Val's hand. Bony is what he thought. Dry, firm, and, nowadays, with real strength, but definitely bony.

She asked if he would like some coffee. He said no to the coffee but wondered if he might have some water.

When she returned with a large tumbler of cool water, he said, "You asked me something?"

"Mr. Burnet, I love my grandson more than you can possibly imagine. I know how he is feeling even before he does. I know that since summer last year he had been almost despondent. He was uncommunicative, and, while that is not totally uncharacteristic, he was careless of the feelings of others, and that is. He had gotten physically stronger and coarser, but all the joy had gone out of him. Since he constitutes what little joy there is in my life, it goes without saying that the joy had gone out of mine, as well. Some time back he came to visit, a changed person. I have never seen him so happy. It was apparent to my daughter and me that both conditions were affected, if not caused, by you. Can you explain to me why I have suffered the past year on your account?"

For the first time in his life, Buck had a clear understanding of the term *taken aback*. There wasn't a lot of lace around this lady's borders. He was impressed not only with her lack of hesitation in confronting him, but also with the spareness and density of her language. He wanted to do justice to her question, and he took an inordinate amount of time formulating his reply. Most listeners would have, from impatience, broken in on his thoughts; but she quietly bided her time, her eyes never leaving his face.

"I have to tell you," he said, "that the earlier depression was on my account. His recent happiness is on his. Having said that, it's a story that needs telling, and I ask you to let me tell it in my own words and at my own pace. I don't expect it to make me any less of a villain, but I am easily sidetracked, and I want to make sure I cover everything."

She wondered about his speech. She didn't know a great many workmen, but the ones she knew didn't speak anything like this. His phrasing and word selection were different from normal speech. They were consciously correct. He spoke as if he were picking and choosing words as he went, which is something we all do, but at some point the words must be ready to hand. She wondered if its slowness was due to the picking or just a natural regional pattern.

As he spoke Buck realized that the telling of the story was, at least in some measure, the reason for his being here. He told her about that first day on the workboat at the Exxon docks in Venice. He told her about his mood and the series of assumptions he had leapt to when he saw Val on the fantail.

"For all that I look like it, I am not a mean man, or even unkind. So I am hard-pressed to explain why I was both of those to Val. I was in a bad mood, and I was caught off guard; but those aren't all the reason. Val looked almost a caricature of what he was: educated, sensitive, slight, weak, physically inept, and pampered. None of those are qualities that you look for in a hand. Anyone taking him on was sure to have to spend a great deal of time teaching him the very basics of the trade and guarding him from himself and the myriad things on a rig that can snatch a hand or snuff a life before you know it. I am not averse to teaching, but this was equivalent to getting a first grader in high school. So it was asking a lot to take him out green; but that still doesn't explain it.

"The fact that he looked pampered is a little closer to the point. We don't get pampered people in the oilfield, much. Most of us come from working-class backgrounds, at best, and high school is generally tops in the education department. That doesn't mean we're stupid. On the contrary, I would match the brains of my crews with a similar cross section of office workers anywhere in the world. If we are deficient, it is culturally, and we are conscious of that. Our isolation and the little interaction we have with others tend to reinforce that difference. It's not so strange that we resent it. After all, it only arises because of a lack of opportunity.

"Up to now, what I have told you about my assessment of Val was accurate. He was all of those things, in spades. Where I completely missed the mark was in the assumption that he had a powerful father."

As Buck spoke Sylvie came to understand that he was flogging himself every way but physically. All this talk of boats and rigs held absolutely no interest for her. The world he spoke of was precisely the one she had spent her life trying to keep Val away from. Why would anyone be drawn to a life where that life could be forfeit, leaving all those who loved him and cared for him bereft? How could someone with an intellect and an education spend even one day among people like this brute? God help her, when Val as a little boy first started coming up with the stories about Buck Burnet, she should have made it clear to him that they were just stories, instead of nodding and expressing wonder. But who could know that it would turn into a lifelong fascination? What would have rendered the man able to see Val's quality? Here he was, in her place, using her time and droning on about things that could only upset her further.

"If I knew it, why did I let him try? That's what you or anybody would ask, but you would only be asking a question I've asked myself a hundred times, and never answered."

Sylvie had missed a significant part of the story. She briefly considered asking him to go back but then remembered she wasn't interested in the story to begin with.

"He didn't drop into the gulf so much as the gulf rose to get him, then took him down as the boat dropped and moved away from the platform, stripping his hands free of the rope and lining him up to be crushed when the next swell flung the workboat back against the platform. When that happened, most of him could be seen above the handrail at the stern, though how his legs kept from being crushed I'll never know."

Sylvie's eyes widened as she realized that she had actually come very close to losing Val. She could see Buck's lips moving, but there was no sound coming from them. Fear of Val's being killed and relief that he hadn't been created a vortex in her mind that allowed nothing else. Her hands reached for the arms of her chair as she tried to steady herself and regain some semblance of rational thought.

"So a series of bad decisions on my part became another story about me. You would think divine intervention would have humbled me…that I might have taken it as a sign that Val was special, and to be treated so. But no, if anything, the incident intensified my mood, and I stayed angry for a week. I spent every waking hour thinking about Val and ways to make him quit. I was amazed when he showed up the next time. This time I recognized the defiance for what it was. He may not have been a man in any other respect, but he had a will.

"Over the next few months, I didn't see much of Val. I tend to spend my days between the living quarters and the rig floor. Most of his time was spent out of sight of those, around and under the outside of the rig or down in the working spaces. When I did catch sight of him, before he was aware of my presence, he appeared relaxed and happy. I'm sure Davis was…"

She stirred, reconsidered, stirred again, and, unable to contain herself, said, "What do you want from me, Mr. Burnet? Absolution? Bless you, father, for you have sinned? You come and tell me you are turning my fine grandson into a brute, and you expect me to be happy because he now is a man, according to the code of some hairy-chested Troglodytes. You tell me that you almost killed him, that you hated him and treated him like scum, and that he has now been made like you, and you want…

what? You want me to congratulate you? You want me to thank you for making my grandson what I have tried to avoid these many years? I think not, Mr. Burnet. I think not. I have heard quite enough, Mr. Burnet. Please be so kind as to leave, now."

Buck could not remember ever having been talked to that way. He rose in a state of shock. All Sylvie could see was the huge person getting up slowly and turning toward the door, but in Buck's mind he was scuttling away in full retreat. He wanted to protest. He wanted to tell her all the reasons she shouldn't feel the way she did. But the reasons weren't there. She had every right to be upset. He had treated her grandson unfairly, and feeling like this, the first time ever, he thought, was his just reward. The fact that he felt differently about Campbell now didn't matter to her. He picked his way through the shelves, at pains not to knock over one of the racks and make a bad situation worse. Sylvie made it to the door ahead of him and held it open, ushering him out. On the sidewalk he turned to her, intending some form of farewell, but no words would come. Sylvie looked defiantly into the pirate face and realized she was seeing his eyes for the first time and seeing — could it be possible? — contrition? Regret? Sadness? Surely not. She closed the door, a little more firmly than necessary, she thought in retrospect.

CHAPTER XVII

Lunch with Earl Guidry

Back in the sunlight, Buck stopped at the curb to let his eyes readjust. He hadn't accomplished what he wanted to, whatever that was. In fact he felt like he was on the negative side of where he had started out this morning. He wasn't going to leave town before lunch, in any case. His breakfast had been home cooking of a high level, and lunch would surely be, as well. With nowhere else to go, he walked back to the cafe. He might have a piece of pie right now, if it was fresh out of the oven.

Fresh out of the oven it was, and with a little dab of vanilla ice cream on the side. Hot, fresh dewberry pie, so good, as they said around here, it would "make you slap yo' mama." In fact, that was what the large, loud lady who ran the place said when Buck asked about the pie. He was sipping his coffee when the deputy came in.

"Well, what did you think of our Miz Sylvie?" he said heartily. Deputy Guidry was a hearty guy. "She's sumthin', ain't she? Did she pull out the shotgun?"

The questions came so fast that Buck's nod covered them all.

"She's over there every day, nine to six, hell or high water. She doesn't get many customers that walk in the door. I don't know how many customers she's got or who they are, but little trucks come and go, and there must be enough of them to keep her afloat. She reads a lot of books, and I'm sure she enjoys that, but I don't see how she can afford to keep that place open just for the sake of old John's memory, especially with that expensive ventilating and air conditioning system going all the time. That must cost a pretty penny, all by its lonesome."

Buck's expression seldom gave anything up, but deputy Guidry's practiced eye detected a flicker of interest at the mention of John. Buck recognized the patter of the natural-born gossip. Usually he had little time for such people, but time was all he had today, and information on Val's family was his expressed reason for being here. Besides, he liked the deputy, who seemed to have good information. His comment about the ventilation system had already filled a tiny hole in his mind.

"Sheriff, if you don't mind, I'd like to ask you something."

"Deputy Sheriff," Guidry said. "Ask away."

"A while ago, when we were talking on the sidewalk? Did you have a backup behind me somewhere?"

Buck fancied that he could see the thoughts on the deputy's face, and he wondered idly what kind of poker player the deputy was. The sheriff decided something, and one of the most engaging grins Buck had ever seen spread across his face.

"I have to tell you that, under normal conditions, a man who looked like you, in a Rolls-Royce—I'm sorry, a Bentley, for God's sake—sitting on Main Street in the middle of the morning with no apparent business...normally I'd have backup. But this morning I didn't, because I knew I wouldn't need it. It didn't take more than fifteen minutes to find out who owned that car, and I knew that you couldn't be anybody but Buck Burnet. I wasn't checking you out this morning; I was meeting you. Now, can I ask you something? Why a Bentley?"

Buck's eyes dropped to his coffee cup.

"A friend of mine who worked for an oil company took a job in Tunisia. They were caught up in moving and needed some ready cash. It was his wife's car, and I think it may have been one of the reasons that they needed to get a high-paying job overseas. They couldn't find a buyer right away, so I took it off their hands at a price just over what it would take to be able to keep looking them in the eyes. I had intended to sell it as soon as I could, but, to tell you the truth, I like the damn thing. It's hard to imagine a ride being worth that much money, but it's just that little bit better than anything else I've ever had, and I can't seem to part with it."

Guidry said, "You told me you were looking for information about the Campbells. If you've got a few minutes, I can fill you in on the parts I know."

Buck's settling in the back of his chair was all the deputy needed.

"John was her husband," he said, answering the unasked question. "He was from an old family. They were good family here from way before the war."

Buck signaled for another cup of coffee. If they were starting at the Civil War, this was liable to take a while.

"They owned a good-sized plantation out north of town. The old man at that time was a member of the state legislature. He wasn't too strong for the Confederacy to begin with, but when one of their boys came home on leave and got himself killed by a bunch of outlaws right in front of the house with his mother watching, they decided they had had enough of the Deep South. They sold the place and packed up and moved to Texas. John's granddaddy either didn't get the word about the move or didn't like the sound of Texas, because when he got back from the war, he came back here to Hickory Flat. He had the slave they had sent him off with, a fashionable war injury, and a classical education, and that was it. The slave was no longer a slave, obviously, but their relationship didn't seem to be any different than it had been when they left. It's likely he would have died in the Reconstruction South and his part of the line with him, but he was a tall, good-looking fellow, like John was, and he caught the eye of the oldest McNeil girl, and she married him. Her grand-daddy had been a sharecropper, but her daddy had gone north before the war and come back a carpetbagger. He had managed to buy up most of the farmland north of town, including what had once been the Campbell plantation.

"Well, that was one Campbell with more money than he could spend in a lifetime. His son, John's daddy, went up north and got himself a classical education, and came back fired up to start a college, right here in Calcasieu Parish; and he did. The administrative offices of McNeil State College are what was originally the main house of the Campbell plantation. The reason it's got *State* in the name is that John's daddy was no businessman. He built some nice buildings and got some good people down here to staff it, but he couldn't keep it together by himself, so the state waited till he had sold off all his land keeping it afloat, and stepped in and took it over before it went under. That was when John was at university. I take it John was a pretty accomplished scholar, because he came back a doctor in literature from Oxford or Stanford—one of those schools in England. The college here hired him on as a professor of English, and he did well. Within just a few years, he was the head of the department."

Buck and the deputy both ordered lunch, it having become that time. The lunch was meatloaf and fresh vegetables, with dewberry pie for dessert. The deputy seemed partial to pie, himself. Buck thought the meatloaf was excellent. Give Buck a choice between meatloaf and duck a la orange, and he would pick the meatloaf every time. A distant girlfriend had once accused him of having "industrial taste." Buck always thought it said more about her than him.

"That slave that John's grandfather brought back from the Civil War?" The deputy's whole face seemed to form a question mark. "One of his descendants cooked that very pie you're eating. Another one works as a housekeeper for Miz Sylvie and her daughter, and another one is a deputy with me."

Buck was hoping this was an aside and not a side track, and so it proved to be. The sheriff settled back into the main narrative.

"Did I mention that John was a good-looking sum'itch? And tall — really tall? Well he didn't have a lot of money, but he had a lot of appeal, and he was the subject of many female conversations around here, I can tell you. He went so long without getting married that the talk naturally tended in the direction of homosexuality. Well, there wasn't anything to that. My personal opinion is that John didn't have a big need for other people, of whatever sex. He had his books, and he had his students. He had inherited a pretty substantial library, and he had added to it, and there's an eternal quality to the students at a college. There they are, year after year, forever young and trusting, their minds just opening, waiting to be formed. A large number of them ripe as peaches on a tree, and soft…and snuggly."

Buck lost the deputy momentarily while he considered just how snuggly they might be.

"I don't know if John ever indulged, but if he didn't, it wasn't for lack of opportunity. I suspect he could have had half of his female students if he had wanted, and it would certainly explain why he wasn't bedding any of the locals. It would be hard to compete with the fountain of youth. My feeling is that he didn't. John had a pretty strict sense of right and wrong. I think he would have considered it taking advantage. I, on the other hand, probably wouldn't have seen it as that. I would have been able to make up an acceptable story for myself, but I don't think he could have. Not being able to make up that kind of story for himself is what finally killed him. There was some talk that he had a black mistress. That would be another reason for why he wasn't sexually 'active,' but I have to tell you that I never saw any evidence of it, and never heard anything that would really credit it. As far as I know, John stayed at home with his books. Then he was invited to present a paper at some kind of conference in Montreal, Canada, and didn't come back. Not for two or three months, anyway, and, when he did come back, he brought Miz Sylvie with him. I think it's real handy the way college professors can drop everything like that with no repercussions. If you or I took off, they wouldn't even remember our names when we showed back up. Obviously Miz Sylvie was the talk of the town. Hell, she was the talk of the parish—this whole part of the state. She was beautiful. That was there for any fool to see. Still is, in my opinion. The big thing was she was French."

Buck apparently got some coffee down the wrong pipe, because he started coughing.

"Are you all right?

"I'm all right; I'm all right. Just something I said. I talked to her," Buck said, "and I didn't hear a trace of an accent."

The deputy laughed. "You didn't say something derogatory about the French, did you? She doesn't have an accent. She doesn't have an accent in French, either. When she talks about it, she talks like it's some kind of defect in her makeup. She says it's something about her ear, or the way things are passed around in her brain, but she can't reproduce an accent, even if she tries to. She's not like we talk about being French, though. She's real French, from France. She was up there in Quebec teaching little Quebecoise how to speak proper French, but she is that died-in-the-wool, born somewhere just outside and educated in Paris, real, sure 'nough French. There's always been a competition around here about who's got the most class, English people or the French people. There's even some kind of division of the French people into French and coonass. But all the people around here would agree that real French from France *is* class. The whole parish felt like they were upgraded by having somebody like that living here.

"Hell, it gets even better than that. A few years back, a cousin of hers visited her and Valerie. He was one for chasing the ladies, anyway, but one time he had a little too much to drink and got to chasing Sadie around the tables here at the cafe, and I had to put him up at the jail for a while till he sobered up. Normally, Sadie wouldn't have objected, but he had dropped his pants and his shorts off and had a hard-on like a pump handle, and she wasn't sure but what something that size would hurt her. She must have got to thinking about it, though, because she was seen in his company, frequently, after he got out of jail. Anyway, while that fella was staying with me, we had the opportunity to chat. He told me that their family in France was descended from royalty, and that Sylvie would most likely have been a duchess or countess or some such if she had gone back to France. This lady was considered high-class even in France." The last was said with particular vehemence. So much so that the cafe went momentarily silent while everyone checked to make sure there wasn't something more than a conversation going on. While the deputy was getting himself squared back up in his chair, a man Buck would have taken for a judge in any setting passed behind the deputy and patted him on the back.

"Hello, Judge," the deputy said. "How you doin' today? How's Miz Marjo?"

The judge, two tables away and moving, allowed as how everything was great.

"Anyway, everybody around here, including me, fell in love with Miz Sylvie, and John Campbell's stock went up considerably. They seemed to have the perfect marriage. Two beautiful people in a beautiful antebellum house. Social prestige out the wazoo. A new little baby girl that was lovely to look at. The security and prestige of a college professorship. The salary of a department head. But there, as somebody said, there was the rub.

"It's only my opinion that Miz Sylvie was motivated by a need for money. Anyway, it became obvious through the years that she was not totally satisfied with her little corner of heaven. John began to sell insurance on the side. Nobody in town would have chosen that for him or believed he would have chosen it for himself, so it was assumed that the idea came from Miz Sylvie. Oddly enough, he sold a lot of insurance. People wanted to have him into their homes, and if the price of that was a little whole life, then they were happy to pay it just to count him as a friend. The rich people bought from him just so Miz Sylvie would be sure to attend their parties. She was, hands down, the belle of any Calcasieu Parish ball. The future looked bright for the Campbell family. The daughter, Valerie, was developing her mother's looks and grace, and her father's scholarly bent. For his part, those who knew John well didn't think he was looking all that good. His performance in class was listless, and he didn't seem to walk as tall as he had. He loved his daughter, and she adored him, but with her was the only time anyone saw him smile anymore.

"The business did so well that John had to give up his teaching, pretty much leaving his students in the lurch."

A thought that had been niggling at Buck for some time became conscious, and Buck said, "And you were one of those students, weren't you?"

"Yes," said the deputy, momentarily at a loss for words.

"And you know who said 'there's the rub,' and who wrote it and when it was written."

The deputy was caught off base, his 'good ole boy' persona down around his ankles.

"Yes," said the deputy, "yes, I was one of his students. My high school teacher took me to him. Hell, it wasn't really high school. I was the only one in the senior class. John Campbell took me out of the swamp and opened my eyes to a 'whole new world,' as they say."

The thought made the deputy uncharacteristically reflective, and for the first time Buck thought he might stop, unbidden.

Looking over Buck's head and speaking quietly around a toothpick, the deputy said, "I had a semester to go when John resigned from the college. I quit school in retaliation and went to work as a deputy. Strange how a kid's mind works, isn't it? I changed the course of my life to spite a man who had never promised me a goddamn thing. I don't know why I reacted so strongly. His giving up the quest for truth and beauty for that of 'filthy lucre' seemed a personal betrayal, and I wanted to hurt him back. And it did hurt him. I could see it in his eyes every time we met, which was pretty frequently. At first I took satisfaction in it. Later I came to regret it.

"John started a full-time insurance business, and it flourished. All the contacts he had made through the years stepped up, begging him to let them invest in it. All the banks were after him to borrow their money. John was hiring people right and left, building a building out south of town. He bought this store over here, so Miz Sylvie could start her own business. I'm not even sure they knew what that business was going to be. Everything was coming up roses, and it looked like John was going to be rich. But John wasn't any more a businessman than his daddy or his granddaddy. And it wasn't very long before those people who had been begging him to take their money were knocking on his door with different expressions. A more practical man would have hid all he could, declared bankruptcy, and found work somewhere as a professor. I'm not sure anything like that even occurred to John. The only asset he felt he had was the insurance he had taken out on his own life.

"His daughter Valerie was sixteen when she found her daddy dead in their backyard. As violent deaths go, it wasn't messy. He had used a .22 cal. rifle, and everything must have stopped immediately, because there was very little blood. Blood or no, it must have been a horrible sight to that little girl. I've replayed that night in my mind a hundred times, but what comes back to me isn't the sight of John laid out on the azaleas; it's the sight of Valerie standing stiff and white in the kitchen, her mother consoling her, trying to find a way to embrace her, but not being able to get her arms around someone so hard and cold. John did what he did, and I guess, in some weird way, he thought he was doing the best he could for his family, but I wonder if he wouldn't have chosen another way if he had known how it was going to affect them. The insurance money paid off the debts and left them a little bit to live on, but I think for some years now Valerie has been the main financial support. Everybody blamed Sylvie for it, including Valerie, I believe. I think that's the reason they still live together, just so Valerie can communicate on a daily basis how much she loathes her mother. And the mother, wracked with guilt, can't take the basic logical step of removing herself to someplace safe. Valerie's chosen role in life seems to be inquisitor general to her mother, and Miz Sylvie's seems to be trying to save her daughter from something she can't understand.

"Miz Sylvie scrapped whatever plans she had for that store and moved all of John's books into it and made it sort of a bookstore monument to John. It's hard to believe that a single man could have owned that many books, but the number there right now can't vary by more than a hundred or two from what he left.

"This is all just me talking, you understand. Just conclusions based on observations from the outside. To my knowledge, Valerie has never considered marrying anybody. Occasionally she'll pick somebody out, use him until there isn't anything left, then drop him like the stick from a popsicle. There was a time that I wanted to be chosen. I thought I could get to her and bring that sweet, loving girl back to life. Hell, I would have even taken being used; but I didn't meet her standards. Her marks are unfailingly intellectual and, except for the one I believe to be Valiant's father, don't look anything like her own father. Val's father, I think — because, as far as I know, she has never told anyone who the fathers of her kids were — was a young professor in anthropology or archeology teaching out at the school while she was an undergraduate. Handsome guy, very much in John's mold, and brilliant. He's famous now. At least as famous as a person in a very narrow field can get. He's a big deal at a university on the West Coast. And I'll bet you anything he doesn't know he left Valerie pregnant with his son — if, in fact, he did."

Buck's eyebrows were up as he said, "Did you say kids?"

"Two. Val and a little sister, who's—"

About that time the deputy spotted the judge, who was working his way back through the cafe on his way out.

"Hey, Judge. Hey, Judge. Come here a second." He waited for the man to approach. "Hey, Judge. You know who I got here? It's Buck Burnet. Buck, this here is Judge Prentiss."

Buck stood for the introduction.

The judge's expression said, "I know I'm supposed to know the name by the way you say it, but I don't really recall..."

The deputy said, "You remember? Twenty years ago or more. The fight down in Lake Charles at the racetrack over doping? The big roughneck that cleared the stands of all the track people?"

The judge's face still registered puzzlement. Buck wasn't surprised that the judge couldn't remember. He himself had no recollection of the incident. That didn't mean it didn't happen, any more than the deputy's having heard it meant it did. It was Buck's experience that such stories frequently didn't require a real incident to be based on, although he was beginning to remember a day at the races that didn't go as planned.

The judge's expression said, "I wish I had time to sit here and play twenty questions, but I got some real pressing business back over at the courthouse, and I don't have time to stand and reminisce with some lowlife roughneck." His mouth said, "Pleased to meet you, Mr. Burnet. Maybe I'll get a chance to see you again."

Buck got the feeling that he hoped it was across the bench in his courtroom. Buck had been watching the judge during the charade about the fight. He was a tremendously distinguished-looking man — tall, with a full head of gray hair. But, where the deputy wore his authority with an easiness that showed you he was still conscious of being a mortal, the judge wore his like a mantle that had been placed there by God, personally. Buck didn't like being in front of any bench, but he decided that he for sure didn't want to face Judge Prentiss in any place where the judge had the upper hand.

"It's Burnet," Buck said.

"I beg your pardon?" the judge said.

"The name's Burnet. Burn-ette. Not Burn-it like the little town in Texas."

Buck knew full well that the judge cared less than nothing about the pronunciation of his name, but he just couldn't resist poking at him.

Nodding absently, with the remains of his question still on his face, the judge backed and turned slowly away. Buck used to try to make mental notes of such chance enemies, but there were so many now, it hardly seemed worth the effort.

Buck said to the deputy, "You didn't tell me you knew anything about me."

"Actually, I did." said the deputy. "Anything? Hell, man, there was a time you were famous around here. There was a new story every week. You were like the oilman's Paul Bunyan or something. I about decided you were a myth—just a compilation of bar stories."

Buck knew that he had been famous in the way that the deputy meant it. He had even been guilty of courting that fame to some extent. He hadn't consciously added to his own illusion, but he had certainly let the stories go on unchecked—not that he could really have checked them. Oilfield hands in those hard days had needed heroes. They were called 'oilfield trash' and treated accordingly. Some large percentage of them *were* lowlife, drawn by the gypsy-like nature of most of the oilfield jobs. But the majority were hardworking family men. During times of reduced drilling, the owners would send the rigs anywhere they could get a contract. The best hands were those who owned property and didn't want to move away from it. The rigs that managed to stay in an area within driving distance from home had first call on them, and those were the rigs with the best drilling records, and therefore the ones with the best hands. Buck didn't stop the stories because it was fun being famous, even on a minor scale, but he justified it to himself by its share in his being able to get and keep the best hands, an effect that had aided him for all of his long career. Only lately had his earlier celebrity seemed other than a blessing, as both his mind and his body seemed less inclined to physical confrontation.

"You know, while I've got you here and talking, I've just got to ask you something," said the deputy. "Now, don't take this wrong, but I just can't not ask it."

Buck had a feeling he knew what was coming, and his mind cast about for a way to get the deputy off the track.

"Were you the one who tore that guy's dick off in New Orleans that time?"

There it was. The one story he couldn't seem to shed. He hated being thought of as the man who had pulled another man's penis off. Why couldn't it be an ear or a nose or even a foot—anything but a penis.

"No," Buck said.

The deputy said, "I heard about that incident when it happened. Every New Orleans cop I ran into for a while had been the first one on the scene. I hadn't heard anything about you in a few years, but as soon as I heard that story for the first time, I put your name on it. I put your name on it just because it sounded like what I had heard of you. But I didn't believe it had really happened. The whole thing was just too incredible. A couple of years later, I'm investigating a string of burglaries, and I get word from the Houston PD that they're holding an old-time police character they think may be good for them. They think he's been operating in south Louisiana. It turns out that they don't know that south Louisiana and New Orleans are two different places. He had operated in New Orleans, but he hadn't been a burglar at the time. He had been a small-time enforcer and bagman for the mob; 'small-time' because whenever it was something important, he would be put with somebody closer to the top. He said he got to going out pretty regularly with a guy who was kin to the top guy in New Orleans—a big hairy guy who was a real sadist. He said this guy told him that sometimes he was paid to play the sadist in club shows that you had to be special to know where and when they were taking place. He wore a leather mask and black leather pants with studs and used whips and such. He said that those customers who wanted to thought they were fake, but he said there wasn't anything fake about it. Sometimes he went overboard and killed somebody, but he said it didn't matter because it was always someone nobody cared about, and it was good for business.

"Can you imagine that?" the deputy asked Buck. "What kind of a person goes to something like that?" Apparently realizing that the answer was obvious, the deputy went on.

"He said they got sent out one night to kill someone. He said it had something to do about a whore that had once been a mistress of the big man. The guy they were going after had kidnapped her or something. He was a big guy who worked for some business in New Orleans. They didn't expect any trouble, and the sadist even tried to talk him out of going, so he could do it himself, but this guy was afraid he would be in trouble if it got messed up, so he stayed with him. He said the whore had set up the hit. He said the mark was big. Really big. Big as his partner. And he didn't look like he worked in any office. My guy wanted to shoot him and be done with it, but his partner wanted to do it with his hands. His partner was acting odd, getting worked up, like it was a sexual thing. They trailed him into Jackson Park, of all places. He said it had a lot of bushes and stuff then. They cornered their man in some oleanders — that's what he said, oleanders. The mark was big, but he was scared, so my guy starts feeling better; and about that time, all hell breaks loose. My guy says he was thrown into a tree. He said it had to be the mark, but he had never seen him move. He's standing there looking at the guy, and all of a sudden, he's trapped in all these limbs and leaves and looking at the sky. He was struggling to get out when he hears the scream. He said it was like every bit of juice he had in his body was sucked into that tree. He said it was the worst thing he had ever heard in his life. He thought his partner must have done something terrible to that mark. He thinks maybe he should stay where he is for a little while. Then he hears a crashing and a thrashing like an elephant in extreme pain was caught in a trap. Then he hears, quite clearly, because I quizzed him on this point, he hears, "He pulled my dick off!" He looks where the sound came from and sees his partner running off into the night, and the mark standing, watching him leave. He decides to be real still until he sees the mark walking away. He said the mark had a distinctive walk. He kind of rolled, like John Wayne. He said that night he went out of the enforcing business and left New Orleans. He says he would be surprised to find out that they ever found anybody to do that mark. He doesn't know what happened to his partner after that."

Once he had finished, the deputy watched Buck carefully, as if he expected him to betray something.

Buck stared at his coffee cup, and said, "That's quite a yarn, Sheriff. You sure that guy wasn't having a flashback of some kind?"

The deputy slowly rested the front legs of his chair back on the floor. "You see, I always had that mark as being you — or your myth, at any rate. I didn't really believe the story, because I didn't believe that any man could actually do it. I mean physically. If there is any part of the human anatomy that would want to stay attached, that would be it. But as I look at you, I'm not so sure that it couldn't be done. I mean, what are you? Fifty? Sixty?"

Buck nodded his agreement that he must be one of those.

"And you're still as big a person as I've ever been close to. You don't look like Mr. Universe. You look more like a Mr. Universe that had the peaks and valleys leveled out. For all that heft, you walk like a much younger man, sort of like you don't put all your weight down at every step. I wouldn't take you on now, with the help of three deputies. I'd have to shoot you before I got within range."

Buck said, "I just have two questions."

He waited for the deputy's nod before going on.

"You said Valerie supported them now. What does she do?"

The deputy said, "She's an English professor out at the college."

"And the other question is how is it that a man who can quote Shakespeare doesn't know that Stanford is not in England?"

CHAPTER XVIII

Sylvie's Home

Early summer afternoon in South Louisiana. The morning had been hot, but it wasn't a patch on this; and soon it would be even hotter. Buck was back in the Bentley. He thought briefly about turning the air conditioning on, but decided it would be too hard on the engine. He was left with nothing really to do. There didn't seem to be any way to get a look at the mother, and sitting here in what felt like a sauna was getting less reasonable by the second.

He caught a motion in the outside mirror, which was still aimed at the storefront. Sylvie Campbell had come out and closed the door. Now, bent over, she appeared to be locking it. Directly she turned around, looked toward the car, and started walking. She looked both ways at the curb, but that was the only time she looked away from his car in the time it took to get to it. Buck, who wasn't really familiar with the sensation, was feeling a little bit of panic. He reached to start the car but realized the keys weren't in the ignition. He was searching for them when she reached the door.

"Exactly what are your plans, Mr. Burnet?" she said. "Do you propose sitting out here all day?"

Since he hadn't yet proposed anything, he couldn't think of anything to say.

A little bit put out, she said, "Come along. Walk with me to the house, and we can talk there."

When Buck mumbled something about customers, she said, "There are no customers. And I can't read with a giant infant sitting across the street in this ridiculous car."

Buck thought that was going a bit far, but he got out and locked the ridiculous car and set off after Sylvie Campbell, who was already on the sidewalk and striding rapidly away. Buck walked behind her until he realized he was watching the sway of her hips. Feeling oddly guilty, he caught up and walked beside her—half ran really, because she was setting a furious pace. She was talking as she was walking, but because of the motion and having to watch where he was going, he was having a hard time catching all of it. They had gone one street north of where the car was parked and were headed east. The street was pure antebellum paradise. Huge live oaks arched overhead, complete with hanging Spanish moss. The houses along the street nearly all had plaques on their fronts proclaiming them state treasures. Buck heard her say something about having to come to some sort of agreement because Val was still her grandson and something about the rest of the story, but he couldn't make out if she wanted to hear it or felt like she should. Finally, when, through having to watch the moss overhead, the tilts in the sidewalk, the curbs, and, guiltily again, her breasts, he tripped, she slowed her pace. He couldn't tell if her slight smirk was because she had caught him looking at her breasts or because of his stumble. It occurred to him that if he had any pride, he would turn around and leave Hickory Flat and her in the past. He decided he must not have any pride.

"How is it you speak the way you do, Mr. Burnet. I'd heard about it, but I must say, I wasn't prepared for the full effect. The right words are in the right places, but there are certain signs—other than the way you look—that you didn't grow up speaking that way. Nobody I know grew up speaking that way. Isn't it just a touch pompous and self-conscious?"

This lady had no trouble putting it right out there. She had to slow down and finally turn around as formulating an answer brought Buck almost to a halt. He said, "I was full grown when I started reading and learned that there was such a thing as proper English. To some extent the reading changed the way I spoke. I consciously changed it the rest of the way, because I believed someone when she said that was the reason she didn't love me. By the time I recognized that for a fruitless quest, I was speaking this way, and anything else would have seemed like backing down. I feel comfortable with it now, at any rate, and any other way of speaking would feel uncomfortable."

Something about the foregoing had interested her because, just for a moment, she looked at him intently. They had stopped in front of a beautiful old masterpiece of a house that looked like it had been part of the set for *Gone With the Wind*. Buck had driven past many houses like this and wondered what they, and the people who lived in them, were like. This one was made of white shipboard lath with working green wooden shutters on tall French doors along the front porch, which spanned the breadth of the house. Sylvie Campbell turned and charged up the front walk, and Buck fell in behind her. Up the broad steps they swept, through a crystal door, into a wide hallway, stairs ahead. She pointed Buck into a room on the left as she skirted the stairs, calling someone's name. Buck found what could only be called a parlor. He had had no real experience with such, but, when he read about parlors in books, this was exactly the sort of room he had envisioned. Rich-looking furniture was set about in unlikely ways. There was a large fireplace and a mantel with a portrait of someone severe above it. Light from tall windows made its way through heavy velvet drapes and fine lace curtains. The placement of Oriental rugs seemed as random as that of the furniture.

The reaction of the chair Buck chose to sit in gave him the first clue that everything wasn't as it seemed. He quickly stood with a clear vision of himself sitting atop a pile of expensive

sticks. Closer inspection revealed that everything was thread-
bare and in ill repair but, as they say, clean. A strange noise
drew Buck from the parlor into the next room farther back. The
two rooms were connected by a wide entrance with yet more
curtains. It was a dining room, and the noise had come from
a far corner. It was dark, and Buck could tell something was
there, but couldn't make out what from across the table. He
stood just inside the entryway, very still, trying to pick up what
information he could before committing himself. Whatever it
was, was alive and being as quiet as he was, probably for the
same reason. Slowly he walked around the table, conscious of
the wood floor and the sounds it was making. At the end of
the table, eyes still adjusting to the dim light, he peered into
the corner, hoping he would see what it was before it fastened
onto his leg with cold, steely fangs. What it was, was a girl
of nine or ten with straight black hair cropped just below the
ears. Her pretty face was turned up as if looking for a spider in
the corner behind Buck. Quickly, she turned to look at another
corner, then, just as quickly, back. She was seated at a table
which had a U cut from one side. She sat in the U, and the table
was pushed against the wall, effectively trapping her. The table
was about five feet square and had nothing on it, though there
was a selection of books and other children's toys on the floor
around it.

Buck realized she had not been looking at the corners of the
room after all. She was looking at him. That is, attempting to
look at him, because she appeared to be blind in front but able to
pick up something from the sides of her eyes. She reached and
grasped as if trying to feel him, though he was a good seven or
eight feet away. She was a lovely little Asian child. Apparently
satisfied that Buck wasn't there to either harm her or give her
anything, her head dropped to the surface of the table, landing
on its tongue, and she licked the table in a quick, sixty-degree
arc to the left, and went back to whatever she had been lost in
when he entered.

Suddenly, Buck was struck on the hip by something that
bounced off toward that side of the room, leaving him to avoid

smashing the dining room table by not falling on it. When he got upright, the something materialized into a dark, round woman of indeterminate age, with ridiculously large eyes, which were on his face, and a similarly large mouth, which was open and screaming. The child was screaming, as well as, Buck supposed, was some part of himself.

Sylvie Campbell came in and added to the din by inquiring loudly why Olivia was in the dining room instead of where she was supposed to be, and why she, the round one, was watching soap operas instead of teaching Olivia her numbers. That conversation continued through another door and out to what Buck took to be the kitchen, leaving Olivia and him to become peripherally reacquainted. She lost interest in him more quickly this time and resumed her task of keeping the two-inch wide, eighteen-inch long strip of table in front of her sufficiently slick with saliva.

The other door actually led to a large pantry with a walkway and space for storage on either side. There was another door to the kitchen—the finest residential kitchen Buck had ever entered. He felt instantly at home in that kitchen. The appliances and cabinets were white. The countertops and floor were white-and-black tile, giving the room the flavor of an old-fashioned ice cream parlor. The kitchen was as large as a lot of houses and, indeed, gave the appearance of having been a separate building at one time. Buck had entered from the south, and there was a large fireplace, which had some utilitarian bars and hooks hanging from and around it, though none of them appeared to have had recent use. The north and south walls were the only ones without windows. The east wall had windows from waist high to the nine-foot ceiling from front to back, and the west wall had a window over the sink, and then more like the east wall between the end of the counters and a door to the outside, which was situated next to the north wall. Sunlight filled the room, and there was that about it that said cleanliness and competence. Buck wouldn't have been able to say why he was comfortable in one place and not another, but this was the first room in the house in which he did not feel out of place. There were two stoves on the north wall, and on top of one of them was a big, blue-and-white speckled coffee-pot. A quick sniff told Buck that it was still worth drinking. Small cups, thick rich coffee with chicory, and lots of real sugar were a true Louisiana luxury, and Buck took some in a cup from a group that were out—mismatched, he noticed. There was a big, solid-looking table that could have been a hundred years old or more, and Buck sat down at it with his back to the east windows, giving himself a position from which he could survey the room. There was a door across from him that he assumed the two women had left through, and presently the dark lady he hadn't met edged in from the pantry. She was of a type that can be found only in south Louisiana, though usually somewhat farther east. She was dark, but more the dark of an American Indian than of an African. Her features were pretty, and her eyes were hazel. She was both less round and younger than Buck's first impression. She was a born coquette, and she never once looked at him straight on with anything other than a knowing smile. She spoke English with a Cajun accent, and she moved in ways that let him know just how tasty the parts were which were doing the moving. A large part of Buck always responded to that, but this afternoon his mind was on other things, and he was too distracted to play the game out with her. Interplay with a natural was always a pleasure though, and Buck enjoyed it. She told him she had been sent to fix him a cup of coffee in the "company" pot. Buck told her that if the coffee from the company pot was any better than that from this everyday one, he didn't believe he could stand it. She laughed politely and said that she had made some biscuits this morning, the big, fluffy kind that "Valiant"—the last said with cut, defiant eyes—favored. Buck said that if "Valiant" favored them, he could probably choke down one or two. Her name was Justine, and as Buck bantered with her, he thought how increasingly rare her type of person was. He doubted that she had heard any of the recent discussion of men's and women's roles, but he'd bet that she wouldn't be interested enough to join it. She seemed just as pleased that he loved her cooking as she would be if he loved her loving, and pleased in the same way. She was obviously intelligent but didn't feel she had to hide anything; consequently there were no complexities to fathom, no tricks to try to see behind. Buck very much enjoyed his twenty or so minutes with her, and her inevitable displacement by Sylvie Campbell came as a bit of a disappointment.

She was a case in another point. She was so complex that Buck hadn't even been able to determine if she were intelligent. He assumed she was, but so far everything she had said to him could have been a product of the right upbringing. Her manner toward Justine was brusque. Justine's apparent unconcern made him think that, either the brusqueness was for his benefit, or that the recent incident involving Olivia hadn't yet been resolved. Justine kept fussing about the kitchen, occasionally glancing one way or the other to see if Buck were watching. Occasionally, he was. Sylvie Campbell drew a cup of coffee from the "family" pot and took a seat at the end of the table, to Buck's left.

"What shall I call you, Mr. Burnet? Around here Buck is a name for a horse, or a dog. I would feel a little silly calling a grown man 'Buck.'"

Buck wondered if she were baiting him, and why she would be. She had been mispronouncing his name, placing the accent on the first syllable. He said, "It sounds like it has a double *t* on the end, but it doesn't. Since it's not a common name, I suspect that a recent ancestor took it on when his real one would have been inconvenient." She smiled dutifully at something that had obviously been said many times. Buck decided not to tell her that it was the truth, and that the recent ancestor was himself. He wondered what the casual adoption of a surname conveyed to her, who probably had a maiden name treasured through centuries. She had changed into a different dress, but one that didn't reveal any more of her body than had the first. She looked like she had a good shape, and not only for someone her age, but that could have been clever clothes selection. Buck had occasionally been amazed at what clothing could do. He didn't like the word *handsome* applied to a woman, but that is what she was. Her hair had been blond, and it was somewhere between that and gray now. That combination can be unpleasant, but in her case, it looked as though the changes were being made on purpose by someone who knew how. She had a broad forehead, a straight, pretty nose, a generous mouth, and a chin that verged on being too strong. Her eyes were a light blue, but didn't seem very expressive to Buck at the time because she obviously disapproved of him, and that's all they had communicated. She cast those eyes on Justine now and confirmed Buck's assessment of the previous situation by bringing up Olivia and why she wouldn't take proper care of her. Justine told her that she could only take so much of being bitten and spat upon, and, when she reached that point, it was better that she and Olivia be apart. Sylvie's expression said that she could understand that, and, while she continued to remonstrate, the heat went out of her voice. Buck asked about Olivia, and when he did, a look of sadness covered her face like a funeral veil. Buck had never seen such sadness and such strength in one person before. The feelings he had had for her when he first saw her solidified, and Buck promised himself that he would become friends with this woman, whatever that took.

"Olivia is Val's half-sister, the daughter of my daughter, Valerie. She contracted spinal meningitis shortly after birth and was left partially blind, partially deaf, and mentally affected. When she was a year old, we were told that, if we sent her to a special place in Texas, they could help her to become an adjusted person. I don't know what they did to 'adjust' her there, but by the time we listened to our hearts and brought her home, she had all these 'behaviors.'"

He thought that an odd choice of words, but later found out that "behaviors" was a word used by mental health professionals to describe erratic speech and actions.

"Justine had been with us long before Olivia came, but she has been a godsend since. There are times when she is the only person who can exercise any control over her. If anyone understands her, it is Justine."

Justine entered the conversation at that point, saying that Olivia couldn't "see very good, and she maybe can't hear very good, but she thinks real good, and everything she thinks is mean."

Sylvie said that Olivia's mother was certain that Olivia had a good brain, but that there was some kind of a block between that brain and her body. As she spoke, her voice became firmer, and she said the last looking steadily into Buck's eyes. He was still thinking about what she had said and didn't have a comment or question ready. He was not the world's best for conversation with a lady, but he wanted to continue this one and felt it was up to him to keep her engaged. Some of his confusion must have shown, because she said, "I must say, Mr. Burnet, I have never been in the presence of such physicality before. As close as this, it is quite overwhelming. It is intimidating and more than a little bit irritating. You are large, but I don't suppose you are any larger than the wrestlers one sees on TV, or the football players. I see occasional flashes of sensitivity, but I look at you and think, 'That can't be so.' Still, you obviously have a mind, and you are here wanting to talk. I don't believe it's your size that irritates me; it's what goes with it. It's an attitude: the way you walk, the assumption that you will be given way. I've seen power worn by other men, and there was some of that in them. I would imagine that Hitler or Alexander gave off such auras. Your size is an accident, Mr. Burnet, a gift from God. It is a reason to be grateful, not smug."

Buck didn't know if he was smug. Neither was he conscious of walking a certain way. It struck him as ironic that the two people she chose for examples were both physically small. If there was an attitude, he thought it was probably due to his position on the rig, which was just one step down from God. His size defined Buck. He couldn't think of a single person who, when asked to describe Buck Burnet, wouldn't start out by saying how big he was. He didn't resent that—he couldn't afford to—and, in truth, he wouldn't have wanted to be any other size. He often compared size in a man with beauty in a woman. There were certain automatics that went along with being beautiful.

A competitor might notice the advantage it afforded and resent it, but people who wanted her attention, which included most of the men, and at least some of the women, in any given place, didn't. Even the people who resented her beauty might feel drawn to it.

Size had its automatics, as well, and most of them were generally considered to be advantages. Buck felt his real advantages lay in the things he was not: slow and dumb. He wasn't as fast as a Joe Tom Wright, but he was much faster than most people seemed to believe possible. He considered speed, not size or strength, to be the difference in any encounter. As he aged he came to rely more on the second thing he wasn't, but he could foresee a time when size, strength, speed, and brains together weren't going to be enough. Buck didn't look forward to that time, but he didn't dread it either. He would no longer be king of the pride, but neither would he have the responsibility for it; because contrary to what Sylvie Campbell thought, Buck very much considered his body and abilities to be gifts from God. He considered his treatment of Val Campbell over the past year a failure on his part, and he didn't know it, but this trip to Hickory Flat was a pilgrimage seeking a means of atonement. His God defined the real Buck Burnet much more than did his size. It was a God of his own making, and what he required of Buck had grown and gained definition over the years until Buck was bound by a code as stringent as any monk's or samurai's. He wouldn't ask for forgiveness, because his God wouldn't grant forgiveness just for the hell of it. His God required something from Buck that showed he merited it. If the offense were bad enough, he wouldn't offer a means of atonement, and those offenses were carried on Buck's heart like pieces of lead.

Buck said, "It's entirely possible that I have an attitude. Do you blame a pretty girl for being aware of and using her beauty? I don't. It takes a person of exceptional mind and will to overcome such influences and become a person in her own rite, and it must be that only a few such exist. I think I have a good mind, but not an exceptional one, and I don't have room in it for worry about which parts of my outward behavior, many of which were formed by those around me, convey an impression that I would not consciously make."

After what had possibly been the longest lecture of his life, certainly the longest to a woman, Buck stopped and went back over what he had said to make sure that it was what he intended. He had noticed a tendency for words to take off on their own and leave meanings behind. He felt like he could have done better but that an attempt to refine it would confuse rather than elucidate. Sylvie Campbell was looking at him as if he were a person for the first time. She was going over what Buck had said in her own mind. No matter how she looked at it, there was no way she could make his little speech other than an original, cogent look at a part of life that she herself had thought about in bits and pieces. She had almost a physical sensation as her opinion of him shifted, as if a heavy door had been cracked open someplace and a slight movement of air had reached her. She surprised herself by being aware of his scent. There was no hint of the cologne, or whatever, which so many American men used. She hated it when the mere act of shaking hands left her own smelling strongly. His scent wasn't as heavy as a European's, but it was decidedly male.

"The person that taught you to read, Mr. Burnet—was she pretty?"

Sylvie's question wasn't as ingenuous as it sounded. She actually had some foreknowledge of the subject matter.

He started to say that she hadn't taught him to read, that she had given him a reason for learning how, but decided that the two might be the same thing to Sylvie Campbell. The question brought up feelings that Buck strove to keep buried but that had formed his life as surely as had his size or the fact that he was born into poverty.

"Was she pretty? She was way beyond pretty, but when I think of her, I recall mostly her scent." What Buck saw was Sylvie Campbell taking a sip of coffee, but the movement had started involuntarily when his thoughts came so close to her own. "You can't recall a smell, of course, but whenever I smell something remotely like it, it's like she is almost physically present. It wasn't a perfume. It wasn't musk. It was its own combination of the world's odors that draw us. That scent went right to the central part of my brain and wiped out any logical activity.

"I had her for a while," Buck said. "Right at first she was as much a prisoner of the thing as I was, but after a short time, I could never pierce her armor again." Buck gave no sign that he recognized the pun when Sylvie Campbell glanced up. "She saw me as an oaf, a moment's diversion. For weeks I stumbled around the French Quarter, alternately grieving and raving. I was by this time aware of what she did for a living, but it's not quite true to say that it didn't matter to me—that I would forgive her. It just was not a factor. It wouldn't have mattered if she had been the wife of Satan or a saint. I was past thought, of any kind."

"When had she taught you to read? It doesn't sound like there was time."

"If I said she taught me to read, I misspoke. She made me feel like that was what it would take to become acceptable to her. Before that I had everything in my life I needed to be happy. What she did was point to a void I hadn't been aware of. I came to believe that filling that void was the only way to become a whole person. Jack London wrote what I took to be an autobiographical novel. I can't remember the name of it, but it struck me as his *Portrait of the Artist as a Young Man*. He speaks at first of being invited to dinner at the home of a San Francisco socialite. He had, until that time, lived in a physical world, and he was aware and totally confident of his position in it. At the dinner table, he slowly realized that he was being ridiculed, and worse, that he had no way of fighting back. He left the place in shame, vowing to become the equal of the diners and worthy of the girl. He was naïve, yes. But there is that about a man, a physical man with a brain, an innocence that is not present in any other circumstance. London became the intellectual he wanted to and validated it by creating things for other intellectuals to ponder; but I've often wondered if he was glad of his awakening. I for one am ambivalent about the small intellect I have managed to cultivate."

Buck was not being self-effacing. He knew his present life was richer for the greater number of things he was able to appreciate, but he often longed for the simplicity of life as he remembered it. He had been preeminent in the role that he had been asked to play. He could be wrong about things, but would it really have mattered if he hadn't known? He could be just as wrong now. The only difference was that he felt badly about it.

"Losing her forced my mind open, and in that sense her presence (or absence) in my life could be said to have been a good thing. Certainly it's a richer world than it would have been otherwise. But after her, nobody was as soft, nobody smelled so good, nobody made me shudder with a simple look—or the touch of a hand. Had I known it was never again to be, I might have picked the best of those available and married. I might not have been happier, but I would have had progeny."

Sylvie Campbell startled Buck by saying, "Sometimes progeny is not all sunshine and roses." She was still at the table with him, and Justine was seated as well. He could see that Justine was taken with the romance of the thing; from time to time, she would dab at an eye with her apron. Sylvie Campbell, on the other hand, didn't have a lot of sympathy for someone she apparently considered to be naive to the point of stupidity. "How is it you had so much time to spend mooning around New Orleans? Did you not have a job? Other responsibilities? How did you make a living?"

Buck said, "I had a job. I haven't been without a job since the age of fourteen." Not truth, but much briefer.

The look Buck gave her was no more than a glance, really, but it did make her aware of the power he was able to muster. She was conscious once again of what she was dealing with. His portrait of himself as a big, oafish child in a world of manipulative adults had lulled her, but the truth must be more complex, as evidenced by the fact that he was here and talking. The very size of him was really quite something. She knew a lot of what was hidden under his clothes was muscle, and she found herself wondering what that must look like on massive bones. The comment about his small intellect was obviously meant to be self-deprecating, but how small, or large, was it, really? It was easy to think of him as some sort of bear, or ape, but if one observed him for any length of time, that impression didn't hold. Thus far, he didn't strike one as being at all feral. He was intelligent. And Valiant liked him.

Buck was unaware that he had piqued her interest. In fact, he felt like he was losing her, that she was reconsidering her decision to let him into her home. He liked her, he liked this house, he liked this kitchen and this coffee, and he wanted her to like him. He didn't try to analyze his feelings. He was content to know them and keen to stay here, enjoying them. In an attempt to put her at ease, Buck asked about her grandson at exactly the same moment she thought of him.

"Valiant is my only reward," she said. "Earl told me you ate lunch together, and I'm sure he told you more about us than I would care for you to know. Earl is a good man and a good law officer, but he is addicted to information. My husband was a good man also, and from the outside he was the strongest and most complete of men. But he wasn't complete, and I was too young to know. I applied pressure in the wrong places, and he came apart. If there is an opposite of that, then Valiant is it. His mother had an appendectomy when she was three months pregnant. I was there when the doctor lifted the womb out of the way. He said, 'I don't believe this little one is going to make it, but I'll put him back just in case.' God help me, I was so embarrassed about his being a bastard that I hoped he wouldn't make it. When she was six months pregnant, she fell down the lower part of the stairs while running from me after yet another argument. We thought she must miscarry then, but she didn't. When he was an infant, he developed pneumonia and nearly died. The doctor told us that one of his little lungs had collapsed and would never function again. If he did live, we would have to restrict his activity because of the reduced capacity. That proved not to be the case. Valerie wanted him to be named after her as some sort of a twist on not needing a man, and I had fought that; but by the time he pulled out of the pneumonia, we both loved him desperately, and we agreed that Valiant was an appropriate name.

"Valerie has never said, but I believe his father is a man who was teaching here at about the right time. I'm sure she never told the father that he had a son, either."

Buck was hoping for a chance to examine her more closely while she was speaking, but her eyes stayed steady on his, and he had no choice but to keep his on hers. He was conscious that she was telling him exactly what he had wanted to know and doing so without pointed questions.

"Grandmothers always think that their grandchild is the best. It must be a miserable person who thinks otherwise; but Valiant *was* perfect. As far as I know, he has never asked anyone about why he doesn't have a father; certainly he has never asked me or his mother. He was born on Christmas day, which I have always tried not to take as a sign. It made him the youngest in his class at school, and he was small for his age. It must have been extremely difficult for him, but he never said so. If he cried, the tears were dry by the time he got home. He wasn't a particularly expressive child. Well then, we are not a particularly expressive family. What I'm trying to say is, he didn't frequently come and want to be kissed and hugged, but I knew he loved me. His presence in the room lit it up. Even Olivia, God bless her, becomes calmer as soon as she knows he is near.

"I'm sure now that Valerie had him purposely to have a man around that she could control. God truly works in mysterious ways, however, because Valiant was ever the least controllable of men. I referred to him as a man because he never seemed to be a boy. He was like having a little adult around. Had he been a different person, it would have been eerie. Even before he could talk, it was as if he weren't talking only because he was considering what should be said.

"His preschool years were spent here with us. We didn't see to it that he was around other children. In truth, he didn't seem to need other children. Consequently, when he went to first grade, he didn't know how to relate to them, or they to him. I know now that there is no such thing as a little adult, and if I had it to do over again, I would have pried him away from Valerie and taken care to socialize him. As it was, he was an outsider from the first. He would have been different in any case, but I think he might have had a happier childhood. He was not good at sports, and I realize that's not an uncommon story in America. Not that one couldn't be a poor player in Europe; it's just that being a poor player doesn't seem to mean as much there. You mentioned earlier that he was able to teach himself, though, and that didn't surprise me. He was always quick to pick up information, but his ability to teach his body was something I noticed when he was in middle school.

"That could be it, you know." When she digressed, her whole manner changed and she became much younger. Her eyes lit up, and she played with the new idea like a cat with a toy. Buck suddenly saw the beauty that the deputy had alluded to. "In France, they play football, as well. It is a different football, but somewhat similar. They don't have just a single team with the best players that represent an entire school, though. Any school will have a number of teams. They will have as many teams as they have boys that want to play for them. That way, on Saturday, when one school plays another, there will be one team with the best players, and they will play at the main venue, perhaps with seats on the perimeter for people who want to watch, but on fields around the outside of that their second and third and fourth teams will compete, et cetera, et cetera."

When she said "et cetera," she said it with an accent and a rising inflection, the first trace of her origins he had noticed. The first *t* disappeared, and the second was hit hard. Buck liked hearing her say "et cetera."

"That way, the boys on the outside fields did not end up feeling as if they were lesser people for not having played. I think this is a much better way, yes? I suppose my point is Val could have learned to play any game if given the chance to practice. It broke my heart each year when he would try out for the teams and not make them. I found it almost a mercy when he quit trying. Anyway, when he was in the eighth, or the seventh, grade, they put up what they called a 'tetherball' on the schoolyard. I suppose you know this game, yes? Yes. Like most sports, it favors the large, the quick, and the strong; but it is one on one. At lunchtime and recess, the children would line up to play, the next in line to play the winner of the previous game. Mostly, I think, for lack of anyplace else to be, Valiant would get in line and take his turn. The game itself must have captured his interest, however, because he began to study it and realized there was a strategy to be used. At fourteen he was under five feet tall, and some of the boys were over six, but he taught himself how to win at tetherball, and after a while he took it over, and nobody else could beat him. He did the same with table tennis. He didn't get awards for excelling in those sports, but he took a lot of satisfaction in them."

Buck wondered if there were anybody in the world, when she spoke of Buck, did so with her eyes shining, taking so much pleasure in her memory of him. He decided that if there had been, he wouldn't be here, poking around in someone else's memories.

"Academically, I think he was bored. There was never any question he had a good mind. Any aptitude test he ever took he was well up on the scale. But his grades in junior high and high school were average, and my feeling is the teachers could have given him worse ones. We weren't as concerned about his grades as we probably should have been, but I don't think it ever occurred to us that we might have been able to influence them. At any rate, influencing Valiant was a very hard thing to do. I think in order to accomplish it one would have to be a paragon of whatever it was she was trying to put across. He saw through things too easily, you see. Words—what one said— meant nothing to him. He knew what one thought, what one felt, just by watching one over time. Early on I despaired of communicating on any but a social plane with Valiant Campbell... That's very odd. Just now, when I said his full name is the first time I've realized that Valiant could be taken for an adjective. It sounds like someone bound for Valhalla, doesn't it?"

She laughed, then, and it was a soft, throaty thing, and it made Buck feel good.

"I don't mean to make him sound odd, or otherworldly. He wasn't at all. But one didn't often put anything over on him. I'm quite sure I never have. He knew all there was to know about his mother and me from a very early age. He didn't judge. He didn't blame. He loved us both and was protective of us; but he knew us better than it behooves any person to be known. Love usually obscures. It, or some form of it, kept you from seeing what your 'whore' was. I don't think it's possible for anything similar to happen to Valiant. I suppose I shouldn't be so sure of that. He is, after all, the grandson of a Frenchwoman."

She caught herself then, and Buck realized that she had given away more than intended. She looked down, in the first conscious move to avoid his eyes that he had noticed. She looked into the rear garden, then, at a large magnolia tree in bloom that Buck had noticed before.

Buck said, "I'm told by those who know him that he credits his grandmother with his getting an education and that you have been a heavy influence in his life in other areas."

She said, "He always knew what I wanted him to do, and in some matters he was pleased to take my advice. I'm sure I tried to control him, however, and I hardly did that."

"Well, I tried to control him, too," he said.

It was odd, she thought. The way he seemed to be changing as they sat and talked. It was as if the driver she was thinking about earlier were emerging and taking the place of the machine. But where the machine lived up to his advance billing, the driver didn't at all. It was becoming more difficult to think of him as the brute she had imagined.

Buck said, "Even while I was giving him such a hard time, I was also watching him and noticing he was almost totally uncoachable. He was far from a sorry hand, but getting to the point of knowing a job was very difficult for him. Once he figured it out and got all the circuits from mind to body lined up, he did it well, but every job took a while. You would think that the smarter a man was, the easier it would be for him to catch on; but a large part of what we do is physical, and Val was so smart, I think it was actually a hindrance. His mind didn't want to let go of a thing and just turn it over to his body. Mike Brown is the same way. They say that the impulse that creates a reflexive move doesn't make it all the way to the brain — that it is short-circuited at the first joint and goes directly back to the muscle that's needed to move whatever needs moving. A true 'natural,' like Joe Tom Wright, for instance, sees a thing happen one time and can step in and just do it — and do it well. It's like the conscious part of his brain doesn't have to become engaged. His whole body is one large short-circuit. You can see what an incredible advantage that would be in a fight and how it must have applied to Achilles or Alexander. When Alexander dropped into that compound in India, facing hundreds of vetted warriors, only a pure natural could have come out of that alive. Of course, Alexander and Achilles had the advantage of considering themselves divine and therefore incapable of making a wrong move; but that may go along with being a natural, as well. They live in a world of klutzes, and it's easy for them to think they are members of a higher order."

Sylvie Campbell was seeing for the first time what Buck was really known for among those who knew him well: the tendency to shift from the present reality to an area of arcane, sometimes unrelated, knowledge that he evidently found to be as real as the present. Since she knew very little of Alexander, she found it irritating and almost broke in to explain that she wasn't conversant on the subject. Luckily for her, she didn't, thereby avoiding a lengthy diversion into the life and times of Alexander. Something else had been bothering her, though, and she couldn't keep herself from asking about it.

"You speak of fighting so easily, Mr. Burnet, as if it were as common as eating or sleeping. Most of the stories I have heard about you had violence as their theme. Yet you seem an intelligent man. How is it that such a man can allow himself to stoop to violence? More, even, you seem to condone violence, perhaps even to enjoy it."

She had noticed before that Buck with a question was Buck derailed. One could almost see the driver breaking down the big machine, setting the various parts on the ground, then picking them back up and putting them together so the machine was headed in another direction. Justine had produced a couple of biscuits, and Buck busied himself with buttering and covering them with what looked like homemade plum jelly. He was always careful to compliment cooks, but in this case a compliment hardly seemed enough. "Justine, ma'am, I have to tell you that these are the best biscuits I have ever eaten. The cook on our rig makes great biscuits, but they aren't this good." He meant every word, too. They were large. They were fluffy. They had a rich golden, chewy crust on the bottom and a rich golden, crispy crust on the top. Justine was naturally dark, but she got even darker and waved his words away with a spatula.

The truth was Buck didn't have an answer to Sylvie's question. The answer lay somewhere in the cultural differences between them, and nowhere were those differences greater or more evident than in that area. Given his circumstances, Buck could no more have avoided violence than he could have avoided his occasional bouts with hay fever. By nature, Buck was one of the least violent of men. He was physically equipped for it, having strength and quickness and good bones, but he lacked the essential qualities that make for a truly violent man: he wasn't driven by a need to prove himself, and he didn't like hurting people. In other words he just wasn't a mean man. But he knew that there were men who were mean, because his size and reputation were like magnets to them. So far, with the help of God, he had been proof against them, but he knew he was coming up on a time when that would no longer be true. He felt that people like Sylvie Campbell lived in a dream world where people settled their differences reasonably and evil was something made up during the dark ages to keep children and peasants in line. He knew evil existed and considered it ironic that it was only people like himself and the deputy — and all the other essentially good people who met violence with violence — that allowed people like Sylvie Campbell to believe what they did. He knew all this, but he had no idea how to convince her of it, so he didn't try. He launched back into the story.

"Watching Val the first time was really when I thought of contrasting him and Joe Tom. There is nothing in this world that is perfectly anything. An engineer friend of mine with a philosophical turn of mind once told me that it was against nature for anything to be perfect. He said that when you get down to the atomic level, there is such a thing as the equilibrium vacancy distribution. That means that in order to get a crystal that has an atom at every site in the crystal lattice you would have to add energy. In other words, there are no perfect crystals. In the real world (equilibrium), there is a predictable number of vacancies, and every other physical thing is similarly flawed. That all is by long way of saying that Joe Tom is as close to a perfect natural as anyone I've ever known, and Val Campbell is as close to the perfect klutz as anyone I've ever known. If a scientist were going to make a study of it, those would be his two subjects."

She said, "I'm sure I didn't understand a bit of what you just said. I'm sure this 'Joe Tom' is a paragon of all manly virtues. I would be much more interested in how kind a man he is, or what kind of a family person."

" I don't know if he would be considered kind. I don't think you could find a single person who would say he isn't fair. The first time Joe Tom and I ever had a discussion, I was in the derrick watching a new morning tour derrickman. We don't get many like Joe Tom out there. I don't expect any industry gets many of them. Most of them end up chasing balls or hitting other people in the head for big money. If you had been at Troy and watched Achilles walking down the paths between the tents, and suddenly he turned and walked into the light of your fire, you would have felt just like I did when Joe Tom came over the rail at the monkey board into the light of the derrick. He had absolutely no fear. There was nothing in the world he could not handle, and he was open to everything. He lit on the handrail and sat watching, interested, like an owl."

Sylvie's attention was beginning to wander. She was not particularly interested in the subject, but she was interested in the interest that Buck apparently had in it, and in his need to tell the story. It was as if these were all thoughts that had been stored up, and his mind was full and had to be vented. She wondered if he had ever said these things to anyone else. She didn't know how she felt about his opening up to her, but she knew she was beginning to feel something, perhaps pity, for him, and she didn't have the heart to interrupt. The ability to look interested in what a man was saying had been passed down through many generations of French gentlewomen.

"If Joe Tom is a hero, then Val is an antihero. His mind is in on everything. In physical tasks, the measure of his success is usually the degree to which he can force his mind out of the way and let his body take over. If you talk to the men on the rig, you will hear that I paid Val no attention for at least a year. That is what they think because that is what I wanted them to think. In fact I was keeping pretty close tabs on him. I didn't like him, and my conscious mind was hoping he would fail, but another part of me couldn't help but admire his tenacity. Everything was a struggle because he had to fully understand it before he could do it. I suppose it's possible that he understands everything it takes to get a car to operate. If he doesn't, I wonder if he even drives."

He certainly drove. She couldn't say if he knew everything there was to know about a car. Sylvie was glad she had waited through the first part of the story. Any grandmother likes to hear about her grandchild. Somehow she was getting some insight into her own grandson through this odd man. She was beginning to see why Valiant might want to do what he did, to go into a really tough world and gather a set of survival tools. His venture into the oilfield was a metaphor for his entry into life. For the first time, she realized that a life in academia might be a bit like being a bird in a gilded cage, and she wondered, not for the first time, where one so young found so much wisdom. She had been terribly worried about his taking leave of his senses and turning his back on life. She should have known to trust him. And here was this huge, curiously diffident man, telling her things that she should have been able to figure out for herself. He sat here now, at her own table, black eyes creating the illusion that they enabled him to look deeper inside her than she wanted anybody to be able to. Even herself?

Sylvie Campbell stood quickly and turned to the sink. "If you're quite finished now, Mr. Burnet," she said, placing the accent a little too much on the first syllable, "you are free to go." A soft exclamation of distress from Justine served only to increase her agitation. "One can't just strut into other's lives and create havoc." Buck felt like she was referring specifically to Val's life, but Sylvie was no longer sure of whose life it was in which he was creating havoc. This was the second time Buck had been dismissed by her, so he wasn't as shocked as he had been the first time. This time, Buck felt like he knew what set her off. He very much did not want to leave.

He told her that he didn't mean to strut, purposely misconstruing her meaning. He told her a story about a little man at a company he had worked for in New Orleans, an executive who had accused him of strutting, as well.

Buck told the story hoping to point out that the meaning of the way he walked was more in the mind of the person watching than it was in his own, but he could tell she hadn't read it that way. He didn't know exactly how she did read it, but he felt like it didn't go any way toward making her want him to stay around and tell more stories. He hadn't had the time to figure out why, but he desperately did want to stay around. It wasn't as if he felt warm and fuzzy in her presence; he was reaching the conclusion that she was exceptionally cool. Campbell had something to do with it. It was as though he wanted her to like him for his sake. She was a woman, and an interesting and vital one, age aside. She had experience and, with it, the potential for passing on knowledge. For whatever reason, Buck wanted to stay there; her body language was telling him he wasn't going to be able to very much longer. There was something about her or the house or maybe even just the kitchen that stroked and consoled at least one of his demons. The wish to stay had already spurred him to an uncharacteristic loquacity, and he felt like she had recognized it for an effect and divined its cause. Buck had never been around anyone quite like her. She was elegant, but not so elegant that it was intimidating. *Reserve* was the word that came to mind. Not *reserved*, as an adjective or adverb, but *reserve*, the noun. There was a stillness about her that had nothing to do with a studied pose. Even when she moved, it was in such a way as to not disturb things around her, as if she could dive into water without creating sounds or ripples.

CHAPTER XIX

Valerie Campbell

If Buck harbored any thoughts that Val could have been the result of a chance meeting of himself and the mother, they evaporated when Valerie Campbell blew in the backdoor. He was even a little let down, as if there had been a whisper of a chance that they had spent a night together. Life wasn't a Dumas novel.

The part of Buck that manufactured such naive and romantic thoughts had gone about them on its own and left the rational mind to follow as it found the time. The fact he had two minds that were frequently at odds didn't surprise him. What surprised him was his romantic side was still alive and active after all these years. It had learned to be very subtle. Somehow it thought its thoughts without coming to the attention of the conscious mind. Because of his schedule, having seven out of every fourteen days with no specific duties or obligations, the romantic side guided him here or there with suggestions recognized as no more than unspecific urges. The conscious mind didn't realize what was up until something concrete resulted — like Valerie Campbell's blowing in the backdoor.

Buck had known he would confront her eventually, but he had expected to have time to get her measure. She obviously didn't need the time to get his, because when she came in, she already knew who was there and how she felt about him. It's not right to say that her face was distorted by rage. It was more like her face was undistorted by rage, the effort required to keep everything in place radiated from her. This lady hated Buck. It is very hard to sustain a high level of hatred or fear or even disgust in the presence of its object. Close-up inspection generally renders the object less evil or fearsome or disgusting than one had imagined it to be. Her hatred fed on Buck's presence, however, as if every look not only confirmed but reinforced her former feelings. Buck later figured out she knew he was there because she had seen his car across from her mother's store on the way home. That was not the first time Buck had thought a Bentley not to be the perfect choice for a toolpusher in south Louisiana, but it was the first time he had a real good, solid reason. He felt his driving it was an extension of the big guy in a big hat and boots syndrome. One figures, "If they are going to look anyway, might as well give them something to look at." In reality, the car had a very comfortable ride and hardly ever needed repair, but it drew a lot of attention. In this case, the attention had given Valerie Campbell just enough time to work herself into a frenzy before pouncing on the driver. The fact it was a Bentley added fuel to her fire, but he suspected any car recognized as his would have had the same effect.

She directed the initial diatribe at her mother, but there was no doubt that its object was Buck. Other than it was clever and grammatically correct, Buck retained no specific memories of what was said. Generally, she didn't see how her mother could have let him in the house, his being the embodiment of Satan. Actually, Buck got the impression that Satan's standing was good compared with his own. He had ruined her son's life and, by extension, her own. He was a cretin. Actually she couldn't say enough about how crude he was. His crudity was sort of the theme of the homily. He was a sadist and a pervert. He had very nearly killed a man a short time ago and undoubtedly had killed an undetermined number before that, and so forth.

Toward the end of the first onslaught, Sylvie Campbell got up and left the room. Justine kept doing whatever she was doing at the sink exactly as if there weren't a screaming woman in the middle of the kitchen. Buck didn't try to counter. There was no opening for a verbal answer, and a physical one was clearly inappropriate. He confined himself to making sure she didn't grab one of the knives that were uncomfortably handy on the counter. It was some time before Buck realized she was delivering a lecture, the title and theme of which was probably something like "Men Are Bad." The lecture had a beginning, middle, and, presumably, an end. She must have had to improvise at first to make Buck the subject, but somewhere in there, he had become merely a symbol for his gender. Her left foot stayed in place the entire time, and she used the right one to stamp for occasional emphasis. She was not really a plain woman, but for some reason she affected plainness. She wore no makeup, and her long shapeless dress covered everything from neck to upper arms to feet. Her medium-long hair was cut in no particular way, and it hadn't been washed in some time. She looked to be slightly overweight, not unpleasantly so, but surprising in view of her mother's and Val's body styles. She looked somehow younger than she must have been. With each stamp of her foot, errant strands of stringy hair would seek out one bad place and then another, causing her to interrupt herself frequently while she fished them out. All the clues had been in place before he met her, but it was only now Buck concluded she was a seriously disturbed person, and he was out of his depth. There were some things he could fix and sometimes other ways he could help, but there wasn't anything he could do here. He became sad for her and Olivia, and before he knew it, he had tears in his eyes. He thought, "This could really get to be a pain in the ass." He tried to blink and get them back in without blotting or rubbing, but a couple had already gotten away and down his cheeks. The next thing he knew Valerie had come to a full stop and stood looking at him with her mouth open. Justine had wheeled around from the sink and was clearly upset at the sight of a grown man crying. About that time the inside door came open, and Sylvie entered, herding Olivia, who was all legs and arms in every direction. The realization that it was more than he could handle was coincident with the one that he was badly in need of getting rid of some coffee.

His words rang like pennies off a tunnel wall. "Could I please use a restroom?"

Probably somebody would simply have pointed out the bathroom, which was behind him to the right, had Olivia not snorted. But she did, and it was obviously taken as the beginning of laughter by the others, who then began to fold up, one by one, in peals of deep, salty laughter. Buck was later to see the laughter as good—a breaker of tension and a cleansing thing. At the time, all he could think of was being its object and its not feeling good. Everyone else in the room naturally assumed that Valerie's words were the cause for his condition. She herself looked almost contrite. Her mother was embarrassed for him, and then a little put out when it became apparent that he didn't seem to be embarrassed for himself. Justine was more than a little put out and started in right then showing him that she didn't have any use for men that cried. Buck tried to think of a way to explain the tears were from another source.

The fact he had cried in public didn't affect Buck very much. While it's true that he didn't remember ever having done it before, it was also something that he had never considered doing, and he didn't have any set opinions about it one way or the other. He was well past caring whether anyone thought him macho or not, and whatever time he spent thinking about it was spent thinking about its cause. Strangely, the combination of his most recent feeling of inadequacy and the earlier one about falling short as a toolpusher seemed to have triggered something that, from then on, had him crying almost at the drop of a hat. It's not the sort of thing he would have wanted to be seen engaging in offshore; but offshore, there was seldom cause. It would happen most often in movies and with children. Of course, the movies that did so were designed for that response, but a child could trigger the tears simply by smiling or moving in a certain way. It became somewhat troubling. He couldn't decide whether it was the natural effect of getting on in years or a problem that needed to be addressed; still he found the sensation not totally unpleasant.

He guessed at the bathroom's location and guessed right. He stood too quickly, and his chair scraped on the wood floor and rapped the wall behind him at the same time his thigh hit the edge of the table, lifting it slightly and dumping bowls and glasses. This bathroom was used infrequently and then only the commode and the sink. The bathroom showed the same evidence of disuse and lack of maintenance as had the living room. The footed, cast-iron tub was full of boxes, and a shower curtain meant to encircle the tub was hanging from only a few hooks. The room itself was large and bright with a southward facing curtain-less window. He was disappointed by the recent turn of events, not the least because he was certain not to be invited for supper, something his taste buds and salivary glands had been anticipating almost since he had come into the kitchen. He still felt no sense of closure, no sense of having accomplished anything, but in view of Valerie's feelings, there was no reasonable way of extending the visit. He told himself he would leave as soon as he had a chance to say some words of parting and thanks to Sylvie.

He returned to the kitchen, looking for a towel to dry his hands. After taking a dishtowel from her, he purposely bumped Justine's hip with his own. She let the beginnings of a giggle escape before she remembered she had no use for him. He decided that their relationship was not beyond repair. The only Campbell lady in the room was Olivia, who was sitting in the chair where he had been. The chair was against the wall, and the table had been moved against her chest, effectively pinning her in place.

"That's the way she likes it," said Justine, seeing his frown. "She can't stand to have things loose or be out in the open."

Once again, Olivia hit Buck with that sidewise scrutiny. Here, in full light, he was struck by her beauty. He moved closer to the table, and she began shaking her head wildly, shimmering hair seemingly standing out by itself. When he took a step away from her, she settled down and began watching him again. First she would show him a left profile, but still with both eyes visible. Her head would go up and down and turn slightly, but the black eyes would stay on him. Then she would give him the same treatment with the right profile. He pulled a chair back to the middle of the room and sat down, pretending disinterest. That hurt her feelings. She made little mewling sounds and rapped her hands sharply on the table. It was behavior that could very well have had nothing to do with Buck, but he didn't believe it. Over the next fifteen or twenty minutes, when her attention would seem to wander, he moved the chair bit by bit until he was seated across the table from her. She reached out, first with one hand then the other. The reach itself meant nothing to him, but she made the same curious little movement with the fingers of each hand, remotely like some kind of sign made by deaf people.

"She wants to smell your bones," Justine said. "That's what she does when she wants to smell your bones." In answer to his look, she said, "Your wrist or your elbow. When she smells it, she knows somethin' about you. Miss Valerie don't like me to say that. She say it's like calling her a dog. I don't think she's no dog, but I sure do believe the Lord give her some abilities he ain't give normal people. Put your hand over there, but watch out! If she find out something she don't like, she can put a hole in it with them sharp little teeth. She's lightnin' fast, too."

Gently, he reached across the table. With surprising strength she grasped two of the fingers and pulled them as close to her as she could. She watched him until she decided he wasn't going to move then very slowly bent her head to his wrist. If she smelled it, it wasn't for more than a moment. Quick as a cat, she licked the wrist once then flung his hand away. He felt he had been accepted.

Buck had been so engrossed in Olivia that he hadn't noticed her mother come into the room. She was looking at him now, trying to figure out what to make of what she had just seen.

What does one say to a woman whose daughter has just licked and smelled one's hand? The truth is Buck understood Olivia's need to smell. He had to smell things himself. There are direct lines going from the sensors in our nasal passages to a place in the middle of the brain. Our brains have developed around and apart from that spot, and it has atrophied as a result; but the connection remains, and Buck believed it could develop and be called upon if needed. Smell is the one thing he knew of that could kill passion for him. It had happened twice that every other sense was screaming "go, go, go," and smell put a halt to the whole thing. There's no telling what kind of information one can get through smell. A dog can tell character. People don't like to be compared with dogs, but in Buck's opinion, dogs came out favorably in the comparison. At any rate, dogs liked Buck after they smelled him, and so did Olivia.

Buck watched carefully for Valerie's reaction. Given the circumstances, any reasonable person would probably already have been gone. Buck thought there was every possibility she would explode again, in which case he would have blamed himself for staying. She had changed into a different colored dress, which showed no more of her body than had the other. This was apparently the first time that his true physical dimensions had struck her. She seemed to be trying to pick a single spot to look at, but her eyes kept circling his bulk as if all the landing spots were slick. Finally her head achieved enough of an angle to let her eyes find his.

"I'm sorry for my behavior, Mr. Burnet. I'm afraid you were unfortunate enough to be the trigger for a lot of pent-up emotions. I don't believe I said anything that was not true, but it was unfair and very impolite of me to carry on that way."

Remarkably, Buck thought, she even managed to blush faintly.

Valerie evidently decided to consider the matter closed and turned from Buck to the stove. Olivia's attention was still on Buck, and she erupted into a series of moves that bore no relationship to themselves or anything else he had ever seen, but that he felt to be an attempt at communication. She broke his heart, did Olivia, and some of that must have shown in his expression, because it made her mad, and she spit at him and slapped at the table, trying to reach him across it.

"She's mad," Justine said, walking to the back of the table and distracting Olivia. "She don't like to be pitied, and I don't blame her."

Buck didn't blame her either and was careful not to be overly sympathetic or condescending from then on. Valerie thought Justine to be reading too much into the incident, though, and scolded her for treating Olivia so roughly. While she spoke, Valerie was moving the table back away from Olivia, causing Buck to move back, as well. In her hand was some sort of heavy cotton garment. He couldn't make out exactly what it was, but Olivia obviously knew, because as soon as she saw it, she thrust both arms straight into the air and started fidgeting again, anxious to get this next thing underway. It was something like a straightjacket, which bound her body to her chair and restricted the movement of her arms. Valerie explained that she was about to feed Olivia and that she felt insecure if not connected firmly to something substantial. The arm restrictions were there to keep her from hitting the food before it reached her mouth. She didn't say it, but he took it that such movements were involuntary. She then took up position behind and slightly to the side of Olivia and began spoon-feeding her, carefully timing the movements of the spoon with Olivia's own, seemingly random, jerks and twitches. Long practice enabled her to avoid disaster, though, and she was not missing.

While Valerie concentrated on feeding Olivia, Buck had time to study her, a task that required no real discipline on his part. She was prettier than he had first thought. She was at least forty, probably more, but time and her genes had been kind. She wore no makeup that he could discern, though he was aware that he could miss really expertly applied and subtle makeup. Her skin was clear and smooth, and her ears were medium sized and translucent, shell-like. Her other features were even and unremarkable, and she showed lines of concentration around her mouth and over her eyes, which would someday become permanent and unflattering. Her body was completely covered by clothing, but her movements hinted at a lushness she seemed at pains to hide. Here, feeding her child, she seemed warm and kind, in total contrast to her entrance just a half hour ago. Her hair seemed to be a permanent nuisance, and as she concentrated it fell farther forward. Occasionally she would throw her head back to clear her eyes, but she must have counted that gesture too girlish, because she switched to a businesslike tucking behind the ear with one index finger or the other. Buck could understand why a pretty woman would not want to be categorized as such, and why she would not play up her physical assets, but he couldn't understand playing them down. He considered good looks an asset, in a man or a woman, and not using them a little silly. He doubted a single ugly person in the world had been made to feel better because Valerie Campbell refused to take advantage of the fact she was fairer than most. She wanted to be taken seriously, but the coquette in her wasn't entirely subjugated, and her unconscious moves betrayed a rusty femininity.

Buck had begun to study her too hard, and the attention made her uncomfortable. He had regressed to the point of wondering why God had made a pair of ears look so much like a dainty French pastry if he hadn't wanted them to be nibbled on, when she asked a question that he missed.

"I'm sorry," he said. "I was thinking about my car getting broken into."

"You don't have to worry about that in this town," she said.

The thing about a social lie is that it makes so little impression it's possible to forget what one said oneself. He caught himself just before asking what she was talking about.

Pausing, a spoonful of food held over Olivia's head, she said," I understand why a boy…uh, a man would want to leave the nest. Why he would want to try outdoor, physical labor… even why he would feel a need for the company of other men…" She hesitated, searching for a way to say it. The best she could do was, "Why in God's name would he stay with a filthy job that had nearly killed him, working for a man who treated him like some sort of animal?" Realizing how accusatory that was, she fumbled for a way to make it sound better but came up with nothing.

He wanted to tell her, when she understood all those things, would she please explain them to him. Buck had started out in the oilfield because he didn't know he had a choice. He hadn't gone there because of reading Jack London or Herman Melville. He had done it because he had had to make a living, and that was the only thing he knew to do. He loved outdoor physical work, but if he had it to do over again, he would opt for an outdoor physical line that would allow him to live in a city like San Francisco or Chicago. There aren't any women in fishing boats or on ranches or on drilling rigs in the gulf; and being heroic and he-mannish with no women around is something like doing a stand-up routine to an empty house. As for why Campbell would stick it out, she was closer to the answer than Buck, because the answer resided within her son. Most men wouldn't have stuck it out. Buck considered himself to be a gentle, fair man; but he had been neither gentle nor fair to Valiant Campbell. Buck was beginning to suspect it had something to do with Val's having no father. Buck knew he had been better off than a lot of boys with fathers, but there was no way Val could have known that. Women tend to make heroes of their fathers, and boys and men do the same for big brothers, or the men they choose for big brothers. Buck was a big brother to most of the men who worked for him. He was their hero, the man they looked up to, the one who protected them from harm, the one who could beat up "your" big brother. He allowed them to put that responsibility on him. Buck felt Val could have been so in need of a big brother that, waiting for him on the dock that day, he had tapped into the other rig hands' feelings; and once he had decided Buck was the one he wanted for a big brother, nothing Buck could have done would have dissuaded him. He felt his nascent theory to be full of holes, and he certainly wasn't going to try it out on the person who had seen to it that Val would never know his father.

Seeing this as a chance to at least demonstrate he could put an intelligible sentence together, Buck cast around for something reasonable to say and was apparently struck dumb by God, because his brain could put the words together, but his body couldn't vocalize them. Valerie took Buck's silence for denial and visibly stiffened. She lost track of what she was doing momentarily and allowed a spoonful of food to linger too long in front of Olivia, with disastrous results. Buck later decided if he had gotten up and at least tried to help Valarie and Justine clean up the mess, he might have salvaged some standing. As it was, Buck only added to the mess and confusion by being something that had to be worked around or moved. Not knowing where everything was, he felt that he would have been even more in the way. He backed all the way to the rear door, and it obviously wasn't far enough. He stepped through the door and on to the back porch and, with nothing better to do, walked on down the steps and into the yard. Shadows were getting long, and there were several live oaks, but the centerpiece of the yard was the magnolia that Buck had noticed from inside the house. The large leathery leaves blocked the sun and left a space devoid of grass beneath it. A magnolia doesn't bloom all at once like most trees. It takes pride in each showy flower, framing each with an area of dark green. There were some old, iron chairs and benches under it, and Buck decided to sit until things died down.

Buck felt if a book was written about him, it would say, "He was not an introspective man by nature," and it would be right. People seemed to consider him quiet and reclusive. In fact he went out of his way to be around people and in places where people were. As he sat, the silence of the encroaching dusk folded over him, and he had no choice but to think. It was still humid and warm, and he felt a sheen of sweat, but he felt as natural sweaty as he did dry. What was he doing here? It was the kind of question he normally avoided, but which cropped up when he was still and alone for any time. Did he have any business being in Hickory Flat, Louisiana? Was there anything to keep him here? Was God in this equation? At times it was easy to see what God wanted you to do. Everything fell into place like one of those kid's puzzles where the pieces are shaped like stars and dogs. This son of a bitch—beg pardon—was turning into one of those million-piece nightmares that are made up of three or four shades of one color.

What was going to happen to him? Oh shit, here we go. But old age wasn't that far away, and not addressing the question was not going to stave it off much longer. Everything he had and knew was on a giant piece of steel in the gulf, and when he was gone from it, he wouldn't leave any more sign he had been there than the mud that was spilled on the deck did when it was washed off at the end of every tour. He saw himself suddenly as a lonely old man striving to connect to a group of people whose own connections were questionable—and at that were infinitely better than his own. He could have walked around the house and left, but he was still reluctant to do that. A mockingbird perched on one of the other chairs and looked Buck over. Something about the presence of the bird made Buck feel better. He considered mockingbirds and doves gratuitous bits of beauty in a normally somber world. He didn't know it consciously, but he also considered them good omens and always felt better after seeing one. Ones like this rangy little guy, who seemed to take a personal interest, were especially soothing to him. In very little time, the effects of the recent disaster in the kitchen had worn off. Buck and the mockingbird watched each other until the fading light rendered them indistinct. Both decided to break the spell at the same moment: Buck heading for the backdoor and the little messenger to his night's lodging.

There was nobody in the kitchen or the dining room—or the salon. The entryway was equally empty, and, less from a feeling he would find someone than from curiosity about what was there, he went through the entryway to the other side of the house. There was another living area of some kind opposite the salon, which had a large fireplace, but no furniture. A double door in the back wall led to a room that was much lived-in. A study, with bookshelves to the ceiling on three sides and a wall full of French windows on the other — there were some books on the shelves, but mostly they contained busts and statues and other things he couldn't make out in the near dark. There was more than one desk and some easy chairs and sofas strewn about almost haphazardly. Buck made out a door on the wall away from the windows, which he felt must go back to a common area beneath the stairs, and another in the wall he was facing. He stood facing, not really looking at the door, thinking probably he had gone far enough.

Sylvie sat in one of the chairs facing Buck, unopened book in her lap. She had had a vague intention of reading, but once she had settled in, she didn't seem to have the strength to pull the light switch. She had been thinking about her daughter and herself and the strange, large man who seemed suddenly to be in their lives. She watched him now, so agile and quiet for someone with so much bulk, discovering the door to her bedroom, totally unaware of her presence. She resisted saying anything because she hadn't resolved how she felt and didn't know exactly how she wanted to treat him. If she waited any longer, she felt sure he would sense her. He was so still he might have been taken for a piece of furniture. Finally, she couldn't pass up the opportunity to startle him again.

"It is my bedroom, Mr. Burnet. Surely you don't mean to go in there."

His reaction was so swift she found herself very glad to be so far away. Had she been closer, she could easily have been hurt before his mind called off the alert. She turned on the light above her head and pushed the shade up to see his face. Such a fierce face to look so much like a little boy, the mixture of anger and embarrassment making him almost pout.

"You do have a way of slipping up on a man, Mrs. Campbell."

"It is you who were doing the slipping up, Mr. Burnet. I was in my accustomed place, slipping nowhere."

The face was all embarrassment now, and confusion.

"I'm really very sorry. I was…I am going, and I wanted to…to…I didn't want to leave without seeing you and thanking you for letting me come here and listening to me."

She regarded him a while longer, then gently dropped the lampshade back into place.

"You needn't thank me, Mr. Burnet. I'm surprised you still feel like it after the way my daughter treated you. You have done me a service. I, for one, no longer consider you a heartless beast and feel better about my grandson's situation. Not good, mind you, but better. You have been very interesting and informative, and I certainly do not begrudge you the time." She was conscious of sounding a trifle Victorian, herself. His manner of speech must be contagious. "Before you go, I must ask you, and please don't take this the wrong way, but if ever I have seen a man who is suited to wear Western clothes, it is you. How is it you dress the way you do?"

Buck was taken off guard. He didn't know if how he dressed had ever before been commented on. He dressed in what he liked. It was as simple as that. He had worn boots and a hat for a long time, but they came not to feel right in New Orleans. He had a feeling the question was class based, like asking a tall, black man why he didn't play basketball. Enough consternation seeped through to his face to tell her she had made a misstep.

"I am sorry, Mr. Burnet. Why any sort of clothes? How clumsy of me. I'm afraid I already had an idea of how you would look based on what I had heard, and you fit it in every way except for the way you dress. Forgive me for being a stupid old lady."

Buck hadn't meant for his feelings to be read, and he was suddenly at pains to allay her embarrassment.

"No, it's perfectly all right; I just don't have an answer for the question."

Then he added, "I'm going to have to find a place to stay and a place to eat tonight. I was wondering if you could make any suggestions."

Happy for a neutral subject, she cast around for things heard and received an actual physical shock when she realized how long it had been since she had eaten out or knew anybody who was staying the night.

"I'm afraid I'm not current on such things, Mr. Burnet. Sorry."

She received a second, even more severe shock when she found herself resisting an impulse to ask him to spend the night here. She could hardly think of anything more wildly inappropriate. Where do such fancies come from?

"That's all right," he said. "I expect something won't be too hard to find. I'll take my leave, then. Thank you for being so gracious. Remember me to Olivia, please."

He turned and walked nearly through the double doors before he turned around. "I don't quite know how to put this… But, if Olivia ever needs something special…like a chair or a machine or something, I would be very grateful if you would allow me to buy it for her."

All he could see of Sylvie was some hair, her bodice, and part of her legs. She didn't move or respond, so he turned again and moved swiftly through the front room and hallway and out the front door. He couldn't know that emotion had rendered her silent. He couldn't see the tears, held back far too long, laying shiny tracks on her face and dripping from her chin.

CHAPTER XX

Evening in Hickory Flat

The glow left by the mockingbird was gone when Buck stepped off the Campbells' front porch and started down the walk to the street. His legs felt heavy, and his body ached in all the places it did when he paid attention to it. He had learned more about Val Campbell, and that had been the conscious purpose of his visit, but during the day that goal had almost been lost in a swarm of thoughts and feelings about other things. One of the developments was the desire to get the Campbells to like him. In that regard he felt he had failed miserably. Given they probably disliked him less than they had, he still had not reached the point of being invited back, and he very much wanted to be invited back. It was clear to Buck that Val Campbell's quiet strength and determination came straight from his grandmother. Sylvie Campbell had a lot of obvious virtues, but the obvious ones weren't the ones that intrigued him. Beauty and dignity and poise didn't explain the strength that could almost be felt around her. There was something about Sylvie Campbell that made him feel that being accepted by her would be affirmation that he was a worthwhile person. Valerie still seemed to hate him, but seeing her with Olivia revealed the warmth and compassion of the person inside, and he didn't think she could sustain the ill feeling if she were around him very much. Olivia herself exerted a strange pull as well. There was something heroic about her refusal to be pitied and her demand to be paid attention. And Justine, a throwback to an earlier time, was a pure pleasure to be with.

The walk back to his car was so pleasant Buck wondered why he didn't drive to small-town Louisiana in the evenings and walk as a matter of course. The air was soft and heavy with the smell of flowering things, there was a full moon just clear of the horizon, and the light from it and the lingering sunset made everything beautiful and young. When was it, he wondered, that he had begun to take pleasure in such simple things? Maybe that ability flowed as one's powers ebbed. He didn't look forward to being old, but there were indications that it might not be all bad.

From several blocks away, he could tell someone was near his car. He didn't really think it was harmed; otherwise, why would the person hang around? But it put an edge on the walk and set him thinking of the Bentley. He had, in the five or so years he had owned it, fallen in love with it. Not passionately, the way young men seemed to love their cars, but comfortably, easily—a love that didn't require thought or accommodation. The car would always be there for him, would always respond and measure up. The thought of possible harm to it was distressing. When he was about a block away, the figure stepped out under a streetlight, and Buck made out Deputy Sheriff Earl Guidry. He was relieved and mildly pleased at the prospect of speaking with the affable lawman.

"Evenin', sheriff," Buck offered.

"Evenin', Mr. Burnet," he said, then, when Buck stood still, added, "This car's been sitting here a good long while. We don't have many car thieves around here, but we got our share of vandals. A car like this here just sort of calls out to vandals, don't you think?"

"Well, now, I suppose that's true, sheriff. I appreciate your watching it, though I would have considered that above and beyond the call."

Buck had meant the remark as a jest, but he could see it wasn't taken that way.

"Calling me 'sheriff' is like calling you Burn-it. It grates just that little bit, especially when the person doing the calling knows better."

"Your point is taken, deputy. Do you have any other points we can go over, being as we have the opportunity?"

The discussion so far had taken place at a distance of about six feet on the sidewalk next to Buck's car. The deputy's car was behind Buck's, and it furnished an intermittent rattle of police calls in the otherwise silent street. The brim of Guidry's hat put his face in deep shadow and made it hard to read. The first mosquitoes Buck had noticed were buzzing around, but he resisted the impulse to wave at them.

In a slightly different tone, Guidry said, "Would you mind telling me where you been the last three or four hours?"

Buck thought it was pretty obvious where he'd been, and Guidry wasn't the detective he thought he was if he didn't know exactly where that was. Why it mattered to the deputy was the real question for Buck.

"I've been visiting in the home of one of my hands, at the invitation of that hand's grandmother." Then, relenting, he said, "I have recently ended that visit at the wish of that hand's mother."

Shadow or not, the relief on Guidry's face was evident in the form of a big smile that showed at least thirty-two teeth. Buck was surprised—floored, even—by the thought there was something between the deputy and Valerie. He was taken so unaware that curiosity overcame his natural reserve, and he said, "Earl, are you still carrying a torch for Valerie after all these years?"

"No, of course not," Earl said. "I just wouldn't care to see her hurt by the big hero from the big city."

"Well, I don't think there's much chance of that. She made what she thinks of me pretty clear, and none of the things she called me sounded like hero."

Earl said, "Sorry about that. I have a habit of wearing my feelings on my sleeve. Are you staying here tonight or heading back to New Orleans?"

Buck said, "I'm thinking about spending the night, but I don't know what might be a good place."

"You might be amused to know that the Lilac Bloom is now an inn of some note. It seems to me you have a little bit of history at that place." Guidry couldn't help laughing at the surprise on Buck's face. "It's true," he said. "People come from all over the world just to sleep in the beds where all that evil went on. At some point Miz Blue had a portrait painter from France staying at the place, and all the rooms and halls are decorated with portraits of the girls that worked there at the time. I have to say, they are very nice portraits, and if the girls really did look like that, I can understand why the place did such a good business."

Buck said, "Is Lilah still…?"

"No. My information is that she lives up in Shreveport now. She's kind of a minor celebrity. She's a big source for writers, and every once in a while, a TV crew will fly in to interview her."

"So, did she sell the Bloom, or…?"

"Yeah. She sold it. And made a tidy sum. The people who bought it are out of Dallas, and they knew what they wanted to do with it. I think they were surprised it was in such good shape. I knew Miz Blue the last couple of years of her residency. She felt like it was time for retiring, and she thought she saw the handwriting on the wall when the Chicken Ranch over in Texas bit the dust. I think the lady that owned that place did a little prison time, and Miz Blue couldn't see herself wearing coveralls. She was already letting the girls go when I met her and not taking any more on. It was just her and Cora at the last. Cora went north with her, but she passed a year or so later. Miz Blue told me some stories about you. She was very fond of you. I bet she would really enjoy a visit."

Buck said, "I will definitely go up and see her. I'm pleased things turned out so well for her. I understand people getting sanctimonious about whorehouses and such, but I honestly believe Lilah did far more good in her life than bad. Her girls were treated fairly and well, and I'm betting most of them were better off than they would have been without her. The customers got a good product for a fair price, and their marriages were better off for it."

Guidry said, "That's probably true. I never did avail myself of her services just because I didn't think it was right, at the time. Still, I was grateful that I was spared the experience of going out there with a warrant or a subpoena. By the time she left, I had become pretty fond of her."

"So, you think that would be my best bet?"

"Yeah," Guidry said, then added, "let me put in a call and make sure they have room." Buck watched the deputy crawl into his car and speak into a handheld microphone. After four or five minutes, he lifted it to his mouth again, then put it down and got out of the car.

"They had a cancellation, so you're in luck. Do you remember how to get there?"

Buck said, "I might have trouble finding my house, but I could find the Lilac Bloom in the dark." Both men grinned. "Where's a place to get a good meal?"

"Well," Guidry said, "that's a little more problematic. Folks around here don't generally eat out in the evening. There's a couple of titty bars on the west side of town where you could get a hamburger or a steak, but I couldn't vouch for the quality…the steaks, anyway. The titties are OK. There's some places along the strip where the college kids hang out, but I don't think you'd want to go out there. About the only place without going into Lake Charles is the country club. One of my cousins is the chef out there. If you go, order the crawfish étouffée; it's the only dish he doesn't mess up."

"If it's a country club, do you have to be a member?"

"Yeah, theoretically. But they don't do a good enough business to turn people away. Hickory Flat isn't really big enough or fancy enough to support a country club, but there are a few wealthy families, and they keep it on the map somehow."

"Would you like to join me for supper?"

"Mr. Burnet, I would dearly love to join you for supper, but I have prior commitments that I just can't cancel."

Buck was genuinely disappointed. The prospect of a lonely meal in a club where he didn't belong didn't appeal to him. On the other hand, étouffée made right was hard to pass up. Buck got the directions to the country club then offered his hand.

"It was good meeting you, Earl."

Guidry took his hand. "Buck, it was an honor."

Guidry had been right about the lack of membership to the club not being a problem. Nobody noticed Buck when he walked in. He hung around the front door for a while then decided that they didn't have a hostess. The lady at the bar told him he could either eat there or at any table he chose. The club had an ornate entrance, but the building had a distinctly temporary feel. The floor gave under the carpet when he walked. He had seen no evidence of a golf course or tennis courts outside, and he wondered what qualified it as a country club. There were maybe twenty tables in the place spread around too large an area. Three of the tables were occupied, and Buck sat down at one as far from those as he could get. The air was cool but dank and musty. The quality of the furniture reinforced the feeling of impermanence. The lady from the bar took his drink order. So far she was the only employee he had seen.

The Lilac Bloom had been a bit of a revelation. He had gone there from his meeting with Guidry. From the outside it looked much the same as it had when he lived there, and he had felt a little glow of nostalgia when he saw it, but the inside had been made over to look like a brothel on a Hollywood set. Everything was heavy materials in red and purples. Dangling stuff tinkled when you got close to it, and the rooms were actually lit with red lights. The only red light in the place in the era of Miz Lilah had been the one over the front door. She had been at pains to keep things homey and tasteful, and he was pretty sure she wouldn't have approved of the changes. Maybe she had commissioned the portraits that lined the hallways and decorated the rooms, but Buck didn't recognize any of the subjects. The paintings looked like they had been done by the guy with the Spanish surname that drew the picture close to the centerfold in every *Playboy*. If the girls had looked anything like they did in the portraits, Lilah would have had way more business than she could have handled. Buck wondered about the kinds of people who travel many miles to sleep in rooms where imagined wicked things took place. He decided he would much rather be in the company of the ones who did the wicked things.

Buck was used to getting attention, and all of the people at the other tables had looked up when he walked through, but the people at one of the tables were doing an undue amount of looking and talking. The bar lady showed back up with his drink and a notepad. She seemed out of sorts, and Buck decided to try to make a friend of her. He glanced at her name tag and said, "Jolie, what would perk you up today?" She gave him a rueful look that said, "I'm too far gone to be perked up." She said, "A little help in this place would be a starter. The cook called in drunk, and the waitress's little boy is sick. The manager is having to do the cooking, and I'm left with everything else."

Buck felt she was right. She was too far gone to be perked up. He said, "Does that mean that even the étouffée can't be trusted?"

"Well, I wouldn't eat it. I'm not too sure the manager would even try to cook it, though. He's not a coonass. He's from Nebraska, and I think he knows meat pretty good. My recommendation for tonight would be a steak. I saw what he brought from the butcher shop, and he had some thick New York strips that looked real good."

"Fine," Buck said. "Bring me one of those, medium-rare, with a big ole baked potato." Buck had himself set for some good crayfish, but he wasn't in the mood for anything bad. The night wasn't turning out well. After she turned away, he very nearly called to Jolie to cancel his order. He would have if he hadn't left his overnight bag at the Lilac Bloom. He felt like his hanging around this evening had been forcing the issue. The realization that he had been hoping to get back into Sylvie's company made him feel immature. He was afraid that horse was long out the gate. Well, there was nothing for it now but to hope for a really good steak and a good night's sleep.

A woman from the table of five came toward his table, and Buck assumed she was headed for the rest room. Instead she stopped and looked at him with a sly, sideways grin. She had had too much to drink but carried it like she had had plenty of practice. She had probably been something in her youth, but it was twenty or more years later. There was way too much tit available for viewing, and her hair was too elaborate. The dress and jewelry were expensive and meant to look that way. Her eyes floated slightly past and then came back to focus on him.

"Hey, sailor. Buy a lady a drink?" Buck's first thought was that she had him confused with someone else, because the way she said it made him think that he was supposed to know her. She had been the odd person out at her table, and, when he had looked that way, she had been the one talking. The two couples with her had been enthralled as people would be who were either hearing an interesting story or listening to someone who could substantially alter their lifestyles. Buck opted for the latter and assumed that, for whatever reason, she wielded some influence in the town. She tried to sit down gracefully, but missed doing it by the last two inches. Her breasts jiggled for what seemed an incredible amount of time.

"Don't remember me, do you?" she said with what appeared to be genuine regret.

She was not the dinner companion he would have selected, but Buck had no reason to hurt her feelings, either. He cast around in his mind but could not come up with a name or even the faintest trace of a memory.

"Same old Buck," she said, "brutally honest." The foregoing was rendered loud enough to carry to the other tables. In a much softer voice, she said, "I'm Marjo Prentiss, nee Baudoin." She said it as if the name should mean something on its own.

Neither name triggered any memories. "This is very embarrassing," she said. "You may not remember me, but I really, really, really need you to act like you do for at least a little while." He let his eyes go wide as if recalling but realized it was too late. "You and I were an item, once. We had a rather torrid little affair, and you wanted to marry me, but before I decided, my daddy ran you off with a shotgun." Buck did a better job with the eye widening this time. "Daddy and Mama were counting on me to marry rich. Daddy always called me 'his little investment.' I did marry rich, but I always regretted losing you."

Either this lady had fabricated a life for herself, or Buck's memory was worse than he had feared. He tried to see past the makeup and the facelift to what she looked like thirty years ago. Certainly she had been pretty, probably beautiful. Say her hair had been black—OK, maybe not as black as now, but it was probably shiny and thick. Her body had obviously been good. No doctor could create a breast that bounced like that, and the rest of her was still trim and shapely. She must have been a knockout. Buck had been a lot of things, but he had never been a lady's man, and he was pretty sure he remembered every girl he had ever been out with. He was certain that he could remember, with exceptional clarity, every "torrid affair." In the period she was talking about, Buck had viewed many girls like her from afar, but he had never even asked one out, much less to marry him. Her expression begged him to buy into the fantasy, so he did, wryly thinking that fantasy affairs were just as good after the fact as real ones—even better, because everything about them was perfect. She had obviously needed such an affair to think about; maybe her marriage was bad, and she had somehow fastened on to his name and built it from there. He considered it unlikely she had even seen him before tonight. She read his expression and seemed pleased that he was accepting the title of "former lover." Had Buck known exactly what that entailed, he would not have felt so fatuously gallant.

Now that they were "old friends," she slipped naturally into the role of raconteur. She was intelligent and funny, and Buck began to feel that he had been fortunate she picked him.

She interested him, and he steered her to her own life whenever he could. Jolie brought his dinner, and he could see the steak had been the right choice. He ate slowly and watched Marjo closely. He was certain now that she had been beautiful, even as a young girl. She was an only child, "daddy's little girl," and a cheerleader and the prom queen, and her childhood had been wonderful, but with the hard edge of knowing that she was expected to replace or create the family fortune. She hadn't questioned their right to ask that of her, or of her ability to deliver. Her mother kept a list of eligible boys and men, and her father made sure there were no serious, unsuitable suitors. She went to college in Baton Rouge because it was felt that her chances for meeting a rich man would be enhanced, but the man they finally decided on was from her own hometown, the son of the head of the only viable local law firm — the de facto owner, after many years of executing wills, of the town and most of the surrounding countryside. Something about this was ringing alarm bells in Buck's mind, but he couldn't see past the red herring of his supposed affair with her. As long as the two of them knew it was make believe, he could see no harm in it. Her husband's father had been an all-American at Ole Miss and a member of the law review after that. He was from a "questionable" family farther east but had achieved "established" status shortly after his move to Hickory Flat when he was named a partner to the old lawyer who had hired him. The son wasn't all that big or athletic, but by the time he got to his old man's alma mater, there had been buildings funded and chairs established, and there wasn't any doubt that he would be on the football team. He, like virtually every other man she had ever come in contact with, had always secretly desired her, but since he was a year behind her, had felt himself to be out of the running.

As she spoke people came and went, and Buck was no longer keeping track of the movement, but the place peaked at about three-quarters full. Jolie was hard-pressed to keep up with the orders. Buck was ready for his bill but was having no luck getting her attention. Marjo sailed on as if she had all night.

Her parents were ecstatic when the marriage was announced, and the haste with which it was put together did not detract from the "finest wedding the town had ever seen," financed with the last of her parent's cash and all their credit. Her husband's father didn't own everything for nothing, however, and, after twenty-five years, her parents still lived a hand-to-mouth existence. She had no children, not by choice, but felt like her husband had several. He was a cold man, and she thought she might have had a hand in making him that way. She had felt something for him at first despite the way in which he was cut from the herd. He had seemed grateful, but no kids came to divert their attention from each other, and it became obvious to him that she was destined to lose what he married her for. He gradually divorced himself from her, although not legally, and made lives for himself elsewhere. She was left to tell her "sad story to strangers and whomever else I can corner."

The last was part of her attempt to amuse, and Buck didn't believe she told the story to all and sundry. He thought it odd that she had opened up to him, however. He was interested in people, particularly women, and most particularly beautiful women, but he was far more at ease if they were prostitutes. He felt a kinship with beautiful women because their looks denied most of them a normal life. Many fathers who would be incensed by being accused of sexual abuse were guilty of treating their beautiful daughters according to sexual impulses they may not even have been aware of. The special treatment continued from teachers and doctors, not always male, and priests and grocery sack boys. It would take an intelligent and extremely strong woman to grow out of that unaffected. He felt like Sylvie Campbell might be such a woman, but she was different from most of those of his experience, and he didn't yet know how much of what she was, was attributable to her having been raised in a different culture.

He had always felt the obvious draw to beautiful women, but once his hormones had settled down to a level that allowed him the odd cogent thought when one was near, he set himself to understanding them. Usually they married somebody rich or someone who showed signs of becoming rich in the near future. These were aggressive guys who thought self, good, and right were interchangeable words, and to whom people were either "his" or the opposition. Occasionally, infrequently in his experience, they got a good man who cherished them into old age and had beautiful children and lived their lives never knowing want or despair. More often, they found out that good-looking rich guys had been raised differently, too, and had problems centering on how much everybody else had to defer to them. In the good-looking, rich guy's opinions, it was everybody, all the time. If the beautiful woman were intelligent, once she got it clear in her mind that he was going to do what he wanted to do, when he wanted, she had a decision to make. The large majority decided that the loss of lifestyle wouldn't be worth the saving of face, and they stuck it out for as long as possible, if for no other reason than to jack up the value of the divorce settlement. Many ended up like Marjo, desperately fighting to hold on to their looks and searching for other ways and people with which to prove their value.

As she spoke, Marjo kept her glass in her hand, sometimes using it to gesture with, occasionally sipping. She had no trouble getting Jolie's attention when she wanted another drink, but the server was gone before Buck could ask for the check. While Marjo was seated, there was no sign of inebriation, and Buck began to feel she could drink at a steady rate all night long.

Buck found himself wishing Marjo didn't have so much chest, or at least that it weren't so apparent. Breasts were some kind of a parlor game that he had never quite figured out. Breasts on their own were fine. He didn't know how much or how little most men liked them. (They were certainly the objects of a lot of male attention.) He didn't consider beautiful breasts a requirement in a potential partner so much as a plus. He liked them in bed, but this public proffering was a distraction, and something he didn't understand. Big-breasted, beautiful women's eyes kept watching yours, though Marjo's didn't seem to be, to see if you did look at them, and when you did, instead of being grateful that you gave them the attention they so obviously wanted, they smirked as if they had won some kind of game—or, worse, started tugging on the front of their dresses as if you were a pervert. He had schooled himself not to look, but it put a hell of a strain on his eyes.

A flash of long, blond hair drew his attention to the table beyond Marjo and a little to the right where a young woman was seated with two men. The first swish had told him she was proud of her hair, and the second one that she was maybe a little too conscious of it, but it wasn't until she cut her eyes at him after the third swish that he realized that she was doing it for him. He couldn't imagine why that should be so. She looked like a beauty contestant, and there was no possible reason for her being interested in an old guy several castes down the ladder. He had nearly decided that he was imagining things when she got up and started walking toward their table. Her walk seemed almost a parody of a movie siren's hip-thrusting slink, but maybe she was just dodging tables. She was certainly a toothsome morsel, and Buck was beginning to hope she was another old flame he didn't remember (more likely her daughter). Then she started talking to Marjo. She spoke in the way of sorority girls of all ages—the exaggerated highs and lows and emphases on odd words, and the stylized pronunciation that verged on being an affected speech impediment. She bent down and hugged Marjo and cut her eyes at Buck as she kissed the air near one ear. Possibly out of deference to Buck's presence, Marjo didn't respond in the sorority-girl language. The girl asked about the "hunk," and Marjo introduced him as an old friend. Her name was Sherry, or one of its variations, and Buck continued to get the impression that she was flirting with him. Gradually, as the two women conversed, Sherry punctuating with cute little squeals and squeaks, he got the idea that they were rivals in some manner and that Buck's attention was just one more little contest. When he thought about it, Marjo's enthusiasm for the discussion was markedly less than Sherry's, and there was a flatness in her tone that hadn't been there before. If he went with the theory they were rivals for more than his attention, he ended up at Marjo's husband, and that was reinforced when it came out that Sherry was an attorney in his father's law firm. He was apparently witnessing the public humiliation of a feminine cuckold by her replacement. It wasn't until Sherry said something about the "judge" that Buck connected Marjo's last name with the alarm bells that were suddenly deafening and the judge that had walked by when he and the deputy were eating lunch. What if, say, the judge's disdain for Buck wasn't the natural one of an educated, powerful man for that of an uneducated redneck roughneck, but that of a hated adversary? What if, whenever one fought with one's wife, a name was brought up—say, the name of some fictional someone who was better than you in every way? Buck thought one might, over the years, develop a serious aversion to someone like that—so serious, in fact, one might consider ways of harming, or even disposing of, that someone. If he wanted to get paranoid, he might tie these two women and the deputy into a conspiracy to get him here and compromised in some way, so the judge could have his way with him, all legal and above board.

Buck's mind didn't have a "race" mode, but it was definitely moving faster than it was used to. He felt that if Marjo were a participant, she was an unwitting one. She would have had to have been a consummate actress to this point, and he didn't think, given the amount of alcohol he had watched her consume, she was capable of it. Besides, if her story played into the theoretical conspiracy, he couldn't see that she had anything to gain by his being in trouble. Likewise, he couldn't really fit Earl Guidry into the role of conspirator. Given, the deputy had pointed him out to the judge and had gotten him here at this point in time, but Guidry would have had to be able to fool him on a number of levels over a relatively long period of time, and, once again, he didn't think him capable of it. Miss America here was a different thing, though; the way she visibly enjoyed dealing out pain to Marjo was evidence of that. The judge didn't like Buck a lot; that much had been obvious at lunch. He also seemed to be the kind of man that liked making people miserable. He and Sherry had to be quite the loving pair. Buck decided that, if there was a conspiracy, Sherry had been here to set him up. If that were true, then the two men at Sherry's table were here to spring the trap, and Marjo's presence was just holding things up. Buck felt like he knew what was going on; he just didn't know what to do about it.

After Buck left Sylvie had sat in the dark going over the day's events. Valerie's entrance had been fortunate, in a way, and in another, not. Fortunate in that she had brought out some feelings she herself, Sylvie, had, and unfortunate because it had cast a pall over the best evening she had had in some time. Something had pulled loose in Sylvie during Valerie's tirade. She didn't understand it yet because it was fraught with emotion. (She briefly wondered if people used *fraught*, or if it was mostly a written word.) And she was having trouble sorting it out. It had to do with her relationship with Valerie, and with Valiant, and not the least with the most recent addition to her tiny circle of acquaintances. This man. This huge, "different" person who had most recently gained her attention. He was no Hector, no Achilles—no prince beloved of the gods. He wore no flashing helm with shimmering horsehair plume, carried no five-layered shield fashioned by a crippled god. He was the warrior with a conscience, the master who plied his trade all unaware of what others thought.

In the beginning year of her second form, she had taken a trip with her mother to Naples. Her mother—"happening" to be there when her latest passion, a dashing, half-wit driver of racecars—would be there with time to spend and had only taken her on a whim. She most surely had regretted having taken her when the prey had gobbled the hook like the simpleton he was. Before her mother tired of her little conquest, which happened relatively soon, Sylvie was left free to wander about the streets of the uncomfortable, old city. She wasn't of an age to seek out museums, really, but they were places one could be without explanations or excuses, and she ended up spending quite a bit of time in them. (When her mother asked where she had spent her time, she told her in cafes and on the streets, thereby denying her the feeling that the trip had benefited Sylvie in any way.) There was a statue in the Museo Nationale that had intrigued her, and she had revisited several times. It was a classic-age rendering of Heracles that nagged at her, simply because it was so unlike the son of a god. The figure leaned on his club, padded by the full skin of the lion. He gazed into the near distance, seeing God knows what, but nothing within sight. He was tired. Thick, heavy muscles lay in slabs upon his large bones, and his waist hardly narrowed the rest of his trunk. His head seemed a trifle small for the body, and his nose was large and hooked, his face very human and not handsome. But he still had power, and he had done what was set before him, and his reward was death. This was not a man who had ever had the illusion of immortality. The day the statue released its hold on her, she fashioned a sign with a borrowed sheet of drawing paper that read, in Italian, "This is not Heracles. This is Ajax." She set it on the toes of the statue's left foot. She smiled now at the childishness of it, but the gesture had furnished closure with something that disturbed her at the time.

Mr. Burnet was that Ajax. He carried about him that sense of things accomplished and wonder at what they availed. He was the reason she was out driving now, though she hadn't known it when she bathed and picked out a frock she hadn't worn in years, when she applied her makeup as if she cared where it went and how it looked, when she got into Valerie's car and realized she hadn't driven since John's death. Another childish gesture, this. She should be home. But she didn't feel like being home. She had been the willing victim of whatever had stopped her life for long enough. She didn't want to think about it. She wanted to be out, to think about things that pleased her, to let fresh currents through, to sit close enough to Mr. Buck Burnet to smell him.

CHAPTER XXI

Rescued

Buck wasn't familiar enough with feeling threatened or worried to know that was what was troubling him now. All he knew was that he was extremely uncomfortable and looking for the quickest way possible out of the country club. The two men at the table where Sherry had been were showing signs of restlessness. They were both beefy and fit and, though they wore suits, didn't look like lawyers or people who would be in the company of lawyers. They could just be interested in the pretty woman, but why two? And why suits? Sherry maintained her nonstop chatter, and to Buck she plainly seemed to be trying to get rid of the older woman. Her voice got higher and louder. She had positioned herself beside Buck and was now talking to him. He had stopped listening to the words earlier, and he tried to catch up. Before he could get the sense of what she was saying, the men got up from their table and started walking toward Buck's. He could tell now that the suits were cheap and well-worn. State police? FBI? There was no way that a physical confrontation could do him any good.

This had all the earmarks of a bad situation. Buck's worst fears were confirmed when the older of the two men addressed him.

"Sir," he said, "why are you molesting this young lady?"

Sherry had dissolved into tears and stood behind Buck with her head in her hands. It was obviously a setup situation, but in Louisiana they could make this stick. Buck liked his chances in the parishes around New Orleans, but he had no friends way out here. He truly didn't have any idea of what to do. Decision time was upon him when the younger of the two reached out as if to grab him by the shirt. Buck's hand locked on to the proffered wrist and fastened it to the table without his thinking. The move gave him a temporary advantage as the young man was left twisted around and in the way of his partner. Buck's brain knew what his body didn't however; this was an unwinnable situation.

Enter Sylvie Campbell, stage right.

"Mister Burnet, please unhand that gentleman. This isn't New Orleans, and that sort of roughhousing isn't amusing in this part of the state. Had I known it would be like this, I wouldn't have accepted your invitation."

Buck would later be able to see the humor in the situation, but at the moment he was as shocked and speechless as nearly everyone else. Sherry's eyes were wide, and, like the others, her mouth was open. Marjo had bumped the table in her haste to get up and was struggling to keep from falling. Remarkable in that was her managing to keep both her drink and her chest from spilling, all while keeping her eyes locked on Sylvie's. The young policeman completely lost track of what he was about and was jerking to unpin his arm, so he could better ogle Sylvie. She was a vision in a little black dress that showed just enough cleavage and leg to convince anyone who was interested that they were the real deal. Only the older policeman was unimpressed, and he was maneuvering to get around his useless partner. Buck himself sat in a caricature of surprise. Sylvie neatly inserted herself between the older man and Buck and continued in the same level voice.

"Marjo, how nice to see you. Catching up on old times with Mr. Burnet, were you? I know I've heard you say that you two were an item in your youth." She conveyed this with a look that said she hadn't believed it. "Unfortunately, Mr. Burnet's dance card is full this evening. Remember me to the judge, won't you?" When she turned to Sherry, she took a step back, forcing the older policeman to take one as well. He tripped over a chair at another table and only just managed to stay on his feet. "You must be the Charlene Black who has so bedazzled Harold." Buck thought, "Charlene...Sherry." The younger woman raised her hand in the briefest of gestures at the mention of the judge. It had the effect of stilling the older policeman. The younger one's face still looked like that of a puppy looking for a treat. "I had thought you couldn't possibly be that lovely. The next time we meet, I'll tell him I was wrong."

Sherry/Charlene was on the fence. Her face became hard when she was thinking, and she was thinking hard now. She obviously didn't know Sylvie or who she was, and she felt she should know anyone the judge/Harold saw on any kind of a regular basis. If this lady did know Harold, then perhaps she should back off. She had a strong feeling that the whole thing was a ruse to protect Buck, and she was on the verge of reengaging the security men. Before she could do that however, there was a shriek that stopped the whole room dead again.

It was unlikely that Sylvie's comment was Marjo's first knowledge of her husband's indiscretion, but it was the trigger that released pent up feelings

"I knew it!" Marjo said, while launching herself at Sherry/Charlene. "The whole town knows you're his whore." She said a lot more in the melee that ensued, but very little of it was comprehensible. She finally lost her drink, and at some point both breasts burst free. Sherry/Charlene showed which side of the tracks she was from by being a much more skilled fighter than her older and more easily winded adversary. Marjo's breasts seemed to have taken on lives of their own and were adding to the confusion, though in nearly equal measures to both participants. He gave the early points to Marjo, but the younger woman was clearly gaining the upper hand. The men in suits were left trying to pull the women apart, and Buck was thoroughly enjoying himself when Sylvie grabbed his hand and motioned him out. In the parking lot, she said, "Meet me at my store and park that ridiculous vehicle somewhere that it can't be seen." On the way out, Buck pressed a hundred dollar bill into Jolie's hand, overpaying by at least twice. Jolie hardly seemed to notice, entranced as she was by the doings at Buck's old table.

The best Buck could do for a hiding place for the car was an empty lot off the alley back of her store. There were trees around it, but anyone intent on finding it could have done so without a lot of trouble. There was a door to the back of her place, but she hadn't said anything about it, so he walked around the block to the front. She was waiting for him with the door ajar, and she closed and locked it behind him. She led him to the back, saying something about how easily he attracted trouble. She motioned him to the same chair he took that morning then walked into a room to the side, saying she would make some coffee.

He was curious about what exactly had been going on at the country club, but he was mostly wondering how and why Sylvie happened to be there. He hadn't yet considered the possibility that she had been looking for him, and he was trying to square her appearance with the impressions he had developed earlier. The woman who had saved him from what could have been a very expensive and damaging situation was younger and more vital than the one he had spent most of the day with.

Sylvie stood at the sink with the coffeepot in one hand and the water running, but her mind wasn't making the connection that would put them together. She stared out a little window into the darkness and tried to gather her thoughts. When she had walked into the country club, she had had a little plan of what to say to Buck, but it had evaporated when she saw what was going on at his table. She knew about Marjo's Buck stories. Most everyone of consequence in town had heard them directly from the author at least once. Sylvie thought it likely that the only one who believed them even a little bit was Judge Harold.

Marjo and Buck was one thing, but Sylvie knew the Black woman for Harold's mistress and a vicious little bitch. Whatever she had up her sleeve couldn't bode well for Buck. What Sylvie had done had been largely from reaction to the events, but she had used up her little store of boldness in the country club. She took stock. Her legs were weak, and the sink was taking most of her weight. Her empty hand shook, and her scalp was damp. She was afraid. Of what? Not Harold Prentiss or his poisonous assistant. Sylvie had owned Harold Prentiss for a long time. Not Buck Burnet. It wasn't strictly true to say she didn't know him. She knew quite a bit about him in the abstract. Abstract being of two dimensions and in black and white. True, the person in the flesh was something else again, but nothing she had learned today made her think him someone to fear. She stood thinking for long minutes until her mind came to what she considered a reasonable premise. She was afraid simply because she was outside her comfort zone. Everything she had done since she took the decision to bathe had been a little adventure, a titillating mental exercise. Once she had stepped into the fray at the club, the game was taken out of the imagination. She could deal with that.

First she'd make the coffee and give herself time to settle down; then she'd go in and have a discussion with the legend in three dimensions and living color. Fill the pot. Measure out the coffee. It hadn't been the crying that did it. She didn't trust tears. It was when he had turned in the half-dark doorway and asked after Olivia. There was nothing false or calculated about that. It was as if he had leaned over and offered her a look into his mind. He was long gone when she focused on the doorway the next time. Something in her released and spilled over, and there was no getting it back in the container. He had been the object of her hatred—a name, a myth, a concept she could point to as the most recent reason for the state she was in. It was the loss of Val that she couldn't face head on. She understood now why Val had made such a radical departure. Val wasn't suddenly wiser than she; he had been wiser almost out of the womb. He had allowed her the illusion that he was hers out of compassion. But he wasn't hers. She had allowed Valerie to blame her for John's death thereby ensnaring the two of them in a sick, symbiotic relationship that had them both loathing her. How could something like that happen? She had wanted security. How could she not, given her own upbringing? She was young. She didn't know much about real people. She had presumed John rich when she married him. She didn't know anything about working for a living. To her one either had the means to carry one through life or one didn't. She pressed for financial independence, as much for him and Valerie as for herself. She had thought him strong, largely because that's what she wanted him to be. She was to blame for John's death. There you have it. She had sentenced herself to nearly thirty years of self-hatred and flagellation. Worse, she had sentenced her daughter with her. Well, the prison doors were open.

"Do you know what was going on at the club?" she asked, as she set the mug of coffee down beside him. He noticed that she was holding a cup and saucer and surmised that she had chosen the mug for him in deference to the size of his fingers.

"Not really. I figure that I was being set up, but I'm not sure why."

"You don't have any idea?"

"Well, the older woman, Marjo, was acting like we had been an item at some time in the past, but I don't think she was in on it. The common thread seemed to be a judge that I met with Earl at lunch."

"Harold Prentiss," she said. "That explains how he knew you were in town."

"Earl was at pains to make sure each of us knew about the other."

She said, "I doubt very much that Earl had anything to do with what happened tonight. There is no love lost between him and the judge. I'm pretty sure he was just taking advantage of an opportunity to twist Harold's tail feathers."

"It sounds like you know more about what was happening than I do."

"That may be so, but we will probably never know for sure. What I do know is that Marjo has been talking about 'her affair with Buck Burnet' since shortly after she and Harold were married. My guess is that Harold heard more about it, and in more detail, than anyone else. It is not outside the realm of possibility that tonight's event was no more than an attempt to reclaim some of his self-respect."

"Do you think they will keep looking for me?"

"If it was set up by Harold, they will doubtless have reported to him already. If they did and he hears I am involved, he will have them stand down. He will not risk crossing me."

That bit of information intrigued Buck, and he waited for a further explanation. It didn't come.

Buck said, "It seems to me that the judge could be a nasty piece of work if he wanted to."

"He's nasty, right enough. Harold is a spoiled child with a temper; but, get him out of his robes and away from his father's sphere of influence, and he is a nonentity. Marjo got what she set out to when she married him, but even she deserved better."

Again there was the suggestion that she had the judge's number, and Buck was really curious about how, but again she went no farther. There were a few minutes of silence while they thought their own thoughts. Neither thought to remark on how comfortable the silence was.

"Is your coffee all right? I forgot to ask."

Buck took a quick sip of the now tepid coffee. He had forgotten to taste it.

"Yes, yes. It's really good. I don't want you to take this wrong, but you look truly beautiful tonight."

Sylvie wondered how something like that could be taken wrong. This night was not turning out at all like she had imagined it, but it wasn't bad. She could tell he was taken with her, and the compliment had been almost boyishly sweet.

She said, "You remember in the Bible when Jesus cursed the fig tree?"

Buck shook his head.

"Well, he did. And from the first time I heard it, I felt it to be inconsistent with the rest of his life. It is said that you hate white-collar workers. But that attitude seems inconsistent with the person I see."

"It doesn't apply to me." Buck didn't have to think about that one. "I don't hate anyone or any group of people. I have contempt for what I call corporate players, but I don't hate even them."

Buck would have left it there, but he could see that she wanted an explanation.

"I hate that our culture places white-collar workers on a higher plane than those of us who work for a living." He amended that, saying, "Those of us who work outside with our hands. But I don't believe we are any better than they are, either, though I might have given that impression on occasion. Both types perform critical functions in society."

It was Sylvie's full intention to seduce Buck Burnet this night, but she wasn't really sure how that went. She had never had to seduce anyone before. Going to bed with someone had been more a matter of choosing from those around her who wanted to, and of those there had never been a dearth. All she could think of now was to keep him talking.

"I've heard it said — and if I'm not mistaken, you said something of the sort earlier today — that you hate privilege and entitlement."

Once again Buck felt floored. Who was more privileged and entitled than French royalty? How could he answer such a question truthfully and not offend her? Or how could he back down from a stance that he had taken publicly and over a long time?

Sylvie could see that she had stymied him once again.

"What are corporate players?"

Buck pulled himself together and mentally thanked her for taking him out of his misery. He wanted this night to go on. "Anybody in a corporation who doesn't pull his or her weight. In some corporations well over fifty percent of middle and upper management can be made up of them. As far as I'm concerned, they are like barnacles on a ship—no, worse than barnacles. Barnacles just slow ships down."

"Are there not barnacles among the men who work with you?"

Buck smiled at the naivety of the question. He was directly responsible for the condition of his ship's hull.

"If you are asking if there are working-class barnacles, the answer is yes—probably in roughly the same proportion as in management. There are barnacles on my rig only to the extent that I allow them. I am notorious for getting rid of barnacles. I have to say, though, that if I liked a certain barnacle enough, I might not be able to spot him as a barnacle. When the CEO of a large company has enough layers of people under him, spotting barnacles would be extremely difficult. Of the few companies I know something about, the company I drill for, Exxon, seems to maintain the cleanest hull. My opinion is that they do that by only hiring quality on the front end. Anyhow, barnacles in the field are much easier to spot. It's easy to tell if a worker is doing his job or not."

Sylvie was nodding as if the question had been rhetorical and he was just confirming what she already knew. She said, "There is one other area of inconsistency that I have been curious about. Were you the one who pulled that man's penis off in New Orleans?"

Now it was Buck nodding as if he knew what she was going to say. He looked around the room. She had turned an overhead light on, and it was better lit than it had been in the daytime. It wasn't a room, really, as it was open to the store on one side. It was just a place to work, yet she had made it as comfortable as most homes. Buck felt relaxed and at ease, and he didn't want to play games with this woman who was rapidly becoming one of his favorite people. Had he ever addressed his legend and told another person exactly what he thought of it? He thought not.

"I'm not sure that anybody pulled a man's penis off in New Orleans."

She said, "I understand that sometimes you operate outside your mind and that you frequently don't remember where you were or what you did."

Buck wasn't nodding now. He thought that the way she phrased the question betrayed knowledge beyond the myth. He had been behaving like a schoolboy in the presence of a favored teacher, but now he looked into her face and eyes. They were beautiful, but he tried to see past them into her heart. For the first time in his life, he understood what it meant to offer some-one his heart—total vulnerability. He could look into those eyes and imagine all sorts of things, but he didn't know if he could stand what would happen when he stood before her stripped of armor. He wondered if he had ever trusted anybody and decided that Bobby Lynd was the only one. Well, he trusted Mike, too. Maybe it was time for another.

"The night of that incident I was with a friend in another part of the Quarter. I don't know how they came up with my name, but the police were looking for me within an hour of when it was supposed to have happened. It didn't take them long to find me, and it didn't take them long to determine that I couldn't have been in Jackson Square when the crime took place. The guys that questioned me were sniggering and snort-ing during the whole interview. I got the distinct impression that they didn't consider doing damage to a man of the vic-tim's sort a real crime. I also got the impression that they didn't plan on investigating it very thoroughly. I'm not even sure they spent enough time on it to determine if a crime had really been committed. A story like that develops a life of its own, how-ever, and by the next morning, every pimp and druggie in the city had a version of it on his lips. You could tell when they reached the punch line by the grimaces that went around. Most of them knew me or knew of me, and by the end of the day, there were many witnesses who had heard and seen the whole gruesome spectacle. I was hands down the puller, and they had even ginned up a pullee: some deluded slob that worked occasionally in the sex clubs who liked to brag that he was a hired assassin and frequently did work for the mob. He was conveniently missing. The police later told me that he had been found shortly after this, dead of an overdose of heroin in a flophouse in Algiers. He wasn't missing any parts. The facts seldom get in the way of a good story, though, and the legend lives."

Buck tried to read her face but found it unreadable.

"So the good news is that I am not guilty of maiming another person. The bad news is that I never worked very hard at making that clear. It turns out that, if you don't mind being considered some kind of freak, a story like that can be very useful. The police weren't impressed, of course. As I indicated they considered the whole thing pretty amusing. I managed to make friends of several of them during the investigation, and that has come in handy over the years. The organized crime people knew the truth as well, but at the time their leader was up to his neck in federal investigations, and he wasn't interested in a fairy tale, even one that potentially reflected poorly on him. But everyone else was impressed, and I suddenly had a lot of respect. That kind of respect translates into your being able to pretty much do whatever you want. I've tried not to abuse that power, but, being human, I'm sure I occasionally do. That story is getting pretty old now. It turns out, though, that you get residual respect even if people don't know why you were originally respected."

"Well," she said, "at least you didn't ever actively lie about it or the other stories."

Buck's face was not one that would be called expressive, but she got the distinct feeling that his expression was pained, now.

"I'm afraid we can't even say that. We can play with motives: entertainment, compassion, self-aggrandizement…But we can't say that I never embellished the legend." That was it, Buck knew. There was no way that a lady with a pedigree like hers was going to continue to put up with a coarse, working-class bullshitter. He had been a fool to think that he could continue to hold her attention. He looked around for anything he might have brought in and set down. She was quiet and still, but he didn't really want to wait for another tongue-lashing. When he shifted his weight forward, though, she spoke.

"Mr. Burnet...Buck, do you suppose you are the only person who ever prevaricated, either actively or by saying nothing?"

Her expression was mild, but her eyes were sad, and for the first time, Buck was looking at a person who lived in the same world as he did.

"We are all of us just people, aren't we? Beyond survival we are looking for a little dignity, a little respect?" She was asking him a real question, but he could tell that she didn't really expect him to answer it. "I have been taken for a grande dame, a lady of refinement and taste. I have, as you say, taken no pains to correct that impression. I'm told that some people even think that I am descended from royalty. I have found it convenient to have them think that. It tends to keep people who might become tiresome at a slight remove, and it has helped my little business. But the truth of my background is more pedestrian, some might say even sordid. Are you familiar with the term *courtesan?*"

Until just a few moments before, Buck had thought he had a handle on the meaning of the term. But now he wasn't sure.

"The most polite word is *prostitute*. A more genteel if less definitive one would be *mistress*. In any case, my mother was one. It doesn't really help that she was somewhat famous for being the paramour of some famous people." Sylvie paused long enough to note that Buck was experiencing a series of emotional reversals. She chuckled. "No, I wasn't a courtesan. I spent most of my childhood and youth in private schools around Europe. I saw my mother from time to time at her convenience, but I don't think she cared anything for me. Wherever I was, people knew who and what my mother was, and I hated her for that. As soon as I was able, I sought work in Canada. When I met John Campbell, I was no virgin, but I was certainly no prostitute."

Buck said, "But Earl said you had a cousin staying here for a while, and he said you were descended from royalty."

"That idiot was a nephew of a man who was close to my mother off and on through the years. There was talk that he was my father. He claimed some sort of a title, if the title had still existed, and was apparently a man of some property. Anyway, the nephew was here on behalf of all the other heirs to determine if I were going to make a claim on the man's estate. He wasn't even dead yet, but the relatives were already circling and fighting over bits and pieces."

"Did you not want to go and see him on the chance he was your father?"

"I had seen him on more than one occasion, and there was never any indication then that we were somehow connected. No. I didn't want to see him. I had no feelings for him. I had thought that I had no feelings for my mother either, but when she died a few years ago, I found myself regretting that we hadn't reconciled."

Buck said, "What did your mother die of?"

She stood with a rueful smile. "She died from what she lived on — a fatal combination of loves for life and thrill. She died in a parasailing accident in the Cote d'Azur. She may have seen it as a fitting way to go and chosen it. She was no doubt getting too old to enjoy life the way she wanted it."

She had walked slowly toward Buck as she spoke, and now she reached a hand out to him. "And now, Mr. Buck Burnet, stand up. We are neither of us going to get to the point by subtle means." Buck stood and took her hand, still not sure what the point was. As she walked him to the back room, she said, "I always wondered why I put this bed back here. Until tonight it has had no use."

When he woke up the next morning, Buck was totally disoriented — time, location…Nothing made sense. Then he turned to see the back of Sylvie's head and a shoulder and part of her back. His first reaction was a warm glow. Then he became uneasy as certain specifics of the evening came back to him. It had been a series of firsts for Buck. It was the first time he had made love and not just fucked. She was the first person he had ever fucked who wasn't a prostitute or something closely approximating one. She was the first woman he had ever been with who came near his own age. He had not been immediately physically responsive. (He was, after all, on in years himself, and his mind hadn't been giving his body any warning.)

It was his first experience with having to use a lubricant, and there was a bit of business around its application. He had been clumsy and hesitant, and for the first time in his life, he worried that he may not be able to perform. Sylvie, on the other hand, had been patient and accommodating. She led him through the whole thing step by step, very much as if he were a boy without experience. Her skin was drier than that of a younger woman, but he could tell that her natural structure was way better than most. He had imagined an older woman's breasts as being shapeless or unappealing in some other way. Hers weren't exactly perky, but they were beautifully shaped and of a perfect size. Her waist was small, and her hips were a woman's hips, and her legs felt wonderful. Once the preliminaries were out of the way, the rest of the evening progressed nicely, and Buck found himself enjoying a richer, more profound experience than any he had had before. He was thinking that he had nearly managed to get through a life without knowing that there was more to really satisfying sex than the mechanics, when Sylvie stirred. She didn't turn but shifted toward him in the bed. He let her move against him then cradled her ass with his stomach and thighs. Yes, the ass was incredible, too. His arm dropped across her, and his hand cupped a breast as naturally as if it had happened a thousand times.

She said, "When I was a little girl, maybe four or five years old, my mother took me to the estate of the man we were talking about last night. It was one of those trips where they would talk about things outside of my hearing. It was a beautiful place with open fields and trees. The houses and outbuildings were white, and there were white fences everywhere. There were barns and stables and animals about. I wandered off, and the adults didn't notice. In one of the stables there was a horse looking over the door to his stall. He was a huge animal — a beautiful, gray Percheron. As I walked by him, he put his head down, and I could feel his breath as he blew. His head was as big as I was, and I put my hand between his eyes. The walls were solid, but an empty stall next to his had been left open, and the wall between the two had openings between the slats. I crawled through, and he backed into the stall and put his head down close to me again. I walked between his legs and made a game of it. Presently I lay down between his front hooves, and there—just there—is what brings the story to mind. If he had moved the wrong way, he would have killed me, but I knew he wouldn't. I felt as safe as I've ever felt, lying under that mammoth beast. That's the way I feel now—the way I felt last night. That's the way your men feel about you, and likely many others. It's not your fault, and it's unfair of us to lay that at your door, but there you have it. It's like your pretty girls. They are not responsible for being pretty, but they are destined to be treated as if they were. I needed last night. I wanted last night. And I am pleased to say that I am very glad I had last night. But I don't want you to feel any sense of debt or responsibility. Last night was my doing."

With that Sylvie threw the covers back and got out of bed. Buck had the brief thought that he hadn't seen many women get out of a bed nude without wondering why. He felt a sudden surge of desire as he watched her slip the little black dress over her head.

"And now, if you don't mind, I must be home and get ready for work. You, my giant friend, must leave before the whole town can see you doing it."

"What if I don't want to leave? What then?"

Sylvie turned sharply and looked into his eyes.

"You don't have to say that. I've already told you, you owe me nothing."

"No, and you don't owe me anything, either. Looks to me like we're starting off even."

Sylvie stayed looking at Buck, her mind obviously on something else. Finally, without speaking, she turned on a heel and walked out to her office. Buck could hear her rummaging in her desk. Directly she walked back in with a letter-size blue-bound book in her hand. She dropped the book on the bed next to him and said, "Buck Burnet, meet Hector Guerrero."

Engraved on the front of the book was, "Buck Burnet: Paul Bunyan of the Oilfield. A Dissertation by Valiant Conrad, PhD Candidate."

CHAPTER XXII

Tom Coleman

Tom Coleman lived in a rented room in a dilapidated house in New Orleans's Ninth Ward. He wasn't looking for a black district when he tore the ad out of the *Times Picayune*, but he wasn't put off when he found out it was. It was one of the few rents advertised he felt he could afford, and the ad offered a noon meal, something he knew he probably wouldn't get any other way. The house was in no worse shape than those around it and was one of the few that didn't have at least one out-of-work adult lounging on the porch or the front steps smoking and/or drinking. The proprietress was a fortyish black lady with a red wig and an imperious manner who told him, "No way. Ain't no way." Her initial objections centered on what her neighbors might think of her having a white man living in her house. Tom liked the house and liked the woman, Pat Goodman, so he kept coming back. Over a period of days, her manner gradually softened, and her objections became concerns for him and how he would be treated by others in her house and on the street. Finally she relented. Tom got the bedroom of what would have been the original house. He had his own entrance to the front porch and a window to the street, and there was a small hallway by the bathroom that led to a door to the main part of the house. There were roaches, but then, this was south Louisiana; there were roaches. The neighbors got used to him over time. It had suited him then, and it suited him now, twenty-three years later. He had been unofficial uncle, tutor, and friend to Pat's children and now grandchildren and believed, hoped, that they no longer thought of him as being of a different color.

It was Tom's habit to rise at ten thirty, do a thirty-minute meditation then get ready for lunch. This morning he had finished the meditation and was sitting in its afterglow. He had started the habit of twice-daily meditations more than thirty years before because all the masters of the mystic traditions he studied under recommended it as a possible path to enlightenment. He didn't come to it naturally or enjoy it. It had been many years of struggle: first, setting aside the time for it, then actually doing it. Wild horses would have been easier to control than his errant mind. After a decade of effort, he considered giving it up, but he still had faith in the message of his teachers. At the end of the second decade, he felt no closer to enlightenment, indeed, frequently felt further from it. He still strained to rein in his rampant ego and fought with the thoughts that would not leave, or slept, sitting upright in the position. At the beginning of the third decade, worsening arthritis had moved him from the floor to a chair. Sometime after that he gave up striving for enlightenment and gave in to his thoughts, watching them as they marched in ranks across the screen of his mind. Strangely, he thought, while the thoughts were no shorter or less frequent, there began to be longer quiet spaces between them. Gradually the thoughts moved away from the center of his mind, and the space that was left was filled or, more accurately, was not filled with a featureless, characterless void that was somehow comforting. Tom Coleman knew of the human penchant for self-delusion and knew that he could be imagining this peace; but he decided if it was delusion, it was better than anything that had gone before, and he would seek comfort in it as long as it lasted. Lately he had begun to be disappointed when the timer went off, and sometimes, as he was today, spent time savoring the wisps of feeling that lingered.

The knocking at his door was insistent and heavy. He lifted one of the slats in the Venetian blind and saw Buck's Bentley, and his heart sank. Buck had never been here before. There had to be something catastrophically wrong. His thoughts flew to Catherine, the iron lady with the velvet center.

As expected, when he opened the door, it was Buck who stood there. He was holding some kind of bound manuscript; but it was a different Buck. Tom looked for the change and finally fixed on his face. There was something about Buck's face that made him seem younger, more open.

"Do you mind if I come in?" Buck said.

"Certainly not," Tom said. "I only have the one chair, and I'm not sure it can support you. Why don't you have a seat on the bed?"

Tom looked at his room through what he imagined to be Buck's eyes. He didn't see anything that would dispel the myth that he was a monk: a single bed with a hard mattress, an end table with a lamp, a small, desk-like table with the single chair, a wardrobe containing all his earthly possessions, a Buddha on each of the tables, and pictures of Jesus and Gandhi on the walls. He briefly thought about putting up a couple of center-folds just to break it up.

"Do you feel good about leaving the car out there?"

Buck said, "I paid the young man with the foghorn voice twenty bucks to watch it."

Tom looked back out the window and saw Caleb, one of Pat's grandsons, leading a tour of kids around the car as if he owned it. The car would be all right.

"This is one of those lines like 'follow that taxi.' To what do I owe the honor of this visit?" Tom said. He normally thought of his bed as firm, but Buck had the mattress and springs down to the top of the bed frame. Tom looked closely at Buck again. There was still something different. Buck didn't have what you would call mobile features, but Tom thought he was seeing anguish in the way they were arranged.

Buck said, "I thought your room would be wall to wall books, but I don't see a single one."

Tom could have told him that he was in the way of losing information these days, not gaining it, but he knew that Buck was just filling space. He pulled the chair opposite Buck and continued to study this man, this rock—this thing he'd been anchored to for a nearly a quarter century. He analyzed his initial reaction to Buck's appearance and recognized his own fear. He poked around in his mind, seeking out and snuffing all the little egoic bits that lived on his relationship to Buck. He couldn't help Buck if he was worried about how what he would say would affect himself.

"I've met a woman," Buck said.

"OK," Tom thought. "Nothing there. That was like saying a morning commuter had run into traffic."

"I think I'm in love with her."

"Up jumped the devil. That's completely outside the norm." Tom had always considered Buck to be in love with several or more women at any given time. With the exception of the Frenchwoman, he'd never even heard Buck speak in terms of one woman.

"But that's not the worst of it."

Was he saying being in love was a bad thing? Nobody knew how old Buck was, but it had to be around his own sixty years. Do people really fall in love at that age? Obviously they do. That was a silly thought. Buck had set the manuscript on the bed beside him. He grabbed it and flipped it up on the table beside Tom. Tom read the title.

"Paul Bunyan, huh?"

Buck said, "I'm sure I've told you about the young man that came to the rig a year and a half ago?"

"Val Campbell. I've met him. Rather impressive, I must say."

"Yeah. Well, it turns out that he literally went to school on Buck Burnet and wrote that book. Apparently I'm not Buck Burnet."

"Who are you?"

"Hector Gonzales."

"Gonzales?"

"Some Spanish name that starts with *G*."

"How is it you're not sure of the name that might be yours?"

"His grandmother told it to me early this morning. I haven't read the book."

"His grandmother? Is she the person you've fallen in love with?" As far as Tom knew about Buck, thirty was about the upper age limit for women to be interested in. There was more than a little Buck Burnet in the look he gave Tom as an answer.

"Why haven't you read the book?"

Now we're getting down to it. Buck looked down at the floor, spread his arms out, and put his hands on the edge of the mattress. He nearly spanned the length of the bed.

"I don't know. I think I'm scared to."

Tom thought that a perfectly reasonable reaction. Buck had obviously undergone some kind of severe trauma before the beginning of the legend. Whatever it was had been bad enough to make him want to forget everything that had gone before.

"When she called me that name, it was like she had stuck a cattle prod up my ass. I drove all the way down here, and I still don't feel right. One thing is for sure: I don't feel like Buck Burnet anymore."

Tom realized that that was what he himself had been afraid of hearing. If there was no Buck Burnet, there was no protection for him and for a bunch of other people.

"And you're here because you want me to...?"

Buck Burnet had been incapable of pleading, but when he looked up, that was exactly what he was doing.

"I want you to read that book and then tell me what it says, in bite-size chunks."

"I'll be glad to read it, but I can't do it today. I've got to be at work in a couple of hours."

"I've taken the liberty of calling Miz Catherine and telling her that you were sick today."

Tom looked at Buck...Hector, and knew that this was what he was supposed to be doing this day. Besides, there was no way he was going to pass up being one of the first to know the true origins of the man he had come to respect and love.

"Are you going to stay here while I read it?"

"If you don't mind. I'm sort of curious to find out what it says."

Tom didn't think pointing out the irony in that statement would be helpful.

"Do you want me to give you information as I read it, or do you want me to read the whole thing first?"

"Whichever. Once you get reading it, just do what you think is best."

"Would you like a cup of coffee? I'm going to get one."

Tom's coffeepot was on a hot plate in the bathroom. Buck hadn't answered him, but he brought him a cup anyway. He opened the blue bound book to the back first and checked for reference pages. As he had hoped, fully a third of the book was taken up with references. He went back to the table of contents and saw that most of the book had to do with Buck's life after he was fourteen. Only two chapters at the end had to do with his origins. He sifted through the first part of the book to get familiar with Campbell's techniques. If he was any judge, and he considered himself so, then Campbell was a good writer as well as a thorough researcher. Each chapter concerned itself with the town or area where Buck lived at the time. He would start off with the stories told, the basics without literary turns, then put in as much backup as he could from eyewitness accounts and newspaper reports. It had not been written to lionize Buck or further his myth. The rest of each chapter, and most of the book, was about the people and culture of each town at the time Buck lived there. Buck was the thread, but the book was really a history of the oilfield, as it moved from place to place throughout Buck's life. Several times he almost got lost in the reading only to remember his purpose and press on. He made a mental note to get a copy of the book and read it when he had some time. He went to the last two chapters.

Tom looked up from his reading and said, "Guerrero."

Buck said, "What?"

"It's not Gonzales. He says the name is Hector Guerrero. He says he is not one hundred percent sure that it's you."

"I don't think it *is* me."

"Why not?"

"Nobody ever said anything about me having an accent or knowing any Spanish words."

"Not everyone with a Spanish name in Texas is a Mexican. There were lots of them living there before the first settlers from the United States showed up."

"Yeah, but they were Mexicans then, weren't they? Isn't that why Santa Ana made the trip in the first place?"

Tom could see Buck was just being contentious.

Tom said, "You know, saying Mexican like that, 'Mes'kin,' is insulting to a Mexican, right?"

"No. In south Texas that's the way even they say it. That's what you got in south Texas, Mes'kins and gringos."

"I can't speak to what they do in south Texas, but I can tell you that, in south Louisiana, calling someone of Mexican descent a Mes'kin is an insult. You might want to keep that in mind in your new circumstances."

"What circumstances?"

"It's beginning to look very much like you're one yourself."

Tom looked closely for Buck's reaction. Surprisingly, he saw the beginnings of a smile.

"Son of a bitch," Buck said softly.

With that the door to the rear of the house opened, and a tall, slender young woman carrying a tray of food walked in. Her skin was the color of butterscotch, and her hair was red and cut close to her skull. She had a regal bearing and wore a beautiful smile that disappeared when she saw Buck sitting on the bed.

"Anaya," Tom said, "This is one of my bosses, Buck Burnet. Buck, this is Anaya Goodman, and on the days when I'm really lucky, she is the one who brings me my lunch."

Anaya looked steadily into Buck's eyes, not daring him really, just putting him on notice. Buck looked at her. She was truly gorgeous.

Buck said, "Maybe that's the way it will be in heaven."

Tom said, "She used to do it all the time, but now that she's grown up, she spends most of her time in New York City. She's a fashion model for some snooty agency.

Anaya looked at Buck and said, "Yes, thanks to—"

Tom stopped her with his hand. "Thanks to God giving you those looks and your hard work. Anaya, do you think there is enough food for Buck to have a plate?"

"Well," she said, "there's enough food cooked for a regular-sized person, but I don't think there's enough food in the house to fill that up." She cut her eyes at Buck and smirked.

Tom said, "Surprisingly, he doesn't eat that much more than me."

"Well," she said, "let me talk to Pat and see what we can whip up. Maybe we can fill him up with cornbread."

She walked over and set Tom's tray on the table beside him. When she walked out, she did so knowing there were four appreciative eyes on her all the way.

Buck said, "She's magnificent."

Tom said, "When she was a kid, she could beat up any boy in the neighborhood."

Tom left his meal untouched and went back to the book. Pat brought Buck's dinner herself, partly, Tom thought, to get a close look at the stranger. Both men were a little disappointed. Behind her came a little boy dragging a kitchen chair.

"Buck, this is my landlady, Pat Goodman, and her youngest—" Pat cleared her throat. "Her next to the youngest—" She cleared her throat again. "This is her grandson Marnier, future NFL champion running back."

Pat was appraising Buck with the frank stare that only young children and older black women can pull off. Marnier (pronounced Maw-ree-yay) looked at Buck from behind Pat.

Pat said, "I didn't think he had no friends. In all these years, he hadn't never had nobody to the house." She looked at Tom. "Are all your friends that size?"

Tom said, "You only need one."

Pat gave a throaty chuckle. "Yeah, I expect that's so."

As Pat turned to leave, Marnier darted out from behind her and tried to count coup on Buck's knee. Buck caught his arm and lifted him up to eye level. Marnier didn't protest or move, just looked Buck in the eye. Buck put him down, and Marnier ran after his grandmother.

"Linebacker," Buck said.

After Pat was gone, the men chatted as they ate.

"I haven't eaten since last night," Buck said. "I was so involved in thinking I just forgot to stop." Then, after a while, he added, "It's not me, you know; it's everybody else."

Tom understood perfectly.

"I've been trying to think of a way to describe how it feels. It's like a deer that suddenly finds itself in an open field. No, it's more like being a warrior and finding yourself stripped of armor; only in this case I didn't know I had been wearing armor."

"Or," Tom thought, "finding yourself mortal after a lifetime of being Superman."

"The only analogy I can think of is the original Hector. The gods were with him his whole life then, suddenly, they weren't. I've always felt protected, but it was something I took for granted. I wish that I hadn't found Sylvie and found out about Hector Guerrero at the same time. I don't know if what I'm feeling is a reaction to one or the other, or both."

Tom thought back to the Lilac Bloom and contrasted the Buck he knew then with the one that sat before him. If this had been the old Buck, there wouldn't be a problem. That Buck had been totally reactive. He had been like a male lion, lounging around, eating and sleeping and taking all the attention as his due. This Buck had an intellect and, perhaps more telling, a conscience. Any moment now Tom expected him to break into Hamlet's soliloquy. As for his being protected, Tom had had no trouble believing Buck's contention that an angel sometimes took over his body. He had been standing on the porch with a shotgun on the day the sheriff's men came to the Lilac Bloom. All he could see was Buck's back, his feet planted and his hips and shoulders moving with machine-like blows. It was a jumble of motion, but he retained one clear image of a man, even bigger than Buck, coming up to Buck from the right and taking a blow in the center of his torso. He didn't bounce and roll like in the movies. The blow seemed to cave in his chest, and he dropped like a sack of meal. The mental image haunted Tom for years after.

"I've always felt that there was one last Neandertal waiting for me out there. There would be an epic battle, after which I would die with dignity saying something wise, or at least memorable. Part of me looked forward to that as a way to break the monotony, a way of getting on to the next thing. But now, I don't want to die. That's all I could think of driving down here. I don't want to die; and thinking it makes me feel funny and weak."

Tom said, "I suspect all the keys are in these last two chapters. He says he doesn't know for sure that it's you, but that's probably just scholarly caution. He must have felt there was plenty of evidence to have included it. What are your plans in regard to this woman — Sylvia, is it?"

"Sylvie. She's French."

Buck smiled at Tom's reaction.

"I know. I know. But, in the deputy sheriff's description, she's 'real, French from France French.' The only plan I have right now is to see as much of her as I can. I'm not at all sure that she'll see me again. We had last night, but she seemed to be coming at it out of a strong biological need. Thinking back on it, I can remember no indication of what she thought of me as a person, or even that she thought of me as a person."

"Yet, you think you're in love with her?"

"I'm pretty familiar with lust, particularly as it relates to Buck Burnet. I think I was in love with her before she took my hand and led me into the bedroom. I hadn't even considered sex before that. Anyway, I plan to be with her in whatever capacity she'll allow."

"Married?"

"Hopefully. In any case, I think my life as Buck Burnet is over."

"What about 'everybody else'?"

"There's the rub. Incredible, isn't it? How so much that looks like reality can hang on a fiction. Of course, I was fully vested. I was playing a role without knowing it. Now I feel like I've been leading everybody down the garden path. I don't think I can say anything about it right now. I think I have to just go on with the play until I can figure out ways of letting everyone down easy. That's the reason I came here first. I know that you never bought into the myth, and this won't affect you."

Buck had always given him too much credit, and he had allowed it. The person Tom aspired to be wouldn't have felt a sense of loss, but Tom wasn't there yet.

"What about Catherine?" Tom said. "I think way in the back of her mind she always thought you and she would be together at the end."

"Yeah, I know. That was in my mind as well. We've both been guilty of using up our credits without regard for the future. She's been in some kind of a funk lately, too. I don't know. I'm certainly not going to lay this on her right now."

Tom knew Catherine was in a funk. It was directly related to the night she had spent with Val some months back. Tom had been worried about her before this. She hadn't been as diligent about looking her best and seemed to be gaining a little weight. He was in full agreement that nothing be said.

"I've got to work out what the hands can do, at least the ones that have been with me for a long time."

"Most of them."

Buck nodded. "Most of them. The one I'm most concerned about is Mike Brown."

Tom was genuinely surprised. "Mike Brown? I would have thought him the one least to worry about."

Buck got up from the bed and put his empty plate on top of Tom's and took both of them to the counter in the bathroom. The gesture was oddly domestic and un-Buck-like. Tom wondered if it were a conscious move or a reflex from his Hector Guerrero past.

"Yeah. Mike's got a lot of strengths, but he's got a little bit of a hole at his center, too. He grew up in a macho family in a macho place, and he just wasn't macho. That happens a lot, I think. Most of the boys in that situation will overcompensate by dressing and talking and acting more macho than everybody else. Some will throw up their hands and take home economics. Mike didn't think that he should have to act like something he wasn't, and he was hurt that his family couldn't accept him as he was. It wasn't until he got away from home that he began to realize that he was a regular person and that machismo wasn't necessarily the way of the world. He fits in just fine, but he's never escaped the feeling that, in some way, he just doesn't measure up."

Tom said, "I understand, but I don't see how that's your responsibility."

"*Responsibility* is not the right word. I guess the only reason I even think about it is because it's something that troubles a really good friend." Tom considered that an exceptional statement but didn't have the time to figure out why. "But there is something about Mike for which I bear responsibility, and I'm only now beginning to understand it. Mike has all the attributes necessary for moving up in an organization like Exxon, but he hasn't moved up, and I'm the reason."

Tom objected. "That can't be true."

"It is true. Way too true for my comfort. I set it up—not consciously, of course, but it's no less true for that. I was a prima donna, and Exxon doesn't have any truck with such. At the time there was a shortage of rigs, and they needed mine badly. Olympia wasn't in the way of firing me, so somebody in Exxon analyzed the situation and came up with Mike as the solution. I suspected Mike was going to stick when he first came out, but I gave him a ration of shit, anyway. Pretty soon he was pulling his weight, and in a couple of years, I gave up trying to make any downhole decisions. By the time he'd been with me five years, he was probably the best drilling engineer Exxon had. Somewhere around that time, I got word through my company that Exxon was planning to make him a superintendent and move him onshore. I raised such a stink that the idea was quashed. They made a couple more stabs at it, but I always managed to keep him out there. Mike always seemed happy, and I'm sure I told myself it was for his own good, but, sitting here right now and talking to you, I have no idea how I could have believed it. They have him teach a course every six months to the new engineers, and for the last ten years, they've been sending the most promising ones to intern with him. Now his time is past. He's out of the rotation, and, at fifty or thereabouts, he wouldn't be considered able to acclimate to the corporate culture. His bosses for a long time have been younger than him — all because I didn't want to have to work with somebody else."

There was no objection from Tom this time. What Buck had related was a clear example of affecting someone else's life adversely. Tom was pretty sure Mike wouldn't have blamed Buck because he loved Buck as Buck loved him, even if he had been unable to come up with the words. But was love ever an excuse for wrong. Was a mother who held her children too close to be excused because she did it in the name of love?

"Does Mike know you did that?"

"I wouldn't think so. The only way he would is if his bosses in Exxon told him, and I don't think they would consider it in Exxon's best interest for him to know."

"That's a significant thing. You're going to tell him, of course?"

"I hope not to have to." Tom let that one sit there long enough for Buck to become restive. Buck said, "The hands will be all right. If I can talk Joe Tom into taking over as toolpusher they shouldn't miss a beat."

Tom said, "I imagine the ones who will miss you the most are all those vendors that make their livings off you."

Buck smiled. "A lot of them I really consider friends, but we'll see how that goes once I don't have any leverage. Some of them could care less who owns the tit, as long as they get some milk from it. Any way I didn't assign work based on who were my friends, although, everything else being equal, friendship probably made the difference."

Buck was looking over Tom's head, thinking. Tom went through all that had been said and wondered if there were anything to add, but it sounded like Buck was doing well on his own. He picked the book back up and turned to the first page of the last two chapters.

Tom said, "Shall we get on with the life and times of the young Hector Geurrero?"

CHAPTER XXIII

Back on the Rig

Mike Brown was lying on his bed on the Hector, reading a Len Deighton novel. He had shifted his body downward so his boots hung off the end, but he was still feeling a little guilty about being on the bed with his clothes on. Deighton had a way of making him laugh at things that shouldn't be funny. His hero was currently breaking and entering a butcher shop while his wife, a doctor, followed him around trying to explain what was wrong with their marriage. As he breaks law after law with no explanation, she grows increasingly alarmed and, when they reach the front door, ends the chapter and the marriage by stepping into a taxi.

When Buck came into the room, Mike said, "Is the rig sinking? Are we blowing out?"

Buck said, "If that's an attempt at humor, it's an extremely feeble one."

"Seriously, you never come into my room. Is everything all right?"

"Everything is all right. God, this place is a mess. What is all this shit?"

Brown's wife, Sandra, was a wonderful woman, but she was a bit obsessive about neatness — OK, more than a bit. Brown preserved his sanity by allowing clutter in his environs at sea. Perhaps he did go a little overboard. His opposite number, Curt Peterson, another engineer and a manly man, occasionally felt compelled to straighten up while he was here. Buck took the back of the guest chair and tipped it, dumping a stack of books and papers onto the deck. He set the chair down in a clear spot and lowered his bulk into it. Brown swung his feet to the deck and sat on the edge of the bed, facing Buck.

"Really, Buck," Brown said, "you're making me nervous. What is it?"

Buck said, "You remember when Campbell and I had that little run-in a while back?"

Brown nodded. That run-in had been the main topic of discussion on the rig ever since. Brown was not likely to forget it, ever.

"Remember his saying that neither of us had a father, and our saying that he must know something I didn't?"

Once again, not something Brown was likely to forget.

"Well, he knows a lot I don't. It turns out he literally went to school on me. He wrote a book, a dissertation, about me."

Brown said, "I knew it had to be something like that. Do you have a copy?"

"Yeah, his grandmother gave me one."

"His grandmother?"

"Yeah, I went to that little town he's from and did some investigating of my own. I met his grandmother, his mother, and his little sister."

"No shit? What were they like?"

"They were real nice. The grandmother in particular is kind of a remarkable person. I'll tell you about them sometime, but right now I want to tell you about the book."

"Well, let me read it, and then we can talk about it."

"I'll let you read it sometime, but right now I just want to tell you some of the things I found out."

"OK."

"First off, what do you think my name is?"

"I'm guessing it isn't Patricia or Rosanna or Dorothy."

"Hector. It's Hector. Can you believe that?"

"That is pretty coincidental."

"Hector Guerrero."

Brown said, "That means 'warrior' in Spanish."

"Yeah, yeah, it's also the name of a Mexican state. I looked it up. My mother was Mexican, or half Mexican. Her progeny is a little fuzzy. That's all if I am really the guy he thinks I am. He says there's no way of saying definitely that I am Hector Guerrero. But he thinks the odds are real good. If I am Hector Guerrero, I have brothers and sisters that are still alive. My mother is dead. She was a cleaning lady in West Dallas. She was never married. During hard times she turned tricks. Including Hector, yo—"

"Yo?"

"*Yo* means 'me' in Spanish."

"It means 'I,' but I get the drift."

"Including me she had seven kids and claimed she didn't know for sure who had fathered any of them. I was the oldest. At the time of my demise—"

"Demise?"

"That means 'death.' That's actually an English word. At the time of my death, she was living with a guy, a real brute, who was a Dallas cop. Apparently he had lived with her off and on for many years. Val's theory is that he was the reason she could never get any traction. He only had one function with the police department. Whenever it was deemed necessary that someone be beaten up, he was the guy who was called on. Sometimes he left her, and sometimes she tried to get away from him, but she never did. Anyway, her thirteen-year-old son, Hector, had enough of his mom's being beaten and took the cop on. The mother and the other kids had to watch the beating, which went on long after Hector was unconscious. The cop dragged the body out of the little shack into a dry creek bed in the back. The kids theorized that he pulled it all the way down to the Trinity River and dumped it in. How do you report a murder to the police when the murderer was a cop? That took place approximately six weeks before I got off a westbound truck in Jal, New Mexico."

Buck sat expectantly, waiting for all the connections to be made in Brown's brain.

"How did he find all that stuff out? What happened in the six weeks? Can a body recover from a beating like that in that short a time?"

"He said it was like following smoke from a fire that happened yesterday. Several people in Jal said the truck came across the line from Texas, so he concentrated his search there. He went to all the cities of any size and checked back newspapers and police reports when he could but never found anything that looked likely. Apparently missing thirteen-year-olds weren't big news in those days. He started putting ads in newspapers, and that generated a lot of leads, but he didn't find anything that fit all the requirements. Finally, some old lady in a retirement home in Fort Worth wrote him saying that she was a nurse who had sat with a dying woman about the right time. The woman told her a story about losing her will to live when she lost her son. She said the woman was pretty, but she could tell she had had a hard life. She was impressed with how much she had invested in a child. She couldn't remember the lady's name but told him how to get to the records. That's how he located the siblings. Once he had interviewed all the people he could find, he tried to pick up the trail. He canvassed West Dallas, hoping for more luck. No hospital or clinic had any records. There were always records of bodies being found in the Trinity, but none of the ones reported fit the description. The time between the dumping of the body and my arrival in Jal is still a total mystery. As far as how quick a body can heal, I don't have any idea. I didn't have any scars or signs of broken bones."

"What happened to the cop?"

"Unfortunately, he's dead. He retired from the force with full honors and died quietly some years later. My mother, Lydia Guerrero, stopped eating after Hector died and died herself.

The cop was already gone, and the rest of the kids got sucked into the system and parceled out to various foster homes. Some were luckier than others. Some of the youngest don't remember Hector. A middle girl was so emotionally scarred by the incident that she was never able to function normally. The next-oldest boy to Hector, Miguel, became a lawyer and a prosecutor, and he tried to make a case for murder, but he could never get enough evidence together to make it stick."

"So all those siblings think you…think Hector is dead."

"Yeah, Campbell interviewed them, but he never told them what he suspected about me. He said he wanted to leave that up to me. He said he didn't know if I would want to reconnect or not."

"Do you?"

"I don't know. That's something I have to think about. Logically I think it all hangs together, and I could be Hector Guerrero, but I don't really feel like I am yet, and maybe I never will. I couldn't walk up to someone and tell them I'm their brother if I didn't feel like I really was."

"What about Buck Burnet? What did he have to say about the legend?"

"Not a lot, really. In the dissertation he stuck to verifiable facts, and there weren't a lot of them around even at the time of the alleged incidents. Every once in a while, he would come across somebody who claimed to have been a witness, and he wrote about what he or she had to say, but most of the people he talked to could only pass along what someone else had told them. He talked to Bobby and Lilah and Laney, the lady judge in Jeanerette, but it sounds to me like their memories had fogged up. Their versions got a little more fantastic over the years. Campbell is thinking, if we ever get the time, we can put the stories together in a fictionalized version and give it the same name as the dissertation."

"Well, there you go. You can use my book as a basis."

"Yeah, that's what I told him. We could use your book as a basis."

"What…?"

"What? Nothing. I can't believe I'm a Mexican."

"Well, half. Maybe a quarter. What nationality was the cop?"

"Polack."

"What was his name?"

"I don't know. I skipped over that when I heard it. I didn't want his name stuck in my brain."

"How do you feel about being a Mexican?"

"Good, I guess. It's the first time I've ever been anything."

"You do possess a goodly amount of swarth."

"I thought you'd be interested."

"I am interested. I'm mostly interested in how you feel about it. That's a lot of emotionally loaded information to be taking on all at one time. So the university...whoever it is who's responsible for passing out sheepskins felt that was worth one? It all seems a little shy of scholarly content to me."

Buck grinned and said, "That's what I thought when I read the title. Val's pretty clever, though. Buck Burnet is the bones of the thesis, but the meat comes in the description of all the little subcultures along the way. West Dallas was its own chapter, but the rest of it was detailing the oilfields that were hot from the time of World War II until about five years ago. Val said it was a virgin area, and his sponsors and the review panel ate it up."

"So it's 'Val' now?" Brown said. "What does 'Val's' mother look like?"

"Why don't you clean this shithole up? You've probably got rats living in here."

"I do, but they leave me alone if I drop enough food on the floor."

Nearly six months after storming off the floor, Val was in the derrick making a trip. The night was fair, and the lights of the gulf coast sparkled in a long uneven string behind him. The moon had been up for a while, and if he looked to the left, he could see its reflection coating the surface of a dead-calm sea. There was a breeze in his face. Earlier the wind had come from onshore, bringing mosquitoes and other bugs to bother him.

There probably were still some on the floor, but up here they had all been blown away. The air was soft and clean. The allergens that normally plagued him on the beach were lacking, and there was nothing between him and the sheer enjoyment of life and limb.

On Val's first hitch after his blowup, Buck had assigned Joe Tom the task of teaching him how to work derricks. Val supposed that was his way of telling him he belonged. It was no small thing. It was unheard of for someone of Val's relatively miniscule experience to snag a derricks job onshore, much less out here. Val had been keen to learn, but in the first ten weeks to three months, he had many opportunities to regret his eagerness. For one thing, it was scary. The main deck of the rig was thirty or more feet out of the water, but it was a broad flat area surrounded by hand rails. The floor was another twenty feet above that and smaller than the area of the deck, but still roomy and surrounded by handrails. The monkey board where he worked in the derrick was an eighteen-inch wide, twelve-foot long piece of metal with holes punched in it and no handrails. He was attached to the derrick behind him with the slenderest of ropes, and when he looked down from the end of the board, the nearest stopping point was the rotary table, eighty-six feet away. On top of that, most of the work in the derrick was performed with the front half of both feet over the edge of the board and his body leaning into the derrick at ten or fifteen degrees, the only thing keeping him from dropping like a stone the rope attached to the harness at his belly. Just forcing himself to rely on that rope was a huge undertaking. Initially, the potential of a fall took up most of his brain, so he only had a very few cells available for learning. For another thing, everything was physically very difficult. If he had come up here when he first came aboard, there would have been no way he could have performed even the tiniest task. As it was Joe Tom had had to shepherd him, continually taking part of the weight when it looked like the strain was going to be too much. When he wasn't in the derrick, he was mixing mud and carrying hundred-pound sacks of clay and chemicals up and down stairs.

When he came down from the derrick each evening, it took all the strength he could muster just to shower and make it into the top bunk. His seven days off were six days of recuperation, and the seventh one of dreading the next.

Finally, everything that happened up here happened fast, and, if he didn't manage to accomplish his part of the cycle in time, it all came to a halt until he could undo the damage. He thought he had worked under pressure as an academic, but the two occupations weren't even comparable. When he dropped a stand of drill pipe across the derrick, it hit the other side with a distinctive series of steel knocks. The rhythm of the engines loading and unloading was broken, and the trip came to a silent halt. People came out of the living quarters to watch and jeer as he worked his way around to the other side and attached the mule to the fallen pipe. The derision of the hands was one thing, but Val could feel Buck watching from the window of his office, and Buck's concerns would be the more practical ones of time and money lost. Nub was very patient, but Val knew that the speed of the trip was one of the things used to measure a driller's performance, and Nub was very proud of his crew's speed and efficiency. The trip to the other side of the derrick, clinging to steel girts and beams, was in itself an enervating exercise and depleted the emotional and physical reserves he needed to get through the rest of the tour. More than once he felt tears of frustration and exhaustion on his cheeks and thought that if he were just a little less stubborn, he would slide down the ladder and give it all up. He had Joe Tom there though, and he knew Joe Tom was not going to let anything permanent happen.

Gradually his body got stronger, and he became surer. The time came when he was able to get through the tour and wake up the next day refreshed and not feeling sore. The confidence that he could handle anything that came up freed his mind and allowed him to think about the job he was doing and ways to do it better. The things that Joe Tom had been telling him all along began to make sense, and his technique improved. Ironically, as he got better the job got easier, and he needed less and less strength to get it done. The last two times he had not only not dreaded coming out but had looked forward to it. The days of dropping stands were over, and when he walked into the mess decks, he could feel the respect of those he respected for the first time in his life. He understood Jack London to an extent he had never thought possible and felt like, had the timing been right, he could have talked to him man to man.

Tonight was his first night as the real morning tour derrickman, and he was savoring the sights, sounds, and smells of the Gulf of Mexico, the world, and the universe—and feeling himself to be a legitimate part. He felt the pride and allowed himself to savor that, too. The trip was a symphony, and he was the percussionist, the clang of his elevators furnishing the beat. The trip was a dance, and he was the lead, moving in perfect rhythm and harmony with the rest of the troupe. He had felt some of this working on the floor, but up here the feeling was distilled and intensified. His personal life was coming right, as well. His departure from the original plan had left an open wound, which had now had time to heal. It was like it had never happened with his grandmother. She even seemed now to approve of what he had done. His mother and he had never been really close, but she was making attempts to communicate. Just last week she had risen early to catch him at breakfast and pass on a concern she had about his grandmother. Apparently she had taken to leaving, sometimes for days at a time. It was almost like she had somebody, but neither one of them could feature that. It must have had something to do with the store. She had ever been closemouthed about what went on there.

There was a slight vibration in the derrick, and he realized someone was climbing the ladder. Soon the distinctive outline of Joe Tom hove into view, and he stepped into the light of the derrick. Val loved Joe Tom and, more, loved the idea of Joe Tom and thought that there would never be a better example of God's intent.

"Worried that I would fuck up?" Val said.

"Naw. I'm not worried about you fucking up anymore."

"I'm not worried about it, either."

"Yeah, and that's why I'm not worried about it. There's derrickmen that have an edge on you because of experience, but I haven't seen one that can do the job any better than you. When you first came up here, I had my doubts. When someone brings me a cutting horse to train, it's usually one of three types. Some take to it so natural that pretty soon all you have to worry about is not falling off. Others seem like they knew about it in a dream, and they have to be waked up and reminded of what to do. The last bunch don't have any idea what you're trying to do and never will. You can teach them to answer the rein or the knee or the spur, but they don't have the moves that would put them in the ring at a show. You were like one of that last group. You had the desire. You just didn't seem to have the wherewithal. I really don't know how you learned to do it. You are a horse totally outside my ken."

Val thought about that for a while. It was high praise from a man who wouldn't have the slightest idea of how to flatter someone. Nobody was going anyplace, and he let himself relax back into the rhythm of the trip. Walk the stand out, squeeze the catch rope, straddle the stand, let it go, latch the elevators. Clang! Walk to the back of the derrick. Val didn't know how you would test the Joe Tom's intelligence, but he knew if you could, it would be considerable.

"Are you worried about me taking your job?" This wasn't a serious question, but Val could tell that, just for a flicker of a second, Joe Tom took it so.

"Naw. You aren't going to take my job."

"Why not?"

"For one thing you aren't interested in taking my job. You don't ask the right questions. You want to learn all the jobs on the rig, but you're not thinking about what's going on downhole. A drilling rig is all about what's going on downhole. If you were thinking about staying out here for the rest of your life, you'd be trying to learn all about bits and mud and logging and such. That's why you see me talking to Buck and Mike and Nub and all the service hands. I'm trying to get ready to take the next step. You love working derricks right now, but sometime soon you are going to realize that it's pretty much the same thing, day after day. That big old brain of yours already knows that, and if it had any intention of staying out here in the gulf, it would already be making plans for moving to driller."

Val knew it was true soon as Joe Tom said it, but he didn't like hearing it. He was happier than he had ever been, and it made him sad to think it would end.

"For another thing, you're not the right kind of horse. You can put a racehorse in harness and, I guess, get something out of him, but he's never really going to be a workhorse. Thoroughbreds don't run quarter-miles, and quarter horses don't run distance. They can do it, but it's not what they're built for, and they can never be truly happy not doing what they do best. Everyone out here likes you and admires you for what you've done, but, in their heart of hearts, nobody sees you staying forever."

Val continued working as Joe Tom spoke. He knew himself to be a romantic, and it became clear to him that, at least in part, he had been on a quest for the "noble savage" and a place where life was simpler, where the difference between good and bad was more clear, where ability and competence defined one, and bullshit took a back seat. Joe Tom was the best example, but, to lesser extents, everyone out here was a noble savage. In one way he felt Joe Tom to be wrong. He could stay and be happy. He was however right in that Val had no interest in moving up the ladder and accepting more responsibility. Having people's lives in one's hands seemed more of a burden than he wanted to bear. He was also right about Val's nature and what he was equipped for. As distasteful as Val found the maneuverings inherent in indoor pursuits, he knew he was better suited for them than most and most likely to contribute effectively there. At the same time, he knew, without knowing how or why, that he would never be more content than he was right here, right now. He had nothing to say and gradually Joe Tom sensed that, rather than bolster Val's spirit as he had meant to, he had had the opposite effect. He backed out of the light and disappeared into the dark, and Val didn't know when it happened.

The tables in the mess decks on the Hector were bolted to the floor, and their arrangement was consciously egalitarian, but there was an unspoken agreement that dictated how they were used. Nobody ever said the seat that faced the door at the second table on the left was Buck's, but nobody else ever sat there. Even visitors instinctively avoided the table unless invited by Buck. This particular morning Buck and Mike Brown were engaged in a typical postbreakfast discussion on the state of the well. The well, as it happened, was going well, with the expectation that it would reach contract depth within the week. Buck and Mike were going over all the service companies who would have to be put on call and the equipment and material that would have to be scheduled. Completing a well was something they had done many times, but it was in both their natures to leave nothing to chance. Business done, Brown made a move to get up, and Buck stopped him with a question.

"Mike, Sandra is some kind of special education teacher, isn't she?"

"Yeah, she's at UT getting her master's in something to do with vision right now."

"What can be done for a child that got some kind of disease when she was a baby and it affected her brain?"

"I know she's worked with kids like that. She's told me stories about them, but I didn't pick up enough information to do you any good. You'd have to talk to her."

"You and Sandra have a good marriage, don't you?"

Brown was surprised by the question and answered lightly, "That's something else you'd have to ask her."

Buck said, "I'm serious. How long have you been married?"

Brown sat back down. "Let's see...I think it will be twenty-six years this September."

"That's a long time. Have you always been happy?"

Brown could see that Buck really wanted to know. "To tell you the truth, it's always been happy for me. Sandra says there have been a couple of periods when she wasn't so happy. I think that's partly because of the way I've had to work, being gone so much. She pretty much raised the kids on her own. Also I was kind of raised in that Texas machismo bullshit. When my mother was a girl, all the women waited until the men finished eating before they set the table for themselves. We didn't do that when I was growing up, but women were still definitely second-class citizens. If a man wasn't demonstrably the head of his family, he was considered weak. I carried some of that into the early years of our marriage, and Sandra took it, but we both sort of grew out of it. Some of our friends think we don't ever fight, but that's not really true. We have disagreements and hurt feelings. What we don't ever do is scream and yell at each other. Neither one of us, no matter how angry, has ever slipped and said one of those things that really hurt. But the answer to your question is yes, I have always been happy."

Buck had been nodding as if the answer was what was expected but maybe not what he was looking for. "What do you think is the secret?"

Brown thought that's what he had been talking about. "You want to know the real reason for my happiness? The key to my long-lasting marriage?" Buck nodded. "The key is marry the right person. When I was a newsman in Dallas, I hung around Will Fritz, the head of the crimes-against-persons division of the Dallas police department. He was an old man at the time and seemed to enjoy telling me stories. He was raised on a horse ranch in New Mexico, and they were artificially inseminating horses in those days. That had to be sometime around the turn of the century. Anyway, Captain Fritz always said that breeding is the key—to horses and men. He said, 'Look at the bloodline. It will always run true.' Sandra was a naturally happy person. Even I couldn't make her unhappy for long. She is happy, and our kids are happy, and for that reason I am happy."

Buck wondered if it could be that simple. Certainly there were people who were normally happy and others who were normally sad. He realized he took it into account when he was hiring and deciding who would stay. He didn't look for people who were ecstatic all the time, but he did watch for potential malcontents. There were people who were only happy when they were indignant about something. Those people were like cancers. Misery did indeed love company. But applying those principles to romantic relationships?

Brown could tell that Buck wasn't a believer. He decided to give it one last shot. "How long have you and I been together out here? Twenty or so years?" Buck nodded. "Would you call that a happy pairing?"

Buck said, "It isn't the same thing."

Brown said, "Yes, it is. It is the very same thing. It's a relationship based on mutual respect and consideration for the other. Marriage carries other shit with it, but a successful marriage is essentially a relationship between caring equals."

Brown knew something in that struck Buck as true because he could tell his friend was thinking it over. Now it was time for Brown to ask, at his age, why Buck was wondering about marriage.

As he was formulating the words, Val sat at the seat next to him, shaking the table. Kids just didn't get furniture. His own son had done away with at least two couches and a chair. It was an odd time for him to be here since he was supposed to be working, but Brown wasn't surprised that Val had no qualms about sitting at Buck's table. In the first months after the blowup, Val and Buck had spent an awkward time of getting to know one another. They both obviously wanted the father-son relationship and thought it possible, but neither had the natural moves. Watching the process had been interesting and sometimes heartwarming for Brown: Buck's crustiness turning into open and welcoming smiles when Val came around; Val's hero worship morphing into a warm and playful respect. Deciding that Val was here for a reason, Brown shelved his question and stood. Both of the others asked him to stay, but he demurred.

Buck said, "Stay. I've got something I want to tell both of you."

Brown sat back down.

Buck said, "I saw my brother."

"What?" Val and Brown in unison.

"Miguel Guerrero. Last days off I went up to Dallas. It took a couple of days, but I found out where he lived and where he worked and where he would be at a time that I could get a look at him. He has an office in one of those towers on west Main. It's pretty cool. All of those buildings are connected underground with big halls with stores and restaurants. It can look like a slow day at street level, and it's a damn ant farm one level down. I could spend a couple of days just wandering around in that maze. Anyway I found out where he parked and the route he took going there from work. The elevators from the odd-numbered floors let out on the street level and the others on the first level down. He was on an even numbered floor, and where they get off, the elevators open out into a space that's open to the sky. They had restaurants around the edges and tables with umbrellas, so I sat at one of the tables with a beer and waited for him. The first day I missed him. He either left early or worked a lot later than I was willing to stay. All I had was Val's description, but I figured if I couldn't recognize my own brother, he wasn't. I saw somebody who could have been him the second day but didn't think him likely. I saw the same guy on the third day and decided I was going to leave. I finished the beer and walked to the bottom of the stairway to street level. I saw Miguel coming out with some other guys, all dressed in pin-striped suits. They were obviously friends and talking over their days, and the whole group stopped, not ten feet away. The other guys were going to have a beer, and they were trying to get Miguel to go with them. He was saying that he would like to but that he needed to get home. This was obviously a typical scenario, and the others gave up without much of fight. The odd thing is I knew for certain that they liked him and respected him and were truly disappointed he wouldn't go. As they left he turned a quarter turn, and we were face to face. He's no little guy, but he isn't my size. It's obvious we had different fathers, but it's just as obvious we had the same mother. Eyes, ears, nose — all the same. He looked at me as if he might know me at first, but I could tell he was running through the memory banks and coming up empty. He didn't say anything. I think he was waiting for me to speak. I just stood there like a post. Maybe he thought I was one of those statues you see here and there in cities. We looked at each other for what seemed like a long time; then he turned and walked in the direction of his parking spot. I don't know how long I stood there, but he was long gone when I was able to move."

Val and Brown sat riveted, both thinking the question was too obvious to ask. "How could you be that close...?" The question *was* too obvious.

"I wanted to say something. I wanted to make a move. All I could think was that I had abandoned him. At some point in that six-week period, I made a decision to get on a truck and get out of Dodge, and I left him and my mother and the rest of my brothers and sisters in the hands of a man that would make a Dickens villain look like a choir boy. I ran out on them when they needed me, and I didn't have the balls to look Miguel in the face and tell him that."

Both Brown and Val were stunned. They looked at Buck, and realizations opened like flowers in their minds. Val was beginning to be sorry he had opened the box.

Finally Brown said, "You've got to realize how absurd that sounds. You were a fucking child for God's sake. If you had gone back, he would have killed you for sure. You cannot possibly hold yourself to that high a standard. That is the most egotistical thing I have ever heard. I've never been disappointed in you before, Buck, but I am now."

Buck's eyes widened as Mike spoke, but that was the limit of his reaction. He looked at Val, but Val was still engaged in his own thoughts. Mike started to say something else; then he shook his head and rose. He got two steps from the table then turned and said, "The shame of it is you are going to regret not making that move; and you know it." Then he turned and walked away.

Val said, "Did you tell Tom Coleman about it?"

"Yes."

"What did he say?"

"Well, he used more words, and they weren't as colorful, but the meaning was pretty much the same as Mike's. He dropped the ego bomb, too. Said he had never realized before how arrogant I was. I believe he used the word *disappointment* to describe his feelings as well."

Val was trying not to laugh, but the effort was screwing his face up. Buck said, "What?"

"I knew, had been told, that you talked like that, and I even recorded what people said about it. I still wasn't ready for the full effect, though. It kills me. It's like I caught up with Bigfoot, and he asked me in for tea and crumpets."

"Well, I'm glad you're so amused, but there was something on the table here."

"Miguel? You and I both know that you are going to take some time to think about it and go back up there and meet him. You're going to like Miguel, Buck. He's a nice guy, and he's got a lot of character. You're going to be proud of him. I'm not sure how he'll react to you, but I'd like to be there to see it."

Buck thought Val was probably right. It was almost a magic trick, though, the way he cut to the heart of something and swept all the bullshit off the table. It occurred to Buck that Val should have been working, and he said, "Did you come in here for a reason?"

"Yeah, I did. I think I'll just catch you at the Mouse's Ear next week, though. This wasn't the right lead-in."

Buck watched him walk away and knew what was coming. It seemed as though, once you took the armor off, there were feelings everywhere, some of them sad.

CHAPTER XXIV

The Mouse's Other Ear

Val was seated at the bar of the Mouse's Ear talking to Tom Coleman. It was late afternoon on Wednesday following the discussion on the rig. Under the assumption that Buck was always here, he hadn't taken the precaution of making an appointment. Tom was informing him that, for the last few months anyway, Buck wasn't "always here."

Tom thought it was taking an inordinately long time for Buck to resolve his "situation." Tom was left having to try to remember which story went with which life and who might be privy to what.

"I don't know where he's been going, but I think it's mostly by car. He's flown to Dallas a few times, so these other trips are to a place or places not that far away. It's very unlike Buck."

"You've heard about my dissertation?"

"Yeah. We talked about all that. Really interesting stuff, by the way. It sort of makes you wonder how much of Hector has been available to his mind all along. Buck has always been oddly unracist for a white man raised in the South. I am, too, but I know why I'm that way. Anyway I was wondering what would have happened if Buck had bought in to the normal bias. You know, hated people of color and finds out he is one. I think he's kind of proud of it. I think he might be disappointed he's only half Mexican."

"Actually, I thought about that, too. About the mind of Hector being in there all the time."

"I think all this has been good for Buck. I think he was just idling along, being Buck Burnet. He seemed to be content to cruise into old age and death. I think he was bored. Your book has given him a lot of things to think about. He seems rejuvenated. I think he's evolving yet again. He'd already come a long way."

Tom had been polishing glasses and straightening bottles behind the bar, but now he came around the end and sat on the stool next to Val. Val said, "I have something to tell him, and the longer I wait, the harder it is."

Tom said, "I don't know if you know it or not, but Buck operates on the wave theory. He says life comes at you in waves. He says when facing a wave, you have three choices. You can ride it, you can dive into it, or you can let it knock you down. Riding it is the best, but riding presupposes that you were ready for it and that you caught it just as it started to break. Letting it knock you down is the worst. You can't run away from it. If the wave is already breaking, you have to go into it headfirst. You may be uncomfortable for a few seconds, but you will live. If you ignore it, it will crush you into the rocks."

Val said, "That's not the cleanest metaphor I ever heard, but I think I know where you're headed. I haven't been running away from it; I just haven't found the right time."

"I think you'll find that Buck is pretty understanding. He's also way more sensitive than people think. The odds are he already has an inkling of what it is you want to tell him. What is it, anyway?"

"I have been offered a faculty position at Brown, and I've accepted it. The head of their Department of American Studies read the dissertation. He called me a couple of weeks ago and offered me an assistantship. He said the only thing he didn't like about the book was that I wasn't one of his students. I thought about it for a while, but it's really too good to pass up. I can only go offshore one more time before I have to be in Providence."

Val realized he had never see Tom smile before. "Congratulations," Tom said. "Wow, you can't get much more prestigious than Brown. What a wonderful start to a career. Buck will be proud."

"You really think so?'

"Undoubtedly. I know he's enjoyed having you with him, but he wouldn't expect you to stay a roughneck."

"That makes me feel a little bit better. You don't have any idea if or when he'll be back?"

"Nope. He came by when he got back from the rig Monday and then left with a packed bag within the hour."

"Well, maybe I'll have one of those margaritas I've heard about." After Tom got started on it, he added, "On the rocks, with salt."

"Of course," Tom said. "I'm not even equipped to make it any other way."

Val sipped the drink as Tom came back from behind the bar with a lemonade. "A while ago you talked about the way you are. What way is that?"

Tom said, "I don't know. What do you mean?"

"What did you mean?"

"I don't remember what I said."

"You were talking about Buck's not being racist."

"Oh, yeah. A Southerner without racial bias. Although that's not entirely true for me, because I'm slightly biased against white people."

"What do you mean?"

"Well, I was raised by black people. Not formally, of course. Sort of by default. My mother was a socially active Southern belle, and my father was a hard-working insurance executive in Atlanta. They only had one child and didn't really have time enough for me, so they sent me to the family farm for the summers, where I was the only white person. The black help in the Atlanta house took care of me the rest of the time. The bad news is, the only nurturing I ever got was from black people. The good news is, you haven't been nurtured until you've been nurtured by a black mammy.

"When I talked about the way I was, though, I don't think I was really talking about that. My best white friend when I was a kid was the little girl that lived next door to us in Atlanta. Her name was Sarah Renker. My family was considered 'old family,' but we were pretenders compared to Sarah's family. They had been in Atlanta since before 'the War' and had been some of the founding settlers of Savannah before that. Sarah and I grew up with both families thinking we would be married. *I* grew up thinking we would be married, and I think she did, too. You've seen that movie *Steel Magnolias*? She was a steel magnolia. She was prettier than Julia Roberts. Hard to imagine, but it's the truth. She was more intelligent than I. She was funny and accomplished and mature. She was 'the' sorority girl, but if you met her away from the other sorority girls, you would never have known it."

Val knew most of what Tom was telling him from his research for the book, but this was the first time he was getting his part of it. He knew about Sarah Renker because when she and Tom split up, it made the Atlanta society pages.

"I was at Auburn, and she was at Sweet Briar, and, Catholic upbringing aside, we decided to consummate the union during the summer between our freshman and sophomore years."

Val thought he could tell which way this was headed, and he started trying to prepare himself for Tom's announcement that he was homosexual. He thought it was all right because he didn't really know any homosexuals, and it might be a way to learn something about them.

"It turned out that what our relationship lacked was physical passion, and consummating without it just isn't much fun. Our bodies performed the expected functions, but neither one of us enjoyed it. All it did was ruin a beautiful friendship."

"OK," Val thought, "here it comes."

"There's an old joke that's not really a joke about there being a lot more mixed marriages if Southern men married the women that they truly loved. Turns out that I can only get it up for black women."

Tom was watching Val's face closely while he spoke, and the play of emotions across it caused him to laugh.

"It isn't as big a thing as it was in the fifties. I'm pretty sure mixed couples don't have a bed of roses now, but then it just wasn't going to happen. You thought I was going to tell you that I was gay. The reason I did that was to give you an idea of how big 'miscegenation' was in those days. The whole thing kind of derailed me."

Val was miffed. Nobody liked getting tricked, and Tom's laughter made it worse. That and the "getting it up" part just didn't fit in with the Tom Coleman that he thought he knew. Tom had gotten his degree, but he had formed a band while in school, and he used up a few years playing around the South. He had joined the navy in 1954 and spent four years on the West Coast and in Asia. After that he was in Ashrams in India, Buddhist temples in Tibet and studied Zen and Shinto in Japan. He spent the time between then and moving back to Louisiana at various places on the west coast of North America. As a result he was considered a "very spiritual guy," or so Val thought.

Val said, "That doesn't sound very much like a guru to me."

"Who told you I was a guru? I've never ever said I was a guru."

"Well, what are you then?"

"I'm a bartender in a whorehouse in the French Quarter, with no claims of being much of anything else."

"What about all that spiritual training you had? Did that all come to naught?"

"No. Time spent in spiritual pursuits can never be wasted, even if it doesn't make one visibly different."

"If you're not a guru, what are you, religion-wise?"

"I am nothing religion-wise. I have rejected all forms of organized religion. No, rejected is too strong a word. I have studied all forms of organized religion and found them to be based on good ideas but structurally lacking, all in the same way."

"What do you mean by structurally lacking?"

"They all require people."

"You can't have a religion without people."

"There you go."

"OK. So you don't have a religion, and you aren't a guru. What are you?"

"Spiritually? For many years I considered myself a spiritual seeker among spiritual seekers. I have finally formulated what it is I believe, but it doesn't have a label. I suppose I would have to call myself a practitioner of what it is Tom Coleman believes."

"And what is that?"

"You want me to distill many years of thought and practice into a couple of easy phrases?"

"In spite of myself, I'm interested. I have the time, and I could use another one of these excellent margaritas, as well."

"I can get you the margarita. You can't know what I know without going through what I did, and that is the point. Each of us is on his own."

Tom was back behind the bar. Customers had filtered in while they talked, and he had other orders to fill. Val sipped his drink and watched the comings and goings. The girls were quite pleasant to look at, and he marveled again at how little they fit the chippie bill. Once he was caught up, Tom came back to Val's end of the bar.

"I can't tell you what to think, but I can get you started on your own thoughts."

"OK."

"Get you a Bible and tear out the pages that have the gospels. Some of the rest of it has literary value but little else. Go through the gospels and transcribe only those phrases that are direct quotes of Jesus. Then go through that list and do away with the ones that were obviously made up by the original authors to bolster their claims that Jesus was the son of God and wanted them to start a religion. That one about Peter and the rock comes to mind. Then get you a little book of sayings of the Buddha called the Dhammapada. There are some things in there that were obviously made up after he was dead, too. What's left gives you something to live by. Read those things until you understand them. You don't need anybody else's interpretations."

While Tom was talking, he was looking directly into Val's eyes. The good-old-boy bartender had disappeared and left a person who was serene and absolutely sure of what he was saying. It was exactly the analogy of the gooney bird and the albatross. Tom was relatively inept in the everyday world, but mysticism was his element, and he flew in it effortlessly.

"Once you understand the principles—there aren't very many and they're simple— practice them. Don't preach them; practice them."

When Tom disengaged, Val felt like he had been in a struggle. He wanted to keep the discussion going, but the margaritas had slowed his thinking, and before he could come up with a question, Buck sat down on the stool beside him. There were two other men, obviously friends of Buck's, that sat down on the other side of Buck. Val was having trouble focusing, and his mind was still on the conversation he had had with Tom.

"Buck," he said, "what do you think of homosexuals?"

The man on the other side of Buck, the smaller one, said, "Queers? Whatever makes your worm squirm."

Buck turned away from Val, and Val couldn't see his expression, but the other man became suddenly and deeply involved with the drink he had just been served.

Buck turned back to Val and looked at him, seemingly trying to determine if it was a serious question. Finally he said, "The ones I have known, with the exception of a group that I met early on, have been people pretty much like you and me. Some I liked and some I didn't, but I don't think it's appropriate to judge people based on, as my coarse friend here points out, what makes their dick stiff."

Val spent some moments trying and failing to figure out what made a stiff dick less coarse than a squirming worm. He said, "Do you think they were born that way, or did they just decide to be that way?"

"Most of the ones I talked to about it were adamant that it was something they were born with. I'm sure that's true for some percentage of them, but I don't think it's true for all. Nature loves a Gaussian distribution. I think you could put born homosexuals at one end of the curve and confirmed heterosexuals at the other end. There's a lot of people gathered up in the hump in the middle that could go either way. For them it's pretty much what they want to call themselves. Your eyes look a little glassy. What has Tom been feeding you besides a lot of bullshit?"

"Margaritas, but I think I'm going to have to switch to wine."

"Yeah. That'll help sober you up. Tom," he said, looking down the bar, "let's have one of those famous margaritas."

Catherine sat on the little loveseat Buck had given her when she refurbished her apartment. She had loved this place, imagining that it suited her personality, but as she looked around now, it all seemed a little too much. She tucked her legs under her in a move that was consciously girlish, and she felt the leading edge of a painful thought that would not be let in. She had made her choices and lived her life as she wanted. She always knew the piper would be paid, but he had shown up sooner than anticipated. She looked at Val asleep on her bed and let her heart break yet again. There had been no real need to undress him, but she had allowed herself that small indulgence. He was so beautiful lying there: the taut, resilient skin; the flowing muscles hardened by work. His genitals weren't pretty, but they weren't as ugly as most and, she remembered fondly, were put to better use than any of the others she had seen. Her eyes went to the painting over her bed. (Her mother wouldn't have approved — not of the content but of the colors.) They then traveled across the ceiling to the pattern on the wall at the foot of the room. She realized she was distracting herself to avoid thinking. Only the dark tan and the stubble kept his face from being angelic. He was the cause of her distress. No, that wasn't it. He was like the chemical that you dropped in a liquid to get solids to form and sink to the bottom — a catalyst.

She had been happy. She thought, happier than most. He had given her a pair of glasses — no, wait…He had taken a pair of glasses off her, and, after that, when she looked around at her life, nothing was as it had seemed. She hadn't had much time for people who were depressed believing that everyone was the agent of his or her situation; but what she had been going through for the last months was almost certainly depression, and she hadn't asked for it. She was up a good fifteen pounds, and there wasn't makeup enough to keep the tiredness and disappointment from showing on her face. The real trouble was she was having a hard time caring about it. It took an effort of will just to get out of bed in the morning. Val was the cause of it, and then Buck had started acting strangely. He wouldn't say that he had found somebody, but it was obvious that he had — and not someone he could just work in, someone for whom he was at least thinking about changing his life. Then a couple of hours ago, he had dropped the big bomb.

The party had been pretty far advanced when she got downstairs. Once she had found out Val was there, it had taken God's own time to get presentable. Val and Buck had already eaten, and they were back in the salon at the eight-top in the middle of the room. Several of the girls were sitting with them, but they scattered when they saw her. Val had learned he was going to be a professor (wasn't that just perfect), and spirits were high. There had obviously been a lot of wine drunk at dinner. There, too, were two of Buck's oilfield buddies that were infrequent visitors. Sam O'Baugh was a city salesman for some kind of service company. (She'd once asked what the difference was between a salesman and a city salesman. Buck's answer had been vague, but he seemed to think that a city salesman's job had been distilled to *only* partying and playing golf.) O'Baugh was a good-looking little guy with a sort of off-hand, redneck charm. He was also reputed to have a big dick, but she had never been intrigued enough to find out for herself. Luke Metcalf was the better looking, more interesting of the two. He had his own company and didn't seem to depend on Buck's business alone.

He was kind of like a domesticated Buck. He wasn't Buck's size, but there was still plenty there to hang onto. She would gladly have taken him upstairs, but that hadn't happened. She knew he was faithful to his wife, but he was attracted to her and tempted. He was nervous when she was around and at pains to look at anything but her. He was the only one who looked up, though, when she sat down. The lack of a stir she attributed to her status as "one of the guys," a designation she was not happy with, but then, what was she going to do? Val was hunched over the table on his elbows, eyes half shut with a stupid grin on his face. Catherine had never seen Buck drunk, but even his eyes weren't tracking very well. O'Baugh was holding forth about women, a subject he thought he knew a lot about.

"I mean," he was saying, "I wouldn't want to be one. For the same reason I wouldn't want to be a banana in a room full of monkeys. Just thinking about getting pawed by some hairy dude like Metcalf makes my skin crawl." This evoked a quiet laughter. That was something she had forgotten. He was a funny guy. "They say every man has a feminine side. In some cases it's hard to imagine, but a few years ago, I actually got in touch with my feminine side. That's what they say, 'Get in touch with it.' It's supposed to make you more sensitive or caring or some such shit. In my case, it backfired big time. Turns out my feminine side is a thirty-six-year-old lesbian. Her name is Cassandra, but she likes to be called 'Butch.'" This got a bigger laugh, even from Catherine. As soon as she sat down, he had started playing to her. O'Baugh was a smoker like herself, but she didn't allow smoking in the Ear. Nobody ever smoked around Buck, anyway. Sam's hand kept going to his shirt pocket while he talked. "I tell you what, that son of a bitch got me into a lot of trouble. As you know, I am usually the consummate gentleman, but she is randier than hell and not shy about it either. She'd be pinching women on the ass and squeezing titties, and guess who took the heat? Finally one night she caught me asleep and suggested something to Rose." Rose was Sam's long-suffering wife. "Next thing I know, Rose was whomping on me with this big-ass dildo that Butch had smuggled into the house. Rose never did tell me what Butch said, but she told me that, if I didn't get out of touch with my feminine side, she was going to divorce me and take me for everything I had." Even Buck was laughing out loud, now. Val was straining to catch up.

Luke thought it was funny but was embarrassed that he thought it was funny. Knowing that he was playing straight man, he had to ask, "How did you get rid of her?"

"Well, as you can imagine, she was reluctant to depart. She finally agreed to leave if I would give her free rein in a whorehouse for three days. The cheapest three-day deal I could make was at that trailer house in Morgan City across the river. I was down two thousand dollars and developed a serious case of the clap, but she kept her word, and I haven't seen her since."

Catherine wasn't laughing, and eventually the rest of the table realized it. She was in no mood to be company for anyone, much less a bunch of drunken men. When she had come down, it had been in hopes of getting Val up to her room, but one glance had been enough to tell her that wasn't going to happen. She wasn't stupid or delusional. She knew very well that she and Val were not to be. All she wanted was one more night of the purest pleasure—to feel and savor youth and goodness. Instead she was left with what her life had turned into—a constant, deafening dullness. Buck obviously had something going on, and it wasn't within walking distance of the Mouse's Ear. The Ear had been her base for many years now, and the base of the Ear was Buck Burnet. He didn't seem to know it, but it could not exist without his patronage. When the forces of evil include those who are entrusted to counter them, there can be only one outcome. Only Buck had kept the wolves from the door, and she was getting the definite feeling that his attention was elsewhere. Due probably to her dour presence at the table, first Metcalf and then O'Baugh begged off, Metcalf to home and O'Baugh to another party. Buck was looking at her with what she could only think of as concern. Ironically Val was the one who had failed to catch her mood. He had tried vigorously to hold the party together. While they had been talking, the salon had emptied out, and she, Buck, and Val were the only occupants. Val got back from the restroom and sat between Buck and her.

"Buck," he said, "there is one point I would like to ask about. In all the fights for which I could find credible witnesses, once you had won the fight, you backed off. You always backed off. You never delivered the killing blow — not even with that highway patrolman in Cameron."

"It was Grand Isle," Buck said.

"No. It was Cameron."

"I was there. It was Grand Isle."

"You were there for sure, but it was Cameron. The guy that owned the bar has a picture that he took of you standing over a guy lying on his back on the ground, in front of his former bar."

Buck thought about that. "Maybe his first bar was in Grand Isle. I would have had no reason to be in Cameron then."

Parsing that one out was clearly beyond Val at this point. After some minutes of trying, he said, "Anyway, that guy was a certified sadist, and you didn't see fit to punish him. Yet the guy in the supermarket in Jeanerette was in for some very un-Buck-like pounding. The witnesses said you were bouncing him off the concrete floor long after he had stopped moving. I was just wondering what there was about him that made you do that."

A lot of Buck's "friends" (friends in quotation marks because, in Catherine's opinion, most of them were his friends because they depended on him for their livelihood, in one way or another) liked to sit around and rehash these old stories. She generally dropped out of the conversations when they started because they were always violent. Buck would listen to them patiently but usually didn't join. She had the sense that he was embarrassed by them and would as soon they didn't exist. She was curious about how he would handle this. He was looking at Val and thinking, but she couldn't tell what. Finally he stirred.

"I don't know if that's so, and I have no idea of why it might be, assuming it is. There was something odd about it on the front end, though, aside from the fact that it had been a long time since anything in the way of violence had come up. I had seen the little family on the way to the butcher shop in the back of the store and hadn't made anything of them. The man gave me a hard look, but that's not uncommon. On the way back, I noticed the little girl, who struck me as too pretty to be in the group. I was looking at the left side of her face, and as she looked at me and smiled, she turned so she was looking at me head-on. The right side of her face was dead as a stone, and it gave her a clownish look—like the masks of tragedy and comedy blended into one. The last thought I had was what kind of a blow would it take to do that to a child's face."

Val nodded, not quite up and down, as if what he was hearing confirmed what he already thought. He said, "And yet, that face could have had a hundred causes."

Buck looked at Val for a long time, then, eyes going to the table in front of him, said, "And yes, that face could have had a hundred causes."

Catherine never found out if Val knew more than he was saying about the incident. She half expected him to say something like the girl had been born with a disfiguring disease, but he didn't. His final phrase was the last intelligible sounds he made that night—make it, that morning—save one that he muttered as she was putting him to bed. Buck, however, not realizing that his conversing partner was brain dead, held forth on a variety of subjects. It was all what he took to be fatherly advice and, she had to admit, sounded interesting and useful. Since it wasn't meant for her, however, she allowed her mind to wander into other areas. When Val's head was absolutely on the table, she got up to go to him and tuned back in to Buck who was saying, "So that's why I bought a house in Hickory Flat." If he had physically hit her, the effect would have been no different. "Hickory Flat," she thought. "What in the world is Hickory Flat? Where is it? Who is it? What is Hickory Flat?" She searched her mind, but Buck's monologue hadn't made the secondary tape. She tried to get Buck to go back to what he had said while she was trying to get Val to his feet, but Buck just looked at her stupidly as if wondering what she was doing there. Finally his mind engaged enough to come over and put the unconscious Val on his shoulder and follow her onto and off the elevator.

Buck dropped him onto her bed like a sack of corn and looked at her with a stupid, crooked smile and said, "Have fun."

She could have hit him, but she didn't. "Buck," she said. "Buck, what were you talking about buying a house in Hickory Creek?"

She hadn't meant to sound hysterical, but the room went still. She looked across Val's inert body at Buck, and her jaw literally dropped. His expression was such a mixture of compassion and guilt that she went still herself, and something in her chest that had been wound up uncoiled. The man she was looking at was not Buck Burnet. He was somehow younger and far more vulnerable. Something that Tom had said weeks before came back to her—something about Buck's not being Buck. He had made light of it, and she let it pass, but here it was right in front of her. When she left California, she had vowed to never become dependent on a man again. This had happened so slowly and subtly she hadn't even known it. Strangely, she thought, she was at peace. Reality was something she could look at and deal with. Buck sat down in the reading chair, and she walked to the phone and called downstairs. Tom was still there, and she could tell he had been waiting to see if he would be needed. He said he would make coffee and bring it up. She rang off and pulled the loveseat around so it was facing the bed and Buck's chair.

At first Buck was so apologetic as to be nearly useless, but the coffee helped, and he gradually came around. Other than owning the building and leasing the space to her, Buck really had nothing to do with her business, but she knew that was not the common perception. As soon as it became known that Buck was no longer around, she would find herself at the mercy of several entities, none of them benign. Buck had already been thinking about her situation and had what he thought would be a solution. As he first described it the pieces were inchoate and the overall scheme seemed quixotic, but as he sobered up, he managed to fill in the empty spaces. He saw her core problem as being that what she was doing was illegal. He thought that making her business legal was the first step. He had been talking with the operators of the boutique hotel alongside her space that he leased to. They were a Swiss company that had twelve or thirteen similar holdings at various jet-setting hot spots around the world. They were amenable to taking over her space after Buck remodeled it to their specs. They would train her in Switzerland while the remodeling was taking place, then she would manage the hotel. They would also allow her to buy into the company and become an officer. Those terms were currently being negotiated by Buck's people, and, if she decided this was the way to go, she would become a part of them. The company was very conservative and very well funded. Buck said they typically acted as if they were doing him a favor, but occasionally they would betray their eagerness to acquire the Mouse's Ear. Apparently they felt like its proximity to their current space had helped rather than hurt their previous business, and they were planning on using its cachet in future marketing schemes.

By the time she let Buck go, he was so tired he was almost stumbling. She felt oddly as though she had been the one consoling him for a loss. She stayed where she was and thought and rethought everything that had been said. Personnel turnover in her business was high. If she had as much as three months to wind down, the girls would be gone by natural attrition. There was no way she could see it as anything but a tremendous parting gift from Buck. She began to let herself be excited by the prospect. Only when she had come to this conclusion did it occur to her that they hadn't discussed what had happened to Buck at all. Sighing, she rose and lovingly peeled the clothes from the young body. She sat back down on the loveseat and considered the things that must be done. She had a few plans to work out herself.

Catherine had gotten no more than two hours' sleep after planning the day's activity. She had been very sure about her decision in the early morning hours, but now she was losing heart. Val sat beside her in her car, idly watching the people passing by on his, the passenger, side. She had let him sleep until after noon. He hadn't been ready to wake up, but her window of opportunity was narrow. Sharon always ate at this little place on Cleveland before she went on duty Thursdays. She'd seen her go in about five minutes ago. She thought she could see her through the window at a table in back. She'd been telling Val what she thought since they left the Quarter, but he was being very uncooperative. He hadn't even commented on her car (a convertible Mercedes with a certain number on it). Young men always adored the car. That's why she had bought it. She thought this was one of the best ideas she had ever had, and she didn't understand his reluctance.

"Look," she said, "I'm not trying to be a matchmaker. I've never done this before. I've never even thought of doing it before. Yes, Buck did happen to mention that you were having trouble getting started with suitable girls, but that had nothing to do with this. I know this woman. She's the right age, the right intellect, from the right background. She's had trouble meeting the right kind of man—so much so that she hasn't dated since she went back to school. It's like I've been working on a jigsaw puzzle, looking for a certain piece. You are that piece; I know it in my bones."

"Catherine, it's just not realistic to think that you can put two people together and have it work out."

"Realistic? Realistic? Are you under the impression that we live in reality? The world, life, is what we make of it. None of us lives in reality. We have a group of wants and opinions, and we're either happy or sad depending on how well reality matches up, but nobody just takes what is and is happy with that. I haven't thought about it before, but now that I say it, that could always be the best way to handle things. What are you going to do? Wander around waiting for a lightning strike until you get tired of looking and take the best of whatever's there? That love-at-first-sight thing is a load of crap, Val. I've tried it, and it is one hundred percent bogus. Who's to say that a knowledgeable outside agent, who, incidentally, has been matching people up for years, isn't a better way to go than trusting to dumb luck?"

Val thought she had struck a chord, there. Many of the cultures he had studied had arranged marriages, and there was nothing to indicate that they were any less successful over time. In fact, now that he thought of it, he seemed to remember some recent studies that indicated just the opposite.

Val said, "How do you know her? Was she a prostitute?"

She turned quickly to look at him, frowning.

Val smiled and looked at her for the first time that morning. "It would be a plus."

She looked away and said in a different tone, "You are the only man I know who could say that and mean it."

"Even Buck?"

"Buck would say it doesn't matter, but I don't think even he would count it a plus. I'm not going to tell you her story. I'll leave that up to her. I will tell you that she is good all the way through. She had a bad time for a while, and I did what I could to help her. I haven't had any contact with her since she got accepted to Tulane."

"If times were hard, how could she afford Tulane?"

Catherine turned to look back at the restaurant. "Scholarships."

"Scholarships?"

"Scholarships. She's a very intelligent woman."

"What is she studying?"

"Studied. She's going to be a doctor."

"A medical doctor?"

"What other kind is there?"

It was Val's turn to look at her and see if she were kidding. She was.

"When you said studied, did you mean that she was all the way through?"

"She's a resident at Charity Hospital. She's going to specialize in children's diseases."

As soon as Catherine said it, she had to turn around to make sure the air in the car hadn't actually crackled. The haze was gone out of Val's eyes, and he was looking at the restaurant for the first time. "What did you say her name was?"

"Sharon Miller. She's wearing those green things they wear." This she said as Val was getting out of the car. He came around to the driver's side.

"What if there's more than one young woman in green scrubs?"

"Pick the one that looks like a fashion model." Then, after a pause, she added, "Val…"

He turned in the middle of the street.

"I'll miss you."

He said, "Not if you keep me updated on where you are."

With that he turned and headed into the restaurant. She watched him go to the back where she thought she had seen Sharon sitting. After a minute or so, he dropped out of sight behind other diners. Nothing hurt so bad and felt so good as an unselfish act.

CHAPTER XXV

Sylvie's Mind

A bit of time for thought, that's what she needed. At Lake Charles Sylvie turned left onto the eastbound I-10 feeder road and eased up the on-ramp. The drivers of the cars behind her let her know that they thought she was being too cautious.

A lot of things had changed during the years of her self-exile, not the least of which was the addition of this four-lane highway cutting through the bottom part of the state. Buck had told her she should go by way of old Highway 90 — that it would be a more pleasant trip. But she remembered bridges and lots of turns in New Orleans getting to the airport, and I-10 dumped you off right there. She had not been prepared for how fast the cars would be going. She eased it up to seventy then set the cruise control the way Buck had showed her.

He had bought her this new car because he said any single person in America had to have one. He said you could walk in Paris or New York, but you couldn't walk in rural south Louisiana. It had seemed far too extravagant when he first suggested it, but he insisted, and she finally gave in. Now she could meet him at the airport in New Orleans without his having to drive up here. Truth be told, he had been spending so much money on her account that the car almost seemed a drop in the bucket. It was a Japanese model, and that was another change. Japanese no longer meant cheesy. This was a really nice automobile. Buck said the Japanese cars were far better than the American ones now. It was very easy to drive. All she had to do was stay in this lane and make sure she didn't run into anyone from behind. There didn't seem to be much chance of that.

She had tried to hide the car from Valerie by leaving it near the bookstore, but that didn't work for very long. When Valerie asked about it, she told her that her business was picking up and she needed it for work. She was pretty sure Valerie didn't believe her.

The business picking up part was true; business was booming. Most of their travels took them to cities where she had customers, and she and Buck had visited them and some new ones. It was astonishing how much a little personal interaction helped her customers to think of her first. She should say, helped them think of her and Buck. They all seemed very impressed by him and conscious of his presence, though he usually just hung around outside waiting for her. Chicago, New York, Mexico City, Miami, LA, Toronto—they had been to nearly every major city on this continent, as well as once to Paris.

At first she had thought he was doing all of it to impress her and must be depleting some sort of retirement fund, but there didn't seem to be any sign of winding down; he didn't act like a man who was worried about running out of money. She had asked him about it, told him he needn't do all this for her sake. He said he didn't do it for her: he said he did it to be with her. He said if they lived in five-star hotels the rest of their lives, their heirs would still have plenty of money.

Before they went to Paris, she had asked him to buy a cowboy hat to wear. He didn't want to, and he said something that indicated his sense of humor was even better than she had thought. He said, "For a man, wearing a hat and cowboy boots is a lot like wearing a nice little frock; if he doesn't believe it a hundred percent, he's not going to pull it off." The words were funny, but the thought of him in a "nice little frock" actually made her laugh out loud. He said cowboy boots were too uncomfortable to walk around in, but he did buy a nice-looking hat. It looked very natural on him — so much so that it made her wish he did wear Western clothes.

It had the anticipated effect in France, too. The women were crazy about him. They thought he must be a movie star. They crowded around and oohed and aahed and ooh-la-la-ed and asked him to make a muscle so they could feel his arm. They were shameless, propositioning him while she stood right there beside him. The ones who couldn't speak English asked her to translate for them. She loved it, and Buck didn't hate it. Buck was a handsome man, but in that hat he was very close to irresistible.

Highway 90 to New Orleans was a charming drive, dotted with beautiful little towns and wonderful fields and estates. A bayou ran along at least one side of the road, and huge live oaks lined the other side. I-10 was undoubtedly quicker and more efficient, but had nothing else to recommend it: flat, ugly rice fields, spindly trees, and people who drove way too fast.

She had been at a loss when Buck had asked if he could see her again. The legend had served its purpose for her during that first night. In its place was a real human being with all the complications and inconveniences that entailed. She had just rid herself of a burden, and the last thing she wanted to think about was taking another one on. It took her a couple of weeks to think it all through and answer one of his calls and another two before she allowed him to come up. He was obviously infatuated with her, but she didn't have a lot of room in her life for that sort of thing. The sex took awhile to get right, but early on she began to feel comfortable in and then had come to enjoy his company.

Never had she known anyone so at odds with what was on the surface. Children, in particular, brought out a gentle side of him, and he always got emotional talking about Olivia. He

391

really was interested in Olivia and had been looking around for ways to help her. The wife of one of the men he worked with—Mike, she thought—was a teacher at the Texas School for the Blind, and she taught children like Olivia. Buck was hopeful of getting her down to see the child. Buck thought a lot of her and was sure that she could help, some way. Of the two of them—Buck and Sylvie—she was far the harder person, but she felt like being with Buck softened her somehow. At first, she had wondered what he saw in her and didn't think there was any way this—whatever it was—could last. Gradually she came to believe he really liked being around her and that, maybe, what he'd been calling love wasn't just infatuation.

She didn't know if she knew love from anything else. She called what she felt for Val and Olivia love, and that seemed like a safe premise. She didn't think she had loved John. His looks had fit the bill, and being the wife of a *professeur* seemed like the ultimate mark of respectability; but what she'd taken into consideration before she'd accepted his proposal—none of that had to do with anyone or anything other than herself. Even some large portion of what she felt for her grandchildren was self-centered.

She'd been hiding her relationship with Buck from everyone because, initially, she hadn't thought it would last, and their not knowing would save a lot of explaining. And ultimately she thought that Valerie might have a major problem when she found out. Val might be all right with it. Only Justine suspected. No, not suspected. Justine knew. How she knew was a mystery to Sylvie. She thought Buck was the catch of the century. Justine...Now, there was someone who loved unconditionally. Sylvie had only relatively recently come to realize how much their little family depended on her, and it struck her now that she did, in fact, love Justine. Maybe she did have the capacity. Maybe her feelings for Buck weren't flawed.

She was on a causeway now over a swamp. The swamp was full of dead trees that looked like bristly telephone poles.

Could that be a good thing? Miles and miles of swamp and a causeway that rivaled that over Pontchartrain.

She had asked Buck about the "Buck Burnet Legend" two weeks ago and asked him to tell her the absolute truth. He begged for some time to think about it, so he could make sure what he told her was right. When he came back, he said some of the stories were true. During the time from when he was fourteen to when he was thirty, there were eight or nine occasions when he was involved in something that he had no memory of. Since then there had been maybe two more incidents. The rest of the stories just happened around him. He hadn't tried to quash them and had let himself be eased into the role. He had certainly garnered a lot of mileage from being the legend, but being Buck Burnet carried its costs, too. The older he got, the less he felt like the man he portrayed and the less able to bear the responsibilities and burdens of other people's expectations. He didn't know if he could make the change, but he very much wanted to be Hector Guerrero and lead a normal life for the time left. She really had to work on learning to call him Hector. He fit the role of Buck so well, though. There it was — other people's expectations.

Baton Rouge. At least it still looked like a town in south Louisiana. Buck said this right turn was the last one, and from here it was straight to the airport, about an hour away. She checked and found herself excited to get there, excited to see him. The car was perfect. It drove so well, and she wasn't a bit tired. Leather and wood, quiet and smooth — perfect. Buck — Hector was...perfect. Was that what kept her from leaping into the chasm? The feeling that there were undetected flaws? Terrible things that she didn't know? Somehow that didn't work. He had been in the open under scrutiny for too long a time to be harboring dark secrets. The truth was that, especially with her, Buck Burnet-Hector Guerrero was an open book. No, the problem was hers. Somehow she felt she didn't deserve perfect. Was leery of reaching for it for fear of having it snatched away at the last moment.

The truth was she didn't deserve it. She had hated her mother because of what she was, not because she had treated Sylvie badly. Her mother deserved better than she got from her daughter. John deserved better from his wife. She had ruined him—there wasn't any question in her mind—and made an emotional cripple of her daughter; and tried to ruin her grandson, the only beautiful thing to have come from the whole, sordid mess. Her whole life, she had been thinking only of herself. And now? Now that there was truly something good in front of her? What now? Could she finally get away from herself and become, and relish being, Mrs. Hector Guerrero? Ah. There it was. Moisant Field at New Orleans.

CHAPTER XXVI

The Rig Finale

Days, like trolley cars and grizzly bears, have personalities. The day the Neandertal showed up at the Hector was schizophrenic. It started out friendly enough. The temperature was mild, and the sky was cloudless. There was a soft breeze, but the gulf was flat, and there were birds in the air. Mike Brown stepped out onto the landing at the end of his little hallway and breathed deeply. "Beautiful," he thought. The day would reveal the other side of its nature when he went to the mess hall for breakfast, but for now he was enjoying the morning.

Buck was retiring. He hadn't announced it to the crew yet, but he had told Mike last night in his office after supper. It was a surprise to Mike. In fact, he was beyond surprised. Buck was certainly old enough to retire, but somehow Mike had never considered its happening. He and this rig were synonymous. Hell, they had the same name. Buck as anything but a toolpusher on an offshore rig just didn't compute. He had bought a house in a little college town up between Alexandria and Lake Charles. Alexandria? A house? There were a lot of guys who thought about retirement. There were some guys who *only* thought about retirement. Until last night Buck had never even mentioned it. Buck said he had met a woman and thought he might be in love with her. He wasn't giving her name out yet because she hadn't told her family about him. Her family? How old was she?

"Buck, I know sex with a young girl must be great, but what are you going to talk to her about?" Mike had said. "And you bought a house? Buck, remember that dumbass that came into the bar in Venice that time that had inherited the money from his aunt?"

Buck said, "The one that bought a house for a woman in Alabama, and she wouldn't let him into it? I promise I won't turn it over to her until I know if she'll let me in. Besides, she already has a house. One that's much bigger and nicer. And, she's no young girl."

"Buck, what are you going to do in a little town? Raise a garden?"

"I'm not sure that I'll *do* anything. If I can be a part of this lady's family, I'll do that. Hickory Flat is closer to Dallas, and hopefully I'll be making trips up there to see my original family. Other than that I don't have any real plans."

"Hickory Flat? Isn't that where Val is from? Buck, are you marrying Val Campbell's mother?"

"No, it's not Val's mother, but that's all I'm prepared to say about it at the moment. And I'd appreciate it if you could keep the whole thing to yourself until we can get everything squared away. It's kind of complicated."

A thought came to Mike, and it got out of his mouth before he could grab it. "Buck, did you find Madeleine somewhere?"

Buck looked blank until he could figure out whom Mike meant. When he did figure it out, he laughed. "No. This lady has elements of Madeleine, but she's way more than that."

"How long have you known her?"

"A few months."

"That's not very much time."

"How long did you and Sandra know each other before you got married?"

"Yeah, but Buck, we were young and stupid and lucky. Really, really lucky."

"Well, for the first time in my life, when it comes to women, I feel lucky. Really, really lucky. Mike, I think this is my Sandra."

Well, he had him there.

Mike said, "How old is she?"

Buck said, "I'm not sure. We haven't had that discussion. I'm guessing she's about my age…maybe a little older."

Mike looked like Buck had hit him in the forehead with a hammer. Nothing he knew about him would indicate Buck might go out and take up with an old lady. Buck thought he was kidding at first, but when the stunned silence went on, he reached over and shook Mike. Buck said, "Is that so shocking?"

Mike said, "No, no, it's not shocking, no more than if I heard Hugh Hefner was going into a monastery. It's not shocking at all."

Buck said, "This is different from anything I've known before. I know you're concerned about me, and I appreciate that, but I would really like to see you get around to just being happy for me. I think this would have happened if we had met at any other time in our lives. It seems like bad luck meeting this late, but maybe it's good. Maybe all the bad shit is behind us, and what we have left will be nothing but good. We made love early on, so we know everything there works, but our second time together was a weekend in New York City, and we were having such a good time we never got around to sleeping together. Now that I think of it, I think this could only have happened now. I don't think I was finished enough to appreciate it before this."

Mike could see that his initial reaction had been based on his ego, on how Buck's decision affected him. He looked at his old friend and thought, "What did I think — that this would just go on forever? Why shouldn't Buck have some of what I've had these years with Sandra?" He found himself hoping with all his heart that Buck's lady was everything Buck thought she was and more. He said, "When do I get to meet her?"

Buck said, "I'll bring her to Austin the day after we've told her family and determined there isn't something there that will keep us from doing it."

"Fair enough," Mike said. Mike hoped he would get to meet her in Austin, but there was something tenuous and brittle about the whole thing. Like Rhett and Scarlet's relationship just before Bonnie dies. It created a tension in him—something that wouldn't be eased until he saw Buck well and truly happy.

"Who's going to take over the Hector? Nub?"

"I'll offer it to Nub as a courtesy, but he won't take it. I'm going to give it to Joe Tom if he wants it. I'd like to sell it and the other two rigs, but with so many stacked out right now, it's not the time to do any selling."

They had talked for another hour. Mike went back to his room and went to bed, but he didn't go to sleep. He was genuinely happy for Buck, but the decision had put his own life into a tailspin, and he was kept up worrying about that. He was nearly fifty years old. Although he probably had enough money set aside to retire, he could find nothing in himself that wanted or needed to stop functioning in a competitive environment. His was a unique situation. Although his masters were pleased with the work he had been doing, he wasn't sure they would have another place for him. A lot of his value to them had been his ability to work with Buck. He felt like they might see him as a remora attached to Buck's shark. Indeed, that's how he sometimes saw himself. Normally he would have worked a few years offshore then been given an assignment onshore, possibly as a senior drilling engineer or even a superintendent. From there he would have worked up the ranks. His company, Exxon, had an unpublicized but very effective program for finding and developing talent. Rule number one: only hire the best. They had a team of people whose jobs were to regularly visit colleges and universities and sift through the various candidates, keeping tabs on them from as early as late in the sophomore year. Mike was himself one of those candidates. Exxon's interest in him waned, however, when his grades dropped in his senior year. When they hired him, they might have taken into account his having to work as a night watchman that last year, but they certainly considered his experience offshore. The point is that he already had an asterisk beside his name in the folder they would open when they heard about Buck's retirement. Exxon was sucking in people as smart as Mike all the time, and the ones who were drilling engineers in the gulf were at least twenty years younger. He might have had a couple more cards to play because of experience, but the real problem was that Mike was making the money of someone in senior management. The number of drilling engineers in the world making that kind of money had to be very close to one. If he were one of his bosses, he wouldn't linger very long over that decision; and that was another thing about Exxon—emotion did not play a part.

Then there was the home front. Sandra had recently finished advanced degrees in special education and snagged a job at the Texas School for the Blind and Visually Impaired in Austin. She had spent the first fifteen years of their life as a stay-at-home wife and mother and had gotten her first degree at the age of forty. She was extremely proud of her accomplishment and loved her job. He had a feeling that if he went to her and said he had a new job and they were going to have to move to Houston or New Orleans, the answer would not be a resounding, "Yes, let's do it." His home life was good and mostly because of her. His being gone more than he was home all these years could have been disastrous had she been a different kind of person, but it had made her even stronger and more self-reliant. Mike had no intention of checking to see how self-reliant she had become. The kids were almost gone: Sam was in the fire department, and Angela was in school at UT. Austin was a nice town, and they had lived there for a long time now. They both had roots down. He could start a consultancy, sit on wells or set up some kind of advisory deal. He had decided finally on going back to school, getting his PhD, and maybe teaching or doing research. Even that wasn't like jumping into a feather bed. It had been almost a quarter century since he had thought about an integral. Whatever he did was going to be a big change and would require guts. The expression in the oilfield was "ass." "Balls" was roughly equivalent, but "balls" was brash and carried with it a certain amount of bravado. "Ass" meant something else—something quietly constant over a long term. People like Buck and Joe Tom had ass and didn't even know it. It was hard for them to understand people like himself, who had to think about it and, even then, not always make the mark. Mike knew his ace in the hole was having a rock at home, and that's the thought that allowed him to finally get some sleep.

He turned from watching a freighter work its way toward the Mississippi, and the act of facing the living quarters caused something to sink in his stomach. He chided himself for letting the night's worries return, but as soon as he walked into the mess decks, he knew they hadn't been the cause. There, sitting at Buck's accustomed place, was the Neandertal that Buck had been talking about all these years. He didn't know how he knew that. The man was hairy enough, but he didn't have a sloping forehead or recessive chin. He grinned as soon as he saw Mike, as if to say, "I know who you are and what a pussy you are." Mike got his breakfast and took the tray over to his regular spot, sitting directly opposite the Neandertal. People around him were talking, but it wasn't the usual spirited discussion. He introduced himself to the man and asked him who he was and what he was doing here. He said his name was Asa Butler, and, as for what he was doing here, he was here to "kick Buck Burnet's ass." Mike didn't have any trouble believing that; he had feared as much already, but the open declaration surprised and dismayed him.

Mike said, "Even if you could do that, we don't allow fighting on this rig at any time. What you better do is get your ass down there on that boat that's tied up to the landing and wait for it to take you onshore."

Butler said, "Why would I do that? Because you say so? How are you going to make me do that?"

Mike looked around at the men at the other tables. He knew everyone had heard every word said, but they were all looking in some other direction. No help there. Butler still had that infuriating grin on his face. The man's shoulders were sloped so much that you couldn't tell arm from shoulder. His shoulders attached to the head just below the ears. His forearms were thick and heavy and lay like two bags of throwing chain on the table in front of him. He had the legal right to kick the man off the rig, but the problem was enforcing it. The Coast Guard had jurisdiction, but he wasn't too sure how they would react to the call that "there's a big bad man out here threatening to kick our asses." Sitting here Butler looked taller than himself but maybe not as tall as Buck. He thought to get up and warn Buck, but, too late, Buck had just walked in. Mike could tell as soon as he saw him that he had already known. Butler's grin never wavered as Buck stopped and looked him over. Buck was somewhere around sixty-four years old, and right now he looked every bit of it. The Neandertal was at least twenty years younger. Buck's expression was still impossible to read, but it was obvious he was not overjoyed at the meeting.

"Buck," said the Neandertal.

"Butler," said Buck.

Butler said, "I told you then that this day would come."

As he walked toward the counter to get his food, Buck said, "I don't remember you saying anything at our last meeting. What are you doing out?"

"I been out for a while, Buck. I got rehabilitated and found Jesus, and they let me out. I just come off parole. None too early from the looks of it. Are you still getting around OK? Without a walker, I mean."

"What does Jesus say about your being out here?"

"He ain't said anything, but he don't like unfinished business any more than I do."

Buck took his tray to a table at the other end of the mess hall and sat with his back to Butler and Brown.

Butler looked at Mike while he spoke, but he was talking to the whole room. "Buck Burnet, big-time hero, sucker punched me, knocked me out with a bat or something while I wasn't looking, then beat me up so bad while I was unconscious that

I spent eight months in the infirmary before they could bring me to trial. And they convicted me and sentenced me to forty years on bullshit. They couldn't prove me guilty of a single crime. They found me guilty by putting together a jury of people who were scared of me and put me away just so they wouldn't have to live in the same parish with me. Does that sound fair to you?"

Brown was watching the other men in the room, and, it seemed to him, the consensus was that it wasn't fair. This must be the man from the grocery store in Jeanerette. How long ago did that take place? Had he just been waiting for Buck to get old? Mike was really getting concerned. This wasn't anything like a match between equals. Mike looked at the force of nature sitting across from him and then down at Buck, and Buck seemed somehow diminished. He got up and took his tray to the scullery window then went over and sat down beside Buck.

"Buck," he said. "I'm going to go call the Coast Guard and get a cutter out here."

Buck said, "You can do that, but it won't accomplish anything. They can't get here in time and couldn't do anything if they did."

"Well, let me get a bunch of men together and pile on him and tie him up."

Buck moved his lips so the ends turned up, but the result wasn't what you could call a smile. He turned his head to look at Mike and said, "Mike, remember what Krishna said to Arjuna? 'Do what's put in front of you to the best of your ability.' That's what I've always tried to do. There's certain things that are fated. Do you think Hector was looking forward to meeting Achilles? I've always known this was going to happen. I didn't really think I was going to be able to just slip into the twilight and live out my years in peace. It was always going to be this guy or someone like him."

Mike had heard of Krishna, but he didn't know who the fuck Arjuna was, and he knew that the Achilles-Hector match hadn't turned out very well for Hector. He didn't understand Buck's being so fatalistic. He wasn't a superstitious ignoramus for God's sake; he was an intelligent, modern person. Mike was getting increasingly agitated, and the whole day was developing a surreal quality that he was learning to hate. He got up abruptly and bolted from the room. Butler was saying something as he left, maybe to him, but he didn't catch it. He went first to his office, where the microwave radio was located. He called his office in Houston and asked them to send the Coast Guard and Exxon security. Then he went out and spent ten or fifteen valuable minutes searching the platform below decks before going up to the rig floor and asking if Nub had seen Max.

Nub said, "No, I haven't seen him. 'Course I don't usually see him in the normal course of events, but it seems to me I haven't seen him a lot more than I usually don't see him, lately. If I was you, I'd ask that elect—"

Mike had been looking into the derrick. "Is Joe Tom in the derrick? I didn't see him around the mud pumps."

Nub said, "No, Joe Tom is off on vacation this week. His youngest girl is a barrel racer, and she's entered in some kind of a big show in Fort Worth or some—"

Mike said, "Joe Tom never goes on vacation. Is this some kind of cosmic conspiracy?"

Nub made as if to answer the question, but Mike was already down the ladder to the pipe rack. He spent another five minutes finding Dee Toombs, the electrician, and five more wangling out of him that Max was in Mobile selling one of his boats and that he should be out sometime today. Sometime today wasn't going to do it. There were only three people on the rig potentially capable of dealing with the Neandertal, and two of them were gone. What were the odds of that? He kept thinking of how happy and at peace Buck had seemed when they spoke last night. The sky was still clear, but Mike felt as if it were overcast and stormy. In the last twenty years, Mike had gotten away from the habit of distrusting happiness, from always waiting for the other shoe to drop. But now that feeling was back in spades. He was sick to his stomach with dread that the Neandertal was going to kill Buck. Mike had run out of options. His mind was still making small, swift circles, but his legs were leaden, and he could hardly make them take him up the stairs to the mess decks. Just as he got there, the door burst open, and men streamed out headed down the hall to the outside. Mike went with them and got pushed to a corner of the landing platform at the base of the helideck stairs. His heart was racing, and he realized he was afraid. Afraid? Of what? Afraid of Butler for Buck's sake? Or just afraid because that was his normal state? Buck came through the door and put his back to Mike, forcing him against the handrail as he ushered the Neandertal up the stairs. As Butler cleared the first step, Buck kicked the back of his foot and tripped him, causing his head to strike the corner of one of the steps farther up. His head was turned, and Mike could see the genuine look of surprise on his face. Buck vaulted up and landed with his boots in the middle of Butler's back, then jumped ahead of him and stood at the head of the stairs, waiting. Incredibly, Mike heard a distinct chuckle as the Neandertal got to his feet. He said quietly, "This is going to be more fun than I thought."

Mike had to push his way through the people at the top of the stairs to get out on the helideck, and by the time he got there, Buck and Butler were squared off in the middle of the big O painted on the deck. The heliport was a square about forty feet across. Around the edges was a chain link fence about eight feet wide laid out almost flat to form a sort of safety net. It was one of many nods to safety in the oilfield. Mike had always felt that if you were on the safety net, you were already in deep shit. There must have been forty or fifty people standing around the edge of the deck. They formed a crescent with the thick center in the corner where the stairs came up. Mike saw Nub and wondered who was taking care of the well.

The combatants were trading blows, and Buck seemed to be holding his own. The Neandertal was shorter than Buck, but his arms were so long that it gave Buck no advantage in reach. So far Buck had slipped all Butler's punches. He was landing jabs, but they didn't seem to be having any effect. This close you could hear every sound, and the landing blows were a combination of a slap and a thud. The Neandertal's body registered each of them, but it was only the slightest tremor; his head never snapped back, and his expression never changed. There was blood coming from his nose or his mouth. Buck moved in a circle around him, looking for an opening. Butler stayed planted in the center of the O, turning to keep Buck in front of him but, ominously, biding his time. Finally he moved, so fast that Mike didn't even see it. He caught Buck off balance, hit him somewhere in the chest or on the arm. The sound of it wasn't a solid crack, but Buck stumbled to the side. He was out of position for only the briefest moment, but Butler stepped to the left and put one of those pile-driver fists into Buck's midsection. This was a solid sound with the addition of all the air coming out of Buck. Buck went down, but he rolled to the outside and stood with his guard up. He was backpedaling now, and he was obviously hurt. Mike said to himself, "This is insane. This can't be happening." He looked at the people around him, and they were all watching the fight as if it were a show put on for their amusement. Buck wasn't moving as well now, and Butler was going outside the O after him, but he was still keeping Buck to the outside. Buck had been around the deck twice, and he was mostly just avoiding being hit, trying to catch his breath. Then Butler connected with a right cross, and it almost took Buck's head off. He went down for sure, and the Neandertal just stood there with his fists up, grinning. Buck pushed himself to his feet and staggered, lurching to the left in the same direction as before. His arms were up in a semblance of a stance. Mike's eyes were filled with tears. He realized how much he loved Buck and how much he had always counted on him. Buck passed him on his circuit and his breathing was labored, raspy. "Buck," he said. "Buck, just lay down and he'll stop." Knowing as he said it that it wasn't the truth. The Neandertal was ten feet from Mike, and he could see his face as if under a microscope. He saw the tiniest flicker in Butler's eyes and realized why he had been keeping Buck to the outside. He was afraid of falling off the helideck. Buck finished off his third circle on the far side and was down on one knee. Butler was moving in for the kill. Suddenly time slowed down, and everything was happening in slow motion. Mike had never before experienced such clarity. He heard a voice say, "Now." His head went down, and he was moving forward and from somewhere long ago came the words: "Head outside. Drive with the legs. Through the dummy. Go through the dummy. Pump. Pump." Mike took the Neandertal from the side. It was like hitting a brick wall. If Butler had been prepared for him, it wouldn't have worked, but he caught him off balance and moving that way. When Butler realized they were headed for the chain link net, he tried to fall and grab it, but their combined momentum was too great; they were over the safety net and in midair before he could do anything. Butler went off almost horizontal, but Mike, being much lighter and with his legs still pumping was over the top of him and starting a long, lazy turn. He pushed off Butler and stayed straight to keep his rotation slow, but it had a sideways component, and he couldn't control it enough for a clean entry. Hit wrong on a sixty foot fall, and the water would be like concrete. He spotted the surface in time to make some adjustments, but his left side took a lot of the force. He let himself go deep before folding, so he could look up and see what the Neandertal was doing. He was floating inert just under the surface. Mike swam up and grabbed him by the collar and managed to get his head above water, but when he tried to swim for the leg of the rig, the Neandertal's bulk and his own exhaustion made it impossible. Suddenly Butler was lifted out of the water, and Mike rolled over on his back. Floating felt like all he could handle. He saw the edge of a ship, and then he realized there was someone in the water putting a belt around his chest. The Coast Guard. When he was lifted, he went past the cutter however. He was being hoisted by a rig crane to the main deck of the rig. He looked down and saw the Neandertal splayed out on the deck of the cutter and was filled with emotion. His whole body was racked with feeling, and when the crane set him down, he had trouble standing. He was so tired. All the people who had been on the helideck were down here now and clapping, slapping him on the back and congratulating him. Mike couldn't process what had happened. All he felt now was a huge sense of relief. Buck was at the end of the deck smiling, obviously proud for him. Mike wanted to say something, to tell Buck how much he thought of him, but there was so much to say he was speechless.

Buck said, "Pretty good work for a self-professed coward."

Afterword

The screen door of the little café slapped as someone left. Buck liked that sound. The places where he could hear it were fewer and fewer as air conditioning took over the South. There had been lots of changes in his lifetime. It was senseless to even think about which ones he liked and didn't like. They had happened and that was that, but he could still allow himself a little nostalgia about the things he missed — like the slapping of a screen door. The screen door squeaked again as it was opened, and the doorway was almost filled as the Neandertal walked through it. The café was dark, and he stood in the middle of the room while his eyes adjusted. The wood floor groaned with the weight of him as he walked over to Buck's table and looked down.

"Buck," he said.

"Ace," Buck said.

"Buck. The son of a b…gun almost killed me."

Buck smiled crookedly. "Yeah. Kind of magnificent, wasn't it?"

Butler sat down at Buck's table and ordered a glass of tea from the lady who came over.

"Magnificent? Maybe if I had been looking at it from some other angle. I thought he was just supposed to get in the mix. I'm not so sure he isn't a fighter. His timing was too good to be accidental; and I never felt him coming."

"He's not a fighter, but he's plenty brave. He's been down on himself for not being brave. What he's not is macho. I'm sorry you almost got hurt. He surprised me, too."

"I don't know how I landed, but the boat was halfway to Venice before I came to. That's when I got scared. They had me all shackled up, and I thought I was headed back to Angola, this time for life."

Buck said, "It took me some time on the radio to convince them that you were one of my hands, and the real miscreant had gotten away. You look so damn much like a criminal. I'm just glad it worked out as well as it did. Speaking of landings, my jaw is still sore, and I had trouble breathing for four or five days."

Butler grinned. "I'd be lying if I told you I didn't get some satisfaction from landing a couple of good blows. Anyway, what was that about tripping me on the stairway? I couldn't believe you'd done that."

Buck said, "It didn't look to me like you were really into it. I was just trying to give you a little incentive."

"Well, then, you can't really bitch about me hitting you a little harder than I needed to."

"True."

"What is Brown going to do now"?

"I don't know for sure. Exxon doesn't seem to want to lose him. Last time I heard, they were talking to him about some kind of job for mentoring all their drilling engineers. Anyway, thank you for doing it. I owe you one."

"No, Buck. No, you still don't owe me. Like I told you before, I owe you my life. Maybe if I had been killed, we'd have been even—but maybe not even then. Lying there in that hospital bed for all that time was the only way I was ever going to come to my senses. When that verdict was overturned, I knew I was getting a second chance, and I knew you'd been doing God's work that night in the grocery store."

Buck was looking down as Butler spoke, and Butler said, "Anyhow, I hear you're moving up this way—that you're getting married and settling down."

Buck said, "Well, I don't know about marriage yet, but she is going to move into my house. I'm on my way up there today. Her grandson is coming in from the East Coast for the weekend, and we're going to ask his permission. I had lunch with my brother in Dallas yesterday, and next week I'm going back up there to meet the rest of my brothers and sisters. I'm going from having no family to having a bunch of it, in a short period of time. By the way, Buck Burnet died when I left the rig. My name is Hector Guerrero now."

Butler smiled and put a big hand over the table. "Congratulations, Hector. I hope you have a good life."

Hector took the hand. "You, too, Ace. And I'm looking forward to your bringing your family up to Hickory Flat to visit us once we get settled."

ACKNOWLEDGEMENTS

Buck Burnet does not exist. He is a composite of a number of people I have known, most of them in the oil field: John Bradbury, Tommy Parkhill, Lynn Boyd, George Butler, John Zeise, my brother Bryan and others. Joe Tom Wright is my uncle by that name, as I remember him, except he wasn't black and he died in a car accident at 25. Some of the other characters have their own names and are as I remember them. Some have made up names and don't necessarily resemble anyone.

Bob Carnes

www.ingramcontent.com/pod-product-compliance
Lightning Source LLC
Chambersburg PA
CBHW050747030726

47505CB00002B/433